a cowboy *never* quits

CINDI MADSEN

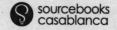

sourcebooks casablanca

Published by Casablanca, an imprint of Sourcebooks
P.O. Box 4410, Naperville, Illinois 60567-4410
(630) 961-3900
sourcebooks.com

Printed and bound in the United States of America.
OPM 10 9 8 7 6 5 4 3 2 1

To anyone dealing with anxiety, you are brave,
you are strong, and you're not alone.

Chapter 1

OF ALL THE PLACES JESSICA COOK HAD THOUGHT SHE'D spend the eve of her thirty-first birthday, a correctional ranch for teens wasn't one of them. Which was par for the course, really. None of her plans for life had gone the way she'd originally intended.

If she dwelled on that right now, she might lose the battle to hold back her tears, so she swallowed the lump in her throat and shoved that thought away to lament over later. The faces looking back at her were a range of ages, from the couple in their sixties to the three ridiculously handsome males in their late twenties to early thirties.

Don't think about the hot cowboys, either. She'd expected grizzled men with gray mustaches—which the eldest Dawson *was* sporting in the most Sam Elliott of ways. What she hadn't expected were the three dudes donning cowboy hats, some seriously sexy scruff, and jeans tight enough to display…well, something she hadn't noticed or thought about in quite some time, and she was totally going to stop thinking about it now.

While the five people on the other side of the wooden-walled office all wore kind expressions—save the furrow-browed one in the middle who'd hijacked the meeting about a minute in—Jessica's nerves stretched tighter, her panic ratcheting up a notch. She couldn't fail. Just couldn't.

She cleared her throat again since the last time didn't take. "Look, I packed a couple of bags, dragged my pissed-off teenage daughter here—thereby ruining her whole life, as she told me multiple times during the two-hour drive. There's gotta be something I can do. Some deal we can make."

The leather of her seat creaked as she shifted. "I'm not asking for charity. I…" To her dismay, her voice cracked. "Well, I guess I am asking for a pinch of it. Your place came so highly recommended and has so many amazing reviews. I especially like that it doesn't seem like a prison."

Gruff-and-Grumpy's brow furrowed more, making it clear she wasn't winning any points. She really should've paid attention to names. Their names had all blurred together as they'd introduced themselves, her anxiety making it impossible to focus on anything besides the fact they were western-sounding names.

"What I mean is, it's more open than I imagined," she continued. "Admittedly, I was afraid there for a bit that I was driving to some cabin-in-the-woods type thing. An elaborate setup to lure people out here so you could murder them and dump their body in the trees or something…"

Eyebrows raised all around, the offense transferring to the elder Dawsons, who'd been halfway on her side a moment or two ago. *Dammit.* Her mouth never knew when to stop. Where was her filter when she needed it? *Great job, Jess. Insult the people you're begging to help you. Excellent strategy.*

Maybe in this instance, in spite of things not going according to plan, she should've made a more solid plan.

"Shit, I'm doing this wrong," she said, dropping all pretense that she had any clue how to go about this. Her heart beat with a thready rhythm as she scooted forward. "I have a teenage daughter who needs help." She didn't want to end up as a case study about how rebellious teens who became moms too early had children who repeated the pattern. "It kills me that I don't know how to help her, but I've tried, and it didn't work, and now I need help." The squeeze in her chest made the next word come out rougher than the rest and about as desperate as she felt. "*Please.*"

Gruff-and-Grumpy opened his mouth, but his mom placed her hand on his arm and aimed a kind smile at Jess. "While we're real sympathetic to your cause, we have a large staff to support, the program isn't free to run, and even if you had the money, we're already runnin' at full capacity."

As Jess had packed in a wild rage, the scent of the jail cell she'd bailed her daughter out of still lingering, along with the image of her sitting there with that smug teenage boy who'd gotten his hooks into Chloe, she'd been so sure that all she needed to do was drive to Silver Springs. She thought if she could just meet the people who ran Turn Around Ranch, she could get them to take in Chloe. Usually she was pretty good at convincing people in person. The combo of friendly and refuses-to-take-no-for-an-answer was how she'd climbed her way to the top of every job she'd had. Not easy for a girl with nothing more than a GED.

The youngest and friendliest of the cowboys thrust a clipboard toward her. "You can fill out a form and put her on a wait list."

Gruff-and-Grumpy's flinty-gray eyes were still on her. The way he studied her left her gut churning in a not-altogether-unpleasant way, which made no sense. Every one of them had done a double take when she'd said her daughter was a few months shy of sixteen. It happened a lot.

Comments about how she wasn't old enough to have a teen-age daughter. People asking if Chloe was actually hers—most any time you put "actually" in a sentence, you should rethink it. Jess had been the age Chloe was now when she fell in love with a cute, rebellious boy with a tragic back-story. Her common sense had been left by the wayside, and she'd made bad decisions. Not so much sleeping with the guy, but not seeing through his lines until it was too late. Although, for the record, she was all for being a lot older than fifteen when it came to sex, especially in her daughter's case.

I want her to have a better life. If this is the only way to keep her from having to go through what I did, it'll be worth her hating me for a while. Even as she thought it, a raw spot opened up in her chest. She and Chloe used to be so close. Before the boy. Before the promotion that left Jess working extra-long hours, often late into the night.

It's my fault. Which is why I have to fix it.

Jess eyed the extended clipboard. The guy who offered it didn't seem to know if he should keep holding it out or not. "By then it might be too late." By the time the ranch made it through the wait-list, Chloe could be even more entangled in her boyfriend's web. Even if she didn't get pregnant—because heaven knew the lectures on birth control had been lengthy—she would end up heartbroken, with nothing to show for it but a criminal record. "I know way too much about regrets and too little, too late."

Chloe was too young to understand the way a stigma could follow you around your entire life. It hadn't ended. Jessica still got the looks. The comments. So much judg-ing, which she should be above caring about—and was most days. But that had changed on the night her own now-estranged mother's words had come back to haunt her. *You keep that baby, and all you'll do is ruin both of your lives…*

Jess knew she should stand up, hold her head high, and go and collect her daughter from the porch swing where she was undoubtedly still sulking. But she'd done enough research to know that this was where she wanted her daughter. A friend of a friend had sent their teen here and claimed he came back a different person. Jess didn't want Chloe to be a different person. She wanted back the girl she'd lost about six months ago.

A hint of sympathy flickered through Gruff-and-Grumpy's eyes, but then the firmness crept back in. He reached up and readjusted his cowboy hat, which set off some kind of wave that made the other two brothers do the same.

Seriously, why do they have to look like they belong on the cover of Ride a Cowboy Weekly?

Wait. That sounded dirtier than she meant it. Not that she'd exactly take it back.

They practically dripped masculinity, their bodies speaking to hours of manual labor, and the effect kept hijacking her jumbled thoughts. It'd been so long since she'd more than half-heartedly checked out a guy that apparently now she couldn't even handle being in the presence of handsome men.

Back when she was in her early twenties—before guys discovered she came with baggage and a five-year-old—she used to be fairly decent at flirting her way into getting a guy to help her out with things like clearing that late fee or giving her a few more weeks on the rent. Once she'd even talked her disgruntled landlord into mowing the overgrown lawn he was harping on and on about. Clearly, she'd lost it, because the expressions aimed her way were immovable ones that conveyed disbelief in exceptions or wiggle room. Or the charity she'd shed her pride to ask for.

A spinster failure-of-a-mom at thirty-one. *Well, it took fifteen years, but Mom was right.* Just when she'd been so cocky about how much she'd accomplished. Now she wanted to Frisbee the employee-of-the month plaque she'd received from her boss last week, for all the good it did her.

"We're sorry you drove all the way here only to have to turn back," Mrs. Dawson said, tucking behind her ear the sandy-brown and gray strands of hair that'd fallen from her bun. The woman had a frail sense about her, her skinniness and the dark circles under her eyes speaking to a recent—or possibly even current—health issue. "I can give you some referrals, and I'll see if my contacts know of a good counselor in your area."

In a daze, Jess blinked at the woman, defeat weighing against her chest and tugging down her shoulders. She truly had failed. And curse her DNA for passing on traits she wished it would've held back. In a lot of ways, her daughter was too much like her: stubborn to a fault, blind when it came to guys, spurred on by the words *no* and *can't*, and turning the word *guideline* into *loose suggestion*.

If they simply returned home, it'd be harder and harder to keep Chloe from bad influences. This past year she'd struggled to fit in at school, and her solution had been to find the worst possible group of "friends." Friends who ditched and smoked pot and encouraged Chloe to sneak out at night so she could go meet a guy like Tyler. He was two years older and a whole mess of bad influences on his own. Rebellious, disrespectful, and mysterious—the same things Jessica had been attracted to at Chloe's age.

Not that her daughter was blameless. Chloe had made plenty of bad choices. She'd dived fully into the party lifestyle, snuck out yet again, and gone on the joyride in the stolen car while under the influence. It was a slippery slope, which was why Jess wanted her at the best place in the state.

Even the others were out of her price range. A counselor might be as well. Maybe they'd just move to a different state entirely. Leave it all behind and eat…ramen. Get a nice box hut under a bridge. Really live out the scenarios people had thrown at her when she'd refused to give her baby up for adoption.

Feeling both levels of failure, Jess shakily stood. "Thank you for your time."

"I'll walk you out," Gruff-and-Grumpy said, and she wanted to shout that she didn't want chivalry. She wanted her daughter enrolled in their program and a way to pay for it.

"It's fine. I've got it. Unless you're scared I'll just drive away without my kid, and then you'll *have* to take her."

"Well, I am now." An almost-smile crossed his face.

She almost returned it, but her lungs constricted more and more as she walked toward the door.

There in the corner, she caught sight of a wall of flyers on a corkboard. Along with a schedule that outlined class time, equine therapy time, and a few other events she couldn't quite make out, she saw a neon-yellow paper with the words HELP WANTED across the top. Even better, it was for a job here at Turn Around Ranch.

"You guys are looking for a cook?" It was as if she'd stepped out of her body and someone else had taken control—someone crazy and reckless, personality traits she'd tried very hard to suppress through the years. When you had a kid who depended on you, impulsiveness went out the window, and recklessness wasn't an option. Still, even as she told her mouth to hold up before it landed her in trouble, the next words were pushing from her lips. "You're in luck. I just so happen to be one."

Those dark eyebrows lowered again, only visible under the brim of his cowboy hat when he was giving the signature scowl he'd given her from the moment she'd stepped inside the office. "You're a cook?"

"Oh, we've been looking for a cook for forever and a day," Mrs. Dawson said, scooting to the edge of her chair.

Hope edged in desperation bobbed up inside Jess. She'd told her boss she needed some time off, and he'd been super understanding. He might not be as cool about her taking…a month? Two? Whatever. This was her daughter. Jobs came and went, but if she lost Chloe, she'd regret it forever. "Perhaps we could help each other out. If you let my daughter into your program, I'll stay and cook while she's here. The only other thing I need is a bed to sleep in. I'm not even picky as to where that bed is."

"Under the stars, then?" the looming cowboy next to her said.

"Okay, I'd prefer a roof over my head. Like a lean-to, at least."

That almost-smile quivered his lips, but he tamped it down. Why was he so determined to keep up the steely front? Or maybe it wasn't a front. Right now, she didn't care, and since she clearly wasn't going to get anywhere with him, she turned to Mrs. Dawson. "I can have a list of references to you within a matter of hours. My bosses all love me." At least that was true. At one point she hadn't known how to balance books or create databases, but she'd learned. Cooking had never been high on her priority list, but she could learn to do that as well. There were Google and the Food Network, and she could make a box of mac and cheese like nobody's business. How hard could it be?

"The job entails cooking rather large meals," Mrs. Dawson said. "We've got the ranch hands, the staff of the teen camp, and the teens. We're talking about thirty people, Monday through Sunday, morning and night."

Holy shit. "Great."

"Wade?" Mrs. Dawson glanced at the man standing next to Jess. Ah, yes—that was it. *Wade.* It fit him perfectly, too.

"Can you give us a moment?" he asked, cupping Jess's elbow and nudging her toward the door. Perfect. The first time a hot guy so much as touched her in over a year, and it was to kick her out.

"I can start tomorrow. Tonight, even," she added. "Just point me toward the kitchen." *So I can study it and figure out what everything is.* She hoped the assumption they kept food more on the basic side was correct. If these cowboys wanted quiches, well…well, she'd figure it out.

Note to self: Google quiche and find out what exactly that is.

Wade propelled her across the entryway, his long strides impossible to keep up with. He turned gentleman again as he waved a hand toward the chairs on the wooden porch. "Please have a seat. I'll be back shortly."

The door closed before she could add any more special

skills: she could balance a ledger, fold clothes into perfect squares for display tables, and deliver food to people who were never happy and make them smile anyway.

Chloe sat on the suspended swing, her legs idly swaying the seat meant for two, and her jaw tightened as Jess sat in the rocking chair to the side. Other than the occasional comment about Jess ruining her life, the silent treatment had been in full force during the trip and was obviously here to stay. Her daughter even crossed her arms tighter. Sometimes it killed Jess how much Chloe was like her, save the blue eyes, which was the only thing her dad had left either of them with.

Jessica opened her mouth to start spouting her list of reasons this was the right call—from how she was only doing this for Chloe's good to how bad decisions had consequences. Then, of course, she'd add that she loved her no matter what. Since those type of remarks had gone unanswered during the drive here, she figured there wasn't much point. Either she'd get the job on the ranch and have more time to try to get Chloe to see the light, or they'd go back home, where she'd have to find another drastic measure to employ.

Chapter 2

"I DON'T THINK IT'S A GOOD IDEA TO HIRE HER," WADE said as soon as the office door closed behind him. He stood across from his brothers, Brady and Trace, who flanked their parents. Usually they had a bit of a monarchy when it came to decisions.

Ma was the queen, and everyone did what she said. Dad helped enforce and carry out her wishes. But she'd gotten so sick over the winter—pneumonia right on top of acute kidney failure—and her stint in the hospital had scared them all. They'd had a big family meeting about the need for her to slow down, which everyone agreed on, and how much they could realistically take on. Since Wade was not only the eldest, but the best at making decisions based on logic instead of empathy, they'd agreed to let him call the shots for the most part.

In theory. This was the first test, and they were failing.

"Ma needs help," Brady said, as if Wade didn't know.

"I realize that. But having Ms. Cook work here is a conflict of interest if we accept her daughter into the program. No one else's mommies are here, and we do that for a reason." Most of the parents had a hard time with the tough-love method the ranch's staff needed to enforce, especially at the beginning. For about half the kids, stricter rules would've been enough to keep them out of trouble in the first place, but there were usually other issues at play, too. It took time and manpower, along with the right combination of manual labor, pushing, and love to figure out what those were, which was why enrollment was capped at fifteen. Taking on another teen would make it sixteen. "Don't you remember how we decided we're not running the Island Ranch of Misfit Toys?"

Ma frowned at the moniker, regardless of it being perfectly accurate. Not that Wade would give up the brothers he'd acquired through the years, or how many teens' lives he'd seen change because Ma and the rest of the staff showed so much love toward them. But they were all only human, and they also were all tired and worn down.

"What about Liza?" Wade tried, thinking he could use Ma's empathy to get her to see his side of the argument. Their counselor was fairly new to the ranch and had her hands full with three-year-old twins with enough energy to outlast that annoying pink bunny who was forever pounding his drum. "Adding another person for her to counsel would strain her schedule, too."

"I can help watch the twins easier than I can stand in that hot kitchen," Ma said. Which was the opposite of the relaxing she was supposed to be doing. If she'd just take some time to heal, she might actually get better.

"I'm sick of stew and chili." Trace leaned around Ma to address Dad. "No offense. It's good. It's just week three, and my stomach can't take much more."

"We can all help out in the kitchen, then," Wade said, and the skepticism spread like a river, flowing from one face to another. Sure, they'd claimed to be willing to help out before, but that kitchen was stifling hot, and cooking on that large scale wasn't for the faint of heart. Not to mention taking a spin there meant wasting daylight on chores they'd later have to attempt in the dark.

"We've upped the salary twice and advertised the position going on four months now," Trace said. "All we've had is that one lady who took a look at our kitchen and claimed we didn't have the gourmet setup she needed."

Yeah, that lady would most likely have made food they couldn't even pronounce, heavy on the vegetables and fancy dressings that didn't fill up growing kids and grown men for a day of nonstop work. Most people in town already carried a steady job or two, and while the ranch's staff had come a long way in opening the townsfolk's eyes to what they did, plenty were still leery about being around the teens. A lot of the kids did have rough pasts, and just when they were starting to buck the stigma, there was an incident at another alternative camp where a troubled teen boy got hold of a knife and hurt some people. Now everyone in Silver Springs was happy to have a good ten miles between them and the ranch, and a few commented they'd like even more.

Of course that incident had happened the month after Ma got sick.

"Brady, can't you ask Tanya about borrowing their cook for a few more meals?" Wade asked. "Didn't you say they're slower than usual at the dude ranch?"

Brady had been friends with the girl next door for most of their lives, and Wade hoped that borrowing their chef—who was also a bit on the fancy side—might buy him time to find someone better suited to the position.

But Brady shook his head. "The guy's on vacation right now, and he's not coming back until their next booking in a couple of weeks. And before you ask, Tanya's got enough on her plate, too."

Wade wanted to argue he wasn't going to ask, but that'd be a lie.

Trace pushed off from the edge of the desk, picking up his gloves, which meant his mind was on getting back to work—where all of their minds should be considering how much they had to do. "Why are you so against Jessica anyway? She seemed nice."

Nice. Young. In over her pretty blond head. There was one problem right there. As he'd sat across from her and she'd pleaded for them to take her daughter, he'd experienced a mushy sensation he hadn't felt in a long time. He'd reminded himself that he disliked people who insisted exceptions should be made specifically for them. That *he* was the one who had to say no because so many of his family members were bleeding hearts who'd take in anyone. Dad rivaled Ma in that area, and if she hadn't gotten sick, they both would've been agreeing to anything Jessica asked for. Which, again, was why he'd taken over the enrollment process for the teens who didn't come through the state.

If they hadn't been making a shopping list for their next supply run into town, his parents wouldn't even have been here. Wasn't that the way timing always was? A real bitch, one who seemed hell-bent on making his life more difficult.

"We can't make exceptions," he said. Not for blond women with big brown eyes that held an admirable amount of determination, misplaced or not. He was sure she heard a lot that she looked too young to have a daughter in her teens, and he'd nearly put his boot in his mouth by saying so. Obviously it hadn't been easy. The hints she'd dropped had him reading between the lines and experiencing a twinge when she added that sentence about living with regrets and worry over it being too late.

That *please* she'd added, so raw and vulnerable, tugged at him, too. He'd shoved away the weak emotion, only for her to surprise him with the funny retort about the lean-to. The more he thought about the woman, the more conflicted he felt, which only brought about more complications and reasons to say no.

Brady stood, and Wade steeled himself to go tell Ms. Cook that he was sorry, but it wasn't going to work out. Then his brother clapped him on the back. "I hate to do this to you, Bro, but you've clearly made up your mind. You'll just pull rank and argue if I don't play a little dirty. So this is me reminding you that we're a democracy. Time to put it to a vote."

Wade automatically shook his head, his argument poised and ready. "We don't have a bed for either of them. I refuse to let her daughter stay with her while the rest of the teens have to clean their bunk rooms and participate in meetings and group chores. It's not fair."

Brady held up his hands. "By all means, we'll keep it fair. I'm sure we can find an extra bed. Until then, she can use a camping cot."

"Jessica can take Nash's cabin for now," Ma said. "Who knows when he'll be back."

If he'd be back, but Wade wouldn't say that to her, just like she'd never say it aloud because she believed giving voice to your worries only made them bigger. Nash hadn't been an official part of their family until he was sixteen, after spending a court-ordered six months here at the ranch. Since discovering he was good at the cowboy thing, he fed his restless energy and paid his bills by working the rodeo circuit.

"And if he does come back while she's here," Trace said, "he can just stay with me."

"Or at the main house," Ma quickly added, and Trace gave her shoulder a reassuring squeeze that infused her with more hope—hope that Wade worried was dangerous. What else was new? Too much hope, too many people, and too much shit to do to ever actually get it done. That might as well be Turn Around Ranch's theme.

Brady turned to Wade. "Sounds like it's settled, then. Jessica's got the job. Do you want me to go tell her the good news, or do you wanna do it?"

———————————————

When Chloe pictured hell, she always thought there'd be more brimstone and fire. Who knew it'd be endless stretches of land, dotted with cows chewing like they meant to show off everything in their mouths, and a house that could only be described as a run-down log cabin? The horrible, all-is-lost sensation clenching her internal organs at least matched—if not exceeded—expectations.

She glanced at Mom, hoping against hope that she'd say something like "Okay, now that you've been scared straight, we can go back home."

But she was an expert at recognizing when there was no changing Mom's no into a yes, and the stubborn set of her chin made it clear that if she had her way, this would be Chloe's new address.

Angry heat coursed along the now-familiar path it'd

seared through her veins on the drive here, over and over, until it was all she felt. The anger was better than the help-lessness and the hurt, so she clung to it. How could Mom overreact like this? For so much of her life she'd done the right thing. Colored inside the lines. So many of those days and nights she'd spent alone while Mom was working.

She'd had no one, but then she'd managed to make a few friends and learned how fun it could be to let go once in a while. Then she'd met Tyler. Spending time with him and her new group of friends calmed her nerves and helped quiet the doubts constantly running through her head. About if anyone liked her, and if people were talking about her, *and, and, and,* until she couldn't breathe. She'd hid the panic attacks from her mom—from everyone. Maybe getting drunk or high wasn't the best way to numb herself, but it was better than being flat on her back on the floor, unable to breathe.

Ironic that she hadn't told Mom about the attacks because she was sure she'd freak and send her to a psychi-atrist, and after one joyride in a *borrowed* car, Mom was full-on trying to enroll her in cowboy boot camp.

What if they force me to wear cowboy boots? That's gotta be cruel and unusual punishment. Surely even out here in the sticks they had their limits.

Chloe's fingers itched to grab her phone and check it, but Mom had confiscated it, along with her laptop. Fat lot of good that would do anyway, since she doubted this place had a Wi-Fi hot spot. Now she didn't know if her friends were trying to get hold of her, or how many times Tyler had texted to check on her. Or if his parents had grounded him, too, although they didn't seem like the grounding type.

In her defense, she *had* tried to talk him out of hot-wiring the car, but he'd given her that impatient look that meant she was being too uptight. As he'd pointed out, the car was old and always parked in the same place, just gathering dust, so he was actually doing the person a favor by running it. Seemed to make sense at the time. They were going to bring the car back before anyone realized it was gone, just as soon as they picked up food from the convenience store a couple of miles down the road.

It would've been harmless if Tyler hadn't sideswiped another car on the way. Just her luck, there was a cop at an intersection who witnessed it and pulled them over, and then all hell broke loose.

Demanding they get out of the car.

The blinding beam of a flashlight right in the eyes.

Watching Tyler walk and turn and stand on one leg and blow into a Breathalyzer.

Being shoved into the back of a cop car.

Admittedly, getting dragged down to the police station beside her handcuffed boyfriend wasn't the highlight of her sophomore year. All she'd wanted in that moment was her mommy, and then Mom had come to pick her up, and now she was the *last* person Chloe wanted.

The need to know what was happening finally overpowered her death grip on her vow of silence. "What's going on? What are we waiting for?"

The rocking chair Mom was seated in creaked against the wooden porch that faced the empty vastness, and she slowly turned her head toward Chloe. "Just ironing out details. I'm hoping to get a temporary job here. That way I can be around as you go through the program and actually have a way to pay for it."

Tightness claimed Chloe's lungs, restricting her from getting any air. "Mom, I've learned my lesson. Please, let's just go home. I'll do better."

"We already had that arrangement when you flunked your last chemistry test, remember? And when you came home after curfew for the second time in a row, and I was sure you'd been drinking, but gave you the benefit of the doubt after you assured me someone had just spilled a beer on you." Mom's eyes went shiny, which made Chloe feel shitty, but she refused to burst into tears. "Then you snuck out, and I warned you. I distinctly remember saying the words 'last chance.' I thought it'd sunk in, so imagine my surprise when I thought you were sleeping in your bed and got a phone call to come pick you up from jail. *Jail, Chloe.*"

"I remember. I was there." Snapping didn't help her case, and Mom's spine straightened, like an exclamation point to her decision about forcing her to stay at this awful place.

"Well, since I was *also there*, I can assure you, this ranch is an upgrade. It's not so bad, and there are people here who can help you. If you'll just give it a chance—"

"I'm sorry. About snapping at you, and about sneaking out, and about ending up in jail."

Chloe treaded carefully, already feeling like the water was rising so fast that all the paddling in the world wouldn't stop it. She had to try, though. "Give me one more chance. I swear this time I'll do better. Just please, please let's go home."

The screen door opened with a screech, and the tall cowboy dude taking up most of the doorway frowned at the mechanism that opened and closed the door. "Needs some WD-40," he muttered, and for some reason that upped Chloe's apprehension about what he'd say next.

She wanted to tell him she didn't belong here and that her mom was overreacting, only her words died on her tongue as he peered down at them. He reminded her of Mr. Gordon, the math teacher who most of the students were afraid of, even the bad ones. No one dared to talk back to him.

Mom stood, wringing her hands in front of her, and Chloe's heart hammered a rapid rhythm that left her dizzy and thinking she might be on the verge of another panic attack. "Did you need my references?" Mom asked. "I can make a few calls and—"

The guy sliced a hand through the air, and Chloe thought she needed to learn that trick because it immediately made Mom stop talking. "No need."

Mom's shoulders slumped; Chloe's hopes soared.

"You're hired," he said, and her and Mom's body language switched, desperation replacing every other emotion inside Chloe as happiness and relief flitted across Mom's features.

"Thank you so much," Mom said. "You won't regret it."

Regret. That could be the title of Chloe's life right now. And as she gazed out at the miles and miles of nothingness that had just become her home for the foreseeable future, she decided she'd prefer brimstone and fire.

Chapter 3

WHILE JESSICA HAD BEEN SINCERE WHEN SHE PROMISED Wade he wouldn't regret giving her a job, clearly it didn't comfort him any. She'd thought he was grumpy before, but his grumpitude had kicked up a few notches since the meeting he'd had with his family.

"You might want to hold off on celebrating," he said, as if she'd been jumping up and down with joy. "There are conditions. Several of them."

Announced in that death-toll tone, it was hard to stifle the worry and doubt that tried to creep over her. Was she in over her head? Totally.

Would she figure it out? There wasn't any other option.

"Why don't the two of you come on in, and we'll go over all the rules and talk terms. Then you can decide if you still want the job."

"I'll want it," Jess said, lifting her chin.

Wade gave a sort of half grunt, half huff, and then turned and went back inside. She assumed she was supposed to follow, so she gestured for Chloe to come on. Naturally, her daughter took her sweet time obeying, but gradually pushed to her feet.

"What job could you possibly do here?"

Well, on the bright side, her daughter was talking to her again. Jess would've preferred a less snide tone, but she supposed beggars couldn't be choosers. "I'm going to cook for the people on the ranch and at the camp."

A snort-laugh escaped Chloe, and even though it was at Jess's expense, it still caused a glimmer of hope. She hadn't heard her daughter laugh in a long time. "You can't cook."

"I do all right, and I'll learn whatever else I need to."

"Do they know you don't have any experience?"

Jessica whirled on her daughter, suddenly afraid the position she'd managed to get her hands on for them would be yanked away and she'd have to start this painful process over somewhere else. "Would you rather end up at a military-type boot camp? Juvie? Because right now, those are looking like your options." The officer at the station had given them a lengthy spiel about how these incidences often snowballed and led to worse crimes, and while Jess wished it'd scared Chloe more, it had certainly terrified her. "It might not feel like it right now, but I'm doing this for you."

"Mom, it was just a stupid joyride. One bad decision."

"A stupid joyride? That's what you call fun these days?"

The epic eye roll made an appearance. "No, I mean—"

"And it was more than one bad decision." Jess ticked them off on her fingers. "Sneaking out, underage drinking, and *stealing a car and driving under the influence.* You're lucky no one was seriously injured. Or worse."

"Okay, I made a lot of bad decisions that night, but I'll do better." Fear flickered through her big blue eyes. "Please don't take me away from my friends. Away from Tyler."

The sorrow in her voice tugged at Jess's heartstrings, but she'd let her motherly affection soften her too many times before, enough that things had spiraled completely out of control. No more, though. "A guy like Tyler will break your heart and never look back."

"He loves me."

She gently placed her hand on Chloe's shoulder. "Love doesn't land you in jail in the middle of the night. That's stupidity, alcohol and drugs, and a guy who only thinks about himself."

The screech of the screen door jerked Jess's attention to the impatient cowboy in the doorway. "You coming?" he asked.

"We're coming." She gestured her daughter ahead of her, and they walked across the foyer and into the office. The two other cowboys were no longer in the room, leaving just the elder Dawsons, Wade, Chloe, and Jess.

She and Chloe sat in the chairs on the lonelier side of the room. Instead of rounding the desk to take a seat, Wade perched on the edge and leaned forward, forearms on his knees as he outlined the terms. Chloe would stay in the girls' cabin with the other teens and follow every rule, no exceptions. Jessica would be staying at a cabin on the other end of the property and be at the main house at the crack of dawn to start breakfast. The teens were responsible for lunch. Then Jess would prepare dinner and help serve it, and under no condition was she to interfere in the program or the tasks they assigned to Chloe.

The *no this, no that* sermon continued, and Jessica automatically glanced at Chloe to share a silent *yeesh, this guy's intense* look, the same way they'd done when they first ended up together in the principal's office.

But Chloe's eyes stared blankly ahead, her features carefully shuttered and devoid of emotion, and an intense ache radiated inside Jessica's chest.

In this scenario, *she* was the bad guy, no matter how

many rules Wade spat out, and for a moment, she reconsidered if this was truly the right move. It had been all she'd wanted a matter of minutes ago, but now...

She just wanted her daughter back.

That first time she'd been called into the high school because Chloe was in trouble, Jess thought *they* were overreacting about the abrupt change in her daughter's attitude and dipping grades. Maybe if she could go back in time and put her foot down, things would've never gotten so bad. But she didn't have a rewind button to press and make it right, and she'd tried her way. There were bigger things going on—she was sure of it—but Chloe wouldn't let her in. After Jess had picked her up from jail, that rift had only widened.

This is the way I get her back. It has to be.

So she nodded and put conviction behind her voice. "I understand."

"I'll need it in writing," Wade said.

Again, she nodded.

"Chloe will need to turn over her phone and any other electronics she's brought."

Chloe paled, her eyes going wide. "No electronics at all?"

"You'll earn computer time. You'll see the desk and the computer as we walk past the main room. Fair warning: Many sites are blocked, and your sessions will be monitored."

Chloe finally looked her way, and the mix of anguish and pleading shot Jess right through the heart. "Mom?"

"Her phone and other electronics have already been taken away," Jess numbly said.

"But I get to call people one last time to explain, right? Even prison allows a phone call."

Mrs. Dawson scooted to the end of her chair and aimed a reassuring smile at Chloe. "Sugar, I know it seems a bit like a cage now, but how much freedom you have is up to you. You'll see that it's more like summer camp than anything."

At least Chloe was polite enough not to voice the skepticism that crept onto her features. Her chin quivered, and her tough-girl facade cracked. As tears bordered her eyes, Jess rethought this plan yet again.

Hot salt-water pricked her own eyes, her throat burning with the effort to choke back a sob.

"Ah, here's Liza," Mrs. Dawson said, glancing toward the woman who'd knocked lightly on the open door. "She'll take you to the girls' cabin and get you all settled in. We'll give you a moment to say goodbye to your mother."

"No need." Chloe shot out of her chair. She stormed past and strode over to Liza, who gave Jess a kind smile she couldn't return—not without bursting into tears.

"We'll take good care of her," the pretty brunette said.

Then they were gone, and Jess couldn't move, couldn't talk. Couldn't do much besides focus on breathing and how each gulp of oxygen tore at her lungs.

The retreating footsteps sounded loud in the quiet, each one echoing in her ears.

The toes of Wade's boots encroached the spot of floor where she'd homed her gaze, and she slowly glanced up at the tall pillar of a man. She nearly asked if she could talk to anyone but him right now, but he flashed her a sympathetic look. There was a hint of fear in his expression, too, most likely over the worry she was going to start crying, which was a very real possibility.

"It's not uncommon for them to refuse to say goodbye," he softly said.

"At least I get to see her, right?" She couldn't imagine how hard it must be for most parents to have to leave when every motherly instinct was shouting at her to go collect her baby.

Somehow she pushed to her feet and forced her wobbly knees into motion. She turned to Mr. and Mrs. Dawson. "Thank you for giving us a chance. I promise you won't regret it."

Unlike Wade, they seemed to find it comforting.

Then Wade placed his hand on her lower back, a move she found more comforting than she should. "Come on. I'll show you to your cabin."

———————————

The walk across the yard had been silent, and Wade wasn't sure what to say. Now he felt as though he'd been too harsh. His mood swings were driving him crazy. Usually he wasn't a mood swing kind of guy. The other odd thing he couldn't shake was the urge to give Jessica a hug and assure her it'd be okay.

No guarantees; that was one of their rules. They believed in their program, but the teens had to do the work, and unfortunately, they couldn't force people to heal and change.

Man, would that make their jobs a lot easier, though, if they could.

Another rule was not to cross lines, not with staff, not with parents. No crossing lines in general. They couldn't deal with the teenagers' drama and help counsel them and their families as efficiently if they were experiencing drama of their own. It was also why he hadn't been on an actual date in over a year.

Okay, one of the reasons why.

He readjusted his grip on her suitcase handle, transferring it to his other hand. At first she'd refused his offer to carry it, but when it didn't exactly roll on the dirt and grass, he'd grown frustrated watching her struggle and plucked it from her grip. Evidently she'd expended all of her energy talking his family into taking on her and her daughter because she'd let the suitcase go without a fight.

Again, that urge to make her feel better rose. He cleared his throat. "The cabin you'll be staying in while you're here belongs to one of my brothers, so you'll have to forgive the lack of decorations."

"I'm not much for decorations anyway. Who has the time?"

The path was more well-trodden and dustier here, each step sending up small puffs of dirt that mixed with the scent of the spring plants finally taking hold and turning the ranch green. "Not sure when it's last been cleaned, either."

"I don't usually have time for cleaning, but I do know how if it's needed." She reached up and twisted a strand of hair around her finger. "Seriously, I appreciate the chance. I'm sorry you got outvoted… Well, not really sorry, but more… You know what I mean." She ducked her head, and he cracked a smile.

"Not sure that I do. I think I've just been insulted."

She laughed, but a sort of sob topped off the noise, leaving him with that conflicted sensation. Damn moods. They should know better than to be so affected by a beautiful woman.

He opened the gate along the fence that served as a second barrier to livestock that managed to escape the corral, and then made sure to secure it behind them before heading down the dirt path to the cabins where he and his brothers lived. "Kids get their feelings hurt often. They're supersensitive and have short fuses. But they also have short memories. Most of them get over things faster than adults."

Jessica hugged her arms around herself. "I'm afraid you're underestimating the type of stubborn that runs in the Cook family."

"Since you talked your way into a job despite it breaking all the rules, I think I have an idea of what that looks like."

The smile that spread across her face kicked him in the gut.

"Wait. Your last name's Cook." He'd referred to her by it earlier and had even just written it on the paperwork she'd signed, but the irony didn't hit him till now. "And you're going to be our cook. Does that mean I call you Cook Cook?"

She tilted her head, and the sun highlighted the golden curls that framed her pretty face. "What is this? The eighteen hundreds? I thought you guys were advanced out here on this ranch, Cowboy Dawson, not still livin' in the Wild West."

He arched an eyebrow. "Ha-ha."

"Seriously, you look good for a guy in his two hundreds." Her eyes widened. "I mean, not that you look good. Not that you *don't* look good. I just…" She gave a cute self-deprecating giggle and shoved her hands in the pockets of her jeans. Her big brown eyes lifted to his. "How about you just go with Jessica? Most of my friends call me Jess, but after you read the riot act to me in the office, I'm guessing friendships between the help are frowned upon."

"Oh, so I'm the help? And the riot act? *Really*?"

The smug curve of her lips lit up her entire face. Then she glanced over her shoulder toward the main house and the bunkhouses where the teens stayed. She exhaled a long breath. "Thank you for making me smile when I didn't think it would ever be possible again."

"Chloe will be okay. Liza and the rest of the staff, they know what they're doing." He was getting too personal, breaking those rules she'd pointed out he had, but he couldn't seem to help sidling closer to the line. "You'll be okay, too. Just takes time."

She nodded, not so much like she believed him, but more like she didn't know what else to say and hoped he was telling the truth. He hoped so as well.

"Here we are," he said, slowing at the sidewalk that led to the steps of the porch.

"Key?"

"Hanging up inside on a hook in the entryway," he said, and when she scrunched up her eyebrows, he added, "We don't have much need of locking our doors out here. If it makes you feel better, feel free, of course."

She scuffed the dirt with her shoes—thin, sockless shoes that were meant for offices and sidewalks and wouldn't survive long on the ranch. He wanted to say so, but since they'd sorta started getting along, he decided to keep his mouth shut. She'd figure it out soon enough.

"Is there a way to get my car any closer to the cabin?"

"Not *your* car. That's why there are so many trucks around." He walked up the steps to the porch and set her suitcase on the weathered wood. It needed a coat of varnish if he or anyone else ever got the time—so in other words, it'd wait. "But if you need help hauling anything, you can hardly move without running into someone who'd be willing to give you a hand. If you need to borrow a truck, we can arrange that, too." He peered down at her, noting she barely came to his collarbone. "Do you know how to drive a stick shift?"

"It's been a while," she said, a hint of longing in her words. "So long I've probably forgotten how."

"I can give you a refresher course if you need me to."

A mischievous gleam hit her eyes, the corner of her mouth kicking up, and his pulse ratcheted up a notch. Then he put what he'd said together with another way it could be taken, and he got the type of jolt he experienced when he got too close to the electric fence.

Jessica reached for the door handle. "See you bright and early tomorrow morning. Sure you all don't want to eat breakfast more in the nine-ish range, rather than at six thirty?"

For a second he wasn't sure if she was kidding, or if she was already pushing the rules. See, this was why he wasn't supposed to go making jokes and indulging in borderline flirting. Or thinking about how long it'd been, or how much he'd like to follow through on that refresher course.

She nudged him with her elbow. "Don't freak out. That was a joke. I'll report for duty at oh-five-thirty so I can figure out the kitchen and get the food done on time." She flinched a little as she said five thirty, but then she flashed him a smile. He could see she was still on the verge of breaking and suspected she'd disappear into the cabin and cry.

Not much he could do about it, and he had work to do. He wished her a good day, told her to call the office if she needed anything, and headed back toward the corral, where several calves were waiting to be doctored.

Halfway there, he glanced back toward the cabin. He could already tell the woman was going to be trouble with a capital T.

Chapter 4

AIDEN WAS BRUSHING DOWN THE REDDISH-BROWN COAT of his horse, Koda, when Brady walked through the doorway of the stables.

"Hey, can you wrangle up a cot?"

"You want me to rope it?" Aiden teased. Words like *wrangle* didn't used to be part of his vocabulary. Neither did words like *stability* and *family*, and he was only now starting to believe they truly existed.

Brady cut the strings on a bale of hay. He tossed flakes over the stalls to the rest of the horses, who'd begun nickering as if they were starving, even though Aiden had fed them some oats before he'd taken Koda out for a ride. "Maybe if I give you an object to rope that doesn't move, you wouldn't miss."

"Low blow," Aiden said, but he laughed. Horses came naturally. Roping not so much. He tossed the brush aside and double-checked the lock on the stall since Koda liked to play Houdini sometimes. "Where do you want the cot?"

"In the girls' cabin. Just set it outside the door."

"New recruit?" A year ago, he might've said *new prisoner*, but his perspective had changed—in spite of how hard he'd tried to hold on to his old opinions.

"Yeah, new recruit and a new cook. A woman showed up and begged us to accept her daughter into the program, and it just so happens she's willing to fill the cooking position, so we jumped on it."

Aiden tossed a flake of hay to his horse and then swiped his hands together. "By 'we,' I'm guessing you mean everyone but Wade."

Brady chuckled. "Not only are we at capacity, but he didn't think the girl and her mom should be here at the same time. Breaks too many rules."

So had Aiden when he first arrived. He learned quickly that you follow the rules or else, and while Wade played enforcer a lot, he was always fair. Sometimes annoyingly so. Exceptions were part of life, but not where Wade Dawson was concerned. For months they butted heads, but somewhere along the way, mutual respect had grown on both sides.

When it looked like he'd end up in the foster system yet again, Wade was the one who drove several hours to Grand Junction to plead a case in favor of Aiden staying at the ranch to train the horses. Aiden had stood in the courtroom, sure he was hallucinating as the guy who didn't believe in exceptions made an exception for him.

A few months later, the Dawsons brought up adoption. It was weird going from loner to a guy with parents and five brothers overnight, and sometimes Aiden worried he'd wake up and find out it'd been a dream. Or he'd screw up and they'd tell him to get lost.

After all, how many people would want to adopt a sixteen-year-old problem child? Not many, which was why he worked long hours and suffered through homework. His adoptive mom wanted him to graduate from high school, and he wanted to make her proud.

"Is the new girl any good at math? I could really use a tutor." A free tutor. Allie, who ran the schooling side of the ranch, had helped as much as she could, but she was always busy, and unfortunately he didn't connect with her teaching style. But he didn't want the Dawsons to spend any more on his education than they already had. Thanks to not giving a damn about his grades or school for several years, he was taking about two years of schooling through a homeschool program that'd cost a pretty penny. Money the Dawsons shelled over like it was nothing, even though he knew they had a lot of stressful expenses that kept them up at night, especially when the hospital bills from Ma's stay got thrown into the mix.

"No idea." Brady folded up his Swiss Army knife and put it back in his pocket. "But I'm not sure it's a good idea to get too close just yet."

"You don't think she'll stick around?"

"Oh, her mom was determined. More like…" Brady pressed his lips together as if he wasn't sure how much to say.

"Not my business. I get it."

Brady brought his hand down on Aiden's shoulder. "More like the opposite. This place is your business now. Part of being a Dawson is working this ranch. She just got into some trouble back home, and we're gonna have to tread carefully. I know Wade's given you the speech about not getting too close…"

Aiden nodded. Like with everything else, the Dawsons had taken a bigger chance on bringing him on board because he was around the same age as a lot of the teens who came to the camp. It complicated things and made every teen girl who landed here off-limits, not that he'd been thinking that. He just desperately needed a tutor. "Got it. If you know of a homely male tutor who works for free, though…"

Brady laughed. "You'll be the first to know."

"I'll go see about that cot."

About fifteen minutes later, he approached the girls' cabin. Liza was outside, giving the new recruit a tour, from the looks of things.

"Brady asked me to leave this cot here," Aiden said, lifting it as if they'd need proof. "If no one's inside, I can carry it in, or I can leave it by the door."

The girl with Liza glanced his way, tipping her chin up enough that her blond curtain of hair fell from her face. Her cheeks were splotched in red, a sure sign she'd either done some crying or was about to, and he wished there was a way to reassure her it wasn't so bad without sounding like a creep or an infomercial.

"How heavy is it?" Liza asked.

Aiden did a bicep curl with the folded gray frame and mattress and shrugged. "Not heavy to me."

New Girl rolled her eyes. While a fraction of the disdain was aimed at him for a move she probably viewed as showing off—although if he were going to flaunt his strength, he'd pick something heavier, like a bale of hay or a calf—he recognized the closed-off posture and sour expression. The chip on her shoulder. He'd worn both and then some when he'd first arrived at Turn About Ranch.

There was something else, though. Her blue eyes were tight with resentment and sorrow, and a hint of the loneliness that settled over you when you didn't feel like you had a single soul in the world you could count on.

Empathy pinged through his internal organs. He'd felt like that more times than he could count. He tipped his head at her. "Hi, I'm Aiden."

She hugged her arms tighter around her middle and turned to Liza. "Can I go to my room now?"

"Sure, Chloe. You might want to take your cot, though, or you won't have anywhere to sit or sleep," Liza said, and Aiden headed toward the steps.

"I got it," he said. "As long as the coast is clear."

Most of the ranch was open, but a handful of doors had keypads on the outside and inside: Liza's office, where she counseled with the teens; the room where Penny, the medication manager and on-site nurse, saw patients; and the boys' and girls' cabins, since they were locked internally and externally at night and checked at varying intervals. It was the one high-tech part of the ranch. Now that he was on the other side, Aiden knew it was a combination of safety measures for the teens and for the Dawsons, but mostly involved legal liability reasons.

Liza had him stand back as she unlocked the door and made sure the girls were dressed and aware a male was about to enter the room. Then he carried the cot inside and set it up in the biggest corner. Liza rattled off a few instructions that clearly went in one ear and out another, and Aiden had a sense of déjà vu. Wade had given him a similar speech, he was sure, although he hadn't heard a word.

When he straightened, Chloe's eyes met his. Her expression seemed to say *Please don't leave me here like this*, even as her mouth stayed in a tight line.

Once again, he wanted to spout reassurances and tell her it wasn't that bad, but he knew it wouldn't make any difference. Even more troubling, he had the urge to grab her hand and race her out of here.

She was pretty. He shouldn't notice, but it was one of those things he couldn't help. Back in the day, he used to have a soft spot for good girls in search of a bad boy. With his cowboy boots and button-down shirt in place of his former biker boots and leather jacket, he no longer looked the part of a bad boy, although he wouldn't go calling himself a good one.

He wasn't sure *reformed* was the right word for him, either, but he was trying. This girl, who looked like she shouldn't belong here but had the attitude that said otherwise, was the kind of trouble he no longer raced toward.

He'd be cordial. Polite. And he'd find that male tutor he'd jokingly mentioned to Brady. That and work ought to keep him plenty busy.

Hopefully busy enough to prevent him from thinking about the pretty new girl and how something inside him tugged every time their eyes met.

Because he'd already had more than enough trouble in his life.

Chloe watched the backside of the cowboy as he walked out of the room, leaving her with a bunch of strangers.

Not that he wasn't a stranger. There was something about the way he looked at her, though, as if he understood. Which was stupid. He was part of the enemy. She just hadn't expected a teenage cowboy to be one of her prison wards. Especially not a cute one.

Another thing that didn't matter. She already had someone, and Tyler was probably so worried about her. She couldn't believe she wasn't allowed to call him and at least let him know what'd happened.

And how long was she going to be here? She only had another two months of her sophomore year, and she had big plans for summer. They didn't involve being here, that was for sure.

She eyed the windows at the back end of the room.

"Hi, I'm Izzy," one of the girls nearest her said. "That's Danica and Desiree. We call them the Double D's."

What was it with everyone formally introducing themselves? Like it was the fifties or some shit. This whole place had a stuck-in-time vibe, and it felt as if her skin wanted to crawl off her and flee.

Wooden walls. Permanent cloud of dust that smelled faintly like manure. Liza had been nice enough until the prying started. She claimed that Chloe didn't have to answer the questions she wasn't ready for, but Chloe had remained silent. Mom was the one who wanted her here; let *her* give them all the information. It'd be wrong, but right now she didn't give a damn.

If she could stop the tears that kept burning her eyes, that'd be great. Where was a bottle of vodka when you needed one? Or a vape pen. Tyler always had a loaded one in his pocket.

"I overheard your name," Izzy said, "so instead of pretending I don't know it, I'm just gonna use it. Hi, Chloe. Nice to meet you. The windows are all sealed shut, by the way."

"Isn't that a safety issue? What if there's a fire?"

"The locks disengage if the fire alarm goes off. Same with carbon monoxide." Izzy flipped her multicolored braid over her shoulder. Her growing-in roots and pale freckled skin made it clear she was originally a redhead. "Or I guess we could always break the glass. But that also would set off an alarm."

Great.

Chloe flopped on the cot, wincing when it was harder than she'd expected. "How long have you been here?"

"About a month. It's not so bad. Not that I'm not counting down my time, but the horses are actually pretty cool. The horseshit on the other hand…"

"Horseshit?"

Danica sat up in her bed. Or was it Desiree? Whichever one had bronze skin and corkscrew ebony curls. "One word: bandanna." She gestured to her face. "You'll want to wrap it around your nose and mouth."

Just like that, Chloe's sense of dread grew, the black heaviness coating her insides. Since she didn't want to talk to anyone besides Tyler, she kicked off her shoes and lay back on her prison-issue cot. Her breaths quickened in that way they did before she couldn't breathe at all, and she wished again for something to dull her emotions.

At least she'd been cured of wanting her mom. She never wanted to see her ever again. What kind of mother just dumps her daughter off at a cowboy camp for delinquent youths? As if that was going to fix everything and make her care less about her friends and her boyfriend, who were way too far away.

Loneliness pressed in on her, along with a sense of betrayal, and Chloe closed her eyes and let the tears freely flow. Her eyelids wouldn't work as a dam for much longer anyway, and if she turned toward the wall, no one would have to see that she'd broken.

That she *was* broken.

Chapter 5

WAS THAT HOW BISCUIT DOUGH WAS SUPPOSED TO LOOK? It was lumpy. And dry, yet wet. Jess's biceps complained as she worked to stir the dough with the whisk again, which made her feel wimpy on top of the drowning sensation already churning through her.

How'd she get in so far over her head?

Since her efforts didn't change the dough's appearance, she decided it was mixed enough. Maybe the dry pockets were what formed those little bumps on the tops of home-made biscuits.

But seriously, why would anyone make these from scratch when you could buy those nifty tubes? Sure, there were those few terrifying seconds where your nerves were on edge, waiting for the jack-in-the-box *pop*, but then it was over and you could just set those perfectly rounded dough blobs on the pan.

Jess consulted the cookbook she'd been handed this morning.

"Unless you have your own recipe," Mrs. Dawson, who'd insisted she call her Kathy, had said, and Jess told her she'd be happy to use the one they usually went with. Mostly because she didn't have her own recipe, and Google had an overwhelming number of options.

As if that wasn't mind-boggling enough, people in the comments section didn't just say the recipe was good or bad. No, they were like *I added two pinches of chives, cut the butter and salt in half, and substituted the milk for the blood of an almond, and you should, too!*

At least recipe books didn't have a comments section. No froufrou options. Just cut and dry, although she did wish they had more pictures than just the after image.

Jess leaned closer to the page and muttered the instructions to herself. "'Roll out the dough to one inch thick…'" She glanced around for a ruler. Was that a common kitchen tool? How precise did she need to be? What if it was one and a fourth inches? What if she undershot it?

The kitchen door swung open, and she fought the urge to hide. She wasn't doing anything wrong. Just fudging a few details on her résumé, and who *didn't* do that?

"Just checking in," Wade said. As he stepped farther into the room, she took in his fitted jeans, worn more at the thighs they hugged, his navy shirt that made her think his gray eyes held a hint of blue, and then there was the pale-brown cowboy hat.

I wonder if he sleeps in it.

Or maybe he's bald under there.

She snorted, and he gave her a disconcerted look. "I'm good!" *Crap.* Her voice came out way too high-pitched, and the tilt of his head said he'd noticed. Did he also notice her checking out his arms? He'd rolled up his sleeves, so it was hardly her fault that her eyes went right to that impressive line in his forearm.

Priorities, Jess. Find a way to make him go away so he doesn't realize you don't know what you're doing. "Isn't there a saying about too many chefs ruining the broth?"

He stepped closer. "You're making broth for breakfast?"

Her sigh filled the room. "Of course not. I'm making

biscuits. Your mom said you guys used to have them a lot, and that everyone's been missing them."

Wade put a hand over his stomach. "It's been too long, that's for sure."

"Well, you won't have to wait much longer. Unless you keep distracting me." As she made the shooing motion, some of the dough flung from her fingers, and a couple stray pieces landed on his shirt.

He glanced down at them, and she flashed him a Cheshire cat grin. If he didn't leave, it would be that much harder to pretend to know what she was doing. The pressure inside her had already built and built until it was at the explosive point.

"Fine," he said, wiping at the biscuit shrapnel. "I'm going."

Jess kept her grin plastered in place and adopted a sing-song tone she so didn't feel. "See you out there."

His hands came up in surrender as he backpedaled. "Did they tell you that one of the teens has a peanut allergy? Most everything's been checked for it, but we always reread the labels, just to be safe."

Oh, good. More pressure. Still, she made a mental note, because she didn't want to be responsible for hurting one of the teens here.

She'd already done a number on her daughter.

Don't think about that, or there will be tears in the biscuits. If she were going to cry, she might as well add a sad rendition of "Happy Birthday" and throw herself a full-on pity party. Yay for being thirty-one!

Wade disappeared, and she blinked at the recipe again. How was anyone supposed to function this early in the morning? She'd given herself an extra half hour in the kitchen, and it still might not be enough.

Halfway through tossing ingredients into the largest mixing bowl she could find, she'd brewed a pot of coffee, and she decided a second cup was in order. The fridge was sadly short on creamer—she always had a supersize bottle of the chocolate kind at home—so she used milk and then quickly got to work rolling out the biscuits, using her knuckle as an inch marker. Then she popped them into the oven.

"Dammit. I forgot to preheat." She set the temperature and added an extra five minutes onto the baking time to make up for it. Then she cracked eggs over a skillet and scrambled them.

Humming a tune, she moved back to the giant fridge and freezer and dug out a can of orange juice. Popping and sizzling noises came from the skillet as she was trying to mix the giant concentrated ice cylinder into the water. Half a second later, a burned scent hit her nostrils.

"Shoot, shoot, shoot." She dropped the wooden spoon in the pitcher and rushed to stir the eggs. The bottom section was way too done and the top a bit runny, so she flipped the whole thing like a pancake and lowered the temperature. Then she fished the spoon out of the orange juice and continued prodding the orange iceberg floating inside.

The timer on the oven went off, and she yanked open drawers, searching for the potholders. Man, she really should've found them *before* the timer went off. Next time, she'd do just that and have them out and ready.

Finally she found a pair—way too far from the oven, if you asked her—and slipped them on.

She opened the oven door and peered inside.

The biscuits had all sort of run together and were black on top but still doughy on the inside. "Um." After a couple seconds of deliberation, she decided to lower the temperature and give them a few more minutes.

Since she'd used the method twice now, she certainly hoped it worked.

Speaking of… That same charred scent from earlier hit her again, and she slammed the oven door closed with her hip and picked the skillet of eggs off the burner.

Cheese. Cheese fixes everything. Sending up a prayer, she moved to the fridge and searched for some. She couldn't find a block of it, but there was string cheese, so she grabbed it. The stupid packs were sealed tight, more effective than a lock on a door, and she finally used a knife to slice a few open. Then she draped strips of the mozzarella across the top of the eggs.

"Okay," she muttered to herself. "What's next?"

She glanced at the oven to see how long the biscuits had, only to see she hadn't reset the timer. A quick look inside made it clear they were done. Beyond done, really.

Well, that's what jam is for.

A few minutes later, she stepped into the large dining room where—*holy crap*—there were a lot of people assembled. They'd mentioned the large staff, and that she'd be cooking for around thirty, but there were a few extra people she hadn't met yesterday, all the teens, and Liza, the younger-than-expected counselor who'd taken Chloe. She had two wiggly little kids seated next to her. Twins—she'd bet money on it—a boy and a girl, both blond with cherubic pink cheeks.

"Breakfast is ready," Jess said.

"Thank goodness," a few voices muttered, and there was an "I'm starving" thrown into the mix.

Kathy started to stand, but Wade, Trace, and her husband, Randy, told her to stay seated. Jess could tell that the family matriarch didn't like to be treated as if she was fragile, and while there were those hints about her recent illness, she still managed to exude energy, a smile constantly on her round face.

After a moment of Kathy huffing and crossing her arms as she settled back in her chair, Wade stood. Apparently he was the designated spokesperson. "Everyone, this is Miss Jessica, our new cook."

Jess gave an awkward wave as she searched the crowd for Chloe, needing to see her. To check on her. She'd said she wouldn't interfere, but she wasn't going to *ignore* her daughter.

Evidently her daughter was planning on ignoring her, though. Her head was down, and Jess couldn't get her attention.

Please look at me.

I love you. I'm sorry.

To herself, she chanted the plea that'd been on repeat for twenty-four hours: *Please let this work.*

The way everyone turned to her, along with the vague realization Wade's deep voice had been filling the air, left her trying to piece together what he'd said. Obviously something meant for her.

"Hmm?"

"I said we'll make official introductions after we eat, since everyone will be able to focus better then. I thought

I'd assign a couple of people to help you carry in the food. That work?"

She nodded. "Perfect."

Wade rattled off names, and a teenage boy who'd sat away from the rest of the group pushed to his feet, as well as two of the teen girls who'd been seated by Chloe. But not Chloe.

And she still wasn't looking at her, and it was all she could do to walk to the kitchen instead of becoming that mom who flung out her arms, dragged her kid into a hug, and cried "my baby" as tears rolled down her cheeks.

Yeah, that'd make a big impression on my first day. She somehow doubted the Dawsons or the rest of the staff would find it endearing, and Chloe would definitely never talk to her again.

Just keep swimming, just keep swimming, she told herself, proving that she was a mom to her core, and the ship of being cool ever again had sailed.

A few minutes later, the food was on the center of the table and people were passing it around. Jess winced as they scooped eggs onto their plates, hoping breakfast tasted better than it looked. Sure, there were some burned pieces here and there, but those were easy enough to pick off, right?

The biscuits received a lot of puzzled glances, so clearly they hadn't turned out exactly like Mrs. Dawson's, despite coming from the same recipe.

"Mom, this is yuck," Liza's son said, sticking out his tongue.

Liza shushed him and gave Jess a friendly smile. "Life with picky three-year-olds. One day they like hot dogs, and the next they won't eat anything but chicken *N-U-G-G-E-T-S* shaped like *D-I-N-O*"—she paused for a second, her forehead crinkling—"*S-A-U-R-S.*"

Jess appreciated her trying to make her feel better, and man, did she remember those toddler days when saying the wrong word aloud could incite a riot, but the little boy wasn't the only one who was making a sour face. Or eyeing the food like it'd been beamed down by aliens.

Jess picked up one of the biscuits. She stuck a piece in her mouth and fought back a gag. "Must be the change in altitude. Or the fact that I don't usually make such big batches. Or…" *Shit.*

This was it. The moment they all called her the fraud she was. Sure to follow was her public firing, and now Chloe hated her, and they'd have to leave before she got help.

Kathy leaned forward, peering around Wade to meet Jess's eye. "It takes some getting used to, cooking for this many people. Don't worry, you'll get the hang of it."

"I will. I promise." Jess made the mistake of glancing at Wade, whose eyebrows were drawn low under the brim of his cowboy hat, and she swore he could see right through her.

She'd show him. She'd do whatever it took to make a decent meal.

"Wade," Kathy said. "Introduce Jess around as we eat. Y'all, thank Miss Jessica for this meal."

Thank-you's came from every direction, and she fought the urge to apologize to them all. Then she was introduced to the counselors, Nick Sutherland and Liza Reynolds. Liza and her twins, Everett and Elise, also lived in one of the cabins on the ranch, and Liza mentioned getting together sometime.

"If you don't mind a messy house and rambunctious children," she added.

Jess smiled across the table at them. "I don't mind either." In fact, as hard as it'd been, she occasionally missed those years when Chloe was a toddler. So sweet and innocent, and Jess's toughest parenting decision was whether or not to let her daughter solely subsist on mac and cheese and Goldfish crackers. Sure, there'd been a lot of times she didn't know how they'd make it financially, but compared to picking up her daughter from jail, she'd take worrying over money any day.

At least having a poor mom wouldn't completely destroy her daughter's future.

Trace, Brady, Wade, and Aiden, the teen boy who'd helped carry in breakfast, took care of a lot of the ranch work, as well as helped out with the camp. Randy, Trace, and Brady doubled as class instructors, and Trace ran the equine therapy program with Aiden's help, while Penny took care of any medical issues and medication—they also had a doctor and psychiatrist who visited regularly—and then there was Allie, the education coordinator.

Jess could feel the sense of community among them, all these amazing people who worked together to help teens at one of the roughest points in their lives. It helped buoy her mood, giving her renewed hope, along with confirmation this was the right place for her daughter.

Everyone was responsible for taking their own dish into the kitchen, and as the teens placed their plates in the dishwasher, Jess was introduced to the nine girls and seven boys in the program. Save Chloe, for obvious reasons.

As everyone was filing out of the kitchen, Jess stepped in

front of Chloe, unable to help herself any longer. "How was your night? Did you sleep okay?"

"Like you care," Chloe said, and the ache that'd made a home in Jess's chest rose up again, throbbing with a vengeance.

She worked to keep her voice calm so they wouldn't end up in a screaming or crying match. "I care. I wouldn't be here otherwise."

"I wish you weren't here." Finally Chloe looked at her, but her features were set and cold, so at odds with how her daughter used to be. "I never understood it when my friends said they couldn't talk to their moms. Now I get it. I'm actually jealous of the kids who don't have to see their moms." With that, she charged out of the kitchen, and Jess pushed a hand over her heart—not that it helped the ripping sensation.

As if that wasn't painful enough, she noticed Wade had lingered, leaving him witness to the whole exchange.

"I'm not interfering. I was just asking if she was okay…" She turned to the sink, twisted the knob for hot water, and dumped dish soap into the mix. Her cooking skills might be subpar, but dishes were easy enough, and right now, cleaning things—being in control of something—seemed like the perfect place to focus her energy.

Wade backed away and left her to it, and Jess scrubbed as if the dishes had personally offended her. Honestly, she'd probably offended them with her loose definition of the term *food*, but they couldn't back-talk her or storm away, so win?

After all the dishes were cleaned, dried, and put away—possibly not where they'd originally started the day, but she'd done her best—Jess checked the time. Since the teens made their own lunches, that left her approximately seven hours to figure out how to make an amazing dish for dinner. Something that might redeem her and allow her to keep her job for one more day. Then she'd deal with the day after that.

That was how she'd dealt with life during the hardest times. An hour at a time, a day at a time.

Naturally, she ran into Wade as she was coming out of the house. She didn't know what it was about the guy that left her so unsettled. Possibly that he was meeting her at the worst time in her life, and while she wanted to stick with that claim, she had a feeling her nerves would go into a tailspin around him regardless of when and how they'd met.

The dogs at his feet raced over to her. They didn't jump but pranced around her ankles, eager for attention. The bigger of the two was a mottled mix of white, brown, and black, one of its eyes blue and one brown, and the other was a black border collie.

She bent down and patted their heads, wishing she had something to offer them. Maybe *they* would eat what she'd cooked this morning. Strike that. They'd already accepted her, and she wanted to remain on their good sides.

Booted footsteps hit the porch, and she ran her gaze up the denim-clad legs to the shadowed face of Wade Dawson.

"I know, the biscuits were awful, and I promise dinner will be better," she said before he could, because it seemed better to confess to that instead of being a horrible cook.

"Those were biscuits?" he asked, a smart-ass smirk on his face. "I thought you'd gone fancy on us and served us English scones."

"And what do you know about English scones?"

He reached up and scratched at the scruff on his neck. "That they could double as rocks…"

She bit back a smile. "That's when Americans make scones. Actual English scones are delightful—more like our biscuits. Well, not mine, but…yeah."

"You've been to England?"

"Well, no." That was supposed to be a trip she went on after graduating from high school, which was another one of those plans that hadn't shaken out. "But I've had high tea with scones and clotted cream and jam." High tea was something her mom used to treat her to way back in the day, before ugliness had overtaken their relationship and the toxicity had led to Jess cutting her mom out of her life. She hadn't thought about that in years, and a pang of longing she thought she'd rid herself of went through her.

"Ah, so you were broadening our horizons." One corner of his mouth quirked up. "On the benefits of eating charcoal."

She rubbed the soft ear of the collie. "Yep. By the end of the month, you'll all be vegans with a penchant for charcoal."

He shuddered, and she was pretty sure it was more over the lack of beef than the charcoal. "If anything, I guess this will be good. We'll be able to add diet camp to our résumé."

Her jaw dropped. It was far from PC, even if a little bit funny. Honestly, she'd hardly been able to shove any food down herself, and she'd only done so out of sheer force of will. Even the orange juice had been runny—or at least her cup had. Someone else complained it'd been too strong.

She'd botched the entire meal, and she still wondered if the other shoe was going to drop. If Wade would politely fire her, now that they no longer had an audience besides the canines, and then she'd have to beg for the second time in as many days. While her pride would balk, she'd do it.

"Come on," Wade said, quick and sharp, and she straightened and put a hand on her chest.

"Me?"

"I was talking to Quigley and Dundee." He snapped his fingers and pointed at the older, boxy pickup truck Brady was tossing supplies into, and the dogs sprinted over and leaped in the back.

"Quigley and Dundee?" She wrinkled her nose. "Really?"

Wade arched an eyebrow. "Have you seen those movies?"

"No. They look—"

"Careful," he said, pointing a finger at her. "They're heroes 'round these parts."

"They're fictional."

He shook his head and gave a loud sigh. "I warned you. Them's fighting words. Ones I can't allow on this ranch, at least not until you've watched the movies. You can find them in the living room, in the big bookshelf next to the Bible."

She wasn't sure whether he was joking or not. This was a new side of Wade, one that did funny things to her tummy. With the knots of worry that he was about to give her the ax loosening, she was able to take a moment to appreciate the beauty of the ranch sprawling out around the cowboy. The stretches of endless green with the picturesque white-capped blue mountains serving as a backdrop. The big wooden barn that showed signs it used to be quintessential red, with the large corral that fed into it and was currently filled with baby cows who frolicked around with their tails in the air and their mamas who looked on with exhausted expressions. A couple of cats were lounging in the flower beds, creatures and life stirring everywhere she looked.

If she'd come here for any other reason, she might even call it charming and idyllic.

"Well, I best get to work," Wade said, reaching up to his hat and giving it a tip—like he was one of the heroes in those movies he'd mentioned.

Jess stepped forward, her mouth opening as if that crazy, impulsive girl she used to be had taken the wheel again. "Do you need help? With whatever you're doing?" After the disastrous breakfast, she felt compelled to prove her work ethic was solid, and that she'd be worth keeping around regardless.

"Dressed like that?" he asked, and she automatically looked down at her V-neck T-shirt, skinny jeans, and ballet flats.

Her defenses pricked up. "What's wrong with the way I'm dressed?"

His gaze ran slowly down her before coming back up to her face. "Nothing. Not sure they're fixing-fence clothes, though. And after tasting your cooking, I'm not sure I trust your help."

"You know what?" Jess stormed past him, planning to stomp down the porch steps so he could hear how pissed she was. What a conceited ass! She hoped his hat *was* covering a bald head. It'd be the perfect match to his lacking, definitely *not* charming, personality.

Wade caught her arm. "Don't go gettin' all hurt. I thought we had a teasing thing going."

She spun to face him. "Bringing it up once was objectively funny. Twice is borderline mean."

"I'd say something about you feeding us those biscuits being borderline mean, but I'm guessing that'd cross the line."

Her teeth would crack if she clenched them any harder.

"Wade? Ready to go?" Brady called, and Wade glanced at his brother but didn't release her arm.

"I just thought maybe you could tell me more about the program and what exactly it entails while we work." Maybe she'd be better at fencing than cooking.

Sure. They'll hire you on as the worst ranch hand ever. Hey, if it meant not having to eat her cooking, they just might. Stress built in her chest and crowded her lungs. She had to do better next meal. And what was she thinking, asking to go along? It wasn't as if she didn't have enough to do, especially since she might need to run into town for supplies, and she wasn't sure where town was or how their supplies would be.

As she opened her mouth to tell him never mind—and she was going to do her best not to add an expletive or let her irritation show, because he was her current employer after all—he inclined his head toward the truck.

"Well, come on, then. Daylight's a-wasting."

———————————

Brady shot him a look over the top of Jessica's head, one that silently asked what he was doing.

Hell if he knew. She'd asked about coming along and wanted to know more about the program. They threw the teens right into labor-intensive tasks, so she might as well see for herself what that was like.

That's not the only reason, his brain whispered, even as he tried to tell himself it was. That it didn't have anything to do with the big, brown eyes and blond hair, and yeah, of course he'd noticed the curves. Hips and breasts and the curve of her full lower lip, and he knew he shouldn't be thinking about her lips at all. Or her other curves, for that matter.

Even if her hip lightly pressed against his as he made the turn that'd take them to the upper field. Her thigh was flush with his, too, and when he reached over to shift, it left his hand and the gear shaft between her knees.

"Sorry," he said gruffly. "Not a whole lot of room."

"No worries," she replied, but it was soft and automatic, her thoughts off somewhere miles away. Most likely on her kid.

That was the other reason he'd told her to hop in the truck. Standing on that big porch, her hands twisting in front of her, she looked as lost as the teens on their first day at the ranch. He'd also caught the tail end of what'd happened with her daughter in the kitchen, and he couldn't help it... That same damn urge to make her feel better took hold.

Completely better was out of his league, but he could at least give her half a hand.

Part of him wanted to push her hard. Give her a dozen chores that'd leave her exhausted and covered in dirt and see if she'd flee. That'd keep him and—even more importantly—his family from getting attached. They'd been down that road before, and he wasn't traveling it again.

Admittedly, the second he'd tasted her awful cooking, he'd thought, *That's it. Now they'll let me fire her.* But then she'd smiled and chatted with the entire staff, including

Liza and her kids, in that genuine, caring way people simply couldn't fake. Not without him seeing it.

Then again, she'd obviously lied to them, and he cursed himself for not personally calling her references and finding out more about her. That was the problem with being too desperate for help. It made you too careless. Too quick to believe anything.

As they drove over to the stretch of sagging fence, his thoughts volleyed back and forth. What to do. What to say. It wasn't his style not to make a decision and stick with it. Then again, he'd been outvoted.

"How far does your land go?" Jess asked, scooting forward.

"Eight hundred acres total. Five hundred that are farmable and three hundred for grazing. This stretch of land is where the cows are currently grazing, although the grass is sparse enough we're still feeding them hay every morning while we wait for it to fill in and grow a bit more. And still they've been wearing down the fence, always thinking the grass is greener on the other side."

"Is it?"

"It's alfalfa. If they eat it now, not only will several of them eat too much and bloat themselves, then we can't bale it come summer and they won't have anything to eat next winter."

"So yes," she said, and he bit back a smile.

"Technically, it's not grass."

"Well, you do strike me as a 'technically' guy," she said with a laugh, and he wasn't sure how he felt about her laughing at him. Probably about how she felt about him poking at her cooking skills.

Brady snorted, making it clear he'd tried to hold back his laugh and failed.

"How many sons do your parents have? And no daughters, or did they flee to greener pastures?"

Wade glanced at her, then gestured for Brady to do the storytelling. He was better at it anyway.

"Sometimes it's hard to keep track, and it's constantly changing." Brady braced his hand against the glove box as they turned off the road. The shocks were beyond worn, leaving them to bounce around the cab like popcorn. "No daughters—yet."

Jessica cocked her head.

Yeah, Brady hadn't done as good a job at giving her the rundown as Wade had expected, almost as if he was making a point to be brief and leave Wade to do the filling in. "We tend to collect people. I often refer to Turn Around Ranch as the Island Ranch of Misfit Toys."

He pulled up beside the weakest stretch of fence and cut the engine. The door squealed and complained as he pushed it open. The old Dodge was from the late seventies, and the engine and transmission had been rebuilt, but Wade clung to it because they didn't make things as sturdy these days. Not that he was going to give up his nicer, newer Dodge Ram. That was for pulling horse trailers and taking women on dates. If he ever did that kind of thing again.

He climbed out and offered a hand to help Jessica do the same.

Two steps out of the truck, she stumbled into a clump of Chico brush that came up to her knees and would probably scratch up her ankles in no time—if the ants didn't get to the exposed skin first. He really should've made her change, although he wasn't sure if she had anything proper to change into.

"You're gonna need boots if you plan on doing ranch work." He reached inside the truck, grabbed his gloves and a spare set, and handed the newer pair to her.

The dogs came bounding over, and like earlier, she bent down to shower them with attention like the spoiled dogs they were. She twisted to Brady, her fingers still scratching a trail over Dundee's back. "You were telling me about all your brothers."

"I was?" Brady asked as he lifted the fence stretcher out of the truck bed.

"Well, I was going to ask for more details, and you were going to happily provide them." She smiled extra wide, and Wade shook his head as he grabbed his fencing pliers and began to remove the staple from the wooden post so he could tighten the wire.

"Wade's the oldest—and the biggest rule follower, as you pointed out."

Jessica laughed, and a sensation Wade hadn't felt in a long time swirled through his gut. It should be irritation, but it definitely had more of an attraction vibe.

"About two years later, I came along." Brady secured the stretcher on the end of the wire and began cranking it. "Nash is around my same age. My parents adopted him when he was sixteen, after he'd gone through the program."

"That's whose cabin I'm staying in, right?"

"Right," Wade said, because why should Brady have all the fun? Plus, it made Jessica turn to him. He secured the top strand to the post with a staple and then told Brady he thought they should replace the middle strand of wire to dissuade the cows from pushing into it. The old one was sagging and rusting, and trying to tighten it would only make it more brittle.

"I'll get the wire," Jessica said, and he and Brady watched as she struggled with it for a handful of seconds. "Um, it's heavier than it looks. Also, I know that it's called barbed wire, but why's it have to be so poky?"

"To persuade the cows not to push against it." Did hefting the coiled roll out of the back with one hand make him a show-off? Possibly, but he caught Jessica eyeing his arms, so he'd happily be a show-off.

Brady gripped the end of the wire with his thick gloves and began walking toward the other post. "Nash discovered he was good at the cowboy thing, and now he works the rodeo circuit. He sends Ma postcards from everywhere he stops."

"It's what keeps me from hunting him down and kicking his ass for not coming home more," Wade muttered, and Jessica arched her eyebrows.

He wasn't going into that. He understood Nash's nomadic tendencies hadn't gone away, but like he said, Ma got attached something fierce. With each month, each holiday that passed that Nash didn't come home, she worried more and more.

"Trace was the baby for a while, but then my parents adopted Nash's biological brother, Nick, after he became a ward of the state. He was twelve at the time, and as you heard this morning, he's one of our camp counselors now. We thought we were done, but then, just over a decade later, Aiden came along. He's the newest addition."

"The kid who helped with breakfast. At first I thought

it was odd he wasn't sitting with the other teens." Jessica picked her way closer to the post Brady was securing the wire to. "How old is he?"

"Sixteen."

"And he came along, like, through the youth program?" Jessica swept a section of hair behind her ear. "Sorry for all the questions. I'm just curious. I've never met a family quite like yours."

"Yeah, he got into trouble, and a judge sent him to us," Brady said. "He has a gift with the horses, and he's a good kid who needed a break. None of us wanted him to leave when the time came, and...well, he's our family."

"I admire that." Jessica stuck her hands in her back pockets, and the move emphasized the curves Wade was doing his best to ignore. "So, what's the program like? It sounds like a lot of the kids stay. Or want to."

To keep from focusing on her too much, Wade decided to answer the question instead of letting Brady take it. "Plenty are ready to put it behind them, although Ma keeps up with everyone who's come through the best she can." Using the hammer end on his fencing pliers, he secured the wire in place and then wiped his forearm across the sweat beginning to form on his forehead.

He turned to Jessica to finish answering her question. "Each kid needs something different, so it's not a simple one-size-fits-all approach. Liza is our new counselor, and she and Nick work alongside Allie on the curriculum. Allie's also got a background in psychology and sociology and has worked at the ranch for seven years. Together, they dig and find what each kid needs, and then they give them the tools to deal with whatever they've got going on. Meanwhile, we work them hard. It keeps them busy and gives them a sense of purpose. You're going to see Chloe exhausted and in the middle of something she doesn't want to do, but—"

Jessica held up a hand. "Don't interfere. I heard the speech."

Wade's defenses went up. The speech was important, just as no drama and not crossing lines were important. He probably shouldn't have brought Jessica out here. She didn't need to know so much about their family, and her prodding questions were starting to remind him of the last woman he'd let into his life.

"Hold these for a sec, will you?" he asked, and Jessica stepped up and held the pliers for him while he grabbed a fence stay and twisted it into place.

"How did the ranch start anyway? And what came first? The animals or the alternative youth camp part?"

Wade glanced at Brady, silently telling him he thought she'd gleaned about enough information.

"Dad inherited the ranch, and Ma started the camp. Now"—Wade took the pliers from her and moved to the next section of fence to do to it what they'd just done to the other—"Brady and I need to focus on our work because this is only the first of many things that need to be fixed and done today, and all these questions are slowing us down."

Jessica brought her shoulders up, clearly catching the brush-off. Since he'd already offended her, he might as well finish and hammer home the point that question time was over.

"Let's stick to what you need to know. Our mom tends to overdo it. She used to juggle things that three different people do now. Four counting you. She got sick last winter, and she needs a break, which is why we hired you."

Jessica hugged her arms around herself. "I swear, I'll help out as much as I can."

If he was going to let her close to his family, he needed to find out more about her. See how big a liar she was, because people who lied about one thing often lied about many. Maybe he should have the sheriff conduct a background search. Most everyone else at the ranch had to go through one because they were working with at-risk youth, and they couldn't have untrustworthy people around the kids.

"Why don't you tell us about your previous cooking job," he said more than asked, and now Brady was the one shooting him a look.

Wade's mood shift had thrown Jess off for a moment or two, and the demand he had followed up with didn't help.

"Admittedly, it was more of a short-order-cook type of situation." Mac and cheese for Chloe while she made soup for herself. Waffles when she'd made boiled eggs, and of course then she'd had waffles, too. She made a hell of a waffle. Well, Eggo made them, and she heated them up in the toaster, but who didn't love those little waffles? Maybe she'd go into town and buy them in bulk. Surely no one would complain about waffles for breakfast. Especially if she added bacon.

When Wade's steely-gray eyes bored into her as if he were drilling for all her secrets, she forced herself to remain firm. Worrying about his mother was admirable. In fact, right now she wished her own child cared that much for her health. But her teenage daughter's attitude wouldn't stop her from doing whatever it took to keep this job.

Same to Gruff-and-Grumpy and his mood swings. She'd given him a break, thinking she'd misjudged him, only for him to do a one-eighty and turn combative at the drop of a hat. Just not his hat, and she was back to hoping he was bald under there.

"Do you need me to hold the wire in place?" Not only did she want to steer the subject in a different direction, but she needed something to keep her hands busy. Perhaps she should've continued to simply stand back and admire the juxtaposition of the green baby alfalfa and the rustic fence that had tiny purple flowers growing around the fence posts.

"I got it," Wade said, juggling his pliers to the other hand. He used a giant staple to secure the wire, the little barbs sticking fiercely into the air and catching the sunlight. They made her think of a certain cowboy. How, if you hit in the wrong place, you'd get jabbed. Evidently she'd have to talk to Mrs. Dawson to learn more about the ranch. Or maybe it was a sensitive subject, and she should just keep her head down and work, work, work.

Not like she didn't have enough of it. Her boss hadn't exactly been thrilled when she'd called last night and told him she'd need more like a month off, rather than a week. In order to ensure she didn't lose her permanent job, she'd offered to work from home while doing her temporary one. Between cooking sessions, she'd be entering massive amounts of data into the company database. On the bright side, it'd help keep her income steady.

"Speaking of food, I should probably get back and start prepping dinner. Until I get more familiar with cooking on the grand scale you do here, I need to check out which recipes I have that are easy to triple." Back home, that'd mean ordering nine entrees instead of the three that she and Chloe liked to order so they could share, experience more than one dish, and have leftovers for the next day. She doubted they had a lot of takeout places in Silver Springs. "How far is the house?"

She really should've paid better attention to directions and distance.

"A country mile," Wade said, and she wondered if he was trying to piss her off, or if it was just a natural talent.

"What's a country mile?"

"Means we've never had anyone officially come measure, but it's about that far. Give or take."

"I have a feeling it'll be more give. Give me crap. Give me an extra mile to see if I can hack it. But I've got news for you. I've got a long history of proving people wrong, and I'm not about to stop now." She turned, head held high, and strode toward the ranch.

"Jessica," Wade said, and her stupid, traitorous stomach completed a somersault. Stupid cowboy and his stupid deep, sexy voice.

She turned, deciding she'd be generous and accept his apology. *If* he made it good enough.

"The ranch is the other way." He tugged off one glove and sighed. "Here, I'll take you."

"I'd rather walk, thanks," she said, and then she started in the opposite direction, her head held slightly less high, but she was doing her best to at least keep it level.

"Dundee, go with her. Take her home, 'kay?"

A few seconds later, the mottled shepherd appeared at her side. Between the canine and the cowboy, she far preferred the dog, so the joke was on Wade.

Dundee stayed by her side, nudging her once when she drifted too far...whatever direction left was. Within a few minutes, she caught sight of the familiar cabin and stables. Her ankles were itchy as hell, but she was sure if she reached down to scratch them, Wade would somehow see or sense it, and that felt like admitting defeat.

As if she didn't have enough reasons to pull off dinner, she now had another one. To see the look on Wade's face when he realized he'd been wrong to judge her and question her cooking skills.

Even if he'd also been right.

Chapter 6

"WHAT WAS THAT ALL ABOUT?" BRADY ASKED, JERKING harder than necessary on the wire.

A fence done in anger was a tight fence, so Wade tugged right back. "I don't think she's got any experience cooking. Don't tell me you enjoyed your breakfast."

"It was…interesting."

"I'm looking out for Ma."

"By scaring off the only help we've had in months?" Brady lifted a hand, cutting off Wade before he could reply. "She'll get the hang of things. Everyone who's started here gets a little leeway as they learn the ropes. Just because you think she's hot doesn't mean you should revert to elementary school behavior and be an ass to her."

Wade scowled at his brother. "That's a low blow on two counts. I never said I think she's hot."

Brady made a *pfft* noise. "You don't have to say it. The way you look at her says it all. It's been quite a while since I've seen you look at a woman like that."

That was part of the problem. "If anything, that's another reason to keep her at a distance. Not only is she a single mom with a daughter at our camp, but she also works here. That's a whole lot of drama, and we have a no-drama policy, remember?"

At one point or the other, every one of the Dawson boys had brought drama knocking on their door, and over half those times had involved a pretty woman. Those were the times every part of the ranch suffered, and they'd all made a vow to do better. To stay focused on what was important.

"Because poking at her about cooking and sending her stomping across 'a country mile' isn't drama?" Brady asked, the smart-ass.

Wade sighed. "Can we just fix this damn fence and get to the cows?"

"Can you just admit you think Jessica's hot?"

Wade focused on the task at hand, ignoring his brother. The loud *tap, tap, tap* of pounding in the last staple helped.

"That's a relief, actually," Brady said, speaking loud enough to be heard over the hammering. "Now I can ask her out."

Wade whipped his head toward his brother, who let loose a smug laugh.

"Just admit it. If she was an ugly dude instead of a pretty woman, you'd have insisted we fire her already."

"If you'll remember, I voted for not hiring her in the first place. I'm just trying to be supportive of the *majority* decision. And when no one has the heart to fire her after dozens of inedible meals and we still need a cook, just know it's coming out of your salary."

"Sure," Brady said as he gathered the tools and spool of barbed wire. "My huge salary that barely covers living expenses, and that's as long as I stay on the ranch." He tossed everything from his arms into the back of the truck, and Wade added his tools to the mix with a *clank, clank*. As they walked toward the cab, slipping their hands out of gloves, Brady shrugged. "Honestly, I was just glad to have something besides chili."

Funny enough, as Wade had been forcing down the

burned food, he was thinking he'd *rather* have chili for breakfast. Beyond tastes and likes, though, he was worried that Ma would offer to help or take over in the kitchen to spare feelings, and then she'd be doing even more when she needed to be resting and healing.

Which meant he couldn't soften toward Jessica like everyone else already was. Clearly he'd need to be the bad guy who told her she was going to have to figure out how to make a decent meal or find another job.

Cold maybe, but didn't he get extra karma points for at least hoping she'd get better?

So far, they'd woken up at the ass crack of dawn, shoveled shit, and made themselves sandwiches for lunch. As Chloe returned to the stables for whatever hellacious task came next, she automatically reached for the phone in her pocket before realizing it wasn't there.

She turned to Izzy, the chatty girl who'd been her shadow since this morning. "What do we have to do to get Wi-Fi time?"

"Do all your chores, complete your classwork. No talking back, no being late. Basically fall in line, and tomorrow you can get twenty whole minutes of monitored online time. If Liza or Nick approve it."

Ugh. Surely prison would allow more. She really needed to talk to Tyler. Then, if she had time, she'd talk to her friends and tell them all that her mom wasn't cool anymore. Nope, she'd gone crazy and dragged them to the middle of nowhere for torture, and news flash, demons wore cowboy hats.

Aiden turned to address them as they walked into the stables. "Good news. After we saddle up the horses, we get to go for a ride."

"That's good news?" Chloe muttered. "I think you've forgotten what *good* means."

Aiden flashed her a smile—oops, she should've kept that in her head. Was that enough to lose her internet time?

The other detainees moved toward the stalls, and Chloe stood in the center of the room, the scent of hay edged with horseshit filling her nostrils.

"You ever ride a horse before?" Aiden asked as he approached her.

She shook her head. "No, but I have ridden a city bus with worn-out shocks, and I'm assuming it's about the same thing."

He cracked another smile, and it brought out deep grooves in his cheeks. Objectively, he was cute, maybe even hot. There was something about the combination of wholesome cowboy and bad boy that made her pulse quicken. Again, not that it mattered. She was taken, and when she got out of here, Tyler would be waiting.

But it was nice there'd be some eye candy to help break up the monotony.

"I'll help you out for your first ride." Aiden led her to a stall that held a horse with a tan coat and nearly black hair—a color he and Aiden shared, actually. "This is Rowdy, and he's a buckskin gelding. Don't worry. He's not as wild as his name implies."

Chloe glanced at Aiden, who was grinning like he'd told a great joke. Okay, so he was cute but had a weird sense of humor. Wasn't that always the way?

Tyler wasn't so much funny unless he was high and simply thought he was, but making people laugh was more her gig anyway, or so she liked to think. Although she hadn't felt very funny for the past year or so. Mostly because life had seemed too serious for cracking jokes.

Have I even laughed in the last two or three months?

There was that time that Trinity tripped on the cement curb while going into school. Although I was a bit too nervous we'd get caught to laugh as much as I wanted to.

"…over his head like this…" Aiden demonstrated how to put on the bridle and saddle, and Chloe did her best to pay attention in case there was a pop quiz that might earn her more internet time. But when he gestured to Rowdy and told her to "hop on," that familiar squeezing sensation climbed up inside her and seized hold of her lungs and throat.

Not now. There was never a convenient time for her anxiety to hit, but she hated that she couldn't worry about anything—even small things—without it taking over. And no matter how many breaths she took, she never got any air.

"You okay?" Aiden asked, and she focused on his intense green eyes. On those dark eyebrows that framed them so nicely.

Chloe reached up and scratched at her neck, trying to loosen the fist she felt around it. "I don't know how to ride a horse. I'm guessing it takes more than shouting 'whoa' to get them to stop. He's, like, really big, too. He could throw me off and stomp all over me."

Aiden reached out and snagged her hand. He slowly guided it to the neck of the horse and held it there. "He's well-trained, and I promise I won't let him stomp on you."

"Let him? I'd feel better if you'd just said he *won't* stomp on me."

"He won't. Do you want me to ride with you? Show you how to guide him and get him to stop?"

Chloe glanced at the other teens, who were mounting their horses like it was nothing.

"Don't worry about them," Aiden said. "Most of them needed help in the beginning, too, boys and girls. In fact, when I arrived at the ranch, I didn't know the first thing about horses. I preferred motorcycles, actually."

"Wait. I thought the older guys were your brothers," she blurted out. As usual, she had a way of inserting her foot in her mouth instead of thinking before speaking, and now he was going to hate her, and she was pretty sure everyone here hated her already. In fact, she suspected the only reason Izzy talked to her was because she didn't have anyone else. Or maybe she wanted something.

The lung-tightening sensation increased until the pain from going without oxygen radiated through her entire body, causing her limbs to tingle.

"Whoa," Aiden said, releasing her hand from the horse and gripping her shoulders.

"Did you just"—Chloe wheezed and fanned her heating face with a hand—"use the same word on me"—another wheeze—"as you do to stop a horse? Do I look like a horse?" Her voice pitched up. This was too much. If she confessed to the panic attacks, would that make Mom more or less likely to get her out of here? She needed less stress, not to have heaps of it dumped on her at once.

Aiden's low laugh vibrated through her, drawing her attention back to him and those green eyes. "Not sure what to start with. As for *whoa*, I say it a lot. Said it even before I came here, and yes, the Dawsons are my parents and Wade, Trace, Brady, Nick, and Nash—who you haven't met yet and probably won't—are my brothers. But they weren't my family until about six months ago, and I'll tell you something I don't normally tell people."

Chloe focused on him, waiting to hear his confession. Maybe he knew how to escape. Maybe he could help *her* escape. Or at least find a way to get a message to Tyler.

Aiden leaned closer and lowered his voice. "Sometimes I worry I'll do something that'll make them kick me out of the family."

"You can't just kick someone out of your family. Or maybe you can. It certainly feels like my mom wants to get rid of me."

"I thought your mom was the new cook."

"She is, but…I don't want to talk about my mom." A different kind of ache settled in her chest, one that made her feel weak, which was why it was easier to let anger take the controls.

"Okay," he said placatingly. "Let's get back to riding so we don't get too far behind everyone else." Until he'd mentioned the others, she hadn't even realized the buzz of conversations and stomping of hooves had quieted. "I'll be next to you the entire time, I promise."

She nodded and inhaled, surprised to find her lungs halfway functioning again. "So you're saying you won't do the thing where I think you're holding the bike and then you let it go without me knowing?"

That same smile spread across Aiden's face, and she found one corner of her mouth twisting up as well. "You'd know if I bailed off the back of the horse."

"Again, the answer is 'No, no I won't.'"

"No, Chloe. No, I won't." Aiden told her to hold on to the saddle horn. Then he guided her foot into the stirrup and boosted her up. A couple of seconds later, he swung into place behind her. He reached around her, his chest bumping her back as he gathered up the reins.

He made a clicking noise with his tongue, nudging his heels into the horse's side, and Rowdy trotted out the open stable door. Aiden explained how to steer the horse right and left and how to get him to stop. It involved more than saying "whoa," although Chloe still said it because it seemed like the thing to do.

As she grew more comfortable, her muscles relaxed. Over and over, what Aiden had told her cycled through her brain, and finally she had to ask.

"When you say when you first came here... Does that mean...?" She focused on the smooth leather of the reins. "Did your parents dump you off here, too?"

"That'd require my parents acknowledging my existence. The court ordered me here, and I was mad as hell. I was determined to bide my time and escape..."

Her skeptical side rose, and she glanced over her shoulder at him. "Is this some bit you do, where you tell the new kids how this place changed your life, so they should totally fall in line or some shit?"

"Nope. You asked, and I answered. I don't even work for the camp really. I just train the horses and help out where I can."

"How long do we have to ride?"

"We can head back if you want to."

Chloe turned the horse around, and yeah, it was nice to

know how to do that, but she wasn't falling for…whatever this was. Did they think she was a simpleton? That they could sit her in a room and ask her about her life and then put her on a horse and that'd fix her?

She was here for one reason—because her mom got knocked up in high school and was overly paranoid that Chloe was headed down the same troubled path. She and Tyler hadn't quite crossed that line yet, but when they did, she knew to be careful. She had no plans of becoming a teenage mom.

As soon as they reached the stables, she dismounted, so quickly she almost landed on her butt.

She shoved the reins toward Aiden as soon as he dismounted, but he shook his head instead of taking them.

"You have to put Rowdy away. Make sure he gets water, then take off the bridle and saddle and brush him down."

This was ridiculous and time-consuming, and the stables smelled awful. "Am I supposed to talk to him, too? Tell him all my woes?"

"If you want. He's a good listener." Aiden gave her a crooked half smile. "Hardly ever interrupts, except to beg for more hay or grain."

Chloe rolled her eyes. She tugged the horse toward the stall where he'd originally been.

"Chloe?"

She glanced back at the enigma of a boy. One minute he was calming her down, and the next he was irritating her. She didn't know what to make of him.

"I'm gonna say something that would ruin all the street cred I used to have." Aiden took a few steps closer, glancing around at the other people in the stalls before his gaze returned to her. "This place did change my life. I'm not telling you to fall in line, but I had no one for a long time, and trust me, pushing everyone away is just a good way to end up alone and miserable."

"Well, I don't push everyone away. My mom pushed *me* away, and I have plenty of friends, as well as a boyfriend who'll be waiting with open arms once I get to go back home. I'm glad it worked out for you, but I'm not like you. Not like anyone here."

With that, she grabbed a brush and got to completing the chore so she could make it through another hour that would take her that much closer to getting the hell out of here.

Chapter 7

WADE WATCHED JESSICA MOVE AROUND THE ROOM. SHE smiled and laughed with the rest of the staff as they ate their burgers.

Good burgers at that. Not that burgers took a lot of effort, but the meat wasn't charred or raw, and after that awful breakfast and skipping lunch in favor of getting more work done, he'd downed two and was considering a third.

Aiden came over to the table where the meat and the fixings were and squirted ketchup on his double-patty, quadruple-cheese burger, and Wade kicked himself for not being as inventive.

"How's it going?" Wade asked as he grabbed a bun. During his years of being constantly shuffled around, the kid had gotten super behind at school. To make up for it, Aiden often burned the candle at both ends, same as everyone else here, but on top of caring for the horses and other ranch work, he went to his room at night to do homework.

"Pretty good."

"How'd Chloe do with the horses?"

"She'll get the hang of it. She's on the angry, bitter side for sure, but there's something else in the mix. Before I could put my finger on it, she got pissy and shut down." Aiden shrugged, and Wade glanced at the sulking teenage girl who was pointedly ignoring the woman who was angry at him. Jessica had avoided his gaze as she'd dished out dinner, and he didn't know if he should apologize or let her stay mad.

After the fuss he'd made over the awful breakfast, he should at least compliment the dinner she'd made.

"Not that I'm Liza or Nick or anything," Aiden said. "I feel weird even mentioning it. Like a rat." That was his old life training kicking in. The life where he had to look out for himself and was loyal to people who'd turn on him in an instant.

"I was just curious. Don't worry, I won't ask you for a diagnosis."

"Definitely not qualified for that. But after a year of being here, I've learned no one gets out of life for free. We're all fucked up in one way or another." Aiden froze, a grimace on his face.

"I won't tell Ma you swore if you won't tell her I pissed off the cook."

"Deal."

Wade finished adding condiments, cheese, and vegetables to his burger and smooshed the bun over the top of it all. Ketchup squirted out the sides, and he licked it off his thumb as he balanced the plate in his other hand. "How's the homework going?"

"I told Brady I could use a tutor. A homely male one."

"Interesting choice."

"Just trying to stay out of trouble."

"Changing my answer to 'good choice,' then," Wade said, clapping Aiden on the back. As tough as he liked to think he was, he'd had a soft spot for Aiden from the beginning, chip on his shoulder and bad attitude notwithstanding. There was just something about him, and when Wade heard Aiden was going back into the system, he'd known he had to do whatever he could to get the kid back here where he belonged. Pretty soon they'd need another cabin or two just for family members. "I can ask around. See about a tutor."

"It's okay. That costs money, and I'm going to try out a new website that's supposed to be real good at explaining math concepts so they actually make sense."

Wade took a supersize bite of his burger and spoke around the food in his mouth. "Let me know if you change your mind. And don't wait until it's on top of you."

"Yes, sir," Aiden said, because he was still a bit of a smart-ass.

Wade had just shoved the last of his burger in his mouth when he noticed Ma approaching, and he worked to swallow it down so she wouldn't scold him for poor manners.

"Jess seems to be getting the hang of things." *Jess.* Which meant Ma was counted among her friends, while Wade had to call her Jessica. Really, it only proved he was right to try to keep some distance between the women, but he could tell by the look on his mom's face she was already falling for her.

"The burgers were good," he said.

"She's pretty, too. So young to have a teenager already, and yet you can tell how hard she's worked to get where she is."

The safest option was to simply nod, so Wade stuck with that.

"Look at how well she fits in." Ma gestured across the room, where Elise was climbing onto Jessica's lap. He knew from experience those chubby little hands would likely be sticky or covered in ketchup, but Jessica just grinned and began animatedly talking to her, making the toddler giggle.

Her hand brushed over the top of Elise's curls, a move

she didn't seem to be fully aware of, as her gaze drifted to Chloe, who had her head down.

It went against his instincts, letting a teen's mother be around her the entire time she was in the program, yet he still found himself silently urging the girl to acknowledge her mom. To give her that hope she needed.

Family therapy was a big part of their program, and all families were invited for Sunday dinners. It was the touchstone a lot of the kids needed, and while there were plenty of rambunctious dinners throughout the week, ones where a few arguments or fights had broken out, Sunday dinners with the family were sacred. No one ever misbehaved during them.

Part of the reason that worked was because they only saw each other once a week. Then they went to a therapy session and hammered out the harder stuff. If parents couldn't come, Ma wrote letters to update them and keep that hope present, for them and for the teens.

Just acknowledge her, he silently pleaded as the sorrow on Jessica's face grew.

But like her mother, Chloe was stubborn. Obviously held a grudge, too, which solidified his decision to apologize to Jessica for this morning. He'd hate for things to get that grim between him and her, and the longer words went unsaid, the harder it was to spit them out.

As much as he hated to admit it, even to himself, he'd overreacted. Hazard of not reacting in time in the past, but he had to leave that behind where it belonged and focus on the here and now. Right now, his family needed Jessica to stay and make more meals like she had tonight. Nothing said he couldn't be cautious and nice at the same time.

After the kids had cleared the table and headed to their

respective cabins with his parents, Liza, Allie, and a couple of his brothers, Wade wandered into the kitchen and found Jessica doing the dishes. While the teens were responsible for part of the cleanup, including rinsing and placing their dishes in the dishwasher, there were always a few stray pots and pans to be cleaned, along with the counters.

He cleared his throat to announce his presence, and Jessica turned, her hands still in the dishwater. "Hey," he said. Because it seemed like the easiest place to start.

"I know that a few of the burgers were a little too done, and a few probably needed another couple minutes, but—"

"The burgers were good. They're a nice…" He almost said *simple meal* but stopped himself. He liked simple. The entire ranch liked simple. But after their previous conversations about her cooking skills, he worried she'd take that the wrong way. "A nice change from what we've been having."

"Burgers are pretty easy. I mean, cooking them all at the same time was tricky, especially since I didn't realize the right side of the grill was way hotter until afterward… Anyway, what I'm saying is that I realize it's a simple meal, and I have plans for more complex ones, I swear."

Funny that she used the word he was afraid to, although he remained sure it was better her than him. "We like simple. This other cook wanted to make dishes we couldn't pronounce with ingredients I'd never even heard of. I'd rather have simple than fancy."

"Well, I'm far from fancy."

"Oh, I wouldn't say that. You did fix fence in those shoes."

She kicked one off and hooked it on her toe. "I'm going to throw one of my so-called fancy shoes at your head. Knock that cowboy hat right off."

"You think you can do what horses and cows have failed to?"

"Are you comparing me to livestock?"

He picked up a towel and began drying the dishes stacked in the drying rack.

After the last dish was scrubbed clean, Jessica pulled out the drain and watched the water slip away. "One day down, and no one's fired me yet." She raised an eyebrow that asked a silent question—or at least asked for reassurance.

"Nope. If I even tried, my own family would fire *me*."

Her lips hinted at a smile, but it didn't quite take hold. Then she jerked her chin toward the towel in his hands. "Helping out with the dishes made me think you'd come to let me down easy—after I finished cleaning up, of course."

"Sounds like me," he said, instead of rising to the bait. "But like I said, the rest of the family…"

This time her smile broke free, and she raised her hand in a fist. "Team Mama Dawson all the way."

"What makes you think it's my mom? My other brothers are equally responsible for you being here."

"Okay, but saying Team Everyone but Wade seems kinda mean." She gave a nonchalant shrug. "Just remember, you asked for it."

He chuckled. "Good thing you reminded me, because I certainly don't remember asking for it." He tossed the towel aside and spun outward, his butt resting against the counter. "I mainly came to help because I feel bad about earlier. It's my job to protect my family, and we barely know you, so I was just being cautious is all."

"Is that an apology, or you telling me to expect mood swings?"

"Yes," he said, and she laughed.

He twisted to face her, his eyes locking on hers. "I'm sorry about this morning. How was your walk back?"

"It was just fine."

"Glad to hear it."

"I mean, my ankles are still itchy from all those poky bushes, and these fancy shoes—which really aren't fancy at all, for the record—don't have much support."

"There's a place in town called Horsefeathers Western Store. You can get some boots there. If you want. If you plan on staying."

"I do," she said, no wiggle room, and while he originally hadn't wanted her to take the job, her response provided him a measure of comfort. He could appreciate someone who got back on the horse after it kicked them off. He wasn't sure if the horrible biscuits were the horse in this instance or it was him being an ass, but the idea was the same.

Jessica sighed, her chest rising and falling with the motion, and he had to remind himself not to let his gaze dwell there. Lifting it to her profile didn't make the thread of attraction stitching its way through him go away. If anything, it grew as he took in the slant of her nose and the freckles dotting the bridge of it, drawing him right to those big, brown eyes. "I survived, and so did Chloe. And surviving a day means we can survive another."

"Solid theory."

She rubbed her neck, and then her eyes met his. "It'll get easier from here, right?"

Truth or hope? He wished they were the same, but that wasn't the way the world worked. While he liked to take emotion out of things, he also was a firm believer in logic, and logic said she needed hope.

"It'll get better," he said, which wasn't exactly the same as *easier*, and he didn't specify when.

She nodded a couple of times, then wished him good night.

Wade echoed it back, and as he watched her go, he prayed that the way she completely threw him off his game and brought up emotions he usually kept under lock would get better, too.

Chapter 8

"Nothing. For the third day in a row," Chloe told the horse as she led him to a patch of grass near the creek for a breather and a snack. While Rowdy munched, she pulled out the granola bar she'd stuck in her bag.

The crumpled coffee cup was next to it, and she wished she'd thrown it away. Not because she was a neat freak—the apartment she shared with Mom often looked like someone had ransacked the place.

A pang hit her square in the chest. *That* was the reason she should've thrown it away. Mom had handed her the to-go cup this morning and whispered, "Extra strong with lots of chocolate creamer and sugar."

"Great," Chloe had said. "Now I'll have energy for all the shit shoveling."

"I'm trying here, Chloe."

"Then let's go home. Let's try there."

Mom's face had fallen, along with Chloe's hopes and dreams. It'd been five days since they'd arrived. It wasn't *all* completely awful.

Like the horse. Rowdy nudged her shoulder, and Chloe ran her hand up his nose to his forehead, giving him a gentle scratch. Aiden said horses were good listeners, and for the first few days she'd refused to utter anything but instructional words to Rowdy. It seemed like giving in to talk to the horse. Or to the counselor. Or to anyone.

But Chloe felt like she was going to burst with the need

to talk about her feelings and everything that was—or wasn't—happening. While those kinds of conversations used to take place with Mom, that wasn't an option anymore. Especially with anything involving Tyler.

"Mom would probably love to say, 'I told you so,'" Chloe continued, patting Rowdy's muscled neck as he bent to eat more grass. "I only have twenty minutes every other day to even try to talk to Tyler, and without a phone, I have to revert to archaic methods of contacting him. But he hasn't answered any of my messages. Not on Instagram, and not on Facebook, which was really a desperate attempt, since nobody besides adults even uses it anymore. I can't even remember the passwords for my other places because they were all on my phone. That keychain saver thing seems like a smart idea until you realize it made you dumber. Know what I mean?"

Rowdy whinnied, leading her to believe he was pretty tech savvy for a horse.

"I bet he's just grounded. If anything, it'll give us more to talk about when he finally answers, right? I mean, it'd be nice to know that I'm not the only one with a mom who's gone completely crazy." And yet, she missed talking to her. Crazy used to be one of her favorites of Mom's qualities. They'd laugh and dance and eat dessert for dinner. Where other mothers were serious and stern, that'd never been Mom. Not before last week.

Sure, Chloe had gotten in trouble here and there, but nothing to this extent. A few months ago was the first time she'd ever been grounded, and while she hated that Mom hadn't liked her friends or her boyfriend, she'd thought eventually her mother would see past the rough exteriors to the real people inside, the way she usually did.

At the very, very beginning, when Chloe had first told her about Tyler, Mom had asked if he was cute and funny and demanded to see pictures. They'd done some light cyberstalking, and Mom had agreed he was totally cute. The speech about being careful with boys and Chloe letting Mom know when she was ready for the next step was resurrected, but it'd been the kind of speech that left her sure that she could go to Mom. For anything.

But now? Chloe tossed the crumpled cup away from her. Hurt and anger battled it out in her chest, and her breathing grew too shallow. Mom was supposed to be the person who was on her team. She'd *promised* to always be on her team.

Rowdy whinnied again, an edge of concern to the sound this time. She swore he could sense her moods, and Aiden was right about him not interrupting. Rowdy moved closer and stomped a hoof, demanding her attention, and Chloe turned and hugged a horse. Like some kind of crazy person.

Even crazier, it was nice.

Then she heard more hoofbeats and the buzz of voices. Any second they'd have company. She and the other teens didn't get a whole lot of unsupervised time, and her cute jailer who claimed not to be a jailer would be arriving soon.

She slowly let her arms slip from Rowdy's neck, and naturally her gaze fell and fixated on the crumpled coffee cup. On the piece of trash marring the greenery and those tiny purple flowers scattered throughout. Under other circumstances, she might admit the emptiness was prettier and more calming than expected.

With a groan, she picked up the cup and shoved it back

in her bag, where it'd undoubtedly pop up to give her more conflicted feelings later.

"There you are," Aiden said, trotting his horse over to her.

"Don't worry. If I was attempting a jail break, I'd be much sneakier than this."

He bit back a smile, his attempt at a stern expression not working. "They sent me ahead to make sure you were okay."

"And here I am—totally okay. Rowdy just likes to go super fast, and so do I." Chloe gave the horse's side a rewarding pat. "It's painful to wait for the slowpokes, isn't it, Rowdy?"

He neighed, because he was cool like that.

She jerked her chin toward Izzy and Jacob, who were crashing through the trees astride their horses, a reddish-brown gelding named Bud and a white mare they called Spook. "Plus, we're pretty sure Bud and Spook are low-key dating, and we were trying to give them some alone time."

Again, Rowdy neighed, corroborating her story.

Amusement danced across the curve of Aiden's mouth. "How insightful and thoughtful of you two. Can't say I've picked up on that vibe."

Chloe shrugged. "Don't feel too bad. The whole point of low key is that not a lot of people know. Still, I don't want to get in the way of their destiny."

"Well, it's a relief *that's* the reason you raced ahead. Because if you attempted a jail break"—he leaned across his saddle, his forearms crossed on the top of the saddle horn— "I'd have no choice but to personally hunt you down."

Chloe gathered her reins, swung up onto Rowdy, and gave her hair a haughty flip. "I'm afraid you'd like that a little too much."

He shook his head, and the last of the group entered the

clearing. But as Aiden turned toward them, she was almost sure he muttered, "I'm afraid I would, too."

How did one go about picking the right boots for ranch work? Jessica studied the row of pointy-toed shoes. Common sense said she should choose the most boring, sturdy pair.

But they had these cute hot-pink ones with stitched flame shapes up the sides, some that were a mix of pink and lighter pink, and an embroidered pair that made her *want* to rock boots.

They want how much? Jess dropped her hand from the price tag and backed away slowly, as if touching the embroidered boots might make someone run up and demand payment.

Since footwear seemed too overwhelming, she browsed the other sections. Jeans with gemstones and shirts with bling and colorful patterns greeted her at every turn. All this time she thought western wear wasn't her style, but that was because she'd never seen the blinged-out options.

I should buy one for Wade. Just grin real big and present him with the most over-the-top shirt I can find. Ooh, I wonder if they have any with fringe…

Beyond that night in the kitchen when he'd apologized, she and Wade hadn't had many conversations that lasted more than a minute. They mostly exchanged polite hellos, and since she found herself wanting to talk to him more while knowing that was a bad idea, she'd given him a wide berth.

For one, getting attached to the guy was a bad idea. Two, she knew he loved the rules too much to even entertain the idea of crossing lines. And three, if he snapped and went back to being curt, it'd sting, and she'd rather pretend she was killing her first week of work, no complications.

He's still bossy as hell. This morning she'd mentioned she was finally going into town, and he'd told her the rain had made the roads rougher than usual, so take the truck, adding that the keys were in the office. Since she hadn't wanted to admit to another skill set she'd embellished, she'd simply nodded. There was no way she was driving a big manual-transmission truck into town. While there'd been a few spots where her car had struggled, she'd made it. Barely, but still.

"Need help finding somethin'?" a female voice asked, and Jessica turned to the woman who'd asked the question.

To behave or not to behave?

A prank gift was out of her budget, and she and Wade were in a good place, so she should probably keep it that way. *Which means I need to behave, dang it.* Jess dropped the checkered black-and-purple shirt. "Oh, I was just sort of looking around."

"What are you looking for? We have some lovely shirts in the women's section."

"Boots," Jess said. "Let's start with boots."

The sales associate guided her toward the shoe section she'd fled from a few minutes ago, and Jess couldn't help adding, "I'd like pretty ones, but, like, budget pretty ones."

The salesgirl smiled. "I know just the pair."

Jess added the giant tubs of potato salad and ribs next to the bags that held her new boots, as well as a pair of jeans and a shirt that'd been on clearance and matched the boots.

Over the last five days, she'd struggled her way through meal after meal. Some had turned out okay, but there'd been a few disasters in the mix. Like the incident with rolls that hadn't risen and a too-thick soup she'd tried to turn into a casserole. It'd resisted, and soggy noodles in a pan wasn't something you could easily choke down, especially with rocklike dough blobs moonlighting as rolls.

The next night she'd gone even simpler, just baked chicken and potatoes, sans bread. The green beans had boiled over, so while the kitchen smelled like she'd burned the food, no vegetables had been harmed.

Long story short, she was out of ideas and starting to worry about getting fired again.

Which was why, when she'd stepped out of Horsefeathers Western Store and seen the beam of sunshine pointing right to the local diner, she'd decided it was a sign.

Admittedly, when she'd stepped inside the Silver Saddle Diner and had seen the saddle-topped stools lining the bar, she wondered if God just had a funny sense of humor.

But it'd smelled amazing, and simply reading the menu items made her mouth water, so she'd ordered a ton of food, dipping into her savings to pay for it.

Once she returned to the ranch, she would throw it into pans to warm it up so that if anyone visited the kitchen, it would look like she'd worked hard to make it.

A white lie. A teeny, tiny one to get her through to tomorrow. She'd bought extra barbecue sauce to throw on to add her own twist, and she was totally *going to* learn how to make ribs eventually, so…

Who am I kidding? I'm desperate. No other word for it.

The door of the diner swung open, and Winona, the

short, friendly woman who'd taken her order, ran over with another white bag. "You forgot the rolls."

"Oops!" Jess planned on saying they were the frozen, pop-in-the-oven kind. That sounded realistic enough, right? That was how she'd done Thanksgiving the one—and only—time she'd attempted it.

Jessica took the warm bag and hugged it to her, the scent so amazing she had to fight the temptation to take one out and get a sneak-preview taste. "Thanks again. And, uh… Could you not mention to the Dawsons that I was here? I mean, if they straight up ask you, then I'm not asking you to lie, but…"

A big smile split Winona's face, the white of her teeth contrasting with her russet skin and straight black hair. "Your secret's safe with me."

"I'm sure I don't have to tell you that it's hard coming up with new things to make every day. I just needed a break, and I have this other job, and…" Jess reached up and twisted a curl around her finger. "I'm a horrible person. Never mind. Go ahead and call them up and tell them I'm a fraud, and I won't blame you one bit."

Winona lifted one of Jess's hands and gave it a consoling pat. "Full disclosure, we heard you were having some trouble with your biscuits."

Jess's cheeks flamed. She wanted to know how and where and why, and if that meant no one could keep a secret. She glanced around like a paranoid lunatic. The shops lining Main Street were all older brick buildings with varying colors of fading paint. There was the clothing store, a hardware store, a dry cleaner, and a building that used to be a movie theater but had been converted to an Italian restaurant.

Ooh, if I run out of options next week, we can have Italian.

"If you ever want to come on down and hang out in the kitchen of the diner," Winona continued, "I'd be happy to show you a few simple meals."

Jess spun back to face her, abandoning her attempts to look for spies who might out her for buying tonight's dinner. "Seriously?"

"Yes, ma'am."

"I was all set to tackle hug you until you went and called me ma'am." Jess wrinkled her nose. "It makes me feel so old."

"'Round here, people are big on respect, so I call everyone ma'am. And what are you, anyway, twenty-three? Twenty-four?"

"Winona, you're already my favorite person in town. No need to keep up the flattery," Jess said with a laugh. She placed the rolls next to the bags with the ribs and potato salad and slammed her trunk. The latch didn't engage—stupid thing was about fifty-fifty these days. Since she didn't have money for things like spotty latches, she hadn't bothered taking it into a shop. Another slam, followed by leaning her weight on it and counting to five, and it stayed in place.

Winona watched the entire thing with a nonjudgmental smile. It still made Jess feel like a bit of a hot mess, but as a single mom, she'd often lived with things that only worked part of the time. Most everything could be temporarily fixed with a trick, though, and she was an expert at finding the right maneuvers to make do.

With the trunk secure, she asked for Winona's number and stored it in her phone. "I'll definitely be calling to take you up on your offer. Thank you so much."

The time flashed across the screen as Jess closed out her contacts, sending her heart rate into overdrive. She needed to smuggle all this food into the kitchen before the guys returned from whatever they were doing out in the fields today. She called out a last goodbye, climbed into her car, and pushed the speed limit as she drove the mostly empty road out of town.

As she turned onto the road that led to the ranch, her tires slipped. A grinding noise sounded underneath her car, and she winced as she bumped farther down the road. The ruts she'd made in the mud on her way into town had partially dried, and it was like maneuvering around oil slicks, only to find crusty jumps not meant for a little car like hers.

"Oh, crap!" She hit a boggy spot, and she should've been going faster to get through it, but she'd been going slow to avoid the ruts. Jess pushed down on the accelerator, depressing it to the floor. Her tires slipped and spun, mud whipping up and splattering her back window, but the car didn't move forward.

She shifted into reverse and slammed the accelerator to the floor. The bags in the trunk rolled around and thudded against each other as the engine whined louder. She sank a few inches, her car going down instead of backward.

"No, no, no." Not only was it a good half-mile walk to the main cabin, but she'd have to carry the bags, which would probably take two trips and be like flashing a neon sign over her head that screamed she hadn't made the food herself.

After a few more attempts to rock the car back and forth that only resulted in it sinking deeper in the mud, she finally gave up and climbed out.

A wet, sucking noise accompanied her footsteps, and by

step three, the sludge had come up and over the top of her ballet flats to hit her bare skin. *Ew, ew, ew.*

Well, her shoes wouldn't ever look fancy again, that was for sure. Briefly, she thought of switching into the boots, but she'd gotten the cute pink ones, and her flats were already beyond muddy anyway.

Maybe the car just needs a good push. Jessica walked around the car, braced her hands on the bumper, and shoved for all she was worth. It barely rocked before settling into the same exact spot. She bent lower, putting her shoulder against the metal this time. A grunt came out about the same time her foot slipped, and her knee went down in the mud.

"Shit." Actually, there was the silver lining. It wasn't actual shit, so yay? Using the bumper, she pulled herself up and glanced toward the house.

As much as she hated to admit it, she needed help.

Man, she hated asking for help. Most of her life had been about proving that she could make it on her own. Only one thought kept her going: *If I can just find Brady or Trace, maybe Wade will never have to know.*

Chapter 9

WADE WAS BENT LOW, STUDYING THE HORSESHOES ON Thunder, the Appaloosa mare he usually rode. He ran his hand over her speckled gray-and-white coat as he picked up the front leg. There was the problem. He dislodged the rock and clump of dirt that she'd been trying to stomp free.

The stable door opened, and Brady, who was putting up their saddles, turned his head toward the noise.

"Oh, thank goodness," he heard Jessica say. "It's you."

Wade's muscles stiffened. Was something going on between her and Brady? They hadn't talked about her since fixing fence the other day, but his brother had made it clear he saw whatever was brewing between them, even though Wade was still doing his best to snuff it out.

"I went into town," Jessica continued, her voice growing louder, "and on my way back, I got stuck. Which is why I'm covered in mud. I don't suppose you could pull me out and, you know, not tell Wade."

Brady glanced at him through the wooden slats of the stall, and Wade slowly stood.

Admittedly, he experienced a pinch of amusement over the way Jessica paled, her mouth hanging open as she tried to recover.

"*Shit.*"

Wade clucked his tongue and folded his arms across the top of the gate. "Did you hear that, Brady? Girl's got a mouth on her."

"And here I thought you were pretending not to notice," Brady said, ruining his fun.

Wade stepped out of the stall, making sure to secure the lock, and then assessed the woman who threw him out of whack whenever she was around. Mud coated her from the tips of her toes to the middle of her calves. One of her pant legs also had a dripping smear across the knee, and she had a smudge on her cheek, where she must've swept her hair off her face. "How in the hell did you manage to get the truck stuck?"

"I…" She glanced toward the exit as if she might need an escape route, and a prickle traveled across his skin. "I took my car."

"I told you to take the truck!"

"Well, I don't do what I'm told all the time."

"Clearly."

"You're not the boss of me. I mean, you kind of are. But not over what I drive and where I go, so…" She crossed her arms with a huff, emphasizing her cleavage and her annoyance.

Attraction and frustration battled it out inside him, but luckily he was good at suppressing the former. Plus, if she'd just listened, she wouldn't be in this mess. "Oh, good. Then I don't have to waste time pulling out your car. That's a relief because I have a lot to do."

"Well, that's why I didn't ask *you* to help. I asked Brady." She turned to his brother, who raised his hands.

"Sorry, Jess, but I'm not getting in the middle of whatever this is."

"It's nothing! Besides him being mad that he can't control every aspect of everyone's life." She blew out a breath and swiped at the curl that forever fell in her eyes. "You know what? I don't need help. I'll go get the truck myself, and I'll hook it up, and you guys can go about your day like nothing happened." She spun on her heel and stormed out, and Wade let his head fall back with a groan.

"You gonna take care of that?" Brady asked. "Or do you want to wait till we have to pull two vehicles out of the mud?"

Wade shot his brother a look. "I got it." He took a step toward the open doorway but couldn't quite let it go. Not when Brady had also called her Jess, not Jessica. "Why'd she come to you anyway?"

"My guess is because of the exact way you reacted. You're not very forgiving of mistakes."

Wade didn't think that was true. This whole place was about second chances and fixing mistakes. Sure, he expected things to be done right, and if they weren't, he corrected people so they'd learn. What was he supposed to do? Tell everyone to do whatever they felt like, however they wanted to, and then go around fixing it when he didn't even have time to do everything he needed to in the first place?

Brady dug sunscreen and bug repellent out of his saddle bag and tossed it aside. "The scowl you're making and your rant about wasting time are exhibits A and B, Bro."

"If she would've just listened..."

"Not what I'd start with. Especially if you want to get closer to that mouth you mentioned."

"Great. Here I was worried that Ma would try to play matchmaker, but you've got it covered." Wade grabbed his gloves off the top plank of Thunder's stall and rushed after Jessica. It wasn't hard to find her. She'd left a trail of mud and had hesitated at the bottom of the porch.

She glanced down at her muddy self and then at the house, her eyebrows scrunching together.

"I'll grab the keys," he said, moving past her.

A few minutes later, after a short argument where she insisted she could do it herself, they were both climbing into the truck.

The bumpy ride to her car passed in silence as he searched his brain for the right thing to say. His mouth always got ahead of his brain. Not to mention that Jessica had a way of getting under his skin. To think he'd been waiting for their next conversation, only to blow it before it even started.

"There it is," she said, and he didn't bother saying he saw it. Not like he could miss it. It was in the middle of the freaking road. The trunk was open, too.

"Um, just a second." She hopped out and sprinted over to the car. She slipped and righted herself as she picked her way to the back, and as he climbed out, he caught a string of swear words.

He didn't know how literally she'd meant *just a second*, so he made his way over, and she quickly slammed the trunk. She leaned her hip and elbow against it as if she had a body in there and gave him a big fake smile.

"Everything okay?" he asked.

"Yeah, it's just peachy. This is what I do for fun."

"To each their own." He squatted to check out the tires. They were buried deep in the muck, no chance of simply hopping in the car and easily driving out. Once this mess dried, these ruts were going to make their little dirt road even bumpier than usual. "I'll get the chain from the truck and hook it to the front bumper."

"Okay. I suppose I should come see how it all works in case I get stuck again."

"Or you could take the truck next time." It'd popped out without thinking, and he worked to soften his words. "Is my suggestion. Not an order or anything."

"Mm-hmm."

After he turned the truck around and showed her how to connect everything, he grabbed a couple of planks of wood from the back of his truck to help the tires get purchase. "Okay, climb in the truck and throw it in first, while I push the car from behind."

Instead of climbing into the truck, she simply blinked at him. It didn't seem like her usual stubbornness, but maybe he hadn't said the right combination of words. "Please?"

"I…" She opened her mouth. Closed it. Then she spun on her heel and climbed inside the cab. She killed the engine three times in a row before bailing out, and he suddenly knew why she hadn't taken the truck.

"When you said you could drive a stick shift—"

"I said it'd been a while. Which is true. But I only tried it out one time, and I sorta wrecked, so…" She lifted her thumbnail as if she was going to bite it, rethought it once she got a look at her muddy hands, and swiped her palms together. "I don't know how to drive one. Not really. There. Are you happy?"

"Not the word I'd use to describe myself right now." He stepped closer and dipped his head, his eyes seeking out hers. "You could've told me."

"Let's just cut to the point and say that I'm bad at a lot of things. Only one of them that I really care about, and it's why my daughter is here now."

"Jessica."

She shook her head. "Can we please just get my car out and move on with our day?"

The tremble in her voice made him feel like an ass. Maybe Brady was right, and he wasn't the best at allowing for mistakes. Probably due to a combination of being ridiculously busy, forever overworked, and stressed out to the point he couldn't remember what it felt like not to have worries constantly in the back of his mind. But that was no excuse to make the people closest to him—or Jessica—feel bad.

He instructed her to get in the car and hit the gas while he pushed so he could at least get her car onto the boards. He almost told her that she was damn good at getting stuck, but he liked to think he occasionally knew when to keep his mouth shut.

Good thing he had it shut right now, because as Jessica hit the gas and the wheels spun, mud splattered up his chest and sprayed his face.

———————————

Jessica gave a celebratory shout as she climbed out of the car. As frustrating as Wade was, he'd managed to get her car out of the bog.

She turned to suck up her pride and thank him, but those words died on her lips as she took him in. A stripe of mud ran up his chest, and he had splatters on his face and ever-present hat.

A laugh burst out of her, and he cocked his head and gave her an *oh, really* look.

"Thank you. And I'm sorry, but…" She laughed again.

Wade squatted down, she assumed to do something with the car, but the next thing she knew, he'd popped up and hurled a glob of mud at her. It hit her square in the chest, and her jaw dropped.

"Oh, it's on, Wade Dawson."

"Bring it, *Jessica*."

She filled her hands with the thick sludge, and when he dove around to the other side of the car for cover, she slid across the hood, hit the soggy ground on the other side, and threw for all she was worth. The mud ball smashed into his shoulder as he brought it up to block, drops hitting his neck and ear.

"Where'd you learn the slide-across-the-hood move?"

"Getaway driving. Not a stick-shift vehicle, obviously."

"Obviously." He stalked forward. "But that leaves me no choice but to play dirty."

She backpedaled, her arms out in front of her. "I think we're both dirty enough."

He lunged at her, and she let out a high-pitched squeal she wasn't proud of, but there it was anyway. Her feet slipped as she turned to run, and she was going down—before he even got hold of her, too, dang it.

Mud squished between her fingers in the grossest of ways. Come to think of it, with all the cows and horses, there was undoubtedly a fair amount of manure mixed in.

She rolled onto her butt and peered up at Wade's smug expression. "This doesn't mean you win. If anything, gravity does."

He laughed and extended a hand.

She clamped on, let him pull her halfway up, and then jerked, throwing her weight back. Her butt hit the ground hard for as squishy as it was, but it was worth it when Wade tumbled down with her.

She flung mud as she scrambled away, but he caught her foot and dragged her to him. Then she was on her back and he was over her, his palms braced on either side of her head. They were both filthy, and she knew she should care, but it only made her get the giggles all over again.

She brought up one knee and pushed to sit using her palms, right as he shifted slightly forward, causing their hips to bump together. His gaze dipped to her mouth, and her giggles died in her throat.

Her mind did a quick one-eighty, thinking back to when he'd first mentioned driving a stick shift. She'd joked it'd been a long time, long enough she worried she'd forgotten how, and she hadn't been talking about a truck.

It'd been so long since she'd even been this close to a man, and sure, this one pissed her off sometimes. But then he'd say something funny, or he'd give her a look, and… Her heart beat faster. They were already filthy, and her body whispered that it was on board with exploring all meanings of the word.

Her breaths came out labored, and she noticed his were just as ragged.

Did he move closer? Did she?

Did it matter?

The trill of a cell phone cut through the air, and it took her brain a few seconds of her hands patting pockets to realize it wasn't hers. Luckily, hers was in the console of the car, because she doubted it could handle mud.

Wade wiped his hands off on the tiny section of his shirt that wasn't dirty and answered.

Disappointment flooded her as she scooted out from under him, even as she told herself it was for the best. She was already on thin ice, and she'd probably only imagined he was thinking of kissing her. She drove him at least as crazy as he drove her.

"…yeah, I'll call him." Wade's gray eyes tracked her as she stood, and her knees wobbled slightly. "I'll be back in a few." He disconnected the call and slowly slid his phone back in his shirt pocket.

"Surprised your phone still works."

"Life-proof case. I was skeptical, but…"

From mud fights to discussions of phone cases. *Super hot move, Jessica.*

But again, she wasn't trying to make a move. She'd rev it only to kill the engine, just as she'd done with the truck. Too much gas or not enough, and speaking of rusty…

Ew. That makes it sound like my… Ew. Not going there.

Just like no one else has gone there in a long, long time.

Jess cleared her throat. "Anyway, so can I just drive off, or…?"

"Or," he said, moving closer, and her pulse leaped. "I've still got to hop in the truck and pull you the rest of the way out. I'm thinking I'll tow the tin can all the way home just to be safe."

She smacked his arm. "Hey! My tin can has taken me a lot of places." Currently, it also had bags scattered across the floor of the trunk. She'd wanted to right the containers and assess the damage, but she'd had to slam the lid to avoid being caught.

Putting her poker face in place so her guilty thoughts wouldn't show, she shifted her weight from her right leg to her left. "I'm guessing that call was about more work that I'm putting you behind on."

He nodded but didn't add a verbal jab like she'd expected. She wasn't sure what to do with this guy. One minute he'd be so surly she'd have to resist strangling him, and the next he was initiating mud fights and teasing her, his mouth temptingly close to hers. One thing was for sure: she could get into so, so much trouble with this cowboy.

"Well, then. Guess we'd better get back."

He caught her hand and gave it a light squeeze, and before she could even process the sweet gesture that left her even more confused and conflicted, he moved to the truck. He opened the door and peered inside. "Guess there's no point in trying to keep it clean now."

"I'll clean it out since it was my fault."

He shrugged—whatever that meant—and ushered her into the truck. Spots of mud were still squishy while other places were drying, and it was uncomfortable to say the least.

The truck lurched, its wheels spinning in the mud for a second before digging in and sending them forward—the beauty of four-wheel drive and giant tires.

Even in the bigger vehicle, they slid and bumped their way back to the ranch. Just as she was about to thank him, he glanced in the rearview mirror. Thinking they must have company, she swiveled around to see what'd caught his attention.

Unfortunately, her brain was on a delay from everything that'd happened, and Wade was already bailing out of the truck, the words "Your trunk popped open again" trailing behind him.

"No," she screamed, reaching for the door handle to jump out and race him there. Her stupid seat belt snapped her back to the seat. She unlatched it, her heart rate screeching into the danger zone as she scrambled out of the truck.

She knew she was too late but was desperately trying not to be anyway.

Wade peered over the top of the trunk at her, an expression she couldn't read. "Why, Jessica Cook. Looks like you have some explaining to do."

Chapter 10

"I CAN EXPLAIN." SHE MOVED CLOSER, FROWNING AT THE mess. Maybe she couldn't explain. It was even worse than before. The containers had come open, and barbecue-coated ribs were scattered across the floor of the trunk, the potato salad container upside down, smack-dab in the middle of the wreckage.

"That's what I just suggested." His smug grin made it clear he was enjoying watching her squirm.

The screech of the front door announced they were about to have company, and Wade quickly slammed the trunk.

Trace, Randy, and Kathy spilled onto the porch, whatever conversation they'd been having coming to a halt as they stopped to gape at them.

"What in the Sam Hill?" Randy's bushy eyebrows came together as he took them in.

Jess went to run a hand through her hair, but the crusty strands made her abandon her attempt. *Right.* They looked like they'd been in a mud-wrestling competition, which wasn't that far off from what'd happened. "I got stuck coming back from town. Wade helped me get my car out."

"Did you swim there?" Randy asked, glancing at Wade.

"Swimming in mud's not as easy as you'd think." Wade gave her a sidelong glance. "Technically."

She pressed her lips together to stifle a laugh. But wait. Did this mean he wasn't mad about the food in her trunk?

Did he think she'd bought ten pounds of ribs for her own gluttonous enjoyment?

Or was he just happy to have a secret to hold over her head?

Her first thought was *Quick! Destroy the evidence*, even though she was hoping some of the evidence was still edible. Otherwise she'd be found guilty without the added benefit of having dinner taken care of.

"Well, if you're done lallygagging around," Trace said, "we need to doctor those calves."

"Doesn't he need a shower first?" *She* desperately needed a shower.

"What's the point?" Wade asked. "I'll just get dirty again. Maybe this'll help me sneak up on the cows easier. They won't fight the medicine if they think it's coming from a moving clump of dirt."

She wanted to reach over and help him wipe away some of the mess. A shower didn't sound bad, either, and she shouldn't think about how nice it'd be to have company. When it came down to it, she hardly knew the guy, so it was a good thing her body hadn't overpowered her brain.

Except for those five to ten seconds.

Because what she did know was that the idea of him kissing her sent sparks zipping across her skin.

"You go ahead and clean up, though," Wade said, placing his hand on her back. His voice dipped low. "Then I'm guessing you'll have to get to dinner." Mischief shimmered in his eyes. Was he teasing her because she needed to start over? Or because he was going to call her on it if she used the ribs?

"I... About the explaining." Jess hooked her thumbs in

her pockets and rocked back on her heels. "Maybe later, after dinner…"

"Guess it depends on if I get my chores done." A smile spread across his face. "Some crazy chick had me rolling around in the mud."

"I just want to point out that you totally started it."

He arched an eyebrow.

"The mud flinging." Her smile broke free, and she shrugged. "Just saying."

"Well, I'm not the only one who plays dirty." He gave a pointed look at the trunk. "Just saying."

Her hand automatically went to the center of the trunk, silently urging it to stay. Trace walked past, his clipped steps making it clear he was in a hurry, and Wade tipped the mud-crusted brim of his hat at her before following his brother toward the corral.

When she dragged her attention away from his equally coated backside, the Dawsons were staring at her. "I, uh, should've taken the truck like Wade suggested. Like I said, I got my car stuck, and he came to help, and…" Heat crawled up her neck, and while Randy seemed perplexed, Kathy's smile was even bigger than usual. "I'm really sorry about the mess I made of the road. And of your son. If there's anything I can do…"

"Oh, he's been plenty muddy before," Kathy said, swiping a don't-worry-about-it hand through the air. "Don't think he's ever looked quite so happy about it, though." She snickered and leaned against the post of the porch. "I'm feelin' pretty good today. Are you gonna need any help with supper?"

"Oh." It depended on what she discovered when she sorted out the contents of her trunk. "I don't think so," she said, even though right now, she was thinking she needed a whole heap of help.

At this point, she wasn't even sure if there was enough help in the world to save her.

———————

"What are you grinning about?" Trace asked.

Usually that'd be enough to stifle Wade's grin, but right now, it only widened it. He never would've guessed wallowing in the mud could be so fun, but when it involved a feisty blond with a killer arm… If that call had come a minute later, he would've kissed her. "You guys give me crap all the time for being grumpy, then I'm happy and I get crap for that, too?"

He should be glad he'd been interrupted before he could tangle himself in that web, but he could still see her big, brown eyes peering up at him. Feel her pinned underneath him.

"Fine. Go ahead and grin like an idiot, but at least toss me the meds while you do it."

Wade gently tossed the bag with all the medicine vials in it. A few of the calves needed antibiotics, and the thing with antibiotics was how often they had to be administered. It'd mean a healthier herd in the summer, so it was worth it, but it was so dang time-consuming.

"Does this mean you're roping?" Trace asked. "Number Seventy-Eight's calf still needs an ear tag."

He'd forgotten about that somehow.

Well, not exactly somehow. It involved the blond he'd been daydreaming about.

The meals they'd had since Jessica arrived were a bit

like Russian roulette. Sometimes they got burned biscuits, sometimes perfect burgers, and sometimes a mix of tender chicken and granite-hard rolls.

The amount of food she'd had in her trunk from the Silver Saddle Diner was enough to feed a small army, which was about what they were out here on the ranch. The question was, if he hadn't seen it, would she have pretended she'd made it herself?

As if they didn't all know what the ribs and potato salad from the diner tasted like. The only bigger telltale sign would've been Winona's famous pie.

He should be mad that Jessica was basically cheating, but the only emotion that rose up when he thought about it was amusement. Along with a pinch of hunger, because the Silver Saddle had damn good ribs. And rolls. It'd been a long time since he'd gone into town for a meal. It'd been a long time since he'd gone anywhere in general. The kids occasionally complained about their lack of outings and social life, and he'd fought the urge to tell them they were preaching to the choir.

The ranch required constant work, from the land to the livestock, and adding the teen program tripled the chores that needed to be done. It took a few weeks that always felt like pulling teeth for the new teens to become relatively helpful. Honestly, the ins and outs overwhelmed him, and the teen camp was the one part of the ranch he'd rather leave to someone else.

Wade grabbed his rope, and he and Trace headed across the yard. If they were going to the grazing field, he'd hop on his horse, but the corral, while on the larger side, still wasn't big enough to justify that.

He hung his rope on a post, and he and Trace took care of the easier of the calves. Once they were doctored, Wade turned to grab his rope. A familiar blond head caught his eye, although the strands were wavier and slightly damp. She must've just gotten out of the shower. He meant to do a quick scan, but he got hung up on the formfitting studded jeans and pink boots on her feet.

Pink. *Of course* she'd bought fancy pink boots.

"You clean up nice," he said as she moved closer.

"I guess I'll have to see if the same applies to you. If you ever clean up, that is," she said with a laugh that sounded a bit nervous, and he flashed her a smile.

"Did you want to hop in and rope a calf for me real quick so I have time to go shower?"

"Hard pass. I'll cheer nice and loud for you, though."

"That'll probably just send the cows scattering."

She stepped onto the bottom rung of the corral and folded her arms across the weathered top beam. "Then I'll cheer super-duper loud."

Wade shook his head and grabbed his rope, quickly forming a lasso. It'd been a long while since he'd had an audience to impress. The only time he roped for show these days was at the yearly local rodeo, where there wasn't much pressure.

There shouldn't be pressure now, but he found himself wanting to impress Jessica all the same. He was about seventy percent when it came to his first toss. He and his brothers gave each other shit every time they missed, which was also motivating. But animals were predictably unpredictable.

He searched through the brown, white, and black mix

of calves until he found the black-and-white bald-faced calf that belonged to Number Seventy-Eight. He swung the loop over his head and calculated the calf's path as Trace pushed it toward him.

Wade released a shallow breath and tossed. The loop went right over the head, and he jerked back, tightening and securing.

A whoop came from behind him, and he grinned as he tugged the calf over to him and Trace, who shot forward and administered the antibiotics. Wade followed up with the ear tag. Then he slid the rope free, and the calf darted away. Tomorrow he'd be harder to catch, but at least he'd only need a quick shot.

When Wade turned back around, Jessica was perched on the top rung of the corral, giving the calves mushy looks. "They're so cute! Can I pet one?"

"If you can catch one, go crazy."

"Maybe I'll borrow your rope and surprise you."

"The real surprise would be if you didn't try to use it on me."

Her laugh split the air, loud and carefree and cute as hell. She swung her feet, those pink boots bright and impossible to miss. "Aren't you going to say something about my proper footwear? Since my ballet flats seemed to personally offend you, and I'm pretty sure they were destroyed by the mud earlier, I'm extra glad I picked them up."

"*Proper*? They're ridiculous."

"They're cute!"

"At least they have more coverage than your others, but they're going to be dirty and scuffed by next weekend."

"That's why you should take a good look at them now."

She lifted her leg, sticking the boot right in his line of sight. "Admire the pretty."

Oh, he was. From the extended leg to the blond waves to the face he could stare at all day. She leaned forward, gripping the wooden post as she tested how far she could go. "I just want to point out that you said *next* weekend, not this one. Does that mean…?" She lowered her voice, and her eyes locked on to his. "Am I going to be around that long?"

"I certainly hope so," he said, because something about her cut off part of his brain, and now he felt like it was too strong of a statement and he should hurry and fix it. "I put a whole lot of effort into digging you out, after all. I need it to have been worth it."

She tilted her head. Then she reached out a hand. "Help me down. I want to try to pet some of those cute baby cows."

Instead of taking her hand, he gripped her hips. She braced her hands on his shoulders, and he slowly lowered her until her ridiculous pink boots hit the ground. *Let go*, he told his fingers, but they were lacking motivation to listen.

She lowered her arms, her hands brushing down his biceps and coming to rest on his forearms. "About the bags of food in my car…"

"Were you able to save any of it?"

"While it looked like a bottle of barbecue sauce had been murdered, most of the actual meat remained in the to-go boxes. And the potato salad container flipped but didn't open, so it just needed to be rinsed off. The rolls, unfortunately, sopped up a lot of sauce and had to go. I wanted to let you know that I'm going to add my own spin on it. I just…" She bit her lip. "I ran out of ideas, and I bought it with my own money and—"

"It's okay. It can be our little secret."

"That you'll exploit me with later?"

"Naturally."

One side of her mouth twisted up.

"Plus, I'm really hungry," he said, "so at this point, I'm just gonna be grateful for an edible meal."

"Ah!" She shoved his chest. "Just when I was starting to think you might be kinda, sorta nice."

"Spoiler alert: I'm really not."

A curious black calf moved closer, and Jessica's gaze moved to it. Evidently his flirting skills weren't what they used to be if they could be upstaged by a cow.

Another calf stepped up as well, a black-and-white steer that was almost ready to go back to the main field.

Jessica placed a hand over her heart. "Oh, look, they're friends. How cute is that?"

"Pretty sure they just think you might feed them."

"So cynical," Jessica said, clicking her tongue as she shook her head at him. "You can see they have history. I bet they moo about how life was in the big field, and they have big plans for when they get out of this wooden jail."

The goofy grin was back on his face. He could feel it, and as long as Jessica was telling stories about the cows, he was useless to fight it. He didn't even bother telling her that the tiny black one hadn't seen the big field yet.

A tiny squeal came out as she moved toward the cows, her arm extended.

The two calves watched her, glancing at each other as if they did have some sort of history, and right before Jessica's fingertips made contact, they darted away.

Not one to give up, she followed, keeping her movements

slow. She circled the entire corral, the gems on the pockets of her jeans catching the fading sunlight. While they were about as practical as her boots and would also be permanently dirty in no time, he didn't let that stop him from admiring what they did to her sexy backside.

Finally, she managed to pat the black calf on the head.

A few more calves circled her, and she gave them attention they couldn't quite decide if they wanted or not.

"Look, I'm petting cows." Jessica slowly pivoted to face Wade as the runt of the group got extra friendly, rubbing its cheek on her thigh as she scratched the top of its head. "While wearing boots, too." She lifted one as if the bright-pink boots didn't stand out in the sea of black and brown. "Am I a cowgirl now?"

Wade chuckled and shook his head. She was a little bit crazy and a lot cute.

Then the dogs came over, not breaching the corral since they knew better, but prancing around and whining because they'd sensed someone out there was lavishing attention on animals, and they wanted in on the action.

On the other hand, Kita, the mama cat who thought she owned the place strolled past Quigley and Dundee and plopped herself in front of Jessica. She scratched Kita's pregnant belly before moving over to the dogs.

And as Jessica showered them with affectionate pats and ear rubs, Wade started to think he might want in on the action, too.

Chapter 11

"SORRY," LIZA SAID BY WAY OF GREETING AS JESS STEPPED into her cabin on Monday night. Her chestnut-brown hair was piled in a messy bun on the top of her head, and she had a slightly frazzled look in her eye. "The kids were supposed to be asleep already. Normally they're in bed by now, but it's been one of those nights."

Two blondies in pajamas streaked through the living room, the high-energy shrieks miles away from the tired range.

Liza managed to scoop up Everett, and Jess took a few long strides and caught Elise. At her offended scream, Jess bounced her in the air and got a laugh. Possibly not the best calm-down move, but her laughter was catching. After a long week, Jess needed a bit of giggling.

"Okay, it's bedtime," Liza said.

"No bed!" Everett shouted, and his sister chimed in her agreement.

"Yes, bed."

"Story!" Again, Elise echoed her brother's words. Man, it must be hard to be outnumbered. There were a lot of times through Chloe's toddler years that Jess had fallen into bed at the end of the night so exhausted she hadn't bothered with washing off her makeup or even changing out of her clothes. Then she'd wake up to start the circus all over again. Those were some of the longest days of her life.

"I'll read them one if you want," Jess said, twisting her

head so Elise could study the earring that'd caught her attention. It'd been long enough she wasn't totally sure the twins were out of the yanking and putting everything in their mouth phase, but since Elise was merely cooing about how pretty the dangly earring was, Jess thought she was safe. "I don't mind. It's been a long time since I've had requests for bedtime you-know-whats."

Liza glanced around the toy-covered living room. Earlier today she'd mentioned she could use some adult girl time, and when Jess echoed the sentiment, they decided to have a wine-and-chick-flick night. "If you truly don't mind. Then maybe we won't have to sit on toys while we watch the movie."

"Hey, I've watched plenty of movies that way. As long as it's not one with a creepy robotic voice that goes off every time I move, I'll be fine."

"Oh, I tore the batteries out of those toys long ago. You never realize how terrifying Elmo sounds until he's giggling in the middle of the night." Liza shuddered.

"Elmo!" Elise spun toward the TV and pointed at the blank screen.

"No TV. But guess what?" Liza infused her voice with excitement, in that way needed to help sell children on an idea. "Miss Jessica is going to read you a bedtime story!"

"No biscuits," Everett said, eyeing her as if she might have some stuffed into her pockets and was planning on force-feeding them to him.

"Thanks for that, buddy," Jess said with a laugh, waving off Liza's apologetic panicked expression.

They walked down the hallway, and Liza turned into the one on the right. "They're still sharing a room for now. I tried to separate them, but they were so used to each other that they just cried and cried, so I gave in. Even though they keep each other up and give each other ideas." She tickled Everett, who cackled, and then tickled Elise's side.

Jessica smiled at the woman who was quickly becoming a friend. "You're doing a great job." Mom guilt was a very real thing, and she wished that when she was questioning everything, someone would've assured her she wasn't utterly botching it.

At least she felt like she'd done the younger years right, even if they'd been some of her and Chloe's poorest years. There'd been a lot of laughter and lots of cuddling, and she felt that trumped the forever messy house and repeat meals that were higher in calories than nutrition, nary a vegetable in sight.

After Liza kissed the twins good night, Jessica tested the limits of Elise's My Little Pony bed by climbing into it and gathering the twins on either side. One of the best things about reading to kids was how excited they got over every picture and every funny voice, so Jess put on a show for them, exhuming characters she hadn't used in about a decade.

One story turned into two, and it took three until they were both crashed out.

Jessica moved Everett to his bed, pulled the covers up over him, and tiptoed out of the room, gently shutting the door behind her.

The living room was remarkably cleaner, and Liza immediately handed her a glass of red wine. "I was about to plan a rescue mission to retrieve you, but I thought I should have at least a sip of wine in case I was caught behind enemy lines and it was my last chance." She rounded the couch, settled into the far corner, and kicked her feet up on the coffee table. "Thank you so much for doing that. Funny how twenty minutes of silent cleaning time feels downright luxurious."

"It was nice, actually." Jess sat on the other end of the couch, twisting and using the arm as a backrest. "Sometimes I miss the unconditional love that comes along with little kids. How they think you know everything, and when they're sad or hurt, they come running right to you, sure you'll make it better. With nothing more than snuggles and kisses, too."

Liza gave her a sympathetic smile.

"Sorry. Didn't mean to be a downer. I'm probably scaring you."

"I work with a bunch of moody teenagers who are dealing with a lot of heavy issues. It'd take more than that to scare me."

Tears lodged in Jess's throat. This was supposed to be about forgetting and relaxing, but how could she do either of those things? "I remember the first day Chloe dodged a hug when I dropped her off at school—second grade, about halfway through the year. It stung, but I understood. About a month later, I decided she was getting a hug anyway. So I tell her goodbye and go to give her a tight squeeze. Her water bottle was in the side mesh pocket of her backpack and it gets squished between us, enough that it cracked right open and doused both of us. I knew I was a mom before, but that was the moment I went 'Omigosh, I've gone full-on mom.'"

Liza laughed. "There are a lot of nights I just want to not be covered in kids and not answering two hundred questions or dealing with a miniscule scratch that's naked to the human eye but apparently needs three Spider-Man Band-Aids, so I'll try to keep that in mind."

"Well, as they say, there's a season for everything. For a while Chloe was too cool for hugs. But she came back around." A few months ago, Jess had gone to pick her up from school, and in front of everyone, Chloe had yelled, "Guys, it's my mom!" and had run over to hug her.

At the time, Jess had thought she never would've announced her own mom like that, and she'd been so glad she and Chloe had a different, closer, and more open relationship. Her smile fell as she thought of their interactions this past week. "Now she won't even talk to me, and I'm tempted to attack hug her again, only she'd probably shove me away, and that'd hurt worse than her dodging it."

A sharp pain lanced her heart, reopening the wounds she was constantly rebandaging at night when no one could see. She twisted the stem of her wineglass between her fingers as she looked across the couch at Liza. "I'm sure it'd be breaking the rules to ask how Chloe's doing in the program and if she's opened up to you at all. She's never felt so distant. Never been so closed off."

"Jess, Chloe loves you. She might not show it the way she did when she was little, but she still loves you."

Great. Now she was definitely going to cry.

"And it's not breaking the rules. I get emails all the time from parents asking how their kids are doing. Not asking about your child is like expecting lungs to stop relying on oxygen. I can't go into what she and I have talked about, but I can tell you how she's doing." Liza took a sip of wine and then set the glass on the coffee table as she sat forward. Her expression changed from warm and open to slightly more tempered. "Even better, I can get some insight from you if you don't mind me going all therapist on you."

"Hey, if I get to lie back on the couch and rest my feet, I'll agree to about anything." On top of cooking, which she was gradually—often painfully—getting the hang of, she spent a considerable amount of time doing ranch work odds and ends. Today, she'd helped feed cows while sandwiched between Wade and Brady and pitched in with laundry when she saw Kathy wrestling a load into the washer. Being busy helped keep her from fixating on how they'd been there a whole week, and her daughter still refused to acknowledge her presence.

"Let's get right to it, then," Liza said, her voice softening. "What about her dad?"

"I was fifteen, he was sixteen. I told him I was pregnant, and he ran so fast I was surprised there wasn't a hole shaped like him in the door."

"So, her dad was the Kool-Aid pitcher."

Jessica snorted.

Liza patted her knee. "Just thought I'd lighten the mood a bit while I was prying."

Jess took a large gulp of wine to help with that as well. "I appreciate it. Basically, the idiot never wanted to be in her life, and it's his loss."

"I can relate. The twins' dad did basically the same thing. Being a single mom isn't for the faint of heart, either."

"No, it's definitely not. I worked a lot, and there were still too many months when I wasn't sure we were going to make it. About a year ago I accepted a promotion that required more hours and responsibility because it meant more financial security, and since Chloe was older, I thought she'd be fine. But I could tell she was stressed and sad more often than she used to be. Once she started dating Tyler, I saw a change, and all the alarm bells went off."

Mentally calling up the image of the devil-may-care boy made Jess's hands curl into fists. At first she'd been supportive and had again been glad Chloe was so open with her, even after she'd met the disrespectful kid who reminded her too much of her ex. Red flags started popping up right and left, and then she began to dislike him and the way he was treating Chloe enough that she couldn't hide it.

"Probably the same alarms that went off for my mom when I started dating Dan," Jess admitted, even though she hated to. "Now I guess I owe her an apology, but she lost that privilege when she demanded I give up my baby." She worked to swallow past the tightness in her throat. "She also told me I'd ruin the kid's life, and maybe she was right about that, too."

Liza adamantly shook her head, and while her voice still held kindness, it was also firm. "She wasn't. Chloe's lucky to have you. You saw something was wrong, and you got her help."

"Not soon enough." Jess had replayed the past few months again and again, trying to find that moment she could've prevented this outcome. "We were so close, and I'm afraid that closeness led me into a false sense of security. Made me think her teachers and the school were overreacting, and that she'd tell me if things were getting out of control.

"I worked so hard to ensure Chloe wouldn't make my same mistakes, but I managed to mess that up, too. She's too much like me, and I should've seen that sooner."

Liza assured her that she hadn't messed anything up,

that kids were simply kids, and asked about the changes in Chloe's behavior. Jess went for a second glass of wine somewhere in the middle of telling her about how she'd noticed Chloe wasn't sleeping very well and would have breakdowns over homework or going to school, but she'd thought it was normal teenage stuff. Then she'd met her new group of friends and the boy she'd love to personally dump in the middle of a desert. She'd give him a canteen and a map that pointed him far away from her daughter. "I'm sorry. This is turning into the lamest girls' night ever."

"Hey, I'm the one who asked, but I think that's enough digging for now. Just know that having that extra background information will help me help Chloe." Liza picked up the remote and waggled it. "Movie time?"

"Definitely movie time."

Liza pressed Play and poured them more wine, even though Jess had been talking too much to have drunk much of her second glass yet. A few minutes in, as they were admiring the sexy hero, Liza said, "Actually, I might want to dig a little more."

Jessica tensed, not sure she was ready to divulge more when the information she'd already shared had left her feeling completely wrung out.

"What's up with you and Wade?"

That question was much easier and way more complicated. Nothing significant had happened. She enjoyed talking to him, and they seemed to have sort of a truce going—not to mention he could blackmail her over the amazing ribs that everyone had loved, although she knew he wouldn't. "I don't know. He's...frustrating. And funnier than expected. Super bossy, yet surprisingly sweet when he wants to be. Sexy. And in charge of my child's future here at the ranch."

Liza's eyes widened, and the wine must finally have been kicking in because she also blinked several times. "That's a lot of things."

"He's definitely a lot of things." He made her feel a lot of things, too, things she hadn't felt since she was an overly optimistic teenager. "Honestly, I haven't dated in years, and I'm not sure the few short-lived relationships I've had since Chloe was born even count as dating. There was a lot of juggling my crazy schedule and not introducing the guys until I was sure they were going to be around. That was about the time things fell apart, so…"

Jess glanced at Liza, worrying once again that she was scaring her, counselor for moody teens or not. "A lot of it was me. Getting knocked up at fifteen makes you leery of guys and their false promises in general." She scrunched up her forehead. "Wait. I was trying to make you feel better. It's been a while since I've had wine, and apparently this is why."

Liza giggled. "I rarely drink, either—a combination of being the only parent of twins who never stop and the fact that my mom used to drink a bit too much." She slumped back on the couch and shook her head. "Wow, we're really bad at this relaxing, light movie night."

"Truth," Jess said, laughing and setting her glass on the coffee table before sinking back into the cushions. "The lighter answer is, I never knew cowboys could be my type. And while a certain cowboy makes me feel like he might just be, getting involved would be too messy. I'm only here temporarily, and more than that, I wouldn't want to put Chloe's spot at risk."

"Understandable. But just know that Wade is nothing but fair, so you don't have to worry about Chloe's spot."

While Jess had gathered as much over the past week, it still felt too dangerous. For her daughter and for her heart.

Chapter 12

CHLOE HEARD THE HEAVY FOOTSTEPS AND QUICKLY minimized the screen. As if the limited internet time didn't make things hard enough, the fact that the computer was in an area where people often walked by made it even harder.

Eight days. That was how long it'd been since she'd sent her first message to Tyler.

She'd told herself that a week was a common length of time to be grounded, but two days ago, the check mark that said Tyler had read his message had showed up. A response, not so much.

Her two girlfriends had sent a combination of "That sucks" and "Run away ASAP so we can hang out, bitch!"

Over the past few days, Chloe's desire to run away had faded. Mostly because she realized it wouldn't do any good. Mom would just have her hauled back here over and over. It wasn't quite as bad as she'd originally thought. Sometimes she even related to what the others shared during group therapy, although she'd refrained from saying more than the bare minimum so far. Not-so-bad didn't mean she was suddenly happy to be here, and once Mom gave the green light, Chloe planned to bolt fast enough to leave a line of fire.

"You okay?" The familiar deep, male voice washed over her and stirred up emotions she couldn't quite name. Probably because Aiden had become the only friend she could actually talk to. Besides Rowdy, who was going to hear all about Tyler seeing her message but not responding the next time she took a ride.

How dare he leave me on Read! Plastering a smile on her face to hide her raw emotions, she spun around. "Yep. Do you have to use the communal computer, too?"

"Nah, I got a computer in my room now."

Her eyes probably widened a bit too much, and the shake of his head confirmed it. "Don't go getting any ideas. I'd be in so much trouble if—"

"I wouldn't want you to get into trouble," Chloe said, and more than that, she meant it. Her roommates, Izzy and the Double D's, were nice enough, but she was still hesitant to drop her walls. Somehow Aiden had walked through them like a ghost with no respect for the rules, and now that he was inside, she found she didn't want him to leave.

Even if that also scared her. The conspiracy theorist in her whispered that the Dawsons used him as a deep-cover spy, but considering the way they brazenly pried for information and how often everyone here spilled their guts, the spy route seemed unnecessary. Plus, Aiden blurted things out without thinking them through on a regular basis and walked far too loudly to be a good spy.

"How's the math going?" The other day when they were mucking stalls, he'd told her he was struggling with one of his classes.

His shoulders sagged a few inches. "Same as usual. I've caught up with the other classes, but if I can't get through the math class, I'll be a junior forever."

"I could take a look at what you're studying."

"I thought you were a sophomore."

She scowled at him. "I've always been in advanced math classes, but fine, don't take my help." After nearly a week of reaching into her pocket for her phone, only to realize it wasn't there, she remembered not to bother and glanced at the giant clock on the wall. "I can find a more fun way to spend my free half hour." Doubtful, honestly, but she could try. She needed thirty minutes of fun before she had to go sit across from Liza, who was perfectly nice but refused to stop poking around for the key to the vault.

I'm not stupid. I threw that thing away the second Mom pulled up to this place. If Chloe told Liza about the panic attacks, that might increase her time here, and she couldn't risk it. Maybe that was dangerous, but she'd had fewer incidences where she'd had to struggle for breath the past few days, so maybe they were going away. *Please let them go away.*

Chloe stood, and Aiden caught her wrist as she started past. A zip coursed up her arm, and she frowned down at his fingers.

He quickly dropped her arm, his hand going up to rub at his neck. "Sorry. I was just going to say… Yes. Please, *please* take a look at my math homework."

"Jeez, you don't have to beg." She flashed him a smile to make sure he knew she was just giving him a hard time. Then she swung an arm in front of her. "Lead the way."

He moved toward the door and then abruptly spun around. "I'd, uh, better bring it in here. There are rules."

"That there are. Way too many, if you ask me."

The dimples in his cheeks flashed as he smiled. "I'll be right back."

Aiden got a bit lost in the way Chloe tapped the pencil to her full lower lip. Thanks to the fact he kept noticing things like her lips, eyes, and smile, he'd tried to minimize the time they'd spent alone together.

He knew the rules. At first he used to think there were too many, but he'd adjusted and they'd even started to make sense.

But now he was thinking there were way too many rules once again.

"Okay, so if you had six piles of horse crap to clean, but you had a friend who agreed to help you with math so you promised to take care of the six piles she was responsible for, what would you have?"

Aiden tilted his head and pursed his lips together. "A con-artist friend."

"Not the answer I was looking for," she said with a laugh. "But probably a fair assessment." She flipped the page of his textbook, her eyes scanning down the list of problems he referred to as number gibberish. Then she slapped a palm down on the page and looked back up at him. "If you liked a girl, would you leave her on Read?"

The question came from left field and smacked him in the chest before he'd had a chance to lift his mitt. Had she sent him a message? He'd deleted most of his social media accounts. Too many of his old friends were way too eager to get him into trouble.

"I'm sure Tyler's worried about me, and he's probably waiting for me to call, but now that he's seen my message, why didn't he respond?" Chloe toyed with his notebook, lifting the corner of the pages with her thumb and letting the pages drop, over and over. "I'm sure he's just busy. Or maybe his parents got ahold of his phone and *they* saw what I wrote. Before my mom took my phone away, she combed through my messages. She's never done that to me before, and it was so violating."

He simply stared, trying to keep up.

Chloe's dark eyebrows arched. She had these expressive eyebrows that hinted at her emotions, even when she was trying to keep them hidden. She snapped her fingers in front of his face half a second after he'd realized the eyebrow arch had been aimed at him. "Hello? If this is how you pay attention, no wonder you're struggling with your math."

His jaw dropped. "Hey!"

"You're right," she said, wrinkling her cute little nose. "That was a low blow. This stuff isn't easy."

"Does that mean you don't know how to do it and this is you letting me down easy?" The glimmer of hope he'd held on to blinked out. The website that claimed to simplify everything had been too complicated for him, and if Chloe was in advanced classes and couldn't figure it out, he might as well give up now.

"Oh, I know how to do it. And I'll totally teach you. But what do you think? About the message thing?"

He thought the Tyler guy sounded like a tool. Had thought so from the first instance she'd brought him up, and she'd started to do so more and more. But how could he say that without crushing her? "I would find a way to send a reply," he said. Hopefully not crushing, but it was the truth, and she should know that.

"He would talk to me if he could. Something must've happened. I'm not some girl who just *assumes* a guy likes her. We've talked about our future. We have something real."

Aiden nodded, thinking he should've known better than to get sucked into that trick question.

The door opened, and he was glad they were at the large dining table with plenty of space and books between them. Especially when it ended up being Chloe's mom. She was saying something about understanding "the pregnant waddle all too well" to Kita, the cat trailing her, but froze when she spotted them. "Oh. Hey, you two."

Instead of responding, Chloe turned to the textbook, the laser focus she'd lacked seconds ago showing up now. Although he'd bet money nothing on the page was actually sinking in.

"You guys need anything?" Jessica asked. "I could make chocolate milk."

"We're not five, Mom," Chloe said, and this time, Aiden kept his mouth shut, in spite of the urge to say he'd love some chocolate milk.

"How about cookies? I baked some earlier."

"Yes, please," Aiden quickly said before Chloe could deny him another shot at a snack. Chocolate milk was one thing, but cookies were another.

"Be right back," she said, and Kita meowed extra loudly. "I didn't forget about your snack. Come on." Jessica disappeared into the kitchen with the cat hot on her heels, the door swinging behind them.

Chloe un-paused, slumping back in her chair. "She's not the milk-and-cookies type, you know. She took the cooking job because it's the only way the Dawsons would let me stay. *That's* how bad she wanted to stick me here. Honestly, it would've been better if she'd just dumped me off." She repeatedly clicked the eraser top of his mechanical pencil, not seeming to notice the long line of lead. Since he didn't want her to stab him with it, he let her click away without comment. "How does she possibly think things can go back to the way they were before? She ruined that when she brought me here."

All of his life, Aiden had wished his parents would care. Not that he was thrilled to be dropped off here—by his parole officer, for the record, because his parents couldn't be bothered. While he wanted to point out that at least her mom cared, the girl could pull out an icy glare that would scare a polar bear, so again he kept his mouth shut.

He supposed it was easy to take parents for granted when you had them, but he'd sworn he would never take the Dawsons for granted. Not after what they'd done for him, and he could never repay them for giving him a home.

One he really wanted to be permanent. The Dawsons assured him he was family now, but old habits die hard, and sometimes he stopped himself short of truly believing it. He'd already let them in more than he'd ever let anyone else, and that felt dangerous. Caring meant having something to lose, and part of him still expected his new life to be stripped away.

The door swung open, and Jessica walked over and placed a plate of puddle-like cookies in front of them. Flat and brown at the edges, they reminded him a bit of the cow pies dotting the landscape outside. "They don't look very pretty, but they taste good."

Chloe gave them the sparest glance. Then she pulled the math book closer. "I'm helping Aiden with his math, so we need to hit it now."

Jessica nodded. She lifted her hand like she wanted to place it on Chloe's shoulder and then dropped it, the smile on her face turning plastic. "I'll see you guys at dinner, then."

Chloe didn't respond, but the instant her mom walked out of the room, her eyes moved to the door. She exhaled a shaky breath that made him think she wasn't quite as tough as she acted, and he reached over and covered her hand with his. "Thanks for your help."

"Yeah, well, I'm not the total delinquent everyone thinks I am."

"I think you're only half a delinquent," he said, hoping the joke wouldn't backfire. She rolled her eyes, but she laughed. She had a really great laugh, too, one that sent warmth coursing through his chest.

"Let's get you through your math class, and then we'll both work on not becoming tragic statistics."

Wade slowed his steps when he spotted Jessica on the far edge of the porch on Friday afternoon, her attention directed out toward the stables. He eyed the door he'd been planning on walking through, then decided he could spare a few minutes.

It'd only been a handful of hours since he'd had her next to him in the truck, but it felt like forever. More and more, he was finding that their conversations helped him get through the day, no matter how hard or exhausting it ended up being.

"Hey," he said, stepping up next to her.

She gave him a smile that didn't quite reach her eyes and then looked back toward the stables. Or more accurately, at the girl standing in the open area in front of the stable doors. Chloe had Rowdy's reins, but he followed her around without her having to tug, and she turned to the overgrown puppy of a horse and ran her hand down his wide face.

"She looks happier than she has in a long time," Jessica said.

"She's doing well. We don't have to get on her to do her chores anymore, and in her free time, she's been spending more and more time with the horse. Most city folk think it's silly to talk to a horse at first, but there's something therapeutic about telling them all your hopes, fears, dreams."

"Lucky horse," Jessica said, sorrow strangling the words. "She still won't talk to me."

Wade covered the hand she had curled around the porch rail. "Write her a letter. That's how a lot of the other parents communicate with their kids while they're here."

"Let me guess, it's unfair of me to even try to talk to her every day."

"No," Wade said. "This isn't me reciting rules. It's me making a suggestion. For the record, it would probably be more harmful for you to be here and ignore her. She might not act like she's listening, but trust me, she hears you. She notices you reaching out. But sometimes letters are easier. On both sides. You can think out what you say and put down things that are hard to say in person with so much emotion crowding the air between you."

Jessica turned toward him, and the wind stirred strands of hair around her face. It often kicked him in the gut how pretty she was. He'd think he was used to seeing her and being around her, and then she'd turn around to face him or smile and *bam*. But she wasn't smiling now, and the other thing he often felt around her—to find a way to make her feel better—drifted up and began to take over.

"Do you have any idea what it's like to have failed at what you consider your proudest accomplishment?" she asked, and her chin quivered. "For countless people to silently judge you or outright tell you that you'll screw it up, but you stubbornly cling to your stance that you can do it anyway, only to realize fifteen years down the road that they were right?"

Wade leaned his hip against the porch rail, his eyes locked on to hers. "Hey. They were wrong then, and they still are. I've met a lot of kids, and she's a good kid who just made a few bad choices. Teens don't have all of their neural pathways formed yet, and sometimes they make stupid decisions."

"I realize that." She gave a mirthless laugh. "Hell, I'm the poster child of that."

"You're not the only person who's made mistakes, Jessica. While part of our program involves owning up to them, we also don't dwell. It's about the future. It's about learning how to make fewer bad decisions. About thinking through consequences before they're thrust upon us."

She scuffed a pink boot against the floor of the porch, scraping off some of the peeling white paint. "I hate that I'm just supposed to let go of control and hope that I'm making the right choice."

"It was your choice to bring her here. You were in control of that, and I think you made the right choice. I know it's not easy to give your kid over to someone else. But this place, the changes I've seen…" He searched for the right words to comfort her, deciding that the plain and simple truth would work best. "It takes all of us working damn hard, a couple of people with psychology degrees, along with several more who have degrees from the life of hard knocks. It takes a staff of fifteen and constantly working at it, and it's far from an overnight process. Stop being so hard on yourself."

Jessica nodded, but her gaze remained on the wooden planks at her feet.

Wade cupped her chin and gently tipped her face to his. "You didn't fail. You're a good person—an amazing mom."

"I worry I was too lax." Tears formed in her eyes, turning them shiny, and then one slipped free and ran down her cheek. "I was so focused on how great our friendship was that I didn't focus enough on being a mother. And even as I tell myself that, I still miss the way we used to talk. How close we were. I worry we'll never get that back, not after I brought her here. But the alternative was to watch her go down a path that could completely destroy her future."

He stepped closer, until the toes of his boots hit hers, and kept his voice soft yet firm. "And I worry you're not listening to a word I say. No one gets out of this life without making mistakes. Without a few bumps and bruises. It's what we do about them that matters, and you made your best move. Out here on the ranch, we don't know the meaning of the word 'quit.' I promise we're gonna help your daughter." There he went, making promises. Doing things he shouldn't. Feeling things he shouldn't. He wiped her tear away with his thumb. "Okay?"

"Okay," she said, and the amount of faith she'd packed into that word made him that much more determined to keep his promise.

Chapter 13

"THE TRICK IS TO MIX IT WELL WITHOUT OVERMIXING IT," Kathy said, and Jess froze with her hands in the dough, not sure if she'd reached the undermixed or overmixed stage, but doubting she'd accomplished the Goldilocks "just right" one. She wasn't sure she'd ever hit it when it came to baking.

Kathy scooted her chair out from the table where she'd been sorting through paperwork, a pair of tortoiseshell reading glasses perched on her nose, and started to stand. Jess held up a doughy hand. "Don't get up on my account. You're supposed to be resting, and I'm pretty sure you brought in those files because you knew your family would take them away and tell you to relax instead."

"*Pshaw*. Don't you start now. All my boys act like I'm some delicate flower—like they don't remember that I can and have whipped them into shape on several occasions, sometimes with nothin' more than a stern look. I've had to hop on a horse and chase 'em down plenty, too. Once I found Wade and Brady out fishin' when they were supposed to be cuttin' hay, and trust me, there was hell to pay."

For some reason Jess had a hard time picturing Wade ever doing anything wrong, and she found she liked the idea of him being terrified by his mama. "What was their punishment?"

"Oh, they mucked out stalls for a week on top of digging the ditch that runs up the east side of the ranch. I worked 'em till neither of 'em could hardly lift their arms to eat."

"If they were eating some of my rolls or biscuits, that would probably be a reward."

Kathy clucked her tongue and moved over to the butcher-block countertop. "You're gonna get the hang of it. Bread is finicky. Like teenagers. One day it's a breeze, and the next day, you're not sure what happened to your precious sweetie. All those hormones don't help, either." She lightly bumped the plastic mixing bowl. "Not sure what bread's excuse is."

If Jess wasn't covered in flour and dough, she might've thrown her arms around Kathy and hugged her extra tightly for making her feel like she wasn't the worst mother in history.

"We women are the hardest on ourselves about mistakes," Kathy added with a kind smile as if she could read Jess's mind. "Especially mothers. We never feel pretty enough or smart enough or good enough, when the truth is, being a mother is damn hard."

"Keep up that kind of talk, and there's going to be tears in the dough."

Kathy peeked around Jess and peered into the bowl. "Work in those floury bits over there. I'd abandon the pastry cutter and just use your fingers. Then you can work it in better and feel with your own two hands if it's the right consistency."

"Okay, but let's take it to the table to finish them up," Jess said, tucking the silicone mat under her arm and then reaching for the rolling pin and the cup she used as a biscuit cutter. "Then I can sit down."

Kathy looked at her like she suspected Jess was just trying to get *her* to sit down—which was true—but she allowed them to move to the table.

After a couple of squishes, Jess understood what Kathy meant about using her hands to mix. She could feel the dry pockets, as well as the too-wet ones.

"There. That's it," Kathy said, pushing her glasses up her nose. "Now you wanna roll it out so it doesn't get overmixed."

Jess started to overturn the bowl, but Kathy placed her hand on it, stopping her. "Gotta flour the surface first."

"Oh yeah." She'd forgotten that step a few times, and then the dough stuck to the mat, silicone be damned. There were just so many steps to cooking, especially if more than one dish was going, and she always managed to forget something. In fact, if she only forgot *one* thing, she considered it a win.

Kathy sprinkled flour across the center of the mat, and Jessica dumped out the dough. When she remembered to also put flour on the rolling pin, she did a mental fist pump.

"I'd love to know more about how you started the teen program," Jess said. "What made you want to do it, and how you juggled motherhood and having so many sons while running this place." She'd always been curious about people and the different lives they led. Perhaps because her course had pretty much been set when she was sixteen.

The history of the ranch and how the Dawsons had decided to merge it with the teen program especially intrigued her. And yes, she also wanted to know more about Wade, even as she told herself knowing more would only get her in that much deeper. After he'd gotten sharp with her for asking too many questions while fixing fence almost two weeks ago, she'd held in way too many.

"Oh, how long've you got?" Kathy propped her chin on

her fist. "I can't seem to tell this story without waxing on and on."

Jess smiled at her. "Well, I've got till about an hour before dinner, when the hungry descend."

"You might regret not giving yourself a sooner out," Kathy said with a self-deprecating chuckle, but as Jess rolled out the dough, she told her how Randy had inherited the ranch from his father, who'd inherited it from his. She and Randy were high school sweethearts, and they built the big house shortly after they were married. They had Wade, and Kathy got pregnant with Brady while she was going to school. She earned her psychology degree shortly after he turned two. "People in town were a bit judgmental about it. They thought I left my sons too much to go to school and wondered what I'd need with a psychology degree anyway. I felt silly saying I didn't rightly know, but that it intrigued me, so I just stuck with *none of your business.*"

"Always a good answer," Jess said. "I used it many times myself, when people asked how old I was and where Chloe's dad was and a hundred other questions I couldn't believe they'd ask."

Kathy placed her hand on the top of the roller. "Much thinner, and we'll get crackers instead of biscuits."

Jess studied the dough, storing it in her memory. She'd gotten so caught up in Kathy's story that she hadn't been paying much attention to her baking. Story of *her* life, really. She reached for the biscuit cutter. "So, you got your degree…"

Kathy settled back in her chair and glanced out the lace-curtained window. "It wasn't till shortly after Brady came along that I had the idea about helping teens. One of the kids in town had gotten bad into drugs, and he was gettin' in trouble with the law a lot. I heard so much gossip about him and his family, about how he was a bad egg, or how it was his parents' fault for not being X, Y, or Z enough, and I thought if they put half as much effort into helping him as condemning him and his family, maybe he'd have a chance at gettin' better.

"And it hit me." Kathy brought her open palm down on the table, and Jess jumped and then laughed at herself. "Being the dreamer, I bring my idea to Randy. He's Mr. Logical so I think he's gonna shoot it down. Instead he asks what I need him to do to make it happen. I fell even more in love with that man right then and there."

A warm, squishy sensation went through Jess's chest. Her past had left her jaded enough that she didn't usually get mushy over love, but she'd seen the affection and respect and friendship between Kathy and Randy, and they were definitely—as Chloe would say—hashtag relationship goals.

"We took out loans and built the cabins, and since I'd always wanted a big family, we were also trying to have another baby. But I had trouble getting pregnant again. Trace took four years, which wasn't as long as some of my other friends waited, but what was really hard for me was feeling in my bones that our family wasn't complete." Her gaze drifted out the window again, her expression a mixture of sorrow and longing and happiness, and Jess held her breath as she waited for her to continue. "Years passed—a whole heap of them. Wade was sixteen when a judge ordered fifteen-year-old Nash into the program. He was different than the kids we'd had before. Lots of demons. He reminded me of a wild animal that'd been caught in a trap.

"He and Brady grew really close. They were the same age, and they just clicked. And something inside of me felt like I recognized him. I can't explain it." Kathy's eyes glistened with unshed tears as she placed a hand on her chest. She reached out and rearranged some of the biscuits Jess had placed on the pan, adding a bit more space between them.

"I'm always happy when the teens make progress and I see a change in them—and I get attached to each of them in one way or the other—but my heart just soared when we finally got through to him. After that, he was so protective of us and the ranch. Of the animals. You can tell a kind soul by the way they connect with animals." A smile curved her mouth as she looked up at Jess. "Like you and the dogs. And I saw you with the calves, too."

A light, floaty sensation tumbled through Jessica as she returned the smile. "Aww, thank you. The dogs were easy to win over, but the calves took some time. I seriously might want to take home a pet cow when the time comes."

Kathy's laughter filled the air, spreading more warmth and kindness. If baking lessons were like this, Jess would sign up for a hundred. Kathy ran her fingers along the edge of the table, pride lighting her features. "Nash took to the rodeo stuff like a hog to mud, too. He entered the annual local rodeo on a lark and beat boys who'd been training most of their lives. When his stint was up and it was time for him to leave, Wade, Brady, and Trace came in and told me we couldn't let him go back to his abusive father."

Pain replaced the other emotions in her features. "Randy told me that while he understood, and while he didn't like it, we couldn't just keep him. The judge had ordered him here, but he'd release him into the custody of his father. My mama bear came right out, and I told him that maybe if we suggested to the judge we keep him while holding our rifles..."

Jess sat down in the chair she'd been halfway kneeling on, too interested in how the story ended to focus on biscuits. Obviously, things had eventually worked out, but her pulse sped up as she worried over how hard a battle it'd been.

"Not pointing the guns *at* the judge, naturally," Kathy said with a shrug. "Just with them casually slung over our shoulders."

Naturally. Casually. Jess didn't know whether to laugh or cheer, but she totally understood that baser mama bear level. She'd never felt so violent as when she'd met Tyler and seen that he didn't treat her daughter the way she deserved. When she found out he'd endangered her on top of that, the feeling went into overdrive, and she curled her fists as the residual anger flowed through her.

"Ain't nobody mess with my kid and get away with it," Kathy said. "He was ours, so we fought. Social services came out and combed through our life. His dad wreaked havoc—not because he cared about his son, but about the money. He'd get more welfare money if his son lived with him."

Now Jess found her hands needed something to do, which again was silly. This story had to have a happy ending. But at the same time, what had it taken? She grabbed a tiny stray blob of dough and squeezed it between her index finger and thumb like a miniature stress ball.

The chair creaked as Kathy sat forward and folded her

arms across the top of the table. "I think I cried and swore every day for three months—sometimes at the same time. Then we won the fight and he was ours, and I thought okay, our family's complete. But something whispered there might be more." Kathy glanced at the biscuits. "Those are perfect. Why don't you pop them in the oven, and just you watch, they're gonna be the best biscuits ever."

The metal of the pan clanged against the oven rack as Jess slid them inside. She double-checked that she'd set the timer, washed up, and returned to the table where Kathy was sipping coffee or tea that had to have gone cold by now. "How are you holding up?"

"I'm good. Promise."

"Good. Because I wouldn't be opposed to hearing the rest of the story, if you're up for it."

Kathy took off her glasses, folded them, and left them on top of the stack of paperwork. "Let's move into the living room where the chairs are much cushier and easier on the rump."

After setting her phone timer so she wouldn't ruin her first pan of perfectly formed biscuits that she hoped would redeem her—especially in Everett's eyes, since that kid *still* brought up her first gross attempt every time she mentioned food—Jess followed Kathy into the living room. She moved a crocheted pillow that said "Blessed" across the front and sat on the couch next to Kathy.

It hit her again that the woman had raised six sons, as well as having influenced countless other lives. A lot of times Jess felt as if she'd had her hands beyond full with one.

For a moment she thought of her daughter and the letter in her pocket. She'd written five drafts over the weekend and was debating between handing it over herself, asking Wade to deliver it, or asking Liza. Part of her feared that if she handed it to Chloe herself, she'd tear it and throw it in the trash just to spite her. Pain rose up, squeezing her lungs, and when Kathy turned to her, she had to work to suppress it.

"If I get too personal, you just let me know."

Jessica nodded, although she was sure that wouldn't be an issue.

"After twelve years of not getting pregnant, I discovered I was expecting. At forty years old." Kathy twisted her wedding ring around her finger, the modest diamond catching the light each time it bobbed up to the top. "I was overwhelmed and excited and scared and pretty much every other emotion there is to feel."

"I felt the same at fifteen." Even thinking about that time recalled the tornado of emotions that'd swirled through her, fast and hard enough it'd done some long-term damage. "I was silly enough to think that maybe Chloe's father would be a pinch excited, too. Spoiler alert: he was not."

Kathy reached out and squeezed her knee. "I'm so sorry, hon."

"No, I'm sorry. This is your story."

"Don't you dare hold back. This is about us gettin' to know each other. Sharin' our journeys and whatnot."

"I appreciate that. But please, continue."

"We had just adopted Nash's biological brother, Nick, and I thought, whoa, I'm gonna have *two* new kids this year, even though one of them was already twelve." She pressed her lips together. "But four months in, I lost the baby." Her voice cracked. "It was a girl."

Of all the things she was grateful for, Chloe was the very top, and she couldn't imagine losing her baby. Empathetic tears blurred her eyes, and she took Kathy's hand. "I'm so sorry."

"It was a long time ago. I've made peace with it. It was hard, but the boys stepped up and took real good care of me, and of each other. After that I remember thinking, I can't do this anymore. I can't get attached only to end up hurt and crying on the floor. So I told my family we were complete, and we had as many as we could handle. For ten years we went on like that, running the ranch and helping a lot of teens.

"Then Aiden came along, close to a year ago now. He told me he was out of here a dozen times, he was so determined to break free. About a month into the program, he got himself into trouble with a local girl and the town was up in arms. I guarantee he's responsible for these gray hairs." Kathy gestured at the gray sections near her temples.

As horrible as it was, a thread of worry stitched its way through Jess. Chloe was so fixated on Tyler, and as sure as Jess was that hadn't magically changed—unfortunately— Chloe spent a lot of her time here with Aiden.

"Three months he fought being here," Kathy continued, "but during that time, we saw him with the horses. We called him the horse whisperer. That told me he was good people, even if he tried to repress it. He was kinda like a wild horse who needed not to know he was caught. Once he felt the confines drop, he calmed. He slowly began to trust us. Oh, how I cried the day he left."

Now Jess was back to experiencing heart squeezes. She wasn't sure she could get so attached and let go, even though raising more kids and doing the teenage thing again also stressed her out.

"Two months later, he showed up on his motorcycle and said his old crowd was gonna get him in trouble, but he had to go back, or his parole officer would find out he'd left town, and he'd be in even more trouble."

He has a parole officer.

Chloe could have one if she keeps going down the path she started with that manipulative jerk.

"Wade dug a little and found out Aiden's parents hadn't even bothered to see him when he returned home and that he'd spent a few nights on the street. Aiden and Wade, they have a special connection. Wade pretends to be tough, and often he's the strictest when it comes to the rules, but he was the one who asked about adoption—even offered to adopt Aiden himself, although he was worried social services would see him as an undesirable candidate, what with him not being married."

Jess's emotions flipped on her, affection going through her for Wade. He was so brash and gruff in a lot of ways, but then there were those tender fleeting moments. Like on the porch the other day, when he'd assured her she wasn't a failure. When his callused fingertips had gently cupped her chin and wiped away her tears.

"I told him that I was just as attached and braced myself for another battle, but Aiden's parents signed him over like it was nothing," Kathy said, her disappointment in children being treated that way palpable. "He's been ours for six months."

Jess's heart softened. Her anxiety over whether she'd made the right decision melted. The Dawsons and the rest of the staff were such amazing people, and she was so glad they were the ones she'd entrusted Chloe's care to. Maybe she should've been more honest about her cooking skills, but she couldn't bring herself to regret that, either, because she was learning so much, and she felt a bond with several of the people here that she hadn't felt in a long time.

Which also scared her. Getting attached wasn't something she let herself do anymore. "Do you feel like your family's complete now?" she asked, then immediately winced. "Sorry, that's so personal."

Kathy waved a hand through the air. "Like I haven't been spillin' my guts and monopolizin' the conversation."

"Only because I asked, and I find it incredibly interesting. This whole place is so different from the environment I grew up in, and I'm so grateful for the chance to get to know you all."

"Happy to hear it." Kathy took Jess's hand and sandwiched it between both of hers. "We're glad to have you. However long we have you."

A pang went through the center of Jess's chest, even though she'd just reminded herself getting attached wasn't the best idea. She couldn't stay here forever. She had an apartment, as tiny and in disrepair as it might be, as well as a job and a life.

As empty as it sometimes felt.

"As for your question, mostly I feel at peace when it comes to my family. But you know, now I need daughters-in-law and some grandkids. Gotta get my boys married off, regardless of how hard they try to resist it." Kathy's words came out sounding an awful lot like *hint, hint,* and Jess hoped the woman wasn't getting any ideas.

Wade walked into the room, glanced from her to his

mom—who was still beaming—and back to her. "Well if this doesn't look like a whole heap of trouble."

"You have no idea," Jess said.

"You okay, Ma?" he asked.

"I'm great. Jessica is an exceptional conversationalist. She asks me questions and lets me ramble."

"Funny." His gaze met hers across the room, and a jolt shot up her core. "She usually gives me attitude and keeps on giving it."

Jess narrowed her eyes at him. "Oh, *I'm* the only one with attitude?"

The Cheshire Cat had nothing on the grin he flashed her, all false innocence. "I just had to grab the keys to the truck, but I'll see you both at dinner." He headed toward the office, his footsteps echoing down the hall.

"What about your family, dear?" Kathy asked, and Jess realized she was staring at Wade's butt and admiring the nice fit of his worn Wranglers. She jerked her attention back to Kathy, whose smug expression said she'd noticed. "We can wait till the distraction leaves."

"I'm afraid you're getting the wrong idea," Jess said, keeping her voice low and one eye peeled for Wade. "As your son pointed out, we mostly bicker."

"Oh, a man and a woman bickering. Never heard of that before. It's not at all what my Randy and I do now and again. You know, when we get real passionate about something."

Jess pursed her lips and raised an eyebrow, but Kathy hardly seemed admonished. In order to avoid the Wade line of questioning, she focused on the other thing Kathy had inquired about. "My family is Chloe. It's always been just the two of us."

The familiar, achy hollowness in her chest yawned wider and sucked away some of her happy. Now it felt like it was just her all alone. The note in her pocket seemed to be burning into her skin. As silly as it was, part of her was also scared to hand over the note to her daughter because if it didn't work, she didn't know what else to do, and she needed to hold on to that glimmer of hope to get her through her days.

"I don't mean to pry," Kathy said, her voice soft.

"I was the one prying, and now I'm not sure if I can handle reciprocating." The phone in her pocket vibrated and chimed, and she was glad for the excuse the timer gave her. "I'd better go grab those biscuits."

Kathy nodded. "Okay, dear. Whenever you want to tell me about it is fine. I'll be here."

Such a nice thing to say, and yet Jess wasn't sure she'd ever be ready. It wasn't a story of pulling together and love and understanding.

Which was just another reason she needed her current family to have a happy ending.

Chapter 14

CHLOE'S HEART HAMMERED FASTER AND FASTER, LEAVING her a smidge dizzy. Tyler had answered. He'd finally answered!

> **Tyler:** That sucks! I miss you, babe. When are you getting back?

Her fingers flew across the keyboard as she typed her response, her time limit ticking down in the back of her mind.

> **Chloe:** Not sure yet. It'll probably be a month or two, and I hope that's all it is. Did your parents freak?

As she waited for his response, she thought about the folded letter from Mom in her back pocket. Usually she was the opposite of patient, but she needed to be alone when she read it, which meant waiting until tonight after she and her roommates were locked in their room and they were distracted with other things.

This was her only chance to talk to Tyler, and Mom had been part of her not having any space, so the letter could wait.

> **Tyler:** You know how they are. My dad was the

asshole he always is. My mom yelled like
the bitch she is.

As conflicted as she currently felt about her mom, Chloe
still flinched at the way Tyler talked about his. It wasn't anything new. He was super rude to his mom, even when she was
attempting to be nice and offer a snack or ask about Tyler's day.

It was because of how bad he had it at home, though. His
dad never stopped yelling, and he was mean to his wife, too.
Then both of his parents would be yelling, and that was one
reason Tyler escaped with alcohol and weed.

So far, Chloe had only used them to take the edge off
after school or over the weekend, but she'd be lying if she
said she wasn't tempted to take a hit off Tyler's vape pen
in the middle of the school day. If it could take some of the
stress away… But no. She only wanted to check out here
and there, not be high nonstop like Tyler was.

Yes, she understood why Mom didn't like her being with
a guy like him, but Mom didn't understand. Not everyone
had stability at home. Of course, right now she didn't have
a stable family, either, although the other teens in the program were growing on her. Last night she, Izzy, and the
Double D's had had a dance party in their room.

An aggressive dance party, she mentally added, since it
was the term Izzy had used. They'd been doing moves from
popular music videos they'd seen, and they'd formed two
sides. Things had gotten a bit out of control when Dez
threw Danica's teddy bear that she'd had since forever, and
it caught Izzy in the eye. They'd been so afraid they were
going to get yelled at that they'd hovered over her and taken
turns soothing her with all the ice they didn't have.

A giggle slipped out. This morning there was only a hint of bruising, so Izzy had just gone crazy with the makeup. Then, since she didn't want to stand out, they'd all done their eye shadow in varying shades of purple, presenting a united, overly made-up front.

When Jacob, one of the boys in the group, had asked if they were conducting YouTuber makeup tutorial auditions, Izzy had added "aggressive makeup tutorials," and they'd all busted up.

Unlike the teachers at her other school, Miss Allie simply smiled and told them about the time she'd worn blue eye shadow to her prom.

Oops, he's waiting for me now.

> **Chloe:** Sorry it's so rough at home.
> **Tyler:** Nothing new. I miss being able to talk to you. I can't talk to anyone like I can talk to you.
> **Chloe:** For now, we can talk this way. You might even be able to visit me on a Sunday. That's when people can visit.
> **Tyler:** Just let me know when you're back.

Chloe frowned. He probably just knew his family wouldn't let him visit, and Mom would be mad, too. So maybe sticking to online messages was the way to go for now.

She glanced around, doing her best to position herself squarely in front of the monitor. A couple of people were in the next room, the open archway not providing much coverage, but no one was paying close attention to her. Still she kept the screen minimized as she placed her hands back on the keyboard.

> **Chloe:** The one highlight about this place is the horses. Actually some of the people are pretty cool, too. But I can now saddle and bridle a horse all on my own.

The times when she could ride across the miles on Rowdy and feel the wind in her hair were her favorites. That was when everything else in the world fell away. In fact, she couldn't wait to go out to the stables and tell Rowdy that Tyler had finally responded and see what he had to...*neigh* about that.

She snort-laughed at her own joke and then leaned forward as Tyler's next message popped up on-screen.

> **Tyler:** Gotta go, babe.

Well, that was a tad underwhelming. But he'd answered and things would get better, and now she didn't have to keep wondering if something bad had happened.

Wade knocked on the door to Nash's cabin. Or Jessica's house. He wasn't exactly sure what to call it anymore.

Voices drifted from inside, muffled and hard to make out.

"Jessica?" He waited a beat, straining to hear. There was definitely talking; he just couldn't make out the actual words.

Was that a "Come in?"

He tested the handle, and when he found it unlocked, he let himself in. "Hey, I was just…"

Jessica was at the kitchen table, laptop open and her iPad propped up to the side, a YouTube video on cooking playing in the background. Only she wasn't looking at either screen. Her head was on the table, her cheek atop a giant stack of papers.

The cooking personality on the iPad screen was rattling on and on about saffron, whatever that was.

"Jessica…?"

She jerked up and blinked, obviously trying to get her bearings. "Wade. Hey, I was just…" The vague gesture at her devices didn't explain much.

"Learning to cook with saffron?"

"Saffron? I thought that was just a pretentious way of saying yellow." Her eyes rolled to the ceiling as if she'd find the answer there. "Or was it orange?"

He shrugged and tipped his chin at her iPad, and she watched a few seconds, then paused the video. "Oh! Saffron. Of course I know about that. It's a spice I plan on putting in everything from now on. Biscuits. Stew." Her eyebrows drew together as she leaned closer to the screen. "Rice apparently."

"Not big on rice. I think it requires more calories to eat than you get out of it."

"Rice for dinner all week it is!" She gave him a sleepy smile, and his gut tightened in the way it tended to do around her and her smiles. "I was just honing my craft."

It could use a step past honing. Actually, it hadn't been too bad the past few days. Ma had been working with her, and the biscuits she'd made last night had been amazing.

"Yeah, I'm going to start throwing more vegan options into the mix. Lots of tofu. Saffron, obviously. And a nice kale salad." Her big, brown eyes practically sparkled with amusement. "Gotta keep everyone healthy, you know."

"I hope you're healthy enough to survive a hangry mob."

The wattage on her smile kicked up another notch. "Did you seriously just use the word 'hangry'?"

"What?" He sat on the edge of the table, his knee bumping into hers on the way down. "Are you trying to imply I'm not hip? Not up with the times?"

"No, I'm straight up saying it." Her joints cracked as she stretched her arms over her head, and her shirt lifted enough to display a stripe of skin he couldn't stop staring at. "Did you need something? Not that you can't visit, but considering that would mean taking time off, I'm guessing the visit has an attached agenda."

Now that she'd said that, all he could think was that he should visit her a whole lot more. "An agenda, huh?" His gaze moved to her computer screen. A whole mess of figures and words filled the squares.

"My boss back in Denver needs me to keep up on data entry."

"You've been working full-time on that, too?"

"Don't worry. I put in the hours after I'm done with the cooking and the other spare jobs I'm trying to get better at around here. It won't interfere."

Damn. Maybe he *had* been too hard on her. Did she really think he was all work and no play? Sometimes it felt like it, but he didn't want her to think that about him, and he'd rather not analyze why. "Not worried. You definitely pull your weight around here." Occasionally she seemed a bit tired, but he'd assumed she was still adjusting to the early hour. He had no idea she'd been juggling so much, and doing a helluva job, too. "I think you could use a night out."

"A night out? What's that? The term sounds familiar, but it's been so long since I've heard it, I'm not sure I remember what it is anymore. I'm surprised *you* know what it is, come to think of it."

"It's been a while." He glanced at his watch. It was past nine, so going out tonight was a bad idea, and his limbs dragged at the thought of driving into town, much less having to get out of the truck and function. "How about we take tomorrow night off? See if we can't refresh our memories on what that's like. I'll show you around town and prove I'm not a stick-in-the-mud who always has an agenda." He nudged her foot with the side of his boot. "You wouldn't be opposed to feeding everyone to-go food from the diner, would you?"

She cocked her head, a warning filling the arch of her eyebrow.

He gave her his best false innocence look. "What? Genuinely curious."

"Mm-hmm." She surveyed the stack in front of her and fought back a yawn. "Taking a night off together sounds nice. As friends."

Way to be subtle about the friends-only emphasis. It was good. It'd keep him in line, even though he was tempted to gather up the line and toss it like a lasso, only he wouldn't bother keeping hold of the end. "It's a...plan."

He tipped his hat and pushed to his feet to leave her to it.

"Wait," she said. "Two questions before you go."

He slowly turned around.

"One, do you ever take that hat off?"

He bit back a smile. "Occasionally."

She leaned across her table, balancing her weight on her forearms and giving him a tiny glimpse at cleavage. Her shirt was so threadbare he could make out the outline of her bra, and the yoga pants she had on did glorious things to her ass. "Admit it. You're bald under there, aren't you?"

He burst out laughing. "Sorry to disappoint."

"I notice you didn't take the hat off to prove it."

He reached up as if he were going to remove his hat and then tugged it tighter on his head. "What was the second question?"

"Why'd you come over in the first place? I was just teasing about the agenda. If you need help with something, I can help. I'm even mostly awake again." She stood up the rest of the way as though she needed to prove it, going so far as to lift her fists and bounce on the balls of her feet as if he might call her to the boxing ring. She bounced closer, the curve of her grin on the taunting side, and man, he'd never wanted to brawl so bad.

Of course he'd never hit a girl, so he'd have to go for grappling. Take her to the floor. Maybe use his tongue to teach her a lesson.

The temperature in the room shot up as Wade's heart thundered in his chest. Then he was noticing her pink boots, discarded by the door, and the scent that had driven him crazy when she was sitting next to him in the truck, and his one-track thoughts turned to something he needed that she could definitely help with. Desire heated his veins as he let his imagination run free. About closing the distance and pulling her to him for a kiss. About driving his hand through her hair to see if it was as soft as it looked as he traced the column of her neck with his mouth.

He licked his lips and worked to keep his voice even. "I just wanted to tell you that I delivered your note to Chloe earlier. I thought you'd want to know."

Trepidation crept into the line of her posture, and she twisted a strand of hair around her finger the way she did when her nerves kicked in. "Thank you. For delivering it and letting me know. I guess now I just wait."

He nodded. Waiting sucked; there was no way around that. "Give her time. It might not be immediate, and she'll probably fight the desire to reply for a couple of days before she does, but that doesn't mean she's not thinking about you. That she doesn't miss you as much as you miss her."

He supposed there was no use in wishing for a way to get the lighter mood back when Jessica was in the middle of mentally rehashing a situation that'd sent her entire world off-kilter. Along with being a hard worker who was determined to keep on trying till she got things right, she was a devoted mother who'd raised her daughter herself. More and more, he was seeing all her good qualities. Qualities that only made her more attractive, and she was already a knockout in the looks department, something she didn't seem to know, which was ridiculous.

"You okay? Need me to stay?" He wasn't sure where that'd come from, but after a solid two weeks of experiencing the urge to comfort her, he figured he might as well give in to it.

"I'll be okay. Good night, Wade."

"Good night, Jessica."

She walked after him, poised to close the door as he

stepped onto the porch. "You can call me Jess, by the way. I was only teasing when I said you had to call me Jessica. And I'd like to think we're friends now. That's not breaking the rules, right?"

"Not breaking the rules." He should just turn and go. Leave it at that. Instead he stepped closer and cupped her cheek. "I kind of like that I'm the only one who calls you by your full name, and I'm not sure I want to stop." He brushed his thumb across her smooth skin, and her sharp intake of breath sent his desire spiking that much higher. "Until tomorrow. *Jessica*."

Chapter 15

TWO AND A HALF WEEKS INTO HER JOB AT TURN AROUND Ranch, Jess felt like she had a pretty good handle on things. For instance, she knew that when she made scrambled eggs, she had to add two extra eggs to sacrifice to the pan gods, because no amount of nonstick spray made a difference.

She'd added a handful of meals to her repertoire, and after watching a ridiculous number of YouTube videos, she was gearing up for another attempt in the near future at a recipe that used yeast and required kneading. On top of her cooking skills, she could approach a calf without scaring it off and help hold it while Wade, Brady, or Trace doctored it, and she was a pro at steering the truck in a straight line while Wade and Brady fed the cows.

Going out for a night on the town, though?

Her nerves careened through her stomach, wrecking the walls and making her regret everything she'd eaten today. She eyed her limited clothing options. Maybe she should've taken a trip home for more, but the thought of being so far away—in case Chloe decided she needed her in the four or five hours it'd take to get there, gather her stuff, and drive back—didn't sit right. Instead she made do with what she'd brought, along with the clothes she'd purchased at Horsefeathers Western Store.

Now she wished she'd bought a fancy shirt or dress.

More than anything, though, she wished Chloe was seated on the foot of her bed, giving her outfits a thumbs-up or down.

Teens could be brutally honest, but Chloe always soft-ened her honesty with compliments.

"You're too young to wear that" meant her outfit was outdated and lame.

"That doesn't show off your figure" meant the clothes were too unshapely and unflattering.

Most of the times she'd asked Chloe for fashion input were for interviews and work parties and the occasional night at the movies—where she sat next to her daughter and came out of the dark theater with either soda splatters or popcorn grease on her shirt.

This was bigger, because it was…well, not a date. But a night out, and she didn't want to look like a sack of potatoes next to the tall cowboy who'd be by her side.

After sorting through her wardrobe two more times, she decided to embrace their country location. The stud-ded jeans were made of the kind of fabric that helped suck everything in and smooth away what pregnancy had done to her body. She slipped into her lacy, white tank top and grabbed the pink-and-gray flannel she'd bought when Chloe *had* been there to give her opinion. Her daughter had seen the shirts and grabbed one off the rack. "Mom, I know you're not going to think this sounds cute, but some girls have been wearing these flannels around their waists, and it's so cute!"

"Are you kidding me?" Jess had asked, and her daughter assured her it looked good, to which she'd replied, "I know. I wore that exact style in junior high." Back in the days when she had time to worry about being fashionable.

Instead of wrapping it around her waist, Jess pulled the flannel on but left it unbuttoned. She took a luxurious amount of time on her makeup, added hoop earrings, and pulled on her pink boots. While Wade had called them ridiculous, she'd also caught him eyeing them now and then, a crooked half smile on his face.

Maybe I should ask Liza to borrow a cowboy hat.

But then I'd mash my hair, and a cowboy hat seems more like something a person needs to ease into.

The knock on the door sent her pulse skyrocketing, and she forced herself not to sprint to answer. The slight skip couldn't be helped.

Her breath caught at the cowboy on her doorstep. Wade usually looked ruggedly delicious, and while she liked him dirty… *Hold up there, thoughts. Let's go with covered in dirt and sweat and…*

That wasn't helping, so she chose to focus on the man standing in front of her. Black shirt with pearl buttons. Wranglers that hugged all the right places and made her thankful pants like that existed. Black boots and a black hat that perfectly complemented his dark dusting of scruff.

Her fingers twitched with the urge to reach up and feel the stubble against her fingertips. Then her tongue could get in on the action and—

"Jessica?"

The way he said her name, all deep and husky like that wasn't helping her focus on the friendship part of this plan. "Yeah, I'm ready to go. Are you? Ready?"

That crooked half smile she'd just been thinking about twisted his lips. "Figured it'd be good to be ready *before* I picked you up."

"Well, look at you, being all prepared. And sarcastic."

"If I'm going to keep up with you, I've got to start as soon as possible," he said, reaching behind her to close the door. His chest bumped her shoulder, and his cologne invaded her senses and caused her ovaries to stand at attention.

It was because they were so neglected. Yeah. That was definitely the only reason. At the same time, *holy crap*, he smelled good.

"Do I look the part?" she asked, spreading her arms wide.

"Of vixen? Yes, yes you do." He put his hand on her lower back as they walked down the sidewalk and over to his truck, and she might've accidentally leaned into it a little.

He opened the passenger door of the big, black Dodge Ram.

"Ooh, you brought out the fancy truck tonight."

He boosted her when she couldn't quite haul herself into the raised cab. "Figured you might like to remember what riding in a truck without dogs, dog hair, and half a bale of hay dusted across the interior felt like."

As he rounded the hood, she took the opportunity to ogle him again. She also sucked in a breath of his cologne before he climbed in, since sniffing the air like a dog would probably undo the fancy factor.

They made small talk as they drove into town, and as light as the conversation was, the air in the cab of the truck felt heavy and thick, full of possibilities Jess kept telling herself were anything but.

He pulled up in front of a rustic building with a neon sign that announced it was the Tumbleweed Bar.

She started out of the truck, but Wade was there in an instant, offering a hand and helping her down. "Gotta give a guy the chance to open the door for you."

"I guess I don't hang around many gentlemen."

"Why, Jessica Cook. Are you callin' me a gentleman?"

"Don't let it go to your head," she said with a laugh.

"Too late," he said, right next to her ear, and a pleasant shiver ran down her spine. He escorted her inside, and she took it all in. The wooden walls, the stage at the front where a band was setting up, and the giant spool-shaped tables dotting the edge of the floor. There were signs of every kind hanging on the walls, everything from "gone fishing" to speed limit signs and ones with old-fashioned sayings. The mini half-wall by the hostess stand had a deer running through it—the back half on one side, the front half on the other.

"I can honestly say that I've never been anywhere like this in my life."

"Just wait till you try the moonshine."

She peered up at him, trying to gauge if he was joking or not. He grinned, and she still couldn't tell.

"Why, hello there!" Winona gave Jess a huge smile as she approached. Then panic widened her eyes, and she turned to the cowboy next to her. "Wade. You're who I was saying hello to. Obviously." Her long, straight black hair fell forward and tangled with her beaded earrings as she extended a hand. "And you must be Jess. It's a small town, so I've of course heard about how you're out working at the ranch, and it's so nice to finally meet you. For the first time."

Next to her, Wade gave a snort-laugh.

"Thanks for trying to cover for me, Winona. But he knows. About the night I ordered ribs from you."

"Oh."

"Would've known those ribs and that potato salad anywhere," he said.

Jess rolled her eyes. "Yeah, he maintains he would've recognized them at first taste, and I maintain I would've gotten away with it if I hadn't gotten the car stuck in the mud and the food hadn't gone sprawling across the back. Right before the trunk popped open."

They shared a laugh.

"I've been meaning to take you up on your offer, too, but it's been so busy," Jess said.

"What offer?" Wade asked.

"Winona offered me some cooking lessons. You know, for large groups of people, since I'm of course a fabulous cook otherwise."

"She'd *love* lessons," Wade said, and Jess elbowed him in the gut.

"I'll give you a call. For reals this time." She tugged Wade toward the bar and, once they were settled on a couple of stools, added, "You, I should never call again."

"I don't recollect you ever calling me in the first place."

She spun to face him and hooked her boots on the bottom rung of his stool. "I don't even have your number. However, I do know where you live."

"How ominous. All the same, you'd better hand over your phone." He gestured for it, and she unlocked it and placed it in his palm. He entered the number and handed it back to her. "It'll save time the next time you get stuck."

Jess shot him her best dirty look, one that didn't seem to scare him as much as it should. Maybe she was losing her touch. Or maybe it was the way she'd rested her knee against his thigh, her sideways position on the stool closing them into a bubble that was a smidge too intimate. Yet she couldn't bring herself to pop it.

They ordered food and drinks. Admittedly, after a whole lot of cooking, it was nice not to have to be the one who made the meal. Bonus, nothing was burned or just on the verge of edible.

The band began playing as they were finishing their dinner, and several couples took to the floor. Jessica watched them swirl and spin and move across the open area like they meant to use every inch. A few times she flinched, sure some of the pairs were about to crash into each other, but they never did.

Jess grabbed the cloth napkin that'd been wrapped around her cutlery and wiped the salt from her fries off her fingers. "Wow, I've only ever seen dancing like that in the movies. I didn't know people actually did it in real life."

Wade glanced at the floor and then sipped at his beer, a noncommittal noise low in his throat. "Let me guess. You're more of a nightclub girl. Fancy dresses and heels and fruity, colorful drinks."

"I'm more of a had-a-kid-before-I-was-old-enough-to-go-clubbing girl."

There was an awkward beat where Wade appeared to be lost as to how to respond. She didn't want to make him feel bad; she'd only spoken the truth. "My early twenties was when I went to playgroups and tried really hard to make friends with moms who had a decade or so on me. Not easy, since they always looked at me with so much judgment in their eyes that I practically drowned in it. Just when I was about to give up, I met a woman who was more my style. She was a tattoo artist who changed her hair color as often as her shoes, was forever running late, and swore like a sailor. We mostly joined the PTA so that we could tell other moms they were doing a *great* job, even when everyone gave them disapproving looks." She smiled at the memory. "Didn't leave a lot of time for going out."

"I didn't even think…"

"Don't worry about it," she said, waving off his apology. "Happens all the time, and I know you were only teasing. There were occasions here and there when I felt picked on and wished for one night to just go out and leave my responsibilities behind for a few hours, but I wouldn't trade any of that for Chloe. I lived out my wild side for a year, and that was plenty."

"Still." Wade twisted toward her, the lights from the bar flashing through his eyes and dancing across his skin. "I'm sure it wasn't easy."

"It wasn't." She shrugged. Sometimes in life *fair and unfair* and *easy and hard* don't matter. You do what you have to. You keep on swimming.

"You did a great job."

That dull ache in her chest throbbed to the surface and sharpened. "Up until about six months ago, I might've agreed. Hell, even three months ago, back when I thought Chloe's teachers and the principal were merely overreacting."

"We've already been over this, remember?"

She nodded on autopilot. "Unformed neurotransmitters."

"Teenagers. I did stupid shit all the time."

"Your mom did mention one of those times."

His head dropped with a groan. "Oh, great."

She nudged his knee. "It's actually nice to know you're human."

When she started to pull her hand away, he grabbed

hold of it. "I'm doing a bad job of getting you away from it all and giving you the break you need. Which leaves me no choice but to do something I don't normally do." He stood and intertwined his fingers with hers. "Dance with me?"

"You dance?" she asked.

"Not really, but for you, I will. One night only."

"Basically you're saying get it while it's hot?"

"Oh, it'll always be hot." He tugged on her hand. "Come on."

She gave in to the pull—in to the desire to see him dance and to be the one dancing with him. They moved to the edge of the floor and her heart sped up, the fear that the rest of the quickly moving couples would mow them down a genuine concern. Especially since she didn't know any of the steps.

But then Wade drew her close, the heat of his body slowly seeping into hers. "Just hold on tight. I promise I won't let you fall."

She secured her hand to his shoulder and tightened her grip on his hand. She gave one sharp nod to say she was ready, and then they were moving, gliding into the melee at as rapid a pace as the rest of them. Her feet struggled for a beat or two, trying to get the feel of it, but they gradually caught hold of the rhythm.

Wade's hand spread on her back, guiding her with light pressure as he pressed her tighter against him. He did as promised, keeping her moving without letting her fall. Halfway through the song, he whipped her out, spun her around, and yanked her back into his arms.

A laugh spilled out of her as she clung on to him. "Do it again," she said, preparing herself as much as she could.

He whipped her out, spinning her like a top. Her hand slipped free, and she cursed herself for asking to go again, sure she was about to crash and send people and food and drinks flying. But he snatched her other hand, spun her in toward him until they were curled up tight, and then he dipped her. The world went upside down for a couple of seconds before she was back in his arms, their chests pressed together.

"Wade Dawson, you're full of surprises."

"It's pretty much a town requirement to learn the country swing, and believe it or not, I used to be a good boy."

"Used to?"

His hand slid a little lower on her back. "I still dabble."

Her heart skipped a beat, and she slipped her hands behind his neck and linked them. As fun as spinning was, she rather enjoyed this position.

The notes faded as the song came to a close, but her heart continued to pound, and every breath sent her chest tighter against his.

The band announced it was time for the lovers to take the floor for their slow song, and she worried Wade would rush them to the side. But he didn't make a move, simply looked at her. Into the depths of her, it felt like.

While she was trying to keep things lighter, she also didn't want to let go. Didn't she deserve a night of dancing with a hot cowboy who knew what he was doing?

That could apply to other areas, but she'd make sure to stick to country dancing. Yeah. Totally. "Since this is your only night of dancing, I'd hate to cut it short. Especially since I might know how to dance to the next song."

The first chords of the guitar filled the air, slow and steady.

"What if I like it when you're a little off-balance?" he asked.

Oh, he'd been throwing her off-balance since the moment she'd shown up at the ranch. "Don't worry. I'll still let you lead."

Friends danced, right?

Wade's hands drifted lower on Jessica's back as he pressed her closer and swayed to the beat. He could hardly say no to one more dance, not when she looked so pretty and with how much he enjoyed having her warm body wrapped around his.

There was a high chance there'd be gossip about this, and it'd undoubtedly make it out to the ranch, but right now, he couldn't bring himself to care.

Her limited time had him volleying back and forth. Did that make it better or worse to start feeling more? To act on it? On one hand, should he simply enjoy the time they had? On the other, there was all the drama he promised to avoid, and with them working together every day, things could go bad.

Before long she'd be gone, just someone who came to the ranch for a while, like a lot of other people had done.

But she was different from anyone who'd ever worked at the ranch—for one, he'd never been so attracted to a woman before, from her looks to her personality to how she constantly kept him on his toes. She made up these silly stories about the livestock, too, and she'd named the calves in the corral, balking when he told her they just called them by their number.

Way too soon she'd be gone, and like her, he didn't get a whole lot of opportunity for a night out.

Just enjoy the dance. It was one slow song. One great night.

He rested his chin on the top of her head, not setting, only letting it brush, and she snuggled even closer. She was the perfect size. The perfect a lot of things. He wanted to know everything about her, even as the warning bell he'd ignored in the past chimed in his head.

There'd been another woman once, one he wanted to know everything about. In spite of them being total opposites, he'd gotten completely swept up in Serena. In the idea of love and having someone to come home to at the end of the day. At the end of that relationship, he'd wished he'd listened to his instincts and kept his distance. Women like his ex—like Jessica—would never be happy out in here in the sticks for long.

The song drifted to a close, and he cursed it for not being one of those ten- or twenty-minute songs.

"Shall we get a drink?" Jessica asked, slowly lowering her arms to her sides. "I'm not sure if you were serious about that moonshine remark."

"Honey, I never joke about moonshine," he said, and a smile spread across her face, making him vote for enjoying tonight and worrying about tomorrow, tomorrow.

Wade had only had a sip of the famous "moonshine" the Tumbleweed served, and she'd had two. It'd been years and years since she'd been this buzzed. She'd always needed to be sober enough for what-ifs. What if Chloe got sick in the night? What if the apartment building started on fire, or there was some sort of emergency?

Even when Chloe was out and about, it didn't help because what if her ride fell through and Jess had to go pick her up?

The *from jail* had never been there before, and now she knew way too much about how awful that felt—the phone call, the drive over, and the days after.

Wade helped her into his truck via the driver's side door, and when she went to scoot over—since she didn't have the excuse of Brady riding with them—Wade wrapped his hand around her thigh.

"You might as well stay close," he said, firing up the engine. "Brush up on driving a stick by watching me shift."

Again and again, her inappropriate joke about not having driven a stick for a long time rose to mind. Speaking of long times, she couldn't even remember the last time she'd yearned to tangle herself up in the sheets with a guy. The way Wade had moved on the dance floor spoke to other things he'd do well, and it'd been forever.

She'd be rusty, but she was sure she'd figure it out along the way. Like riding a bike.

Or maybe she'd let *him* do the riding.

A giggle slipped out, and he raised an eyebrow at her. She bit her thumbnail. "I'm a little drunk."

"I gathered as much. Don't worry, I'll be the perfect gentleman."

"What if I didn't want you to be?" *Oops.* This was why else she didn't drink. She already had problems with her verbal filter.

His eyes darkened, and his hand tightened on her thigh. "Jessica…"

"I know." Her shoulders sagged. "It's against the rules."

"I don't give a damn about the rules right now," he said, the husky tone of his voice sending a shock up her core. "But you're drunk."

"You gave me the moonshine."

"Exactly. How about you just ride next to me, and tomorrow we'll…?" He let out a shallow breath. "Tomorrow we'll see where we're at."

Disappointment battled rationale. He'd made sense. He was the gentleman he claimed to be, and here she was acting like a teenager. Getting drunk, losing her inhibitions, and thinking that sleeping with a guy would fix everything when all it ever caused was trouble.

And fun.

With trouble.

She studied his dark profile, and a wave of desire crashed through her, weakening the tenuous hold she had on her self-control. "But tomorrow we'll be at the ranch, surrounded by your family and a bunch of teenagers."

Wade shifted into fourth as they hit the road that led out of town. "I know." There was disappointment mixed in with the resolve in his voice, she was sure of it.

Perhaps that meant she had some wiggle room to work with, so she decided to make her case. "Your mom's already getting ideas."

"My brothers, too."

"They see it. I feel it." Vulnerability rose up and tightened her throat, but she forced out the words anyway. "Do you feel it?"

His Adam's apple bobbed up and down. "I feel it."

She wasn't sure if that made her feel better or worse. Mostly she worried she'd regret this in the morning. She just didn't know if she'd regret speaking so boldly or not being bolder.

The rest of the drive was quiet, all except the growl of the engine and the faint radio in the background.

Wade pulled up to her cabin and walked her up the steps. "I'm afraid this is gonna get complicated."

She was afraid it was already complicated. She wasn't even all that buzzed anymore. A bit on the tired side, but as Wade's hand settled on her hip, every cell in her body woke up. He pushed the door open with his other hand, and then his eyes met hers.

"Thanks for tonight," she said. "No matter what else happens, I'll always remember how much fun I had."

"Me too." An eternity ground out, the slightly eerie, ringing silence she'd only heard out here at night filling the air. As soon as he left, tonight would be over. They'd go back to being people with tons of responsibilities and pressure heaped on their shoulders.

His hand dropped from her hip, leaving the space it'd occupied too cold, and then he slowly walked down the porch steps and over to his truck.

She told herself it was for the best.

She just couldn't quite make herself believe it.

Chapter 16

JESSICA WALKED TOWARD THE FEED TRUCK WADE AND Brady were loading with bales. She was in a preposterously good mood considering she'd been awake since 5:00 a.m., when a handsome cowboy had knocked on her door and told her it was time for driving lessons.

Yesterday, Wade had seemed to be keeping his distance, which made their night dancing at the Tumbleweed feel like a good dream she'd woken up from only to discover it hadn't truly happened. She'd spent most of yesterday telling herself yet again that it was for the best. While doing a crap job of making herself believe it. Without tagging along for feeding or having Wade stop by the kitchen, she'd had nothing to focus on besides the fact that her daughter still wasn't talking to her.

She'd poured her heart out in that letter, and she worried it wasn't enough, even as Wade's voice also filled her head, telling her to be patient.

Patience wasn't her strong suit, as demonstrated by how she'd rushed through the dishes and then strode across the yard to the haystack so she didn't have to wait to see if Wade and Brady would pick her up to help feed.

They'd passed her by yesterday, which was another thing that'd stung.

But earlier this morning while they'd been in his truck and she mentioned it, he'd admitted that he'd slept through his alarm after their night out, and everyone was all exasperated about his sleeping in, which had thrown off his whole schedule.

A scary amount of joy and relief had tumbled through her at discovering he wasn't avoiding her.

She watched him now, picking up bales by the thin orange string and stacking them into the bed of the truck. He wiped his forearm across his forehead, and his gaze drifted to her. One corner of his mouth kicked up, and he reached up and gripped the brim of his hat.

Then she was reliving being in the truck with him at the crack of dawn this morning all over again, when he'd been rattling off instructions about clutches and gears as his thigh pressed against hers.

Jessica folded her arms across the top of the truck bed and peered up at the two cowboys. "I figured I'd come help with the loading since I finished up the dishes early."

Wade and Brady exchanged a look.

"What? You don't think I can help?" They threw around the bales as if they weighed nothing, and while she didn't pretend to be in as good shape as they were, how heavy could the bales be?

"Be my guest," Wade said, moving to the edge of the open tailgate and extending a hand to help her up.

She reached toward the middle of the stack, and Wade put his hand on her shoulder.

"Whoa there. How about you start with one a little lower?" He maneuvered her over to the last bale in a row, right at hip level. He and Brady stepped back and crossed their arms, watching her as if she were a TV show.

"Way to add the pressure, guys." She hefted the bale, and it wasn't so much heavy as it was awkward… And actually strike that, it was freaking heavy. She spun, doing her best to tamp down any strain on her features. Twice she attempted to put it into place, but her arms were shaky. If she could just get it three inches higher…

"Want some help?" Wade offered from behind her.

"No, I've got—" She threw everything she had into it—only her foot slipped, and then she landed on her butt and the bale was on her lap.

Sputtered laughter came from above her, and her warm, fuzzy feelings for cowboys disappeared.

The weight of the bale lifted, and Wade pulled her to her feet as Brady secured the bale against the others in the truck.

Jess wiped off her backside. "Am I a cowgirl now?"

"Gettin' there." Wade squeezed her hand, and the warm fuzzies returned. Dang things didn't have any sense and had way too short of a memory. "Cowgirl training mostly goes petting cows while cooing at them…" He lifted his flat hand a few inches, as if marking a vertical scale. "Learning to drive a real truck." A few inches higher. "Horses, then tossing bales."

"Oh, so I skipped a few steps. *That's* the problem." She didn't bother saying anything about riding horses, because while they were pretty and she was okay with petting them with a fence between her and them, she was a little scared of getting kicked or thrown off. Every time she spotted Chloe saddling up, her heart pounded too fast, and she'd wanted to ask if her daughter could skip horse riding. But it was against the rules to be an exception, and the horse therapy seemed to be doing Chloe a lot of good.

That was the beauty of being a teenager. They didn't think about every move they made in relation to how much it could hurt them and how long it'd take to recover from—or if it was something they *could* recover from. Now that Jessica was older, she knew she was far from invincible. Eventually she would gather the courage to take a pony ride, but she'd already learned to drive a giant stick-shift truck today, as well as getting bested by a bale of hay. She didn't want to do too much in one day.

"Guess I'll stick to driving," she said. "Now I can do more than drive straight while it's in low gear and moves itself, too."

Brady grunted with the exertion of lifting the next bale, which made her feel a bit better, even if he'd had to stack it way above his head and had been at this for fifteen minutes already. "That's great because Tanya's gonna be here any minute so we can go to that horse sale near Greeley, and I was worried I'd leave Wade in the lurch."

Wade brushed his hand across Jess's back. "I told him I'd find help somewhere." He leaned closer. "I was hoping it'd be you."

Tingles broke out across her skin, and she stuck her hands in her back pockets so she wouldn't give in to the temptation to grip his shirt in her fists and tug him closer so she could get her lips on his.

Usually she was the timid one in a relationship, but he brought out a different side of her. Not that they were in a relationship, and not that she'd follow through.

Because it was complicated.

Stupid complications. They'd been part of her life for a long time, and evidently they didn't plan on going away.

With the truck bed nearly full, she was only in the way, so she hopped down and chatted with the dogs. She attempted fetch, but Dundee was always faster, so then she had to find another stick to toss. Dundee still tried to get both of them, and often did before poor Quigley had a chance.

Ever the problem solver, she tossed them in different directions.

And the dogs just went after the same one. "Killin' me here, guys."

A big, shiny truck with a horse trailer pulled into the yard, and then Jess lost the dogs' attention as they ran to greet Tanya. She'd heard Brady talk about her a lot, and she'd come over a few times, but it had always been while Jess was making dinner and too busy to chat.

Brady catapulted off the back of the truck. "Catch you guys later!"

Tanya grinned and laughed at something he said as he approached. Then he told the dogs to stay back as he climbed into the passenger side of the truck. A cloud of dirt kicked up behind them as they headed down the driveway.

"Are they—"

"Just friends," Wade said. "They'll both freak out if you imply anything else."

"And they've always been just friends?"

"Ever since they were little. She grew up next door. Her parents run a dude ranch, and a lot of times she and Brady would hit the rodeo circuit together. He'd rope and she'd barrel race. They're the biggest trash talkers when it comes to the local rodeo, where our ranches have a competition of our own."

"Sure. I totally understood everything you said, and I definitely know what barrel racing is."

Wade laughed and jumped off the end of the truck. "Ready to use your new driving skills?"

"For sure." She bumped her shoulder against his as they started toward the cab of the truck. "I did have a really good teacher after all."

"Oh yeah?"

"He was pretty hot, too."

Wade's grin widened.

Jess tapped her lip. "I wonder where Mr. Humphries, my driver's ed teacher, is these days. And if he's single." Holding a straight face became impossible, and she almost shuddered at her own joke, because Mr. Humphries had been in his sixties, with a comb-over and forever messy mustache—and that was fifteen years ago.

Wade shook his head. "You think you're real funny, don't you?"

"I know I am." She punctuated the statement with an over-the-top grin.

He opened the driver's side door for her, boosting her up with a hand on the butt before climbing in after her and settling at the wheel.

She'd scoot over, but that'd mean she'd have to travel even farther when he climbed out of the truck to feed the cows, and she'd hate to waste all those seconds. "You didn't want me to drive to the field?" she asked, infusing the words with fake shock.

"I got a little too up close and personal with your shifting this morning"—he dropped a protective hand over his package—"and it took my legs a good ten minutes to wake up after sitting bitch for that long."

An exaggeration for sure, but he hadn't really fit in the middle, and the gear shift had been all up in his business. In her opinion, that was half the fun.

After getting the hang of going forward, she'd gone to reverse and slammed the knob into the crotch she was currently thinking too much about. Since he'd been the one to mention it initially, that made it okay, right?

They arrived at the gate to the field where they fed the cows, and he climbed out to open it. He gestured for her to drive through, and she eased into first gear, feeling quite proud of herself.

A moment later he was next to her again, smelling of outside and his cologne. Once he'd driven them to the center of the field where the cows were gathering, he shifted into low gear and opened the door of the truck. "I'll give you the signal when I'm done here, and then you can put it into gear and loop around to the far side where we feed the bulls."

On one of their first days, Jess had asked if the bulls were in a separate area because they were bullies, feeling quite proud of her pun. Then Wade told her they were there so the cows wouldn't have calves in the middle of the winter. Apparently the reason farm animals were all born in spring was because the ranchers made it so. Who knew?

She probably would've if she'd thought about it. But big surprise, she'd spent relatively little time while living in the city thinking about cows having babies.

The door next to her closed with a metallic screech, and she watched as Wade climbed into the back and took out his pocketknife. He sliced through the twine holding the hay together and began dumping large, square flakes onto the ground as the truck crept across the field. Without Brady also cutting bales, their strip was a bit longer and thinner than usual.

She caught sight of Wade's swinging arm in the rearview mirror. *Oops. I almost missed the signal.*

She depressed the clutch, maneuvered the shifter into the next gear, and readied herself to quickly hit the gas as she let off the clutch.

In her excitement, she overdid it and the truck lurched forward before dying. In the side mirror, she watched in horror as Wade fell right off the back, a puff of dust rising up as he hit the ground.

"Oh, shoot!" She threw open the door and ran to check on him. The cows ate around him, not bothered in the least by him being in the middle of their food. "I'm so sorry!"

He groaned. "What happened to waiting for the signal?"

"I thought you gave it." She went down to her knees and slowly moved his head to her lap. "What hurts? Should I go get help?" That'd mean hopping in the truck and trying again. Unless she ran.

Maybe she should run.

"I'm okay," he said. "Just knocked the wind out of me for a second."

She peered down at his gray eyes. His hat lay to the side, and she was afraid to pick it up for fear it'd be crumpled. His hair was darker on the top than the parts that stuck out of his hat, probably from the sun, and she raked her fingers through it. "I've got good news and bad news. The good news is, you're not bald."

"Oh good," he said with a chuckle. "It's been so long since some crazy chick knocked my hat off that I wasn't sure anymore."

She laughed and dragged her hand through his hair again. It was longer than she expected, too.

"The bad news is, you have enough grass and dirt in your hair that you probably wish you had less."

"Very funny."

"We already established earlier that I'm funny. Or did you forget? Oh no, does this mean you have a concussion?" She made a peace sign in front of his face. "How many fingers am I holding up?"

"I'm fine."

She picked a couple more leaves out of his hair. "You say that, but you're not getting up."

"You're playing with my hair, and my head's in your lap, giving me a rather nice view of your rather nice...figure."

"Ah," she said with a smile. It'd been a while since anyone had complimented her figure, and she was thinking she might've lost it.

Since she wasn't sure if she'd get another chance, she gave in to temptation and let her fingertips drift across his stubbled jaw for a moment before she reached for his hat and helped him up.

"I've got some more bad news," she said as she glanced at his backside. She was assessing the damage, so it was on the up and up. As was his butt. "You landed in a cow pie."

He wrapped his arm around her shoulders and started toward the truck. "Well, you've got to ride with me, so that's bad news for the both of us."

Trinity: I hate to be the bearer of bad news, but
I thought you should know that Tyler's
been hanging out with Kayla.

A fuzzy, staticky feeling had twisted through Chloe as she read Trinity's message, and with each passing second that it didn't magically change and say something else, her lungs grew tighter and tighter. *There's the panic. And the pain.*

This past week had been a roller coaster with Tyler. One day, he'd be sending her intense messages about missing her and how she knew him better than anyone else. Then he'd spend two days ignoring her messages.

Maybe he was just hanging out with Kayla. Sure, the girl didn't have the best reputation, but then again, Chloe didn't either anymore. Ever since she'd started dating Tyler, people had assumed things about her that weren't true. Even some of his friends had hit on her, which she didn't understand. Did he know? Didn't he care? How could they claim to be his friends and then hit on his girlfriend?

There'd been plenty of rumors about her sleeping with him, in spite of the fact that they hadn't had sex yet. For one, she wasn't sure she was quite ready, and two, Mom's lectures had left her scared of getting pregnant, and while she knew there were preventive measures, fear shouldn't be her main emotion when she thought about having sex.

That didn't mean she wasn't curious, or she and Tyler weren't getting close to taking that next step. Because he loved her.

He did love her, didn't he?

It was just the distance making her question it. She hadn't misread him; she was better at reading people than that. He'd never kept them secret, either. Everyone at school knew they were together. He'd proudly held her hand in the halls. He talked about her and posted pictures of them together on Instagram.

She quickly searched his profile. The only new picture was of his motorcycle, and she wasn't sure if that should give her hope or if it meant he just knew how to cover his tracks.

––––––––––––––––––

Wade had taken countless spills in his life. Off horses, off trucks, off haystacks. He'd been completely unprepared to get bucked off a slow-moving vehicle, but he was far from hurt. He might have a bruise on his tailbone to go with the other bruises he got in a typical workweek.

But Jess kept fussing over him, and he'd be lying if he said he didn't like it. She'd insisted on feeding the bulls while *he* drove, and he'd watched in amusement as she tossed a flake of hay over the fence at them, only for the wind to carry it back into her face.

"Hey, stop it," she yelled at them as they began rutting around and butting heads to see who'd get to eat first. "Haven't you heard? Fighting and acting all macho doesn't impress the ladies these days. Try helping out at home—or in the field. Pitching in with the kids. That kind of thing."

He was glad he'd left the window rolled down so he could hear her commentary, even if it meant some of the hay was getting blown inside the cab. Fighting the urge to help wasn't easy, but she was so stubborn that he knew she'd keep trying until she pulled it off, and in addition to being cute while she was refusing help, he admired her perseverance.

Eventually, she managed to get the last part of the bale over, and she added a fist pump before telling the bulls, "That's right. Just eat your food like good boys."

I'm definitely gonna have to get her on a horse.

Maybe after I've had a day or two to recover from her driving.

After she was done properly celebrating, they headed back to the house. He parked the truck and met her in front of the hood.

"I don't know if you know this, but bulls are boy cows," she said, and he smiled, waiting to see where she was going with this. "And I'm a girl who just took care of those cows." She batted her eyes and grinned. "So doesn't that make me a cowgirl now?"

He chuckled and picked hay out of her hair. "We make quite the pair."

"The dirty pair?" she said, and she waggled her eyebrows.

He shook his head, his mind drifting to all sorts of dirty things he wanted to do to her. He dragged another couple dried-up leaves down her silky strands, right to the ends that rested atop the swell of her breasts.

She stepped closer, her hands going to his hips, and a heavy dose of want tumbled through him. He drifted his fingers across her collarbone. Her shallow breath skated across his forearm, and the want morphed into consuming territory, shoving his sense of propriety aside.

Who cared if they were too close to the house to be looking at each other like this? Who cared if his entire family would witness the hungry way he yanked her to him before claiming those lips?

"Wade?"

Shit.

He reluctantly dropped his arm, blew out a long exhale in an attempt to calm himself down, and slowly turned toward the voice.

Aiden glanced back and forth between the two of them, and awkwardness crept in. Clearly, Wade wasn't pulling off calm and unaffected very well. "Sorry. I just, uh, wanted to ask you a question."

"Shoot," Wade said.

"Remember when I just needed to get away from it all, and you saw that and drove me into town?"

It took Wade a second to fully wave goodbye to the chance to kiss Jessica and switch gears. His brain whirled, searching for the memory, and then it grabbed hold. Right. The time Aiden had been about to crawl out of his own skin. Each kid was different, and what Aiden needed more than most was to feel as though he had some freedom. Some control of his life. The times he lost those were when he'd do something stupid, something they'd all regret after the fact.

Wade had seen that urge overtaking him, so he'd taken Aiden to lunch at the diner. He'd filled the kid up with a double burger, fries, and a milkshake, and for the first time ever, the kid had opened up the tiniest bit. The sense of security and seeing that he could safely talk to Wade led to him doing so more and more over the following weeks. "I remember."

"Chloe's at that point. Trust me, I can tell." Aiden scuffed the ground, his gaze dropping for a beat or two before he glanced back up, renewed resolve shining in his eyes. "I want to take her into town. Just for a few hours this afternoon."

Beside him, Jessica stiffened. "I don't think that's a good idea. Do the kids usually go into town?"

Wade didn't want to have this conversation in front of her, and he also didn't want to snap at her, or even try to explain while Aiden watched. This was why he should've kept his distance. Left that amazing night of dinner, dancing, and drinks in town. Now he felt like he was walking a tightrope.

"Excuse us for a sec," Wade said, and Aiden nodded and backed up. Wade turned to face Jessica and forced his stern expression in place so he wouldn't be too soft because of his personal feelings for her. "You're not trying to interfere, are you?"

She scowled at him. A huff escaped as she crossed her arms. "Not trying, but I do tend to overachieve in a lot of areas."

He appreciated her attempt at a joke, even though she'd delivered it too tensely for it to land.

Worry crept into her features. "What if she tries to run away? Or what if she's in town and—"

"Aiden will take care of her."

"Yeah, but what if she convinces him to drive her back home? Or they get into troub—"

"I know it's not easy to let go of control, especially after everything you've been through with her, but if Aiden says she needs a break, I'd rather she get that with someone I trust. I trust him, and I need you to trust me."

Her forehead scrunched up, making it clear there was an internal battle playing out in her head. She glanced around him at Aiden before her big, brown eyes returned to Wade. "Okay, so what if we just followed behind them a little bit? She wouldn't have to know."

He raised an eyebrow, and her scowl returned. This was usually where he'd be gruff and stern, but he was trying to strike a better balance, one where he was firm yet more understanding. "You brought her here because you knew we could help her, right?"

Jessica shrugged. "You're asking me to accept defeat, and I don't do that very well."

He gripped her shoulders. "I'm asking you to trust the process. Trust that we know what we're doing. Do you trust me?" he asked, and while it was a common enough question, he found himself holding his breath for the answer. Hoping she did.

"I do. That doesn't mean I'll always agree with everything you say."

"*Pfft.* That'll be the day. I'll know it right away because I'll look into the sky and there will be flying pigs."

She tried damn hard to fight her smile but lost the battle. The muscles under his fingertips softened, hinting she was considering giving in. Putting her trust in him.

"Aiden will take care of her," he repeated, because he could tell she needed to hear it. He told her he'd catch her later, and then went to give Aiden a lengthy lecture with lots of rules to ensure that nothing would happen in town that'd make a liar out of him.

Chapter 17

"THIS IS MY NIGHTMARE," CHLOE SAID AS SHE TOOK IN the small-town diner. A moment ago Aiden had been telling her about their amazing burgers and shakes, which she could wholeheartedly get down with. She could even handle that the place went all rustic wood for the floors and booths, and while she wouldn't choose horseshoes and a giant longhorn skull that emptily stared down at you as decorations, to each their own.

But the stools that had saddles where a round cushion should be made her want to sprint right back out the door. *I almost forgot I was in hell.*

Aiden placed his hand on her back and gave her a nudge toward the stools. Dang guy must've seen her urge to flee. "Don't knock it before you try it. They're actually pretty comfy."

"You would say that." She widened her legs and walked around the broad back end of the saddle before plopping herself down in the middle of the worn leather seat. *When in the sticks…*

Aiden settled into the stool next to her, looking perfectly at home in spite of his legs being way too long for the stirrups. When he'd first said he'd gotten permission for them to go into town, she'd thought he was playing the cruelest joke ever on her. That he'd add, "In a month, if you play your cards right," or maybe "Psyche! I totally got you."

Part of her even worried there'd be a line of adults

waiting for them at the edge of the property, barring their escape. While she was getting used to the ranch and loved the times she got to climb into a saddle *with a living and breathing horse under it*, she'd felt increasingly restless in spurts. After her computer session today, she'd been ready to implode.

"Okay," Aiden said, looking at her instead of picking up the laminated menu in front of him and focusing on it. "Let's hear it. What's wrong?"

"I'm on a stool shaped like a saddle. And my horse is an effing pole." Chloe nudged her heels as if she were on Rowdy, then made a big show of trying to see why her horse wasn't responding before knocking on the metal post. "I think he's dead. Rigor mortis has set in."

Aiden cocked his head, his expression making it clear he wasn't buying her bullshit. "Is the guy still not responding?"

If she had hackles, they would've risen. "No, Tyler and I have been talking."

Aiden continued to stare, and the dam of humor and sarcasm she'd erected to hold back her emotions cracked and began leaking at an alarming pace. The betrayal and doubt and panic and pain all rushed forward.

One minute she was grateful beyond belief to have Aiden as a friend, and the next she regretted that she'd made friends with him. He was far too observant, not to mention way too good at reading her. How could he read her so well after such a short time? Most people told her she was difficult to read, and she'd pretty much mastered shoving her feelings down deep, only to deal with them late at night when she was alone.

Which had never happened since she'd arrived in Silver

Springs, so the lid on them kept rocking, the pressure build-ing to a breaking point.

Her breaths grew thinner and thinner until there wasn't any oxygen to be found. Aiden was going to see she was a fraud. Tyler didn't love her anymore. Maybe her friends all thought she was stupid or crazy. Maybe Trinity was being a mean girl instead of a friend.

Even worse, what if she was crazy? What if Liza and Mom found out and she'd be here forever?

"Chloe. Look at me." Aiden reached out and squeezed her shoulder. She saw him do it, yet she couldn't feel it. Everything was getting fuzzy and swirling too fast. "I know something must've happened to make you so upset. Talk to me. Please."

It was the *please* that got to her. It shot through the eye of the storm and provided her a lifeline to use to climb out. Then she could feel his fingers on her shoulder, and she focused on that. On the saddle underneath her and the smells of the diner. Gradually her thoughts and breaths calmed as the real world came back into focus.

She lifted her head and peered into Aiden's green eyes. Eyes the exact color of the clover Rowdy was so fond of. A couple more deep breaths, and her lungs began function-ing normally as well. "What do you want me to say? That sometimes Tyler's amazing, and we talk about anything and everything. We even talk about the future, and he tells me things he says he's never told anyone before…"

Chloe ran a thumbnail along the counter. Luckily, it came away clean, which made her feel better about eating here. "And sometimes he ignores me and takes days to respond, even though he doesn't have limited internet time like I do. He knows that I don't have a lot to look forward to and that I'm waiting to hear from him. And…" Seriously, what was it with Aiden? She'd gone from panic attack to spilling her guts, but talking about Tyler with him was too weird. She was probably overacting anyway. She waved her hand in front of her, as if she could bat away her last couple sentences. "Never mind. I'm sure it's nothing."

Aiden ran his fingers down her arm as he leaned closer, and she didn't pull away. Or even look away. Maybe it was because he understood what she was going through in a way no one else did. He'd told her enough about his old crowd for her to draw some parallels to the people she'd been hanging out with. Yes, she'd done things she wouldn't have if she hadn't met them, but she'd made her own decisions. She wasn't going to cop out and claim peer pressure. Honestly, she sometimes missed the mind-numbing effects going out with her crowd had provided.

"Why don't you tell me," Aiden said, his voice low, "and I'll decide if it's nothing."

Since she was going to cave anyway—she was desperate to talk to someone about it and could no longer count on Mom for that, and Rowdy was awesome but not the best at coming up with solutions—she blurted out the thing that'd sent her into a tailspin. "My friend Trinity said Tyler was hanging out with this girl Kayla. But it's okay for him to have friends," she said before Aiden could say anything she might not want to hear. "So like I said, I'm sure it's nothing. Like I have you as a friend, and that doesn't mean anything."

The corners of his mouth tightened. "Gee, thanks."

"You know what I mean."

"I can also read between the lines and have too much experience with manipulative jerks."

Chloe placed her hand on his knee. "Please don't, Aiden. Don't say something that'll ruin the afternoon and our chance to escape the ranch for a while. Because then I'll start overthinking and worrying again, and my breaths will come faster and faster until I can't breathe at all. I just want to sit on my invisible horse and order a milkshake." She squeezed his knee and implored his eyes with hers. "Okay?"

He covered her hand, and her stomach rose as if her invisible horse had just reared into the air and left her trying to cling on so she wouldn't fall. "Okay."

Aiden glanced across the cab of the truck at Chloe. Yeah, he'd noticed she was pretty. He tried not to notice it so much, but with the sun setting behind her like that, lighting up her profile, it was pointless. The other problem was that the more time they spent together, the more time he wanted to spend with her. It was more than because she was pretty, too.

She was smart. She liked to pretend she didn't have a heart of gold, but he'd seen her around Rowdy. Not to mention all the help she'd given him on his math homework, and often during her free time when she could be doing something more fun. Sure, she could turn icy cold in a flash, but now he saw it was the wall she threw up in an attempt to keep herself safe. And some asshole had broken through and was taking advantage of that.

Aiden tore his gaze off her and checked the time. Wade said they had to be back before dinner, even though they'd eaten, and he didn't argue. They had a whole ten minutes to spare. As soon as they arrived at the ranch, he might lose the chance to really talk to her, especially alone, for a day or two.

That made up his mind, and he slowed at the end of the driveway and put the truck in park.

"Ooh, do I get to drive now?" Plying Chloe with sugar might've been a bad idea. She'd practically bounced through the shops along Main Street after she'd downed a pop *and* a milkshake. Not only was it entertaining, it was also cute as hell, and he'd fought the urge to grab her hand and hold it so many times he'd lost count.

"Do you even have your license?" he asked.

Her smile widened, as if that would be enough for him not to notice the answer was obviously *no*. "You wanna get me in trouble?"

"I'll tell them I fought you for it—that it was all me. They'll believe me, because in addition to being wicked strong, I'm the delinquent and you're all reformed."

"Not that reformed," he said before he'd thought better of it. Honestly, he wished he didn't have any desire to return to his old life. He didn't really. Occasionally he thought about how it'd been easier, freer in some ways—until he'd tangled with the law, that was—but he loved it here. Loved the horses, and the Dawsons were amazing. Kind and funny, hardworking and loving. Even though he balked at the rules now and again, guidelines were better than realizing no one gave a shit where you were or what happened to you.

Part of him still had a wall up himself, worried that if he made the wrong move, they'd send him back.

Like, say, if he leaned across the cab and kissed Chloe.

Extra-bad idea, since he'd already gotten in trouble with the

Dawsons for something similar. About a month into his stint in the program, he'd met a girl from Silver Springs who'd been looking for a way to piss off her parents, and he'd fit the bill. In her parents' eyes, he was the bad boy who'd taken advantage of a good girl, and he'd almost been sent to juvie because of it.

Jess would probably feel the same about him kissing her daughter, and the Dawsons would be pissed, thinking he hadn't learned his lesson.

Chloe would probably be pissed as well, considering she had a boyfriend. Who didn't deserve her.

"Aiden? Is this where you tell me you have a plan? Does it involve spoons and tunneling at night?" She gently nudged his shoulder, and he snapped out of his thoughts of the past and what he wanted to do with his present. It also reminded him that this wasn't about him. This was about Chloe.

He cleared his throat and deliberated on the best way to say something he knew she wouldn't like. *Here it goes anyway.* "Have you told Liza about the panic attacks?"

Her eyes went wide, her lips parting.

"Yeah, I put two and two together. Even someone as bad at math as I am can figure that one out."

As expected, she threw up her shields, the line of her jaw going tight. "That's none of your business." She reached for the door handle. "I think I'll walk the rest of the way."

He reached across her to hold the door closed, only realizing how close it brought his body to hers after his fingers were wrapped around the handle and her lips were mere inches from his. "Chloe, don't be mad. Remember that part about how we're friends? I'm just worried about you."

The ice thawed, and her lip trembled as tears rose to her eyes. *Dammit.* Now he felt horrible and wanted to abort the conversation, even though he knew someone needed to have it with her, and he was afraid he was the only person who'd figured it out.

"My anxiety has just been a little out of control this year," she said. "It's not a big deal."

"Then it won't be a big deal to tell Liza."

Chloe shook her head. "She'll just tell my mom, and then I'll be trapped here forever."

He tried not to let that offend him, since at one point he'd felt the same way. "She won't. The stuff you tell her is confidential. If you truly want to leave, let her help you. It's not like she doesn't know something is up. Once you tell her and start dealing with it, you'll make more progress with the staff and be out of here before you know it."

"I…" Her fingers slipped off the door handle, and then she twisted to face him, her knee bumping his thigh as she tucked her leg under her. "Don't get me wrong. I love riding more than I ever thought, and certain aspects are growing on me." She gave him a small smile as she studied him. "I'm glad I have you to talk to. But I don't belong here. And I need to get back before…"

"Before your boyfriend cheats on you?"

The line of her shoulders snapped tight, and he swore under his breath. That was the opposite of getting her to listen and open up.

"I'm sorry," he said, softening his voice. "I shouldn't have said that."

"No, you shouldn't have." She bit her lower lip. "But maybe you're right. Does that make me pathetic?"

The way her voice cracked at the end killed him. "No. It makes *him* pathetic."

Her smile turned sad, and she returned to facing the windshield, her gaze focused on the road in front of the truck. Obviously that meant she was done talking, and he wasn't sure there was anything he could've said to make her listen. He'd never been good at the talking-it-out parts of a relationship.

Looked like that carried over to being friends with a girl as well.

He shifted the truck into gear and drove them to the ranch. As he pulled up in front of the main cabin, he caught the figure at the window. Wade pulled back the curtain and peered out at them.

With their talk, they'd cut it closer than he planned, only two minutes early.

"Thank you for getting me out for a few hours," Chloe said. "I really needed it, and I appreciate it more than you'll ever know."

He knew. He'd been there. Yet he still didn't have the answers to change it.

The slam of the door echoed in his ears, and Aiden gripped the steering wheel tighter, fighting the urge to hunt down the guy who'd hurt her and give him a piece of his mind.

Chapter 18

WHAT WAS I THINKING? I SHOULD'VE KNOWN BETTER THAN to push my luck.

Jess had come a long way when it came to recognizing what foods felt and looked like before they turned into something edible, and she was forever working on having more patience. Over the past week she'd also watched dozens of YouTube tutorials on dough. While she'd done her homework, she'd thought Kathy would be here to help keep her from screwing up this part of tonight's dinner.

But Mrs. Dawson had gone into town earlier this afternoon, and Jess figured she'd go ahead and get started, an hour-ago version of her far too optimistic.

The door to the kitchen opened and she held her breath, hoping that meant Kathy had returned.

Instead, a familiar tan cowboy hat appeared, the stack of freshly washed dishes blocking the rest of him for a moment before Wade stepped into full view. Then she held her breath for an entirely different reason.

"Hey," he said.

"Hey," she replied, because he hadn't given her a whole lot to work with.

His boot steps echoed through the kitchen, and her heart beat in time with them. Lately she was so aware of every single inch of him, and there were a lot of inches to admire. Last night he'd shown up on her porch and let her know that Chloe was back and safely tucked into the girls' cabin for the night.

She'd wanted to invite him in, but then she remembered they'd decided it was too complicated, so they'd stood in companionable silence for a couple minutes before he wished her good night.

"Just thought I'd sneak into the kitchen and see if there were any leftover brownies," he said. "They were amazing."

Since she was wrist deep in dough, she tilted her head toward the plate on the counter. "I think there are a couple left."

He tugged up the foil and grabbed one of the delectable squares. He took a bite, moaned, and then extended it to her. "Want some?"

Boy, did she.

Although she worried it was a type of move she shouldn't complete, she leaned toward the extended food anyway. It was chocolate, so she could easily argue extenuating circumstances. Of all the things she'd made, the brownies were the best by far.

Wade shoved the rest of the dessert in his mouth and wiped his hands on his thighs.

Jess used her forearm to wipe at the strands of hair that'd fallen out of her ponytail. Then she attempted to alleviate the itchy spot on her nose with the same method. There was nothing like food-covered hands to bring on random itches that were impossible to scratch. "I want you to remember how yummy that brownie was. Maybe for long enough to hold you over till tomorrow."

"Uh-oh." He rested his butt against the counter right next to her mixing bowl and peered inside. "Whatcha makin'?"

"Garlic knots, in theory. I thought I was getting better, but I think I got too cocky." She slapped the wadded-up dough ball on to the floured silicone mat. "Is it supposed to be so lumpy?"

Wade shrugged his big shoulders.

"It said to roll it flat, then cut it into sections."

She grabbed the rolling pin and pushed it across the dough, but it was still lumpy.

He moved to stand behind her, like a supervisor with a clipboard, and she was sure she was about to get an F. "You have to push harder."

"Oh, suddenly you know?" She sighed and frowned at the blob. "This is like the blind leading the blind."

"Guess that means we'll have to feel our way out." His arm slipped around her waist, and he hauled her against him.

The temperature in the room steadily climbed, and with the oven preheating, it'd been plenty toasty already. Jess worked at keeping her voice steady, although she wasn't exactly successful. "I didn't know guys used this show-you-how move with things besides sports."

"Only if the girl is lousy at baking." The teasing note in his voice snuffed out the spark of indignation before it could fully light, and the drift of his fingertips down her arm was even more effective.

His lips moved so close to her neck that she could feel the warm breaths sawing out of his mouth. "Confession time? I also wanted to sneak in to the kitchen to see you. I missed having you next to me in the truck this morning."

"I missed being there, too. But I thought we decided it was too complicated."

He made a low humming noise in the back of his throat. "I rethought it when I was talking to you on the porch last night. And when you bit into that brownie. And pretty much every second of every day."

Static electricity danced across her skin, tempting her to move closer to the guy who'd caused it. "I keep thinking about it, too. But I'm afraid you were right. This is probably..." Her tongue forgot how to work as his hand spread on her stomach.

"A bad idea?" he guessed. "I'm aware." He didn't move. "So...just roll, I guess?"

She rolled her hips, and he groaned.

"Not what I meant, but I can go with it." His mouth brushed her neck, a mix of soft lips and scruff.

Her stomach rose up to kiss her rib cage as tingles coursed down her spine. His strong hands gripped her hips, and then he spun her around to face him. She blinked up at him, each second an eternity. He seemed to be leaving it up to her, which was also probably a bad idea, because she didn't always make the best decisions.

In this moment, though, she knew she wouldn't regret kissing Wade Dawson.

She gripped fistfuls of his shirt and tipped onto her toes, and he crashed his lips down on hers. Relief and yearning collided, and she sank into his embrace.

He boosted her up on the counter, wedging himself between her legs, never breaking the lip-lock. A moan escaped as his tongue swept inside her mouth and stroked hers. As she reached around him and explored the muscles in his strong back, he ran his hands up her thighs, stoking the fire burning inside her.

In the back of her mind, she vaguely heard a sound that didn't seem quite right, but then Wade drove his fingers into her hair and tipped her head to gain access to her neck. The rest of the world faded away as he pressed a hot, open-mouthed kiss to her skin.

"I thought I'd—*oh!*"

Wade sprang away from her, although they were caught and then some. Those streaks of flour and white handprints smeared across his shirt weren't doing them any favors, either. "Ma. Hey." He cleared his throat. "I was just asking Jessica if there were any brownies left."

Kathy's eyebrows arched up over the frames of her glasses, and the lenses magnified the skepticism filling her eyes. "Is that so? Let me guess, she said she already ate them, so you thought you'd go searching with your tongue?"

Embarrassment heated Jess's cheeks, and she scooted off the counter. Naturally, Wade had set her in the flour, so a cloud of the stuff puffed up around her, and as she looked down, she saw the white streaks up her thighs.

Kathy chuckled. "Well, I suspected it'd happen eventually." She set the three bags of groceries she'd been carrying on the counter. "You two want a moment to get your stories straight?"

"No story," Jess said. "We were just making rolls, and then we were...not making them."

Wade glanced at her, his forehead crinkling.

"What?" she whispered. "I don't hear you coming up with anything better."

"You're right." He shrugged, a crooked grin spreading across his face. "Jessica's smokin' hot, and I've been thinking about kissing her for a while. The opportunity arose, and I took it."

Kathy looked them over. "I can see that. But since I'd

rather the kids not see the evidence, why don't you two clean up a bit before you emerge from the kitchen?" She gestured to the bags of groceries she'd brought in. "Kindly put those away after you've cleaned up, and I'll see both of you at dinner."

With that, she left the room.

Wade glanced at Jessica, taking a second to admire his handiwork—from the pink cheeks to the slightly swollen lips to the handprints he'd left on her clothes. She'd left her mark on him, too, and he slapped at the mess, sending puffs of white into the air. "Why is it every time I'm around you, I end up coated in something or other?"

"I'd say flour is a lot better than manure or even mud and point out that *you're* the one who came lookin' for trouble."

"I found her, too," he said, and she shook her head, but she was also cracking a smile.

She wiped at her clothes. "What does this mean?" She looked up, her brown eyes going wide. "Not that I'm saying… This isn't me trying to tie you down or demand a relationship. I just…" She rubbed the back of her neck, and he worried this would be where she delivered a speech about only being here temporarily, and how it was too complicated and they shouldn't kiss again. Now that he'd kissed her, he wasn't sure he'd have the strength to stop. "I haven't done anything like this in a long time, and I feel completely out of my league."

Well, that was much better than he'd expected. He snagged her hand and brought it up against his chest. "It's been a while for me, too."

"I guarantee it's been longer for me."

"You don't have to make everything a competition," he teased, and she gave him a ridiculously cute glare. "As for your first question…" He tugged her closer. He'd resisted for nearly three weeks, but he'd known since the night he took her out to the Tumbleweed that he was fighting a losing battle, and every minute he spent with her wore down more of his reserves. "It means that I like you, and that while you're here, I'd like to get to know you better. Does that work for you?"

His heart pounded as he awaited her answer, so hard she could probably feel it against the back of her hand. It hadn't just been a while since he'd dated. It'd been a while since he'd even felt a spark. Every time he was around Jessica, there were fireworks of some kind or other, and he was crazy enough to like both kinds, anger and attraction.

"It's definitely what I want," she said. "But we should probably do a better job of keeping it on the down low. I'm going to leave eventually, and I don't want everyone to hate me when I go."

"No one's gonna hate you."

Two creases showed up between her eyebrows, and her mouth formed a tight line. "You know what I mean. Your mom strikes me as someone who gets attached, and I'm already plenty attached to her, to Liza, to everyone here."

It should send those alarm bells in his head ringing, considering it was what he'd worried about. Instead, another question invaded his brain and took over. "Including me?"

Jessica peered up at him, her features softening. "Including you. Maybe even a smidge extra." She punctuated her statement by dragging her thumb across his palm, and it soothed and riled at the same time. "But my life's somewhere else, and with Chloe going through so much right now, I especially don't want her to think I'm here partying it up and meeting guys. She comes first."

"I completely understand." He did, and he admired that she had her priorities, same as he did. Family came first. Always.

The tension leaked out of her shoulders, and she sidled a little closer. "Okay, then. I guess that means it's game on."

"Game on," he said. Then he hugged her to him so he could get his lips on hers one more time before they had to return to regular life and pretend he wasn't constantly thinking about the next time he could get her alone.

Chapter 19

TODAY'S LESSON WAS IDENTIFYING TRUE FRIENDS FROM frenemies. Chloe wondered if Mom had put them up to it, but that was overly paranoid, right?

After going back and forth all weekend, she'd confessed the barest minimum to Liza about her anxiety issues during their session this morning. She'd underplayed them, but Liza taught her a few tricks on how to center herself in the moment and advised her to work on logical thinking.

Was it logical that they'd have a lesson with slides and have everyone sit through it when it only applied to her? After all, she'd sat through a class on the cycle of addiction, and she didn't have addiction issues.

Still, she gripped the edge of her desk because some of the items seemed way too familiar.

Left-handed compliments. The girls used to "compliment" her about how good she was, but they'd do it as a way to imply she was naive.

Maybe I was, though.

Actually, I for sure was. A few things she'd learned she wished she could unknow, but you couldn't just go into the world expecting other people to look out for you. Like everyone else, she needed to look out for herself, and that required knowing that certain dangers were out there, sometimes in plain sight.

When she first met Tyler and started talking to him, he used to comment that he loved how innocent she was. That she wasn't like the other girls he'd dated, and yeah, she'd heard he'd dated a lot.

It was why in the beginning she was cautious. She wasn't stupid, and she didn't want to be just another girl on his long list. But they'd have these amazing late-night chats where he'd open up, and every time they were out somewhere talking, people kept asking if she was his girlfriend.

And he'd say, "I wish."

Even now, residual butterflies swarmed through her stomach.

They stilled as she recalled the day one of his friends had nudged him and said, "Tell the truth. Quiet, good girls are the kinkiest, aren't they?"

Tyler had laughed, a smug one that had all his friends shooting him congratulatory looks, and when she'd gotten upset about it later that day when they were alone, he'd told her his friend was just being an idiot. She'd let him convince her it didn't matter.

Was she now thinking it did matter because of all the teen ranch propaganda? Or because he hadn't answered her message from yesterday? Or was she looking for negatives since she was frustrated with him?

Ugh. I don't know anymore. Finally, the presentation ended and it was time for equine therapy, her favorite part of the day.

If she was at her old school, she never would've run, because running and being excited about things wasn't cool, but Chloe didn't have anyone to impress. She almost barreled into Aiden as he was coming out of the stables.

"Whoa," he said, steadying her. A slow smile spread across his lips as he peered down at her. "Hey."

"Hey." It'd been three days since he'd taken her into town, and while she'd needed it and appreciated it, she was experiencing too many roller-coaster emotions around Aiden. One moment there was the comfort of his friendship; then there'd be frustration he'd called her out and pushed her.

And occasionally, like right now, with his hand on her elbow, she'd experience a flutter she had to work to repress.

She told herself it was another side effect of being frustrated with Tyler and his lack of communication. Of course she couldn't tell Aiden about the radio silence because then he would use it against her.

But she and Tyler had a past and—once she got to return home—a future.

Which meant she needed to keep Aiden in the friend zone, where she'd be safe from him and he'd be safe from her.

Chloe pulled away. "I'm going to hurry and saddle Rowdy so I get as much time to ride as possible."

Was that sadness pinching the corners of his eyes? Hurt?

She already had one too many boys to analyze, so she wasn't going to bother with one more.

The picture on-screen blurred as tears filled Chloe's eyes later that afternoon.

Tyler hadn't posted a picture of him and Kayla on his feed, but she'd posted a picture of them on *hers*. They were kissing, and there was even a disgusting "BAE" written across the bottom.

Really?

For weeks Chloe had maintained that she and Tyler cared about each other—hell, months if she included all the times she'd tried to convince her mom that he was sweet but just didn't show it much. That he had it rough at home and needed someone to believe in him.

She believed in him. *She* assured him he wasn't worthless whenever he got down on himself. Sometimes he'd snap at her, but he always apologized afterward, and since he acted so sorry, she would immediately rush to make him feel better.

All her attempts to prepare herself for the worst—just in case Tyler wasn't the guy she *knew* he was—were in vain.

Her heart unraveled a thread at a time, leaving an aching, tangled mess in the center of her chest. *Holy shit, it hurts.*

"Chloe?" Mrs. Dawson placed her hand on Chloe's shoulder. "Are you okay?"

The X at the top of the screen got clicked as quickly as possible, and Chloe stood so fast the chair almost tipped over backward. She swiped the tears off her cheeks and blinked to try to stop more from forming, but it was no use.

"I'm fine," she said to Mrs. Dawson, but the words ripped out of her raw throat with a rough edge. "I'm done with the computer, so whoever's next…"

The last thing Chloe wanted was for anyone to witness her having a breakdown, so she strode out of the cabin as fast as her feet would take her. She glanced at the building that housed her uncomfortable cot and then at the stables.

Stables might mean running into Aiden.

Her gaze moved to the trees. She couldn't go far, but she could go to the edge of the tree line. When she'd walked far enough that the scent of pine was filling her nostrils and the large branches could provide decent cover, she spotted a flat rock. It seemed as good a place as any to get control of herself, so for about fifteen minutes, she sat and fought back tears.

No matter how hard she worked to tamp down her tears, the ripping apart sensation refused to go away. *Screw it. There's no one to exploit my weak emotions way out here anyway.*

Once she let go, the tears ran down her face in a steady stream. More of them came as she worried about what everyone would think. Was already thinking. It wasn't bad enough that she ended up riding in the back of a cop car and then didn't show up at school.

Now she was the girl who was stupid enough to believe a boy liked her, enough to go along with him when he took that car. Regardless of all his justifications, she'd known in her bones it wasn't right. That he was too wasted. Of course she'd known he was being stupid.

He *was* stupid.

That should make it stop hurting, shouldn't it?

Should make her feel less like she'd been discarded. Rejected. Used.

It should do…something.

Why isn't it doing anything?

After she'd cried herself out, she debated her next move. No doubt her cheeks and eyes were red, and going back would mean answering questions she didn't want to. She shifted and felt the square note in her back pocket, the one she'd unfolded and read once a day.

A few times it'd made her choke up, but she'd held back the tears. Held back all of her emotions, really.

She pulled it out to read it again, and this time, she didn't bother stifling any of the emotions the words caused.

———————————

The knock on her door was quiet, and Jess wondered if that was Wade's attempt to be subtle. They didn't have to be subtle out here by their cabins.

Not that they could exactly go all out, either.

Her leg protested moving after being folded under her for so long, and it took a few seconds to convince it to hold her up. She ran a hand through her hair in an attempt to undo the mess she'd made of it as she'd been working her second job and opened the door.

It wasn't Wade.

It was Liza.

And Chloe.

Chapter 20

JESSICA'S HEART SOARED AND DROPPED AT THE SAME time. Chloe was here, but Liza was with her, and that meant something had happened. Most likely something bad. She opened her mouth to ask Chloe if she was okay, but before she could, her daughter took a large step and flung her arms around her neck.

"Mom" came out on a strangled sob, and tears clogged Jess's throat as she wrapped Chloe in a tight hug.

She ran a hand down her daughter's hair and looked over her head at Liza.

"She said she needed to talk to you. In emergencies, we usually do Skype calls, but it seemed silly when you're only a two-minute walk away."

"Thank you," Jess croaked out. "How long do we have?"

"Just bring her to breakfast."

Part of her worried Wade would be pissed about the exception being made for them, but with her daughter in her arms and clinging to her, Jess decided if there was any time to break the rules, it'd be now. Sometimes people deserved an exception.

She pulled Chloe into her cabin and closed the door. After going so long without touching or talking, she was reluctant to let go. She switched to a sideways hug, one arm draped around Chloe's shoulders as she walked her to the couch.

They settled in the center, not bothering to take up

more than the center cushion. A giant lump formed in Jess's throat as she studied her daughter's beautiful, tear-streaked face. "What happened? Are you ready to talk about it?"

"He didn't want me, Mom. I gave up so much, and I believed I was different." She sniffed, and two fat tears ran down her cheeks. "He told me he loved me, but he didn't." Pain twisted her features. "Why didn't he love me?"

Jessica pulled her daughter back into her arms, hugging her and doing her best to hold her together. She stroked her hair and searched for the right words to say as sorrow and rage battled it out inside her. She'd kill the little asshole. He'd done the thing she'd most worried about—he'd hurt her daughter—and she hated that she hadn't been able to stop it. "He's clearly an idiot." *An idiot I'll hunt down, and just wait until I get my hands on him. Then* he'll *be the one crying.*

Chloe sniffed again, and empathy overtook Jess's impulse to do something that'd land her in jail.

"I wish I had the words to make it all better," Jess said, rubbing soothing circles over Chloe's back. "To stop the hurt. I'd also like to tell you it's the last time a boy will ever make you cry. But it might not be, and while I can't wave a magic wand and make it better, I do have a gallon of ice cream in my freezer."

"Double fudge?"

"Of course. I even have fudge sauce so we can make it triple." Jess stood to grab the ice cream out of the freezer. Instead of bothering with bowls, she tucked the icy carton under her arm, along with the chocolate sauce, fished two spoons and of the drawer, and snagged a roll of toilet paper on the way back to the couch.

Chloe wiped the tears from her cheeks with the back of

her hand, blew her nose, and then took the extended spoon. Jess pried open the lid to the ice cream, and Chloe poured a layer of syrup over the top.

They dug in, the exact same way they'd done hundreds of times through the years.

"Wanna watch something?" Jess asked around a bite of chocolaty goodness.

Chloe nodded. "The gorier the better."

"*Walking Dead*, then? Which is what Tyler is gonna be if I ever get my hands on him."

Chloe gave a half laugh, half sob.

They settled in, watching the zombies on-screen feast on people while they devoured half a carton of ice cream.

During the second episode, Jess decided to test the waters and ask a few questions in case tomorrow came and things changed and she lost her chance. "How are you doing? I realize this place takes some getting used to, and I know I already went on and on in my letter about how I'm just trying to do the right thing, but I am." Apparently she hadn't gotten control of her emotions, and with Chloe snuggled up next to her, she wasn't sure she'd ever be able to rein them in.

"No one handed me a parent manual when I had you. The hospital just gave me a tiny knit pink hat and half a pack of diapers, and then, after a nurse made sure I could snap in a car seat, they were, like, 'Good luck with your cute baby burrito. PS, you'll never be able to get the blanket that tight again, but have fun trying.'"

Chloe cracked a smile, and relief flooded the fissure in Jess's chest. "You've done okay. And honestly, what you really need is a cooking manual."

"Ah!" She elbowed her daughter, then pulled her closer and kissed her temple, sure a complaint was about to be lobbed her way.

"You're getting better."

Much better than a complaint—it was a real live compliment! "Slowly but surely. I was sort of surprised they didn't fire me after the first night."

"They're nice people. Nicer than I expected. I still don't feel like I need to be here—"

Jess's shoulders tightened.

"But the last place I want to go now is back to school. He seriously went from me to the girl who sleeps with everyone. I'd say more power to her if that makes her happy, but that was before she went after my boyfriend."

A response about how he was plenty to blame was on the tip of Jess's tongue, but she held it back. She didn't want to put any distance between them now that Chloe was finally talking to her again. It almost felt as if nothing bad had ever happened and ripped them apart.

Deep down, she knew there was more going on with Chloe, and that this was the place that could help her with whatever it was. Already, she seemed more like the old her, even if the side effect had been giving her the cold shoulder until now.

Jess exhaled. "If you want to talk about anything, I'm here, and you know that you can tell me anything."

Chloe's red-rimmed eyes locked on to hers. "I know. But can we just have tonight to chill and forget the rest of the world for a while?"

"As you wish," Jess said, and Chloe rolled her eyes, but it was a lighter eye roll with a lot less disdain than she'd gotten the past few months.

"That's so cheesy."

"I think you're forgetting how cool your mom is." She did her best Amy Poehler in *Mean Girls* impression. "I'm not a regular mom; I'm a cool mom."

Chloe sighed, but she rested her head on Jess's shoulder. Her expanding heart tested the bounds of her rib cage, and even after fifteen years, she marveled that she could love someone so much.

That everything her daughter experienced tied so closely to her own emotions. Tonight was the first time in months that she felt like everything might be okay.

Then Chloe said, "Thanks for the letter, Mom," fast and under her breath, and the hope warming her insides got another boost.

Chapter 21

CHLOE POURED THE BATTER INTO MUFFIN TINS AS JESSICA cracked a few more eggs into the skillet. They were testing the bounds of the leeway they'd been granted by spending more time together, but Chloe couldn't be left unsupervised anyway, so she'd woken up early to help with breakfast.

Jess had texted Liza so she'd at least know about it. Whether or not Wade knew about it and their sleepover yet was anyone's guess. More than once Jess had opened her mouth, wanting to tell Chloe about the night dancing at the Tumbleweed and her adventures in feeding and doctoring cows, but she still wasn't sure what was at the root of everything going on with her daughter, and she was afraid that throwing more changes at her would send her spinning.

Not that she and Wade were really a change.

At the same time, she worried Chloe would view it as her mom getting a vacation from life while she was going through the hardest time of hers.

After sliding the muffins into the oven and setting the timer, Chloe spun to face her, one hip resting against the counter. "Was my dad like Tyler? Is that why you hated him so much?"

Talk about a loaded question. "Yes and no."

Chloe gave her the look she always gave when Jess's reply was vaguer than she wanted. She'd always been curious, always wanted to know how things worked. The little-kid answers had never worked for her. Jess recalled the time she'd explained to her two-year-old daughter about how Santa was going to come on Christmas Eve in a sleigh drawn by magic reindeer.

Her pigtailed daughter had looked at her as though she had a few screws loose and said, "Yeah right, Mom."

Chloe was the kid who wanted to know why birds had to flap their wings to fly but planes didn't. She wanted the scientific explanations. During the two-to-four-year-old period, Jessica had just about worn out Google trying to make sure she gave the correct answers.

"Come on, Mom. I'm not a kid anymore. You don't have to give me the answers about how God knew you'd love me enough for two parents."

When it came to the subject of Chloe's father, Jess always forced back the bitterness and focused on the positive. After a while, she didn't even have to fake it. Dan never wanted to know his kid, which truly was his loss, but she also didn't want Chloe thinking her father was a bad guy, even if she was never going to meet him. "Well, I do love you enough for two people. I've never regretted my decision to have you on my own, and you're the best thing that's ever happened to me."

"I appreciate that." Chloe boosted herself up on the counter, making it even harder to dodge her steady gaze. "But there at the end, I could tell you wanted to say Tyler was like my dad, but you kept holding back. I thought you just looked at all teen boys that way."

"Honestly, I worried I was doing that, too." Maybe parents weren't supposed to admit when they didn't have all the answers, but she'd rather be real with her daughter, and it was a legitimate worry. After all, no one would ever be good enough for her daughter. "He just seemed a little too smooth, and he was disrespectful to all adults, not just me. I remember the appeal of the rebel boy with the tragic backstory. The mystery. Being flattered when he picked me above other girls."

Chloe groaned. "I felt flattered, too. So many girls liked him and were constantly chasing him, and he chose me. A few of his exes tried to warn me, and I thought they were just jealous. It's like now that it's over, I see all the clues I missed." She leaned back and let her head fall against the cabinet behind her with a soft *thunk*. "What a waste of time."

Jess gave the eggs another stir before locking eyes with her daughter. "It's only a waste if you didn't learn anything. I blamed myself, thinking I should've seen the signs, that I should've even listened to my mom—*gasp*."

Chloe cracked a smile.

"But part of going out with your dad had been to piss her off in the first place. I wasn't the perfect daughter she wanted, so I thought I'd show her how wild and unperfect I could be. But it didn't exactly work out the way I thought it would." Jess squeezed Chloe's knee. "In some ways, it also turned out to be one of the best things in my life."

She'd always been careful to avoid the word *mistake* when it came to getting pregnant, because she'd never wanted Chloe to feel like she was one. Maybe Jess's mistakes had led to the path she'd gone down, and it was a hard path she never wanted anyone she loved to have to travel, but it'd brought her here. It'd brought her Chloe.

"You loved him at one point, though?"

"Yes." It wasn't a hard answer, even if it was hard to admit.

"And he told you he loved you?"

Old hurts rose up, not so much over that exact guy but over how it'd felt to be discarded. For that longing to have that special person who'd stick by your side no matter what to be so thoroughly squashed. "Yeah."

"Do you think he did?"

It'd been over a decade since Jess had wondered that very thing. "I think we both confused lust for love, and I guess the side of me that still believes in fairy tales doesn't believe that you'd ever treat someone you truly loved like that. Love means sticking by someone, even if it's inconvenient."

"Like, say if they're shipped off to cowboy boot camp?" Chloe asked. She attempted to smile, but it turned wobbly and a smidge watery.

"Even then. I know I've given you plenty of lectures on safe sex and the way people judge situations they know nothing about, but I maintain it's harder for girls in a lot of ways. After I got pregnant, your dad still had his pick of girls. His life didn't change. Mine did, and again, no regrets. It wasn't easy, though, and…"

"And you want a different life for me. You might've mentioned it before. Like, three hundred times." Chloe reached out and snagged Jess's hand. "I hear you, and I definitely learned a big lesson. I've even learned a thing or two while I've been here, and I understand I'm going to have to get through the next three weeks of the program. But then we're going home, right?"

"That's the plan. As long as you cooperate and talk to Liza—really talk. I get that you don't always want to tell me everything, and while you still can, she's here to listen. She's had training on how to help people, as well as a lot of experience doing just that. I've even had a casual session on her couch."

Chloe sucked in a deep breath and nodded. "Okay."

The last twelve hours had been unwinding the ball of tension inside Jess a string at a time, but that was the word she needed to hear for it to loosen completely.

The door swung open, and when Wade stepped into the kitchen, Jess felt like she'd been caught doing something bad in here for the second time. Funny, since last time he'd been her coconspirator. With her memory of that afternoon flickering through her mind, she was thinking it'd been way too long since those lips of his had been on hers.

Now she was wondering if they'd ever touch hers again. If he flipped out about her breaking the rules and letting her daughter have a sleepover, she wasn't sure she'd want to kiss him again.

Okay, so she would, but she worried she shouldn't. Anyway, she decided to do her best to cut the argument off before it could start. "I know, I'm being the exception, but I put her to work this morning, and she's been a ton of help with breakfast, and we really needed—"

"Liza talked to me last night before she brought Chloe to your house." Wade nodded at her daughter.

"And you said yes?" Affection swelled in her chest before she could warn it not to get carried away. She swore she even heard cartoon birds chirping as they dizzily spun around her head.

One corner of his mouth twisted up, bringing a slight dimple out in his cheek, and he lifted his arm as if he was going to place his hand on her hip. It froze a few inches too short as he seemed to remember they had company, and then he let it drop. "Guess I'm more of a sucker than I let on. Hope you won't use that against me."

"Only whenever it suits me," Jess said with a teasing smile he returned in full. "Thank you for last night."

"I really appreciate it," Chloe added, and Jessica mentally high-fived herself for doing such a good job of teaching her daughter manners. Yeah, she was totally taking credit.

"It can't become a habit, but sure thing. I'm glad it helped." Wade's gray-eyed gaze returned to Jess. "Anyway, I was thinkin' about getting you on a horse this afternoon. Check off another step in your cowgirl training."

Those cartoon birds that'd been flitting around her head crashed to the ground.

"Wait. Mom on a horse?" There was a hint of glee in Chloe's voice, along with a note of mockery. "Can I please, *please* be there?"

"Why?" she asked Chloe. "So you can see me fall on my butt?"

Since Jess was taking credit for things, she was going to have to also take the blame for the falsely innocent expression her daughter flashed her. It was one she'd given on many occasions. "So I can laugh *with you* when you fall on your butt."

"I'll do my best to prevent that from happening," Wade said.

Jess wrinkled her nose. "How necessary is it that I learn how to ride a horse?"

"I guess it depends on what kind of cowgirl you wanna be."

"The fake kind," she said, a note of exasperation in her voice, and Wade and Chloe both laughed.

"It's really fun, actually," Chloe said. "I can help, too. As long as it's okay…" She looked to Wade.

"We can set it up during your free time. As long as it's okay with your mom."

Jess crossed her arms and glanced back and forth between the two grinning faces. "I feel like I've just been ganged up on."

The timer went off, and Chloe launched herself off the counter to check the muffins. She pulled them out and gestured at the perfect golden tops, dotted with blueberries. "Look how much progress you've made with cooking." Her eyes widened as her gaze landed on Wade. "I mean, how much you've improved on your already impressive and extensive skills in the kitchen."

"The jig is up and then some when it comes to my cooking experience," Jess said, and the tension in Chloe's shoulders evaporated.

"Oh, good. My point is that you didn't know how to cook or bake, and now you kinda do—"

"Thanks for adding that 'kinda,'" Jess said, and Chloe laughed.

"Welcome. Anyway, before long, you'll say you know how to ride a horse."

"Kinda," Jess provided, and Chloe laughed again.

"Exactly." Some people who'd overheard them talking when they were out and about had glared, clearly thinking Chloe was being disrespectful when they bantered back and forth, but this was their norm. Joking, teasing. Her daughter knew the line, and while she'd recently crossed it, they'd never have a dictator-type relationship. Jess would do whatever it took to prevent that, as her current predicament demonstrated.

Chloe shook the muffins out on a platter. "I'm going to

take these out to the dining room so we can get breakfast started. Especially since these eggs are looking plenty done."

"Oh, shoot! I forgot about the eggs." Jessica lurched forward to stir them, but the bottoms were already the other side of black.

"Good thing I added that sacrifice to the pan gods," she muttered as she scraped the good bits off the top.

When she turned around, Wade was still standing there, watching her with a smile.

Jess glanced at the doorway, checking the door was closed. Then she threw her arms around his waist and squeezed for all she was worth. "Thank you, thank you, thank you."

He hugged her back, enveloping her in those strong arms of his. "You're welcome. Is she okay?"

"She will be," Jess said, and the rightness of the words sent those happy cartoon birds fluttering around her head again.

Chapter 22

WADE WAS HAPPY FOR THE EXCUSE TO BE MORE HANDS-ON with Jessica as they got started on her horse-riding lessons, but he also needed to remember they had a lot of eyes on them. In addition to Aiden and Chloe, the other kids were walking around the ranch during their free time, and he'd bet money his family was watching every interaction with a microscope, especially his mom.

He kept hold of the sides of Jessica's waist so she wouldn't fall as she attempted to climb on the back of the horse, but resisted the urge to move his hands into butt territory to give her an added boost. "Okay, swing your other leg around and slip it in the other stirrup."

"This is about as uncomfortable as the last time someone told me to put my feet in stirrups," she muttered, and he bit back a laugh.

"See," Chloe said. "I told you it'd hold." She'd bridled and saddled Bud, one of their older quarter horses. Even when he'd been a younger horse, nothing much made him want to hurry, which was why he was great for new riders.

"Teacher's pet," Jessica teased, and Chloe laughed and stuck out her tongue. The girl did seem different today, and Wade was glad he'd approved her visit with Jessica last night. Liza had obviously expected him to say no and had even launched into a spiel about how sometimes girls just needed their mom. He'd cut it off and told her to take Chloe over to Jessica's, and that they could have the whole night.

The fact of the matter was, he'd approve anything he thought would make Jessica happy, and that in and of itself was a problem. He could argue the logic, but logic hadn't driven his decision, and he worried he was getting too close.

That those complications would end up biting him in the ass.

"I don't even know how to work these," Jessica said, lifting the reins. Bud lifted his leg and stamped, and her eyes went wide. She looked like she was two seconds from bolting. "I can learn to ride later. Are you gonna help me off, or should I tuck and roll?"

Wade stepped up to her, putting his hand on her thigh. "Bud's one of my gentlest horses, and I'm right here."

"On the ground. As soon as I start walking, you'll be behind me, and what good does that do me?"

A lot of the teens were hesitant with horses and had to be gently coaxed on their first time, but since Jessica usually jumped headfirst into everything, he hadn't expected her to be part of that group.

"I just feel like it's irresponsible for me to do this when I don't know enough about it." A squeak came out when Bud stomped again, ready to be on his way, regardless of wanting to go the slow and steady route. Jessica gripped the saddle horn so tightly her knuckles went white. "I know. How about we find a merry-go-round, and I'll train there first?"

Chloe swung onto Rowdy like a girl who'd been riding horses for years instead of weeks. "Come on, Mom. We'll start with a slow trot. I want to show you this really cool spot by the creek."

"You go ahead, and I'll meet you there. How long would it take to walk?"

Aiden climbed atop Koda and nudged him up next to Chloe and Rowdy. He glanced at Wade and raised his eyebrows, silently asking what he wanted him to do.

Wade glanced at Thunder, who was saddled and also raring to go, and then returned his attention to Jessica. "How about I ride with you till you get the hang of it? Aiden, can you lead my horse?"

The leather underneath Aiden creaked as he leaned to take the reins off Thunder's saddle horn. "See you there?"

Wade nodded, and he and Chloe took off on their horses. Wade climbed onto Bud behind Jess, and then he was wondering why he hadn't had this idea in the first place.

Considering the way his body was already reacting to being snuggly pressed up against Jessica's ass, this might not be the best idea, either, but sometimes bad ideas were the most fun.

"Sorry I'm being such a baby," she said. "Big animals sort of…make me nervous. I don't know what they're going to do, and I'd rather look at them and even pet or feed them with a fence between us, just in case. And before you ask, yes, it made me nervous to let Chloe ride, but she's braver than I am in a lot of ways, and I never wanted to stifle that."

Jessica glanced over her shoulder at him. "Is it true that horses sense fear? That's my other worry. He thinks I'm afraid, so now he's either afraid or has decided to dump me off in favor of someone who's not."

Wade bit back a laugh because he didn't want to make her think he was making fun of her. "They sense all kinds of emotions, but they're not vindictive—well, not most of them, and definitely not this one. I think it's cute you're afraid of horses."

"It's not cute, and I'm not afraid. I'm"—she lifted her chin—"hesitant."

"Well, I'm taking it upon myself to fix that. If that means I have to ride pressed up against you, I'll make that sacrifice."

Finally, he got a laugh out of her. "How valiant."

"Okay, so loosen the reins, or he'll think you're pulling him to a stop the whole time."

"Staying permanently stopped sounds okay to me," Jessica muttered, her big, brown eyes still locked on to him.

"Just wait. I bet that before long, you'll be begging to go for a ride."

"I don't beg."

He leaned closer, his mouth a breath from hers. "Are you sure about that?"

Her delicate throat worked a swallow. She leaned back against him, and her lips brushed his jaw. "Oh, you wanna play that game?"

Desire drifted to the surface in a hot rush, and it took every ounce of his self-control to act unaffected. Although she probably felt the evidence that proved contrary pressed up against her backside. "Later, I definitely do." He skimmed his hands down her thighs and curled them around her hands and the reins. "Now, focus."

She stuck her lips out in a pout, but then listened as he went over how to lead the horse again. She used her heels to nudge the horse into motion, and as soon as she got the hang of steering, he encouraged Bud to go a little faster.

Over the next ten minutes, Jessica's muscles loosened and she found her rhythm with the horse. Wade held on to her tighter than he needed to and whispered encouragement in her ear, along with directions.

Way too soon, they reached the place where the creek widened and met a meadow. Aiden and Chloe were already there, letting the horses graze as they soaked their feet in the water.

"Now just pull him to a stop," Wade said, and Jessica did as instructed. "See. You're a natural."

"I had a good teacher. And this time, I mean you."

"Who's teacher's pet now," Chloe said, and Wade chuckled and climbed off the horse. Jessica gripped the saddle horn and swung her leg around, but she couldn't find the ground with the toe of her boot. She was about three inches too high.

Wade reached up and gripped her hips, guiding her the last little bit. Then he forced himself to let go instead of holding on like he wanted to.

Chloe gestured Jessica over and demanded she stick her feet in the water, and Aiden made an excuse about checking the horses to give them their space. The smile on Jessica's face was even brighter than it'd been for the last three weeks, the weight that'd been on her shoulders visibly lighter.

Warmth flooded him, reminding him why they did what they did at the ranch.

He wished the reminder of how hard it was to sometimes say goodbye hadn't come along, too, but beggars couldn't be choosers, and now that he'd thought about begging again, he remembered Jessica's remark.

At least I know it's going to end. It won't be a surprise to anyone when she leaves. But while she was here, he was going to make sure to enjoy their time together.

And maybe soon, he'd see which buttons he needed to push to make her beg.

_____

Chloe was right. The cold water rushing over her feet did feel amazing. Boots were good for keeping the muck off her skin, but occasionally her feet felt claustrophobic in them.

Jess wiggled her toes. Man, her toenails needed painting, and her hair could use a trim. Her highlights were practically gone, needing to be redone instead of refreshed, it'd been so long. She was going to need to start being more thorough with the razor, too. While she knew Wade probably wouldn't care, if she was going to be intimate with a man for the first time in longer than she cared to admit, she wanted to feel pretty. Sexy.

Ugh, I shouldn't have had that extra muffin. I should probably think about doing some sit-ups as well. As if a handful of sit-ups would make up for years of neglecting to do a single one.

Am I finally going to cross that line? Or is it a bad idea?

Or do I have fun while I can?

The way he'd asked, "Are you sure about that?" all low and husky, the words so full of innuendo, had made an ache form between her thighs. Having his arms around her and his hands on her only made it grow stronger, and if she thought about it much longer, she might have to dip her whole body in the cold water to cool down.

"So, what's up with you and the cowboy?" Chloe asked, and Jessica jerked her gaze off Wade. *Oops.*

Underplaying seemed like the best way to go, so she decided to cling to it. "We're…friends."

"And I totally buy that."

If she didn't learn to be slyer about checking him

out—or you know, kissing him back—they'd be busted by everyone in the entire camp by the end of the week. "We're slowly getting to know each other. But we're only here temporarily, and my priority is you."

Chloe bent over her knees and swept her hand through the water, her blond curls falling forward. She studied the glittery surface as it gradually stilled, and then pivoted to face Jess full-on. "A few days ago, I might not've said this, but you deserve some fun."

"I don't know. I'm scared of getting too attached. At first he frustrated me to no end, but over the past couple weeks I've seen this different side of him, and then there's watching him work with his hands, and…" She sighed, giving the guy another glance as he bent to adjust the stirrups on his saddle, which showed off his Wranglers rather nicely. "There's just something about cowboys."

"Another thing I can't believe I'm gonna say, but there really is…"

Jessica whipped her head back to Chloe.

Her daughter held her hands up in a whoa-there pose. "Don't worry, Mom. I'm in no hurry to jump into a relationship. Aiden and I are just friends, I promise. But when my horse won't quite do, it's been nice to talk to him. He sorta pissed me off when we went into town because he called Tyler a manipulative jerk."

The kid got a point for that, but that was all she was giving him.

"He's cute, though." Chloe looked at him and smiled. "For a cowboy."

"Chloe…"

"Don't ruin it," she said. "We're bonding over cowboys

being cute, like we would if we were watching a movie and a hot actor came on. Like the universal appeal of Captain Hook."

Ah, yes. Captain Hook from *Once Upon a Time*, the one guy they both agreed was crazy hot. "He's closer to my age." It was her go-to in this argument.

"Yeah, but I could help him apply his guyliner. *Without* stabbing his eye and giving him an eye patch to go with his hook hand."

Jess's mouth dropped. "I only slipped *one time* while giving you the cat eye *you asked for*, and your eye is totally fine!"

Chloe giggled. "Okay, okay, withdrawn, counselor." She reached forward and picked a smooth rock out of the water. "How about Hook's mine because it looks like you've already got a boyfriend?"

A swirl went through Jessica's stomach as her eyes flickered to Wade yet again. Then she turned back to her daughter. "Fine. He's yours for the next three weeks."

It was supposed to be a joke, but it only made her aware of how fast three weeks could go by. With things so much better between her and Chloe, she had a feeling they'd go even faster than the first three, where misery constantly hung in the background and took a bite of whatever good vibes came her way.

"We should probably head back," Wade said. "I've got a tractor to fix, and the kids will have to muck out the stalls."

Chloe leaned closer to Jess, their shoulders bumping together. "Muck means clean horse crap, in case you were wondering. It's as horrible as it sounds."

"Is that why your arms are looking so toned?"

Chloe flexed. "You know it. Gonna flash these at anyone

who brings up my sudden disappearance. Maybe I'll even use them on Tyler. It'd feel really good to punch him in the nose."

"As long as I get a turn after you're through."

Chloe used her newfound muscles to help Jess to her feet. *Maybe I should throw mucking stalls into my workout schedule. Then I can pick up a bale and watch the shock on Wade and Brady's faces.*

Or maybe she'd just stick to the ten to twenty sit-ups she'd attempt before Wade came over tonight. *Yeah, that's plenty. No reason to get carried away.*

"Ready to ride on your own?" Wade asked, bringing both his gray-and-white speckled horse and her reddish-brown one over.

"Depends." She batted her eyes at him and gave him her best flirty grin. "Am I a cowgirl yet?"

"Sure," he said, and she smacked his arm.

"*Sure's* not the same as yes."

Wade handed over the reins, stubbornly refusing to change his answer, dang him. He climbed onto Thunder, and Jess sucked in a deep fortifying breath before climbing atop Bud. From her higher vantage point, she could see Aiden smiling at Chloe, and he definitely checked her out.

Then Aiden turned to mount his horse, and Chloe watched a little too closely.

Don't freak out. She said they were friends.

And admitted he was cute.

One day of peace from worrying about teenage boys and her daughter, and now she had to worry about a different boy and whether he'd hurt Chloe or get in the way of all the progress she was making.

Chapter 23

SINCE AIDEN HAD ALREADY CLEANED KODA'S STALL, AS well as the one next to it, he stepped into the one Chloe was working on. *That* was how much he wanted to be around this girl. He was willing to shovel shit for another few minutes if it meant talking to her.

"Looks like you and your mom made up," he said.

A smile spread across her face, and it sent a twisting, tumbling sensation through his gut. "Yeah. Things are good. I mean she still goes all mom on me, and I maintain she overreacted, but... it just feels so nice to be able to talk to her again, you know?"

No, he really didn't, but he nodded anyway. He'd never been close to either of his parents. But he and Wade had talked some by the creek—about school and where he was at with his math class, and whether or not he was getting enough sleep because Wade had seen his light was still on at 1:00 a.m. and wanted to make sure everything was okay. So maybe someone did go all parental on him, and it was probably weird that he appreciated it, even as he insisted it was unnecessary.

Chloe stuck her pitchfork in the muck and leaned against it. "You're not gonna ask what happened? Why we're suddenly better?"

"Nope." Aiden focused on the task at hand for about a minute or so. He didn't want to say or do anything that'd jeopardize their friendship, so he had to tread carefully. But he told himself that he and Chloe were friends, and friends checked on each other. "I mean, if you want to tell me…"

"I'm afraid you'll say 'I told you so.'"

He didn't remember telling her she should make up with her mom, even if he had thought it. "I'll resist. Even if I think it," he teased, and she laughed.

She tipped onto her toes, glancing at the students in the other stalls before stepping closer. Close enough for him to make out the different shades of blues in her eyes and the slight smattering of freckles across her nose that hadn't been there when she first arrived. "Things sort of deteriorated. With Tyler and me. And I really needed to talk to my mom about it."

Aiden remained perfectly still, all except for the hard swallow. This didn't change anything.

It changed *everything*.

"Well?" Chloe bit her lip.

"I'm sorta scared to say anything. You got mad last time I gave my opinion on the matter, and parameters were drawn."

"Just that you couldn't say 'I told you so.' Yes, he ended up being a jerk, and apparently he's already moved on…" Her voice broke at the end, and she dug her pitchfork into the straw with a renewed sense of purpose, the kind driven by pain and anger.

"I'm sorry, Chloe. But I'd be lying if I said I wasn't glad. He wasn't good enough for you. Not by a long shot."

Her eyes met his, and he felt every inch of space between them, every breath, every everything.

Hope was dangerous—he knew that better than anyone. His luck had changed in the past six months, though, and he wasn't sure if that meant it was okay to hope, or it was more dangerous because he had more to lose.

She'd just broken up with the guy, and clearly he'd hurt her, so Aiden could hardly swoop in now and ask her to give him a chance. After all, he wasn't a great guy, either. His flaws were flawed, and she was going places, especially now that she'd cut the deadweight.

Still, one of these days in the near future, he was going to get up the courage to tell her that he thought she was smart and funny and beautiful. That she was one of the kindest people he'd ever met, even if she worked hard to hide it, and he saw the real her.

If he got lucky and that didn't send her running, he might even confess that he'd like to be more than friends.

The guys had some water rights meeting, which Jess hadn't even known was a thing. Basically, there were water rights and a board of people who said when certain ditches diverted water for the ranchers to use for their crops, and long story short, it meant Wade was busy tonight.

Which gave her one more day to do sit-ups.

Not that she was going to use it for that or anything.

Nope, instead she'd been summoned for a girls' night out.

Last Sunday, after spending a few hours at the diner with Winona, she'd picked up a cute, midthigh purple dress at Horsefeathers to go with her newfound knowledge of how to properly bread and fry chicken, along with the yummiest white gravy to go with it and mashed potatoes. Originally, she'd thought she might wear the dress if and when she and Wade went out again, but she decided to don it tonight.

After all, if anyone would appreciate the extra effort her outfit, hair, and makeup took, it would be other women. Guys usually just gave a "damn" when they approved or a "What's up with that outfit?" when they didn't, but women noticed the little details.

"Wow, look at you! I love how your boots perfectly match the embroidered flowers on your dress," Liza said as she greeted Jess with a hug, proving her point.

"Mmm, you smell good." Jessica picked up a section of Liza's chestnut strands. "Your hair looks amazing, too."

"I almost forgot what it looks like when I actually manage to blow-dry and curl it. I had to bribe the kiddos with a movie so I could have extra time to get ready, but it's nice to remember what it's like to get all gussied up."

Kathy came down the porch steps, her sandy-brown hair also curled and pinned up, and they exchanged more compliments. Over the past week or so, those dark circles under Kathy's eyes had been fading, and she had new life in her eyes. She might still have to grip the porch rail and move a bit slower, but it was nice to see she was on the mend, her demeanor matching her sassy personality.

Tanya pulled up in her decked-out, cherry-red truck, and they all piled inside.

As they started away from the ranch, Liza glanced at her cabin. "I hope Everett and Elise are being good. Isn't it crazy how all you want is a night away from your kids, and then the second you pull away, you can't stop worrying about them?"

"It gets slightly easier as they get older, but it never really goes away." Jess craned her neck to see the large girls' cabin, casting her own last glance. Spending those thirty or so minutes riding with Chloe earlier today had been the best part of her day.

"Don't you worry," Kathy said, reaching over Jess to pat Liza's leg. "Harlow's a sweet girl and a mighty fine babysitter. I let her know that Trace and Randy stayed back, too, so she can just give 'em a call if she needs anything."

The name sounded familiar, and it took Jessica a second to remember that Harlow was the local teenager who occasionally came to the ranch to practice her barrel racing. She also stabled her horse here, as did a few other people in town.

Kathy pressed her hand against the dash as Tanya took the corner onto the main road. "Thanks, y'all, for including me in your girls' night out. Sometimes there gets to be way too much testosterone in that house, and I needed to get away from it all for a bit."

"I didn't know there was such a thing as too much testosterone," Jess joked.

"Oh, honey. You've never lived with seven boys." Kathy's eyebrows drew together, and her head cocked to the side. "Have you?"

Jessica laughed. "No, no I haven't."

"Oh, thank goodness. I was afraid I'd gone and stuck my foot in my mouth, and I'm not flexible enough to pull that off gracefully."

They all shared a laugh, and within about ten minutes they were pulling up to the Tumbleweed Bar. From what Jess had seen, there weren't many options in town of places to hang out or get food. Just the Silver Saddle or the used-to-be-a-movie-theater Italian restaurant and the rustic bar.

As they walked inside, Jess couldn't help thinking of the

night Wade had brought her there. How they'd danced and laughed, and how she'd known then that she'd have a hard time not kissing him.

Turns out she'd been right about that part, and as she and the girls settled at a table, she was thinking about his lips again.

"You look happy," Liza said, flashing her a smile over the top of a cocktail menu. "Is it the guy or the daughter?"

"Yes," Jess said, grinning, that blessed lightness she'd felt since last night flowing through her again. So much nicer than the previous hollow feeling that used to accompany thinking of her daughter. "Chloe seems to have turned a corner, and now that we're talking again, everything feels right with the world. Add in spending time with a certain cowboy and"—she sighed—"I'm really happy."

Liza leaned closer, her analytical side whirring to life behind those sharp, hazel eyes. "Define spending time."

Jessica glanced at Kathy, who gave her a secretive smile. It was a little weird to be told to spill the details with her... guy-who-was-more-than-a-friend's mom there, but she told the girls that yes, they'd shared a kiss. "Which Kathy knows, since she got to see the tail end of it."

Tanya and Liza both spun to Kathy, mouths agape.

"Sorry about that, dear. I noticed there was a spark between you two, but I had no idea I'd be interrupting when I brought in the groceries. Considering you were both covered in flour, it seemed like it was quite a kiss."

"Well, I'd never kiss and tell, but..." Jess placed a hand over her heart and sighed. "Yes, yes it was." For a moment she let herself relive the thrill of having Wade's hands and mouth on her, and she brought up her cool palms to place them on her heated cheeks. Then she reminded herself it was important not only to refrain from getting carried away, but also to make sure no one got the wrong idea. "But we're just taking things slow. It's not like we can get very serious. I'm leaving in a few weeks, and I don't want you all saying *good riddance* afterward."

"Impossible, I can assure you of that," Kathy said. "Everyone's enjoyed gettin' to know both you and Chloe."

Liza nodded her agreement as she squeezed Jess's hand. "After hanging out and laughing more than I have in ages, it makes me sad to think of not having a chance to get to know you."

A squishy, not altogether unpleasant sensation went through her, and Jess was afraid she was getting attached to more than the hot cowboy. Needing the attention off her, she folded her arms on the table and looked at the cute red-head across from her. "Tanya, what do you do? I know you live on the ranch next door, but I wasn't sure if it was more of a horse ranch or a cattle ranch."

"Dude ranch."

"Sounds like my kind of ranch," Jess said, waggling her eyebrows. Now it was coming back to her. Wade had mentioned the dude-ranch thing, but it'd temporarily gotten lost in the melee of everything else she'd learned since arriving.

"You'd think, but it's just a bunch of spoiled business-men who want to learn bonding drills. We do corporate retreats mostly, all that mushy trust-fall, learn-to-work-together shit. Not that I don't believe in it—I've seen first-hand what it can do—but from point A to point B, it's a lot of dealing with overgrown babies and way too much mansplaining."

A waitress stepped up to the table, apologized for taking a while to get to them, and took their drink order.

Once she stepped away, Jessica picked up her earlier conversation with Tanya. "So you've been riding horses pretty much since birth, too?"

"Since I was so small I was practically doing the splits in the saddle."

Jessica had a hard time imagining putting a toddler on a horse. It was so big and kids were so small, and just the thought tightened her lungs.

"Heard you got on a horse today," Kathy said, reminding Jess that nothing she did here would ever be truly secret. Not that she was trying to keep that secret, but she was so used to people only caring if she wasn't in their way or if she was being a good worker bee, getting her work done and taking up as little space as possible.

"It was semi-terrifying, but I did. Chloe gave me the run-down as she saddled my horse, and then Wade helped me figure out the steering."

"I bet he did," Liza said with a giggle, and Jessica shook her head. She didn't confess how much she liked having him snug up against her in the saddle, his strong arms around her. The way he whispered orders in his deep voice, and how her skin had hummed with his closeness.

"At the end of the ride when we were putting the horses in their stalls, Chloe told me about two horses that are in a secret relationship but are considering going public, and I told her about the two baby calves that are best friends but are totally going to grow up to become more. And Wade and Aiden looked at each other and shrugged, as if they were either accustomed to the crazy or glad they had someone on their side to witness it." It'd been so perfect, falling into the back-and-forth she and Chloe had always had when they made jokes and made up stories, which was why she was trying to smother her worries over how close Chloe and Aiden had become.

Luckily, their drinks showed up to help with that. She and the girls chatted and sipped and laughed, so much that Jess's cheeks and stomach hurt in the best possible way. As she was marveling at how much fun she was having, it struck her that she'd never had this before.

Sure, she'd had work friends here and there, ones she caught up with at the office. They might even talk about their weekends, but that was as far as it went. A lot of it was because the other women had families—the more traditional, two-parent kind—or they were single and partied on the weekends.

Neither of those really fit Jessica, so she'd spent lots of nights at home, with Chloe when she was younger, and by herself once her daughter's social life picked up. Never before had she felt this close to a group, and her worries over getting too attached rose up to poke at her.

To warn her it was a bad idea. Most people didn't stick around, and she thought maybe she should close herself off as much as possible so leaving them wouldn't hurt more than it already would.

"Jess? You okay?"

She glanced at Liza, who'd asked the question and brought her back to the present moment. Her friend was also doing that psychoanalyzing thing, her training making her far too adept at reading expressions and body language. Jess twisted the stem of her drink, more to have something to keep her hands busy than anything. "I was just thinking how funny life is. Who knew I needed to visit the sticks to meet so many awesome women?"

Tanya gave her a wide grin with a hint of mischief. "Yeah, usually we do our best to keep that a secret. Keeps the crazies away."

"Well, I hate to break it to you, but you're not doing a very good job because I got in." Jess ran her finger around the rim of her glass and then licked off the sugar.

"You're good people," Kathy said. "I could tell from the very start. Which is why I had such a hard time turning you away. You have to know that ate me up inside. I was so glad when you said you had cooking experience and wanted to take that job that I about leapt out of my chair."

"Then we tasted your cooking"—Liza sputtered, nearly choking on her margarita—"and we had a big meeting about how we had to pretend not to realize you couldn't cook while you figured it out."

The ladies busted up.

"You did?" Jess asked, and they nodded.

Liza wrapped her arm around Jess's shoulders and rested her head against hers. "*That's* how much we all wanted you to stay."

Jess twisted in her seat and hugged Liza back so she'd know the feeling was mutual. "Wait. Was Wade in on the meeting?"

"Heavens, no," Kathy said, waving a hand through the air. "We women meet once in a while to make sure things keep running right and just *let* the guys think it happens naturally. Tanya's an honorary member of the Turn Around Ranch board."

"That's what happens when you grow up next door and spend as much time there as at your own place. You end up in family meetings, where you're told you have to keep information from your best friend," Tanya said.

Kathy cackled—there was no other way to describe it. "Gotta keep our boys on their toes."

"You certainly do a good job from what I've seen." Jess turned to Tanya. "How long have you and Brady been friends anyway?"

A flash of something crossed Tanya's features at Brady's name, but she quickly shuttered it. "Forever. Our families have owned the adjoining ranches since way back when, so I don't have many memories that don't include him. We used to meet up at the halfway spot to ride or fish in the creek. Even now, when I get the urge to strangle one of the overgrown babies, I tell him to come meet me for a bit." She smiled, so much affection in the curve of her lips. "He's pretty much the only reason I haven't ended up in jail."

Hmm. That didn't leave Jess convinced there wasn't more between Tanya and Brady, but Wade had warned her that they both freaked out if anyone implied there was more to it, and she didn't want to ruin the congenial mood. Instead of prying for more on that situation, she turned the spotlight on Liza. "How did you end up at the ranch? Did you grow up in town?"

"Oh no. Just answered a personal ad. I've been here less than a year. I warned them I had twins who were going through the terrible twos at the time, and they told me they'd provide a cabin and said they had a great childcare program, and I came running so fast that I think I left the sign that marked the border of my old town spinning."

"We left out that our childcare program involved mostly cows, chickens, and horses." Kathy beamed and put a hand on her chest. "And one far from spring chicken who never gets enough of having kids running around."

The mushy vibes were spreading inside Jess, softening every organ they touched. Everyone at the ranch worked hard, but none of them was viewed as simply an employee. The bonds that grew between them all went beyond that, and those threads were forming again, tugging at her and leaving her waffling on whether to give in and let herself become a full part of this group, even if only for a little while.

"You guys are all amazing, and I'm glad that you didn't call me a big, fat liar my first day and send me packing. That's not even the alcohol talking, I swear." Jess glanced from warm face to warm face. "Thank you for taking a chance on me. Especially you, Tanya," she added as she nudged her arm, because she didn't want things to get too heavy.

Tanya raised her glass in a toast. "You're welcome. It's easy since I don't have to be there to eat the meals you cook."

They all got the giggles, but Kathy and Liza both chimed in to say how much her skills in the kitchen had improved, and how impressed they were she'd improved so quickly.

"It's called YouTube and panic. Along with a lot of stubborn determination and refusing to say die."

"Hear, hear," Liza said, raising her glass, and they all clinked and drank.

After another hour of chatting, drinking, and laughing, they decided to head home. As they were exiting the Tumbleweed, Kathy wrapped her arm around Jess's waist and pulled her into a side hug. "I'm so glad you came to us. Even if it's just a short while."

Liza overheard and came to join in on the hug, and Jessica held on extra tight, logging the memory away. That way, after she was long gone, she could pull it out and reminisce about the time she fit into the most unlikely group of women, and how they'd reminded her what it was like to have true friends who accepted you the way you were, burned food and all.

Chapter 24

JESSICA SUCKED IN A DEEP BREATH AND KNOCKED ON the door to Wade's cabin. Excitement, nervousness, and anxiety whirled through her gut, leaving it a tangled mess. When she and the girls had arrived home last night, he'd been sitting on the porch. She'd made a joke about him waiting up for her, and he'd teased that he wasn't sure who was driving and thought he might have to go pull them out of the mud.

Even though it hadn't rained and there wasn't any mud to be found.

Then he'd insisted on walking her home.

While dropping her off at her door, he told her he'd like to ask her on a proper date and have her over for dinner at his place. While she was slowly but surely getting better at the cooking thing, she'd jumped at the chance to eat a meal she didn't have to cook.

Her nerves spiked higher as she heard the approach of booted footsteps.

She was looking forward to spending time with Wade, but after her night with the girls, she'd been thinking a lot about the quicksand situation she'd landed herself in.

With every movement, every conversation, every hug and kiss, she was pulled deeper into life here. Thinking about it left her without oxygen, which also fit, because you couldn't breathe after quicksand covered your head.

Wade swung open the door, and her breath lodged in her

throat. He gave her a sexy smile that made her ovaries do a little leap, and then she was thinking oxygen was overrated.

"Come on in," he said, gesturing her inside. Her shoulder bumped his firm chest on her way past him, leaving her thoughts completely scrambled.

Why had she been thinking she should go slow again?

That seemed like a stupid idea.

Thoughts turned even more slippery as his hand came up on her hip bone, his thumb doing an intoxicating drag across the top. "You look amazing."

Since she only had so many nice clothes with her, she'd borrowed a wrap dress from Liza and paired it with her pink boots. She'd shaved her legs—as well as other areas of her body—because while she'd thought nonstop about how she might be getting in too deep, she didn't want to be unprepared in case she changed her mind about how far she should go. Which she supposed was sort of counterintuitive if she planned on sticking to her... Well, they weren't exactly goals. More like safety measures.

Safety's overrated, too. No one ever talks about how safe their epic nights were.

Still, she wasn't sure if she was ready to throw caution to the wind.

"Jessica?"

Her mouth went dry as she peered into those endless gray eyes, so familiar, yet so much left to discover in their depths. "Thank you. You look nice, too. Very clean." That last part sort of popped out, leaving her painfully aware that whatever game she'd had was long gone.

Wade chuckled. "The miraculous powers of a shower and a fresh set of clothes." He slid his hand around her waist and used his forearm to draw her closer. Then he lowered his mouth to hers.

The instant their lips touched, she melted against him. Heat built, slow and steady, and she gripped his biceps, needing to anchor herself to this man, this moment, this kiss.

"I've been thinking about kissing you all day," he said, resting his forehead against hers. "I had a countdown going and everything."

"Mmm," was her reply, since her thoughts were nice and hazy again.

He pulled her farther into the living room, giving her a quick tour before walking out the patio door.

The scent of charcoal and smoke filled the air as he opened the grill. Everyone else was having canned tomato soup and leftover biscuits from breakfast, something she only felt a pinch guilty about since Kathy insisted she was feeling better and that Jess deserved a night off.

Mrs. Dawson probably also thought that if things went well between Jess and Wade, they might find a way to work things out long term, and Jess didn't have the heart to tell her that she needed to get back to her actual home soon. For one, her boss was already getting grouchy about her time away from the office and the tasks she usually handled that she couldn't do remotely, and for another, she'd promised Chloe that if she worked and completed the program here, they'd go back.

A two-hour drive didn't seem like an insurmountable distance, but Jess worked a lot of late nights and some weekends, and Wade rarely ever stopped working. Plus, she wouldn't be able to just leave Chloe unsupervised for large chunks of time, not for a while.

Sorrow drifted up to take a bite out of her happy, and she wished her brain would take a vacation from reminding her that she was wishing for things that weren't possible. When it came down to it, she and Wade had barely started their... whatever this was.

"You're quiet tonight," Wade said after salting the now-sizzling steaks he'd thrown on the grill.

"Just thinking."

"Uh-oh," he teased, and she lightly smacked his chest. He pulled her to him and wound his arms around her waist. "Everything okay?"

"It is now," she said, and more than that, it was true. His embrace held her together, letting her focus on the now. She tipped onto her toes, seeking out that tempting mouth of his, and he wasted no time reciprocating.

An urgent edge crept into the kiss and she clung to him, digging her fingers into the muscles of his shoulders. He spun them around and backpedaled. She wasn't sure where they were headed, but she was all for going along for the ride.

He sat in a patio chair, pulling her down on top of him so that she straddled his lap. Desire flared as his hard length pressed against the throbbing spot she desperately needed to appease, and she brushed her tongue over his.

His groan vibrated through her, driving her higher. His hands slid up her thighs, exposing them to the night air. It didn't stand a chance against the heat building up inside her, demanding more friction, more of his touch, more, more, more...

She rolled her hips and he arched his to meet hers, the delicious movement driving her to the edge of madness.

"Holy shit," he murmured as her lips moved to his neck, and the world spun out of focus as his thumbs drifted up to her inner thighs, rubbing and dragging and *holy shit indeed*.

Vaguely she smelled something, a familiar smell that made her want to swear for a different reason. With her brain in a lust haze, it took her a few seconds to recognize what it was.

Wade's posture stiffened as realization dawned. He let out a harsh curse as he stood, leaving her clinging to him like one of those koalas that didn't want to fall off its tree branch. A groan ripped from his throat as she slid down his hard body, and his chest was heaving with ragged breaths as he rushed over to the grill.

Smoke billowed from the lid, and he jerked it open and swore again.

She hugged him from behind, peeked around his large frame at the grill, and snickered. "See? It's not as easy as it looks."

Using the giant fork, Wade removed the two blackened pieces of meat that closely resembled the coals underneath. "Well, I had a helluva distraction."

"That's my excuse for why I exaggerated my cooking skills. There was this hot, gruff, and grumpy cowboy trying to usher me out of the office, and my common sense waved goodbye."

"Yeah, right. You disliked me from the start. I thought we were going to drive each other completely crazy there at the beginning."

"No, *you* disliked *me* first. And we did drive each other crazy at the beginning."

He grabbed the food, led her inside, and set the plate on

the center of the table, next to a salad. Then he turned to face her. "Want the honest truth?"

She lifted her chin, bracing herself in case it stung. When people gave their honest opinion of her, it usually did.

He placed his hand on the side of her neck, running his thumb across her jaw and undoing her fortifications against him. "We'd already decided as a family that we couldn't take on any more teens, and since the rest of them are bleeding hearts, it's up to me to be the stern one. It's hard enough with most people, but then you came along, this beautiful, determined woman, and once you looked at me with those big brown eyes…" His fingers drifted down her neck to her collarbone, slowly revving her up and undoing her. "I knew that if I didn't slam the lid on my emotions and start super stern, I'd be a goner."

"Fat lot a good it did you," she teased, the breathlessness in her voice making it hard to pull off.

"Yeah, I got outvoted, and now here I am, as predicted. A goner."

Her heart swelled, and she closed her eyes for a moment, soaking in the way his words and fingertips made her feel.

"I've never been so glad to lose a vote in my life," he said, and her eyes popped back open. No one had said anything that butterfly-inducing to her before, yet a voice whispered that guys used sweet talk as a way to get what they wanted. Then they walked away without looking back.

A few minutes ago, she'd been ready to jump Wade's bones outside with all the creatures roaming the trees as witnesses. *Omigosh, what if someone from the ranch had strolled by?* Somehow the people in Silver Springs always knew what'd happened, mere minutes after it happened, too. It had seemed charming until she thought of everyone on the ranch knowing she'd had sex with Wade. Now she was thinking about her very limited experience and if she'd screw it up, and how vulnerable she'd feel during and after. What if it messed up this amazing connection between them that'd kept her going when she was having one of the hardest times of her life?

Her worries formed a mood-ruining tornado that left her fighting off the urge to be a woman who begged for reassurances. Ones Wade couldn't give, even if he wanted to.

"I'm starving. Are we ready to have our super-duper well-done steaks?" Jess dug deep and pulled out a smile. "Lucky for you, I'm used to the charred flavor."

Wade stared at Jessica for a beat, wondering when she'd shifted gears. He felt like he'd been thrown off the back of a truck again. He wasn't normally a guy who said mushy shit about being a goner, and he wasn't sure what reaction he'd expected, but it hadn't been a change in subject.

A kiss would've been nice.

Going back to the way things had been outside when she'd been in his arms and kissing him into oblivion also worked for him.

He had invited her over for dinner, though, and the steaks were done and then some. "Let me grab some plates."

"Need help?"

"I got it," he said. He figured a few minutes in the kitchen would give him time to collect himself.

He opened the oven and swore again. It was a swearing kind of night.

"Is everything o—?" Jessica burst into laughter as she looked at the splattered potato guts that coated the inside of his oven.

"Laugh it up."

"Way ahead of you." She moved closer. "Did you use a fork to poke holes in them before you baked them?"

"Since when are you supposed to do that?"

"Since always—and that's coming from someone who knows the bare minimum about cooking." She began opening random kitchen drawers. "Where're the oven mitts?"

"Don't worry about it. I can get it."

She placed her hand on his arm. "And I can help."

He opened the drawer containing his one oven mitt and gave it to her while he made do with a kitchen towel. They knelt in front of the sweltering oven and picked at the mess, gathering up the chunks they could salvage and putting them in a bowl, and putting the rest in the trash.

"If it makes you feel better," Jessica said, shaking the hair off her face. "I discovered it when I blew up a potato by cooking it too long in my microwave without any vent holes. I was pregnant and working at a grocery store, and I could hardly afford the bag of potatoes in the first place, so I was extra bummed. I totally burned my hand when I pulled out the potato. I probably should've gone to the emergency room, because my palm was one big blister. But I didn't have the money, so I just wrapped it the best I could and went on with my life."

She shook the potato in her hand over the to-keep bowl, dislodging the insides and then discarding the skin. "I got written up for swearing in front of a customer the next day. A box hit my burned hand, and the f-bomb just popped right out before I could stop it. The older woman had on a string of pearls, and she literally clutched them. Accidentally snort-laughing about that probably didn't do much to endear me to her, especially since she'd been pretty horrified at the knocked-up teenage girl scanning her groceries as it was."

Wade sat back on his heels and looked at Jessica, and he could feel the awe creeping into his features. While he realized she had a fifteen-year-old daughter and that she was young when she had her, the logistics, along with everything she must've gone through, only hit him now and then, when she said something like that as if it was completely normal. "How?"

Jessica wiped the last of the starchy potato debris from her hands. "How what?"

"How did you do that? Have a kid on your own when you were sixteen?"

She shrugged. "I guess I didn't see anything but making it work as an option. I wanted a baby no one else seemed to want, and I wasn't about to let them tell me what to do, so I set out on my own. At the beginning I relied a lot on the kindness of strangers, like the woman who let me rent her basement without asking for all the regular paperwork most people require."

"Didn't your parents come looking for you? You were just a kid yourself."

"To my parents, I was old enough to get knocked up, so I was old enough to take care of myself." Her voice wavered slightly, making him think she didn't feel quite as nonchalant as she pretended to be about that.

His knees couldn't handle being on the hard floor any

longer, and they'd gotten most of the mess. He stood and offered her a hand. She took it, and he slipped his fingers between hers.

"Don't look so concerned," she said. "It was a long time ago, and I'm fine. Chloe scared me last month, but she's back on the right path, and all those people who told me I was being stupid and too stubborn and that I'd fail can kiss my ass."

He fought the urge to tell her he'd happily take her up on that offer. This was hardly time for that. Maybe later, though. "Have I told you that I think you're amazing?"

She tensed, and he gripped her hand a little tighter when she started to pull away. He'd let her go if that was what she truly wanted, but first he wanted her to hear him—to really hear him. Someone needed to let her know she'd done a great job in spite of the crappy hand life had dealt her.

"You are, Jessica. I see people all the time who'd use a situation like yours as an excuse, and you just punched life in the face and kept on going. You're an amazing mom. I saw it that first day you showed up in the office. I saw it when you were blaming yourself for your daughter's situation, and I saw it when you two started talking again. After observing a lot of parent-child dynamics, I can tell you without a doubt that you two have a bond that's closer than any I've ever seen. She's a good kid, and you're amazing, and it's a shame that you haven't been told that more."

Jessica sucked in a big shuddering breath, and for a beat or two, he was afraid he'd overstepped. But then she threw her arms around him and buried her head in his chest. "Thank you," she said, and he held her tightly to him. Even though he'd told himself he should simply enjoy the time they had together, it wasn't every day a woman like this came along, and he was beginning to worry about the day he'd have to let go.

When he'd have to say goodbye for good.

Chapter 25

OVER THE PAST THIRTY MINUTES, JESSICA HAD SAT ON the couch in Liza's office next to Chloe as she and Liza explained how much anxiety Chloe had been experiencing this past year, and how it'd caused numerous full-blown panic attacks. Including one on the bathroom floor at school, where she'd struggled for breath for several minutes before she'd managed to pull herself together.

A lump had taken up residence in her throat, and she'd done her best not to cry as she'd squeezed Chloe's hand and listened to the ups and downs she'd been experiencing. About her fears over telling Jess about her overwhelming anxiety, and how her group of friends and Tyler had seemed to help.

For a while.

"I've spent the last few sessions adding tools to Chloe's toolbox," Liza said, scooting her roller chair a foot or so closer to the couch. "Basically, I give her coping techniques that she can pull out and use whenever she gets overwhelmed."

Jess clenched her jaw against the tears that were still attempting to flow as she glanced at Chloe. Her chest was a gaping raw hole, and that sense of failure she'd experienced the first few weeks here had returned, but with an extra twist of guilt. "I'm so sorry I didn't see it. I knew something was off and that you were more stressed out than you'd ever been before, but I didn't know what, or how bad it was. Or how to help, and…" So much for stopping the tears. They spilled over and ran warm streaks down her cheeks.

"It's okay, Mom. I worked hard to hide it. And you were so stressed with your job and the bills, and I didn't want to give you one more thing to be stressed about—especially since I know what stress can do."

It sucked that in trying to give her daughter a better life where they didn't have to struggle so much financially, she'd added stress on both of them. "It's not your job to worry about my stress level, Chloe. It's *my* job to make sure you're taken care of."

"We take care of each other." Chloe tugged a couple of tissues from the colorful box on the side table and handed them to her. "That's the deal, and it's the only deal I'm going to accept, so…"

"At least the stubborn is still intact," Jess joked as she used the tissue to dab at the moisture on her cheeks, then hoped it was okay to joke about that.

"I'm not fragile, Mom. Liza's helping me realize it's not weakness, like I originally thought it was. It's a bunch of different things, but we're focusing on what I can control."

Liza gave Jess a quick rundown on generalized anxiety disorder. She mentioned that the doctor who specialized in anxiety had left a prescription for Chloe, so they also discussed the medication, which was said to be generally well tolerated and one of the fastest acting.

The meeting was overwhelming yet promising, and Jess was just glad Chloe's diagnosis was out there and being dealt with, and that Chloe had someone as awesome as Liza to talk to.

When the hour was up, Jessica and Chloe stood. On

their way out of the office, she hugged Chloe tight. "Have to get the hugs out before you're outside in front of your friends."

"Or you'll hug me so hard you'll break my water bottle and drench me?" Chloe asked, but she was holding on equally tightly.

Jessica laughed. "Totally."

Chloe dropped her arms. "I'm okay, Mom. It actually helps to know this is something I can deal with and not that I'm just paranoid." She tipped her head toward the glass door that would lead her outside. "I've got to get to my next class. Will you be okay?"

"Of course. See you at dinner?"

"Yep. I'm more excited about wieners than I've ever been," Chloe said with a giant grin. It was Friday, and they were roasting hot dogs and marshmallows outside to kick off the weekend. It was part of a reward for a great month, and everyone on the ranch had been talking about how much fun it was going to be.

Jess couldn't resist one last hug, and then she was standing in the doorway, watching her daughter hustle across the yard. She smiled when Chloe caught up to the other kids, especially when she and Izzy launched right into a conversation that required a lot of hand gestures.

Relief flooded her.

Her daughter was going to be okay. They were going to be okay.

"How are you handling everything?" Liza asked from behind her, and she spun around.

"Sorry. Didn't mean to loom in your office doorway."

"I don't have any more appointments today if you want

to discuss anything. I also want you to know that a lot of teens are dealing with off-the-charts levels of anxiety right now in America. A lot of studies blame all the social media time and the fact that they never get to unplug."

"I could see that. I still have to keep up with my other job, but it's been nice to be out in the country where it's so much easier to unplug. I know that Chloe has a hundred more social media places than I do, and while back in high school I'd sometimes hear on Monday mornings about parties that I hadn't been invited to, I didn't have to see them unfolding real time with Snapchat pictures."

"Exactly."

Wade walked up to the group of teens and began talking with them, so much caring in his tenderly firm expression that Jess's heart stuttered in her chest. Last night they'd rewarmed the steaks, eaten the salad and premashed-thanks-to-exploding potatoes, and then he'd asked if she'd be up for a movie, clearly sensing she wasn't ready for more, even if she wanted to be.

"Since you claim to be an aspiring cowgirl," he'd said, "it's high time you see *Quigley Down Under*. Consider it part of your training."

They'd cuddled through the movie, which she'd thoroughly enjoyed—the movie and the cuddling—and as the credits rolled up the screen, she'd said she was tired. Which she had been.

Ever the gentleman, Wade walked her home, and when he kissed her good night, she'd almost rethought going inside alone.

But she hadn't gathered the courage to do anything about it, and she'd been kicking herself all day.

Jess leaned a hip on the doorjamb. "Shifting gears here, but I think I might need you to psychoanalyze me."

Liza laughed and swept her arm toward her office. "Come have a seat."

"Will you sit on the couch by me so it won't be so weird? Although, fair warning, it'll probably still be weird."

Liza sat on the couch, and Jess plopped down beside her, tucking her leg underneath herself as she propped her elbow on the back of the couch and faced her friend.

"Whenever you're ready," Liza said, a kind, encouraging smile on her face.

Was she really going to say this? Out loud and everything? "I've got this hot cowboy who wants to have sex with me, and I want to have sex with him, but I can't seem to… to…" The first part was easy enough to blurt out, but her tongue had suddenly quit working properly.

Liza raised her eyebrows. "Unholster the gun?"

"Oh geez, am I supposed to unholster it?"

"Well, there is the dry-humping option," Liza said with a laugh, and when Jess shot her a faux dirty look, she clamped her lips. For half a second. "Sorry, not sorry. I should probably also add a disclaimer that I'm not exactly using technical therapist terms."

"Nooo," Jess said with all the sarcasm she could muster up, and then she dropped her head in her hands with a groan. "I couldn't afford the therapy I clearly need anyway." She peeked through her fingers. She'd gotten this far. Might as well confess it all. "Honestly, most of my adult relationships have really only reached the dry-humping stage. I could never pull the trigger."

Liza snapped her fingers and then pointed at her. "Pull

the trigger! That's probably a better way of saying it if I'm gonna stick with the gun analogy." She steepled her hands and adopted a more serious, professional facade as she tucked them under her chin. "I mean, go on…"

At this point, Jess didn't have anything to lose, and she couldn't get a better bargain than free therapy from someone who truly cared about her. "Okay, so there's this side of me that feels like once we cross that line, he'll lose interest. Whether it's the faded stretch marks and mom bod, or that the challenge is over or…" Jess thought about all the nice things he'd said last night, and how he'd called her amazing. How he saw parts of her that no one else ever seemed to see. Which made her feel safer and more scared at the same time, in spite of that not making any sense. "I know Wade's different than the other guys I've dated. He's a good guy, and the complete opposite of Chloe's dad, not to mention more mature, because being older than sixteen does that to a person."

With every sentence Liza's forehead crinkled more, and Jess replayed her words, trying to figure out what had been confusing, besides having a perfectly good guy right in front of her and freaking out about it. "Wait. Are you saying…?" The therapist mask dropped, and Liza switched into full friend mode as she shifted closer. "Have you not had sex since you were sixteen?"

The room suddenly seemed too hot and stuffy, and Jess could feel every throb of her rapid pulse. She'd never told anyone, because who would she tell? "It just sort of happened. Or didn't happen." She scratched the itchy spot on her neck. "I didn't want to cross that line again until I was sure about a guy, both for myself and for Chloe. You know how it is. It's hard to fit in anything when you're a constantly tired, overworked single mom. I chose sleep over meeting guys a lot, and the few guys I met just weren't keepers."

Liza nodded. "I get that, I do. But all I'm saying is that there is a giant leap between fumbling teenage-boy sex and sex with a certified man, and you owe yourself that. Even if you decide Wade's not the right man."

Longing drifted up, her stomach along with it. Jess really wanted to experience that. Sex with a guy who'd care if she'd gotten there instead of just taking what he needed and leaving her in the back of the car, struggling to fix her clothes, while he returned to the party.

Liza placed her hand on her shoulder. "Jess, you don't have to keep putting your needs last."

"Easier said than done." Now that it was out there, she was glad she'd told Liza, embarrassing or not. "Have you? Since the twins?"

"No." Liza's shoulders deflated. "Their father hurt me pretty badly, and like you said, it's been nonstop busy, and I can't simply bring a guy into their life. I'm not the casual hookup sort, either. Which means I'm the hypocrite telling you to get back on the horse while I'm standing safely on the ground, never taking any risks of my own in that arena."

"Well, I'd rather have sex with Wade than get back on a horse. I'm sure it'll be a more fun ride, too." Jess laughed, and Liza joined in, but then seriousness crept back into her features, along with a gentle rebuke.

"I'm on to you, you know. You use humor when emotions get too real."

"Guilty."

"Don't get me wrong. You're really funny, and like I said

last night, I appreciate how much I laugh around you. But sometimes you've got to drop the walls and take a chance on people."

Jess nodded because that was what everyone did. But she'd already let Liza in, along with Kathy and most everyone here. Including Wade.

Since heartbreak was on the horizon either way, Jess told herself yet again that she might as well take advantage of the time she had before the aftermath came.

Right?

Chapter 26

FIRELIGHT DANCED ACROSS JESSICA'S FEATURES, HIGH-lighting her smiling cheeks before flickering to her lips, her cute nose, and then her eyes.

Wade fed the fire another log, nudging it closer to the center of the pit with the toe of his boot. His gaze met Jessica's through the flickering flames, and the flush of heat that coursed through him had nothing to do with the fire. It'd be highly improper to stride across the way, lift her into his arms, and kiss her before carrying her across the yard and into his cabin. Especially with all of the teenage witnesses looking on.

Izzy, one of the girls who'd been here the longest, stepped up next to him and shoved a hot dog on the end of her roasting stick. Her parents sent her here after they found some dark poems she'd written, and while sometimes poems were merely art, hers focused on suicide. After more digging, Liza and Nick discovered she'd been the victim of severe cyberbullying, and it'd taken weeks for her to come out of her shell. Now she was one of the most outgoing teens and the first to jump into a new task. She hardly looked like the same girl, the ever-present grin on her face matching all the happy colors in her hair.

At the end of the month she was due to go home, and as he often did, Wade wished he could wrap the kids in bubble wrap before sending them back into the real world. Give them a safer transition.

"Where do I put it again?" Izzy dangled the roasting stick over the center of the fire, where the flames engulfed it. "About here?"

"You'd think you'd want to put it right into the fire, but you actually want to hover it close to the coals around the edges." He raised his voice. "Otherwise it'll just end up black and burned to a crisp. Sort of like how Miss Jessica cooks."

"Hey!" Jessica shot out of her camp chair and walked over, which was exactly what he'd been hoping for. "Do you really want to play that game? Because I seem to remember someone else who cooks like that. I'd say they even burned steaks blacker than anything I've ever made."

He grinned and reached for the packet of hot dogs. He slid one onto the metal end of a roasting stick and extended the handle to her. "Here. I'd better let you cook your own. I'm not gonna be responsible for you having to eat two burned dinners."

"Yeah, that's my job. Literally."

"I must've missed the part where we told you to burn dinner. I thought we hired you to just cook it."

"The level of doneness was left open to interpretation, so really that's on you."

He laughed. He hadn't seen her all day, and he worried she would pull away, the way she had last night. She reminded him of a flighty horse that'd been injured or mistreated. Just when things seemed to be going along smoothly, something would spook it and you'd have to start over. He knew better than to tell her that, though. While it'd taken longer than it should've, he'd eventually learned women weren't fond of being compared to animals.

Jessica squatted next to Izzy and asked her a few

questions, starting with favorite foods and then moving to whether she enjoyed riding horses.

The more he saw her interact with the teens and the rest of the staff at Turn Around Ranch, the more he thought Jessica fit right in.

Which was a dangerous thought, one he shouldn't allow himself to think, no matter how true it was.

"This is taking forever," Jessica said. "This is why I burn stuff. I have no patience."

Izzy tugged Jessica's arm back as she began to extend her hot dog closer to the flames. "No, Miss Jessica. It'll be worth the wait. And I'll sit and chat with you so it won't seem so long."

They both sank to the ground, their legs crossed, and talked as they spun their roasting sticks.

A few minutes later, the two of them came over to the table to dress their perfectly done hot dogs, and when Izzy drifted back toward the glow of the fire, Wade sidled up next to Jessica. A steady current of electricity hummed under his skin at her nearness, but as she licked ketchup off her lip, it spiked and arced and short-circuited parts of his brain.

They were partially hidden out here in the darkness, and he would make sure to keep things lighter if that was what she wanted, but he couldn't stand to be around her any longer without giving in to the urge to touch her. He placed his hand on the small of her back, and a secretive smile curved her lips.

She twisted toward him a fraction, her gaze running up and down him in a way that suggested she was thinking very naughty things he couldn't wait to hear more about.

"You should come over tonight. You'll already have had

dinner, so we'll just stick to"—he lowered his lips until they were right next to her ear and gently bit the lobe—"dessert."

Her sharp intake of breath spurred him on. He was going to have to work to keep himself under control, or they'd need more than partial darkness. She reached up and twirled her hair around her finger, affecting a ditzy vibe. "I'm so confused. I thought we were having s'mores for dessert. That's what the flyer said."

Wade grinned and slid his hand around her waist, hooking it on her hip. "I'd give you a horribly cheesy line about how you'd definitely want s'more, but I'm afraid it might blow my chances."

Jess placed her hand on his chest, right over his rapidly beating heart. "That all depends on how well you can deliver on that line, cowboy."

Not a second too soon, he realized they were about to have company, and they jumped apart like two teenagers who'd been caught.

The kids grabbed more buns before returning to the fire. Right when Wade was about to renew his flirting efforts, a laugh carried over to them, and Jessica turned toward the noise. Chloe and Aiden sat on a log on the other side of the semicircle, cooking their food, their heads huddled together.

Tension crept into the line of Jessica's body as concern transformed her features. Chloe and Aiden's closeness had worried Wade a bit, more because of the rules and avoiding drama than because he thought they'd get into trouble. Honestly, it was also good to see Aiden so happy. Besides, how could he give the kid a lecture when he was muddling the lines as well?

Wade ran his hand down Jessica's arm. "Hey. They're just friends."

"Mm-hmm. I remember saying that same thing about us a few weeks ago."

He laced his fingers with hers. "Come on. I want to show you something."

Her feet remained planted in place, her attention on her daughter.

"It'll just take a few minutes, and they're surrounded by people. Remember how you've got to let the process work without interfering?"

Jessica frowned, but finally allowed herself to be tugged toward the barn.

———————————————

A squeal escaped Jess's lips when she spotted the tiny kittens. She couldn't help it. They were a moving ball of multicolored fluff, all of them nuzzling but wiggling. "They're so freaking cute!"

"Kita came out of here earlier today, so I figured she must've tucked her babies somewhere in here."

There were a couple of gray-and-black-striped tabbies that looked just like their mom, one mottled tortoiseshell, and one ginger tabby. They were squeaky little things, constantly meowing as they walked over one another.

"Can I hold one?" she asked, and Wade nodded.

She carefully picked up the fluffy orange one and brought it close to her chest. Its meows were almost chirps, its eyes were tiny dark slits, not quite open, and its pink tongue stuck out as it yawned. "I've never seen any this young before."

"We have a couple batches a year. We keep a few around to help take care of the mice, and then usually neighbors or people from town take a few."

"Not this one, right? This one's my kitty. I can already tell." She patted the tiny head, her heart melting into a puddle of goo. "Don't worry, I know how to take care of cats. Once you're old enough, I'll feed you bacon, like I fed to your mommy while you were in her tummy."

"You fed the cat bacon?"

Jess put on her best innocent face. "No, where would you ever get that idea? What I meant to say is I work magic with animals. You probably noticed how the baby calves run *toward* me instead of away from me when I go out to the corral now." Her secret was handfuls of dried corn feed. Along with love and cooing noises, of course. Jess lifted the kitten and rubbed its soft fur on her cheek. "A farm cat of my very own." She grinned at Wade. "Am I a cowgirl now?"

His laugh filled the air, the deep noise echoing through her chest. One mushy sensation after another careened through her. The cat and the cowboy, and seriously, was this heaven? Who knew it'd smell like straw and manure?

The mama cat came to see what was going on with her noisy babies. Since Jess knew how strong the protective instinct was, she assured Kita she was only admiring her beautiful babies and gently settled the ginger kitten next to its mom and siblings. It wobbled around, and the mom licked its face so firmly the kitten fell over.

More squeaky noises escaped, and when Jess glanced at Wade, he was smiling at her like she was the adorable one.

He wrapped his arm around her shoulders and curled her to his chest. His lips came down on hers, and after he'd given her a kiss that robbed her of breath and flooded her with endorphins, he said, "You're my cowgirl."

Chloe had noticed Miss Kathy looked shaky, and when she'd approached and asked if she was okay, Miss Kathy told her she just needed to go into the house and rest. Since it was dark, Chloe worried about getting over to the main cabin with only the puny beam of the flashlight—especially if she ended up needing to support the older woman's weight.

She'd waved Aiden over, and they'd walked his mom to the house, making sure she was good and had everything she needed before they started back toward the dimming light of the fire.

Soon it'd be bedtime, and Chloe wanted to keep this awesome night going. She'd meant to say hi to her mom, but then Aiden had pulled her next to him and Mom had headed somewhere with Wade.

Get some, Mom. As long as she didn't think too much about it, Chloe was cheering for her to have some fun while she was here. She never dated, to the point Chloe occasionally worried her mom would be crazy lonely when she eventually went off to college.

Goose bumps prickled her skin, and Chloe hugged her arms around herself to fight off the chill. The fire had been so toasty she hadn't realized how much the temperature had dropped with the sun down.

"Cold?" Aiden asked.

"A little."

He wrapped his arm around her shoulders, and Chloe

sighed at his warmth. Her stomach was doing the fluttering thing it'd been doing more and more around him, and she leaned her head on his shoulder.

As they neared the barn, Aiden slowed. "Chloe, I have to tell you something."

Everything inside her rose up, up, up, and she was afraid of what he'd say and if it'd send everything in her plummeting. She didn't want to make the same mistakes she had with Tyler, thinking a guy liked her when he only liked a challenge or a convenience, or whatever the hell that had been about.

Don't think about Tyler.

"Does that silence mean you don't want to hear it?" Aiden asked.

She licked her lips and exhaled a breath in a vain attempt to calm her rising nerves. "Depends on what you're gonna say."

He turned so they were face-to-face, and when she shivered—partly because of the crisp night air and partly because…she wasn't sure—he ran his hands up and down her arms. "You're cold. We can go back to the fire and talk about it later."

"Are you serious? It'll drive me crazy wondering what you were going to say, and who knows when we'll get a chance to talk alone again."

He swallowed hard, and her heart skipped a couple of beats. "It's just that you're going to be leaving in a couple of weeks, and I told myself I'd say something before then. But if I wait till too close to when you leave…"

Chloe locked eyes with him. "Aiden. Spit it out already." Luckily the words came out boldly, regardless of the way her nerves were misfiring, and maybe she should've stopped him instead. Whatever he said next could change everything, and she really liked having him as a friend.

More than that, she *needed* his friendship.

But she'd also wondered if there was something more, there under the surface of every conversation, every laugh, every lingering look…

"I like you, Chloe. You're smart and funny, and that other guy's an idiot for not seeing the real you. For letting you go so easily. Maybe it makes me the jerk for being so glad, because now I get the chance to tell you that. I'm happy to be your friend, but I also really want to kiss you."

She blinked up at him, so many emotions crashing through her chest that it was hard to pick one out from the rest, but hope and happiness were definitely in the mix. "You do?"

One corner of his mouth twisted up, bringing out that adorable dimple in his cheek. "Don't sound so surprised. I know I haven't been very subtle."

"But, like, do you want to kiss me and hold my hand, *and* do you like me enough that you'd talk to me even if I wasn't here on the ranch?"

He cocked his head like the question perplexed him, and her rapid pulse throbbed through her head, begging him to say yes and wanting to believe it. "I'd muck every stall in the place if it meant more time on the internet talking to you. I've made plenty of mistakes in my life, and I know I'm not good enough for you, either, but I've learned to fight for what matters, and I'm not letting you go without a fight."

He stepped closer, enveloping her in his warmth, his green eyes steady and clear and full of resolve. "I'm gonna be messaging you constantly after you leave, so much you'll probably get sick of me. I promise." He curled her hand into his. "Did I mention in there somewhere that I also think you're really pretty?"

"I think you're really pretty, too," she said, and when he scowled, she laughed. "In a totally handsome, rugged way of course." She slipped her fingers between his much larger ones, a thrill shooting through her as their palms met. "I like how determined you get, like when I show you a math problem and you won't give up until you get it."

He dipped his head, the tip of his nose barely brushing hers. "That's because I have to impress my hot tutor."

"I also like how you don't hold back or hesitate to tell me I deserve better, even though it sort of pissed me off at first."

He flashed her the crooked grin again. "All part of my charm."

"And I really, *really* want you to kiss me," she said, her heart beating a million miles an hour, the cold now far, far away.

He closed the mere inch of space between their lips. The first few seconds were like a free fall, that moment when you've decided to let go and it's scary and exciting and your stomach can't quite keep up with the rest of your body.

Then he slipped his arms around her waist, tethering her to him and making her feel safe enough to sink fully into the kiss. He kissed her carefully, as though she mattered and he planned to take care of her heart, and she was seriously considering handing it over to him.

But then she heard her name—her full name—and Aiden tensed up.

Mom and Wade stood in the doorway of the barn, and

before Chloe could figure out what to say, both of their names were being called from the other direction. They'd taken too long, and she instinctively knew they were in trouble. The kind of trouble that meant she might not get a chance to kiss Aiden again for a very long time.

Chapter 27

"Just friends, huh?" Jess spat at Wade. All this work, all the sacrifices and all the progress, just so her daughter could get in trouble with a different boy. She paced across the office, her footfalls heavy enough to create a satisfying *thump, thump, thump.*

The kids had explained that Kathy hadn't been feeling well so Aiden and Chloe had helped her into the house, which she'd corroborated. The other adults were just beginning to wonder about how long the teens were taking to return around the same time Jess and Wade had come out of the barn. Right in time to witness Aiden kissing her daughter.

Apparently the team at Turn Around Ranch liked to discuss situations and punishments instead of declaring them on the spot, since it helped take the anger out of them. The kids had been sent to their bunks since it was bedtime anyway, and while several of the adults had originally gathered in the office to discuss the situation, they'd taken one look at Wade and Jessica and left them to hash it out.

Despite the twenty minutes that'd passed between catching her daughter with Aiden and now, anger was still one of Jessica's main emotions, along with frustration and that same panic that'd brought her here in the first place.

"Jessica—"

She jabbed a finger at Wade. "Don't 'Jessica' me. I brought her here to get her away from a teenage boy who'd landed her in trouble, not so she could get in trouble with a different boy."

"That's not fair. Aiden's not like that."

"Oh, isn't he? I know that he got into trouble with a girl in town when he first arrived."

"Damn it, Ma," Wade muttered under his breath.

"This isn't your mom's fault. I don't even know who to blame. Maybe it all comes back to me. I should've stopped it the instant I saw it. Even better, I should've asked more questions before handing my daughter over." She paced across the room. "How often does this happen? Has there ever been a teen pregnancy during the program?"

When Wade didn't answer, she spun toward him, another spike of irritation going through her at his crossed arms and scowl, and she hated that he somehow still looked hot.

"Well?"

Wade sat on the edge of the desk, much like he had the first day she'd met him in this office. His face was about as stern as then, too. "This is why I didn't want to tell you our family's whole history. It's not all sunshine and rainbows, something I thought you might understand."

"I do understand that. Better than anyone. That's why I want my daughter on a different path than the one I had to go down. A better path with a brighter future. And you still haven't answered my questions."

"They're kids," he said, as if that explained anything. "We're careful, and there are rules and people are constantly watching them. But as you pointed out as one of your reasons for wanting us to accept Chloe into the program, it's not a prison, and we work very hard to ensure it doesn't feel that way. Yes, some of the teens begin relationships with each other while they're here, but again, they're closely supervised, and no, we've never had a pregnancy."

"At least that's something," Jess said, but it didn't provide any comfort, because she didn't want her daughter to be the first. "But Aiden's not in the program anymore, is he? Does he have rules? Restrictions?"

The line of Wade's jaw went tight. "Of course he does."

"I don't want my daughter around him."

"What are you gonna do? Put her in a bubble? Lock her in a tower?"

"If that's what it takes!"

Wade blew out a breath, and for all she cared he could continue to sit there, seething and doing his best impression of a fire-breathing dragon—not one she would ask to protect her daughter while she was in the tower, that was for sure. "Because of our relationship, I'm going to shove the lecture on interfering, although this is the *exact reason* I didn't think it was a good idea for you to work here while your daughter was in the program. We have a lot of experience with how to handle situations like this. There's a careful balance between finding ways to motivate teens and keep them in line and pushing them so far that rebellion feels like the only answer, so they shut down. There are people out there who think you can beat the stubbornness out of a mule, but you can't. All you do is break its spirit."

Tears burned her eyes, and Jess clenched her jaw. The last thing she wanted to do was break Chloe's spirit. She loved her daughter so much—from her quick wit to the empathy she had for people, so much so that she was often anxious on their behalf, which fueled a lot of the issues that'd gotten her into bad situations.

"The thing we work very hard on here is teaching them as much as we can so that they're equipped to make better decisions. Answer one question for me…" Wade pushed himself off the desk, looming tall in front of her. "Do you think Chloe's gotten better since she's been here?"

That question stopped her short. The same relief she'd felt as Liza explained how they were going to teach Chloe how to deal with her anxiety drifted up and provided a balm to her panic. Her anger and worries were harder to calm. Some choices were practically impossible to come back from. It didn't change her answer, though. "Yes," she said, despising him a little for being so logical when she wanted to cling to her irrationality.

"Either our program works or it doesn't. How is it fair to allow Chloe to get better and change, but deny that the same thing has happened to Aiden?"

"Because I don't care about fair, not right now. That's my kid, Wade!"

"And Aiden's mine!" Emotion broke through, his hard mask slipping. "I love him just as much as you love Chloe, whether it's as a brother or a son, or however you want to define it."

A ripping-apart sensation tore through her, tugging her in two different directions. She wanted to cling to her side of the argument, yet she wanted to go to Wade and hug and soothe him. Sometimes she hated the pressure of being the only parent trying to decide what was best for her daughter. Maybe it made her unbalanced. Just when she was about to confess as much, Wade's mask descended again.

"Tomorrow I'll meet with the team, and together we'll come up with punishments and rules. I expect you to abide by them."

The harsh words took away the mushy feelings she'd been experiencing, giving her emotional whiplash. They also made it clear that she didn't count as part of the team, which stung, even though she knew her work here was temporary and only involved cooking and occasionally helping with the livestock, a service she mostly did because she liked the animals.

She jerked her spine stick-straight and saluted him. "Is that all, sir?"

Without waiting to find out, because right now she couldn't care less, she stormed out of the office, slamming the door behind her.

Chapter 28

GROUCHINESS HAD CONSUMED WADE ALL MORNING, leaving him short-tempered and snappish. His family and the rest of the staff gave him a wide berth, which wasn't exactly easy to do in the small office.

He wished telling himself to let it go worked, but he'd tried. In desperation, he'd also tried to convince himself that it was good that Jessica would be leaving soon. The problem with telling yourself lies was that you were completely aware it was bullshit.

"Does that work for everyone?" Ma pushed her glasses up her nose and glanced from face to face, pausing on his.

He released a measured breath, not wanting to speak to his mother with the edge of sharpness that'd automatically come out all morning. "Let me be the one to talk to Aiden. I'm sure he's beating himself up."

Everyone agreed to that, while Liza was the one tasked with talking to Chloe, both to check in on how she was doing and to inform her of the consequences of last night's actions.

Wade hated that it had to happen at all, to be honest, but order was important, and so were the rules. People had entrusted them with their kids, and no matter what Jessica thought, he didn't take that lightly.

"That's it, then," Ma said, and everyone stood. He turned to go, his thoughts on the massive amount of work he had to do. "Wade, I'd like you to hang back for a minute."

"Ooh, someone's in trouble," Brady said as he passed, and Wade grunted.

Instead of walking past him and out the open doorway, Liza paused as though she wanted to say something as well, but she kept opening and closing her mouth as if she couldn't settle on the right words.

"Just say it," he said. "I'm a jerk. She hates my guts."

"Funny that you go right to Jess."

How could he not? He hadn't seen her all morning. Breakfast was laid out by the time he'd walked into the dining room, and while he'd arrived a few minutes late because he didn't want to end up in another screaming match, he'd at least wanted to see how she was. But there'd only been muffins, juice, and lukewarm bacon.

Liza placed her hand on his arm. "I'll just say this. She's tough, and yeah, she's stubborn—because that's what it takes to raise kids by yourself. You're so used to making all the decisions that it's not easy to let go of that control. Just remember that she's also been through a lot." With that, she walked out of the office and shut the door behind her.

Then he had to face his mom. "Are you feeling better?" he asked as he took the chair next to hers.

"Yes, I'm fine. Just overdid it a bit yesterday. If Chloe and Aiden hadn't helped me inside, I probably would have a sprained ankle to add to my list of weaknesses." Disappointment coated her words—not at the kids, but at herself for needing help in the first place.

"They're not weaknesses, Ma. You're human, and you never let yourself entirely heal. How many times has the doctor told you to take it easy?"

"We're not here to talk about me," she said, and he

sighed. Regardless of there being more males than females out here on the ranch, stubborn, opinionated women were everywhere he turned. "Don't you think you were a bit harsh with Jess last night?"

"Was the entire staff listening at the door?"

"Yes, but to be fair, I'm pretty sure we could've heard y'all's yellin' from the living room."

He pushed his hat farther down on his head, wishing he could pull it all the way over and hide from everything for a while. "I made it very clear from the beginning that we weren't going to make exceptions."

"Yes, and you have your rules about not getting involved and making sure there's no extra drama. Ever since Serena left, you've closed yourself off."

For the most part they avoided talking about his ex-girlfriend, the woman everyone was so sure would be the one, but Ma wasn't exactly wrong. Serena was a journalist who came for a story. She used to say she found love as well. Everyone got attached—him especially—and she moved in with him and continued writing her articles from the ranch. Five months later, she decided she couldn't hack it out here in the sticks, and she'd left without a proper goodbye. Just a stupid note that broke everyone's hearts in one fell swoop.

Ma patted his knee. "I think you're upset at yourself for letting Jessica slip in, which is downright silly. Life is dramatic. People are human—you said as much to me a minute ago. You're no exception to either of those things, Wade Randall Dawson. It's okay to feel somethin'."

"It was a bad idea to get involved in the first place. It's complicating things even more than I worried it would, and she's leaving soon anyway, so we might as well quit while we're ahead." Problem was, it didn't feel like they were ahead. It felt like that day he'd gotten bucked off the truck and lost his breath, only Jessica wasn't there to check on him and run her fingers through his hair, leaving him to sit on his sore ass alone.

"There are a lot of reasons to give up, sure." Ma pushed to her feet and pinned him with her serious look. "You'll have to decide if there are enough reasons to fight."

Jess had taken one of the trucks into town, not because Wade would've demanded she do so, but because the *last* thing she wanted was to end up high-centered or stuck and have to rely on his help.

After finishing up the breakfast dishes, she'd snuck out the side door. As she'd driven away from the ranch, she'd seen the feed truck heading toward the field, the back loaded high with bales of hay, and experienced a twinge at not being there in the cab between Wade and Brady.

It wasn't as if they legitimately needed her, though. They'd managed before she arrived, and they'd be fine once she left.

Somehow she'd ended up in the kitchen of the Silver Saddle Diner, wrist deep in pie dough.

After Jess had fought with an apple pie for a good thirty minutes, Winona had given her an extra-large mug of coffee and sent her out front to sit at the counter. The only thing more depressing than being a single rider on a horseless saddle was being alone at a table for one, but only slightly less so.

A plate was set in front of her with a *clink*.

"Banana cream?" she asked, because it wasn't what she'd expected.

"Plus chocolate." Winona swept her long, black braid over her shoulder and slid a napkin-wrapped set of silverware toward Jess, the bottom of her large turquoise ring making a slight scraping noise.

"It looks amazing, but I thought I'd wait and have a piece of the apple pie I helped make." Her mouth watered as she took in the layers of the pie, banana and a layer of chocolate, topped off with freshly whipped cream. "Actually, you're right. I'll eat both."

Winona glanced around, like she didn't want to quite meet Jess's gaze. "You know I simply adore you, hon, and I'm always happy to give you lessons in the kitchen, but I've got a reputation to uphold, and that apple pie you made…" She grimaced and then softened her expression. "Pies require patience and a light touch, and most of all, they need to be made with love. That pie you threw together was made with…frustration and sorrow."

Those emotions twisted through her again, confirming Winona had a point. Jessica had rolled the crust thin, exactly as Winona had done with the crust she was working on. But it hadn't come up clean, the dough stretching and breaking. She'd gotten irritated and lost her patience and sort of thrown the remains onto the top of the apple mixture in blobs. Then she'd tried to smooth it over, doing her best to pinch the crust together where she could. It…hadn't looked pretty, but she figured it'd taste okay, considering she'd only rolled the dough Winona had already made.

"Did I ruin the entire thing?" she asked, embarrassed at

being on the verge of tears so easily. But Winona had been so nice to take one look at her sad face and give her something to do that'd keep her hands and mind busy.

"Not at all. I whipped up a wad of dough, and after it finishes chilling, I'll put a nice lattice crust over the top of the apples." Winona pushed the plate closer. "Eat. Chocolate will help, and I'll be back to check on you in few."

About twenty minutes later, Jess had finished off her pie and was on her third—fourth?—cup of coffee.

"I might need to cut you off," Winona said, setting the pot out of reach and then folding her forearms across the counter on the other side of Jess so they were eye-level. "Are you shaky yet?"

"No," Jess said as she reached for the mug with a shaky hand.

Winona arched an eyebrow, making it clear she'd noticed.

"I had that piece of pie, so it's not like I'm drinking on an empty stomach." Jess thought her joke comparing the coffee to booze and Winona to a bartender was pretty funny, but the diner owner only gave her a sympathetic look.

"I'm fine." After all, she *was* fine. She was breathing, and her daughter was good, and life was just peachy. Sure, it looked like it'd be another sixteen years before she had sex again, which wasn't depressing at all. By then she might as well just embrace old maid status and give up on men altogether.

She was about ready to do so now.

Except…that damn cowboy made it impossible to simply throw up her hands and say *Oh well, no big deal we didn't get the chance to see how great we could be together.*

More than that, she could see a few of the points he'd made last night, even if her stubborn side didn't want to admit it. She sincerely hoped the program could change teens' lives for the better, and more than that, she'd seen a change in Chloe. Which meant yes, Aiden could've changed, too. Jess was sure he had, and that he was a better person than when he'd first arrived. Even *she* felt like a better person after her time at the ranch. She was more open-minded. More open in general. Happier in a lot of ways.

But she still didn't want Chloe jumping from a bad relationship to one that wasn't meant to last.

Kind of like Wade and me.

"This wouldn't have anything to do with the tall cowboy you danced with at the Tumbleweed, would it?" Winona asked as if she could read minds—and Jess wasn't one-hundred percent sure she couldn't. She reluctantly nodded. "You want me to convince you he's a good one, or that's he's no good?"

"Think you could do that? The second one?" Not that she wanted that. Did she?

Winona flashed her a consoling smile. "Judging from the look on your face, you're already a goner, so it wouldn't do much good."

Jess groaned.

Just when she'd seen Wade's point about Aiden during their heated argument—and had almost admitted as much—Wade had given his decree. Admittedly, she'd be offended if anyone implied Chloe wasn't good enough for their kid, which was what she'd basically done with Wade.

Ugh, ugh, ugh. I suck. If there weren't so many witnesses, she'd thunk her head against the counter a few times, although then she'd still be frustrated, as well as have a headache.

Instead, she took another swig of coffee, trying to focus on the burn and not her depressing thoughts. "I'm getting saddle sore. From a post."

"That's why I put those in. They're kitschy and bring in the tourists, but they also keep them from staying too long."

Jess snorted. "And the creepy cow skull?" She lifted her eyes to stare into its blank ones.

"Bob isn't creepy. He's good luck." Winona tipped her chin up to address him. "Aren't ya, Bob?"

Jess rubbed her fingers across her forehead. "You were right. I've definitely had too many if people are talking to their decorations like that's normal. I'm gonna call it." She stood, tossed a couple of bills on the counter, and fought the urge to rub her sore backside. "Thanks for the coffee and the pie. And for letting me mangle some dough."

"Anytime," Winona said, and then she leaned over the counter and gave Jess a much-needed hug. For such a slight thing, she could really squeeze.

With nowhere else to really go, Jess climbed inside the truck. Wade drove it enough that it smelled like him, a mix of his cologne and sunshine and diesel, and she inhaled because suddenly she found the smell of diesel sexy.

The main problem was that seeing a few of Wade's points didn't change anything in the long run. She was down to two tiny weeks. The last sands were about to fall to the bottom of the hourglass. At the same time, she didn't want to leave things badly with Wade—or anyone else at the ranch, for that matter.

She had more than enough regrets, and she didn't want to add wasting her limited time with Wade to the list.

Aiden glanced up as Wade pushed open the door to his bedroom and stepped inside. He continued to loop the red-and-white lead rope around his hand to his elbow so he could hang it up in the stables later, nice and neat, on the hook where it belonged.

"If I need to go, I understand." Aiden was proud of how steady the sentence had come out. It'd been on his mind since last night, and he'd been alternatively dreading and wanting to get this moment over with.

Wade's eyebrows came together. Aiden could handle any punishment, but he couldn't handle disappointing Wade or the rest of the Dawsons. He couldn't bring himself to regret kissing Chloe, but he regretted that he'd let them down.

"You think I'd tell Brady, Trace, or Nick to leave the ranch if they made a mistake?"

Each thump of his knotted heart ached, and again, Aiden worked hard not to let it show. "No, but they're your brothers."

Wade locked eyes with him. "*You're* my brother, Aiden."

The words made his chest too tight in a strangely pleasant yet uncomfortable way.

"I was afraid you'd be hard on yourself, and that's why I came to talk to you." Wade sat on the foot of Aiden's bed. "Have a seat."

Aiden sat next to him, his rapid pulse throbbing through his head.

"There are rules."

Aiden's stomach bottomed out. "I know. Don't cross the line with the people who come to the ranch. I tried not to like her, I swear. But she's funny and smart, and she gets me. She was dating this prick who didn't treat her right for way too long, and I wanted her to break up with him because of that, but once she did, all I could think was that I couldn't let her go without telling her that I cared about her. I usually keep that kind of stuff to myself, but she deserved to know."

Wade didn't say anything, and he looked up at him, trying to get a read.

"Sorry. Did I need to add a 'with all due respect' or something like that?"

Wade huffed a laugh. "No, what you said just made me think that…I could learn a thing or two from you. About telling people I care."

It took Aiden a couple seconds, but then he put it together. "Chloe's mom?"

"She's…" Wade lifted his hat off his head and raked a hand through his hair. Then he shook his head. "I can't lecture you on not crossing the lines, not when I started crossing them the second Jessica showed up. I'm not going to punish you for liking Chloe, or even for kissing her."

The stress that'd been churning through Aiden since last night slowly leaked out of him.

"But," Wade added, and that made Aiden tense up again. "You guys broke the rules when you came back from helping Ma into the house. I appreciate you watching out for her, and I even get taking your time on the way back so you could talk to Chloe. But we can't let you guys wander off alone—especially since she's in the program right now."

"I'll take her punishment. I'm the one who slowed us down. I wanted to talk to her alone while I could."

"I respect that, but it'd set an unfair precedent. We've decided that you two have stall-mucking duties for the rest of the week, both your usual, as well as the other kids'. You're also grounded from being together, save classes. But you can't linger, and you'll be sitting apart. That's what was decided, and I'll enforce it."

"Math tutoring?"

"Nope. Not this week. We'll reassess next week."

Aiden didn't ask if that meant no riding together. He knew it did, and that made everything inside him deflate. It was fair enough, and better than he deserved, but it meant he and Chloe had just lost a week, and that only left one more where they'd still be constantly monitored. "How mad was her mom?"

"Pretty mad," Wade said.

"Are they fighting again? I'd rather Chloe hate me than her mom."

Wade placed his hand on Aiden's shoulder and squeezed. "They'll be fine. You just worry about you and your studies for now. If you need help or someone to talk to, come see me." He stood. "And no more talk of leaving, you hear me?"

His home was safe; they didn't regret letting him stay. Chloe was okay. It wasn't ideal, but it wasn't as bad as he'd worried. Regardless of how many times the Dawsons had shown up and stuck by him, it still managed to surprise him. "I hear you. Night, Bro," he added as a joke, but there was something real and raw in there, too.

Wade paused in the doorway. "You know that I..." He cleared his throat. "I love you, kid."

Aiden couldn't say it back. Not because he didn't feel the same way, but because his throat was too tight to speak.

Chapter 29

WADE HAD JUST STEPPED OUT OF THE SHOWER WHEN HE heard the knock on his door.

What now? After a long day, he'd contemplated flopping into bed and going to sleep so he could wake up and see if tomorrow was magically better. But he knew he wouldn't be able to sleep. His mom's words had run through his head all day, and he'd decided he wasn't ready to give up on him and Jessica quite yet.

Aiden's words about telling people you cared only drove the point that much further.

They might not have much of a future, but Wade didn't want Jessica leaving before he could make things right. He was going to march over to her place and apologize and see where he stood.

He jerked on his jeans and buttoned them, and another knock came as he grabbed a shirt out of his closet.

The fabric caught on his wet skin, not wanting to cooperate, and he'd only managed to get a couple buttons fastened by the time he made it to the door. He flung it open, prepared to put off whatever "emergency" the messenger was bringing to his doorstep, if at all possible. He couldn't spend another day with the rain cloud that refused to go away constantly dumping on him.

Jessica stood on the other side of the door, and her eyes widened as she took him in. At least that bought him a few seconds to figure out what he was going to say. He'd figured he would plan out more of his apology on the walk over.

"Funny, I was about to go over to your place."

She jerked her gaze up to his. "You were?"

"Yeah. Been working up the guts to go over and apologize all day."

"I'm the one who should apologize," she said, throwing a hand to her chest. "I'd be mad if anyone talked about Chloe like that, and I'm sure Aiden's a good kid—especially since he has you. I just panicked when I saw her kissing him, and I thought 'I can't go through this again.' And I know it's not fair to let the bad decisions I made when I was her age turn me into a paranoid lunatic who locks her in a tower, but she's already dealing with so much, and I don't want a boy to get in the way of the progress she's made. I'd feel the same about any boy."

His mouth hung open a few inches as he processed everything she'd said. He'd never expected her to apologize, and it meant so much that she had, which made it easier for him to make a go of it. "I pushed too hard there at the end. A big part of me wanted to comfort and assure you, but then I realized I wouldn't do that with another parent. It's like when you feel the truck sliding in the wrong direction, and you jerk the wheel and overcorrect and end up in the ditch on the opposite side because you went too far."

"And then you have no one to call for help because you're already there?"

He chuckled, then slowly reached out and snagged her hand. "I'd call you."

"So you're saying you want to stay in the ditch forever?"

"With you in there with me, it wouldn't be so bad." He tugged her inside the house and kicked the door closed, and the knot that'd overtaken his chest loosened when she threw her arms around his waist.

Her silky hair brushed his bare skin as she tipped her face toward his. "You know, I was just fine before I met you. So it makes me kinda mad that all day I felt"—she pursed her lips together—"not fine."

A tight band formed around his lungs.

"But I still am fine," she said. "I don't want you to feel guilty or like I expect you to make my life complete."

Amusement rose up, mixing with the affection and the certainty that this was worth fighting for, even if he only got to experience it for one more week. "Is that you taking back your apology? Or is it just taking a weird turn?"

"I am sorry, no takesies backsies," she added with a smile. "I just wanted it to be a no-pressure apology."

"Because you're fine?"

She gave one sharp nod, but her arms tightened around his waist. "Yes."

"Well, I think we can do a lot better than fine." He lowered his lips to hers, backing her up against the door and pinning her there with his body as he delved his tongue inside for a better taste.

"Wade," she gasped, and the sound sent all his blood rushing south. He moved his lips to her neck, lightly sucking the skin there, reveling in the way she arched against him.

She tugged at the few buttons he'd managed to fasten, undoing them and then shoving his shirt open and down his arms. He groaned as she dragged her hand up his abs to his chest and then slowly back down.

A vixen smile curved her lips when she reached the waistband of his tightening pants, and she dragged her finger back and forth, driving him right to the brink of insanity.

"Jessica?"

"Wade," she practically purred. Oh, if she wanted to play dirty, he could play dirty. He circled her wrists with his fingers and brought them up over her head. He lowered himself onto her, cradling his erection against the apex of her thighs, and she whimpered. He readjusted his grip, holding both of her wrists in one of his hands so that he could free his other to explore.

Hooking his thumb on the hem of her shirt, he slid it up, up, up, stopping at the lacy cups of her bra to drag his thumb over her hardened nipple. She bucked against him, taking him from hard to rock hard, and he repeated the move on the other side.

In one quick motion he released her wrists and jerked her shirt off over her head, and then he leaned back so he could take in the view.

She placed an arm over her stomach, and he frowned and took her hand in his. "You're beautiful."

"I'm…out of practice."

"Pretty sure you don't have to practice being beautiful," he replied. She tilted her head, and he flashed her a smile. "No pressure. If you want to slow down, say the word."

"God, no. I really want to have sex with you." Her cheeks colored as if she was embarrassed by her boldness, but all it did was turn him on more.

"Right back at you. But first…" He dipped his head and kissed her collarbone. Her skin pebbled underneath his mouth, and he moved his lips to the swells of her breasts. A quick flick of his wrist undid her bra, and then he yanked it off and replaced the lacy cups with his mouth.

Her moans spurred him on, telling him just how to lick and suck and, once he'd ensured her breasts had been shown the proper attention, he kissed the valley between them, then the top of her rib cage.

His fingers worked the button on her jeans and undid the zipper. Then he dropped to his knees.

Her lips parted, and she peered down at him through hooded lids. "What are you doing?"

"What does it look like?" He tugged her jeans down, groaning at the tiny scrap of lace between her thighs. He kissed her over the fabric, and she braced her hands against his shoulders, her fingers digging into the skin. "You once told me you don't beg. Do you remember what I said?"

"You asked if I was sure."

"Are you?" he asked as he slipped her panties down, exposing her fully to him.

A string of noises spilled from her lips as he put his mouth on her. He licked and sucked, and after working her up to the point her knees were on the verge of giving out, he looked up into those big, brown eyes.

"How about now?"

Chapter 30

JESSICA'S BREATHS WERE COMING RIGHT ON TOP OF ONE another, and the world around her was still off its axis, her center of gravity now the guy on his knees in front of her. Liquid-hot need pooled low in her stomach, the release she so badly needed so close, if he'd just keep doing that amazing thing with his tongue.

She drove her fingers through his hair, giving the strands a light tug. She'd almost asked if they could just to get to the sex part because she was already naked and exposed and feeling way too vulnerable.

Luckily, Wade's kisses had rendered her momentarily incapable of forming words. He wanted words now, though.

"I'm not sure." She was pretty proud she'd managed to force out the sentence, whether it was too breathy to be convincing or not.

The slow lick he gave her in response made her nearly melt to the ground.

"Please," she said, too turned on to care about winning their game. "I'm begging you. Also warning you that I'll make you pay later, but right now, I just need you to finish what you started."

His strong arms encircled her thighs, and then he was stroking her with his tongue, sending her higher. Sparks of light danced across the back of her eyelids, and every muscle in her body tensed.

The tension coiling inside her body shattered, a euphoric

rush coursing through her as her body went limp. Wade caught her on his lap, holding her tight as she gradually came back down.

"You good?" he asked.

She smiled at him, undoubtedly a sated smile she'd never worn before, and said, "I'm fine."

He pinched her side, and she laughed and wrapped her arms around his neck. "That…that was amazing." She kissed his neck, enjoying the tickle of his stubble. "Like room-spinning, I-didn't-even-know-it-could-be-that-good amazing."

The next instant, he was on his feet and she was in his arms, and she wasn't sure how he'd pulled that off. He carried her into his bedroom and lowered her onto the bed, leaving her at eye level with the significant bulge in his pants.

Desire and nerves corkscrewed through her, making her hands tremble slightly as she reached for the button on his pants. He let out a growl as he sprang free of the tight denim. She gripped him over his underwear, and a rough grunt came from him as she squeezed.

She tugged his boxer briefs down and dragged her pinkie over his hard length. "Now let's hear *you* beg."

He leaned over her, planting a kiss on her lips. "I don't have a problem begging, not when it involves getting to have sex with you."

Jess stroked him, enjoying the way his eyelids flickered and all of his muscles tensed. When she swiped her thumb over the tip, he let out a growl she felt deep in her core. The fact that she could elicit that reaction from someone so strong, so usually in control, sent an enticing shiver of power through her.

Wetness pooled between her thighs, and she was about to be the one begging again. But before she had to, Wade grabbed a condom and rolled it on. He crawled over her, his sublime weight pressing her against the mattress, and she took a moment to soak in the feel of having this rugged man over her, his warm skin dragging across hers.

Forgotten parts of her awoke, throbbing to life and doing their own sort of begging. Wade reached down and hooked her knee with his hand. He tugged her legs farther apart and settled himself between her thighs, his hip bones bumping into hers. She automatically arched against him, moaning at the drag of his arousal against her sensitive, slick, and ready opening.

His eyes locked on hers. A beat passed. Two. Three. He slipped his hand around the back of her head and guided her lips to his as he pushed inside her. She cried out, a small cry against his lips, and he lifted himself onto his elbows.

"You okay?"

She nodded.

"Talk to me. Tell me what you like."

"I don't even know," she said, feeling a blush settle in her cheeks as his eyebrows drew together. "When I said it's been a while, I mean a long, long while. None of the times were very impressive, either, so the bar's set super low."

He frowned, and she placed her hand in the center of his chest.

"I don't mean…" How was she supposed to think of words when he was inside her, stretching her in the most intoxicating way. "What I mean is you've already blown my past, very limited experiences out of the water. Everything from here on is a bonus."

"Screw that. I'm gonna set the bar so high no one else will have a chance of reaching it."

Before she could say she could absolutely get on board with that plan, he used his tongue to part her lips and explore every inch of her mouth. They found the perfect rhythm, one that hit an amazing spot deep inside of her that she hadn't even known existed.

His fingers tangled in her hair, tugging her head one way and then the other as he kissed her jawline, her neck, her collarbone...back to her lips. She scraped her nails down his back and met his thrusts. Pressure built as a floaty sensation gripped her body, and then she was tumbling over the edge, clinging to Wade as she called his name.

As soon as he'd eked out every blissful second, he let go, and they fell to the bed in a tangle of sweaty, boneless limbs.

He curled her to him, and she rested her head on his chest, listening to the steady, rapid beat of his heart.

He'd done what he'd said: he'd set the bar high. And now that she'd experienced sex that was both physical and emotional and hot and caring, she knew there'd be no going back.

Chapter 31

"YOU HAD SEX," LIZA SAID AS SOON AS JESS STEPPED INTO the foyer of her office the next day.

"*Shhh.*" Jess glanced around, checking for people who might've overheard.

"Don't worry, no one else is around. I made sure of it. Not that we all didn't see the way you and Wade looked at each other this morning at breakfast." Liza tried to waggle her eyebrows but looked more like she was alternately confused and surprised. "It was more than *we apologized and we're good*. It was *we've seen each other naked, and we're picturing all the wicked things we did in our heads right now.*"

Embarrassing heat crawled up Jess's neck as another kind of heat twisted through her. Liza wasn't wrong, but jeez, was she really that transparent?

Liza clamped on to Jess's arm, tugged her into her office, and closed the door behind them. "How was it? I'm asking as your friend, but I can pull out the therapist if you want."

Jess perched on the arm of the couch. "I'd rather tell my friend she was totally right about the difference between teenage sex and sex with a certified man. I thought it was only that good in books and movies." She fanned her face and sighed, already planning the next time she could get her lips and body on that cowboy.

"Yay," Liza said, punctuating her words with a clap. "Okay, well I'm just going to live vicariously through you for a while."

"That's fine as long as you promise not to wait as long as I did, because seriously, if I'd known it could be like that, I never would've held out for so long."

"Deal," Liza said with a laugh. "Now, I'm assuming you came in for other reasons besides to give me all the dishy dish."

"I did. I was hoping I could get some time with Chloe today—away from everyone else, if possible. I didn't want to ask Wade because all the line crossing makes it extra complicated, and I'm trying to keep things more separate from now on."

Liza nodded and settled into her roller chair. "I get that. Chloe's in the stables, mucking stalls. Part of her and Aiden's punishment is to take care of all the stalls. The rest of the kids get the week off."

"They're in there alone together?" Jess asked, her feet hitting the floor and getting ready to spring into motion. She was trying to relax, but there was relaxed, and then there was reckless.

"No, of course not." Liza rolled closer and placed a calming hand on Jess's knee. "They have separate times. They can't see each other right now, besides their few shared classes."

That should have provided comfort, but it didn't make Jess feel any better. Aiden was Chloe's closest friend here. She was pretty sure they had, in fact, started as just friends, even though lines had been crossed.

How's she handling the program without having him to talk to? What if it makes her stall out? As a parent, it was always tricky finding the right balance and knowing what would help or hurt and which line of strict and lenient to walk.

Jess bounced her knee, a restless sensation taking hold. "Would it be against the rules for me to help her muck the stalls? After all, I'm breaking the same rules she did."

Liza gave a noncommittal head wobble. "Not quite. You and Wade are adults who don't need supervision. But tell you what"—she smacked the arms of her chair with her palms and then stood—"let's go ask Kathy. I'm fine with it, but I need to check with her before granting you permission."

The words dug at the part of Jess that wished she was a full part of the team. She told herself that would come with extra responsibilities she didn't want and that she had enough on her plate, but it didn't stop a twinge from going through her chest.

The twinge only grew stronger as they walked across the yard, where the twins were dragging around a wagon. They'd filled it with rocks and flowers and were struggling to keep it moving, Elise up front pulling and Everett in the back pushing, as Kathy watched from her rocking chair on the porch.

"Help pease, Miss Jessica," Everett said, coming over and grabbing her hand.

Jess let him lead her over to the wagon. She squatted down to assess the situation. "Looks like you're stuck."

"Miss Jessica knows all about getting stuck," a deep male voice said from behind her, making everything inside her go tingly and warm. She glanced over her shoulder at Wade, who smiled down at her.

"Don't ask Mr. Wade for help, either. He throws mud at you."

Elise gasped, while Everett's eyes widened with interest. "We can throw mud?"

Oops.

"Absolutely not, Everett Scott Reynolds." Liza planted her hands on her hips and gave them the mom stare.

Jess spotted the clod of dirt barring the way and moved it aside. "That'll help, but rocks are heavy."

"I gotta get strong," Everett said, flexing his muscles.

"Whoa. Those are some pretty impressive arms."

He nodded, as if this was a given, and Jessica laughed. She gave the wagon a push, helping the twins roll it over to the spot where they could unload the rocks.

She slapped her palms together and wiped the excess dirt on the thighs of her jeans. Wade was still standing nearby, and while she liked the view, he was making it hard for her to ask Kathy her question.

"Jess wanted to spend some time with Chloe," Liza said, saving her the trouble. "She was wondering if she could help her muck the stalls. That's how much she wants to see her."

Wade's posture tensed, the stern dude who ran the camp back in place.

Jess winced, her nerves kicking up a riot in her gut. She didn't want things to turn ugly, not so soon after they'd so thoroughly made up. "I was trying my best not to involve you."

"Oh, so you were going over my head to my mom and Liza?" The words were half teasing, half assessing as he narrowed his eyes, clearly trying to decide how offended he should be.

She took a step closer to him and scuffed her boot against the ground. "I like to call it avoiding any arguments that might lead to a fight."

"I think Chloe needs someone, Wade," Kathy said, the squeak of her rocking chair coming to a stop. "Aiden has you."

"To talk to, sure. But I'm not helping him with his punishment." It almost sounded like a reprimand, but Jess suspected it was more him trying to balance his stern side with the side of him that was trying to keep the three women involved in the conversation happy.

Since he was working to remain amicable, she did the same. "I can just go talk, but it'll be hard to see her doing all that work without helping, and I'm sure saying that makes you want to launch into a lecture about tough love, but what about kindness? Plus, if you think about it, it's in my MO to help out with random chores around the ranch as needed."

"I'll allow it," Wade said, and her heart skipped a beat. "If," he added, and her heart took a dive, "you also help Aiden."

Jess frowned. "Seems like I'm the one being punished now, mucking all those extra stalls."

Instead of getting upset as she'd expected, Wade tipped his chin. "Fair point."

The drop-jawed expressions on Kathy and Liza's faces made it clear Jess wasn't the only one surprised by the concession.

He ran his fingers along his jaw, and Jess could practically see a lightbulb go off over his head. "How about you help him with his math since he lost his tutor?"

Jess hooked her thumbs in her pockets and shrugged. "Sure. As long as he doesn't care about his grade in math."

"I'm confident you can figure it out," Wade said, taking a few steps toward her. "YouTube it if you have to, like you did with cooking."

Smugness crept into the curve of his lips, as if he was basking in having one over her. Then it morphed into a more suggestive smile, and as he looked her up and down, residual butterflies from last night rose to meet the other ones swirling through her gut. There he went, revving her up and calming her down at the same time.

Basically, the guy made her feel more than anyone ever had, and after a whole lot of emotional dormancy, she didn't know how to best handle it.

Kiss him?

Strangle him?

Dare she even think it… Concede?

She lifted her chin. "Fine."

The wattage of his grin kicked up a notch, and he reached out and folded her hand in his. "Give Aiden a chance. Not for your daughter, but just spend a few minutes with him. For me."

She was about to give a sarcastic response about already agreeing to it, but the way his eyes softened let her know he cared about her seeing the good in Aiden. He'd done as much for Chloe, so she nodded.

He tugged her to him and gave her a kiss in full view of everyone. Then he smacked her on the butt, as if they were on a sports team together and she was getting ready to take her place on the field. "Have fun mucking stalls."

Her eyes couldn't help tracking him as he walked toward the corral, and in the background she heard Everett say, "Ew, they just kissed."

Liza and Kathy, on the other hand, were grinning at her like deranged matchmaking loons.

The twinge she'd felt earlier returned and morphed into a stabbing sort of yearning, one that made her wonder yet again if coming here was the smartest thing she'd ever done, or the stupidest.

One thing was for sure, at the end of it all, it was going to be one of the hardest.

The trick was to breathe in and out of your mouth while trying not to think about how you were inhaling manure particles.

Chloe's arms ached, each movement taking twice as long as usual with the tired setting in, which meant she might die in here. Yep, she was pretty sure this was going to be the way she croaked. Her tombstone would read: Here lies Chloe Cook, an anxious hot mess of a girl who only got to kiss a cute cowboy once before dying next to a pile of horseshit.

Rowdy whinnied as if he sensed her depressing thoughts, and Chloe lowered the pitchfork and walked over to scratch his nose. In addition to the extra chores and not being allowed to ride for the next few days, she couldn't talk to Aiden. She'd smiled at him across the classroom earlier today, doing her best to convey she wasn't mad at him for kissing her.

It had been an amazing kiss. Maybe even amazing enough to be worth all the trouble.

The footsteps made her jump away from Rowdy and scramble to pick up her pitchfork. Then Mom stepped into view, and Chloe watched her face, trying to get a feel for her mood.

"Hey," Mom said, and the way she was studying her made it clear she was trying to see where they stood as well.

"Hey."

"Crappy day?"

"Ha-ha."

Mom swung her arms out. "At least you're here in this stable environment."

Chloe groaned, but a laugh accidentally slipped out, too. "That was cringey."

"Ah. I've embraced the fact that sometimes I'll be a cringey mom."

"If it's any consolation, you're less cringey than most."

Mom threw a hand over her heart. "Aww, thanks." She slipped on thick leather gloves, and Chloe was wondering if she was going to try to ride in those things. The reins would be tricky, and Mom didn't have the greatest handle on them yet.

"Would you like some help?" Mom asked.

"Are you serious?"

Mom grabbed a pitchfork. "Yep."

"What if someone comes in and catches you?"

"I already cleared it. I made a deal with the devil, who is more handsome than you'd expect, and I get to give you a hand and spend time with you. I just have to do some math tutoring in exchange, so we might need to forgo conversations in favor of you teaching me enough math to pull it off."

A string in the center of Chloe's chest tugged. "You're gonna tutor Aiden?"

"That was the deal."

"Are you gonna be nice?"

"I'm not sure. That wasn't part of the deal." There was a teasing note in her reply, but truth also underlay the words.

"I've probably lost some of my credibility when it comes to guys, but it's not the same as with Tyler. I know I chose wrong with him. I fell for his lines, and there were a few red flags I overlooked because…well, because he was really good at manipulating the situation—at manipulating me. I wish I'd seen it without having to go through the crash, but I recognize the difference now. I see through the words to the actions."

Mom nodded, but Chloe wasn't sure what she'd said was actually sinking in.

"You said it wasn't a waste as long as I learned something, and I did. Aiden doesn't only compliment my looks. He told me I was smart and funny, and even when we were just friends, he was protective of me."

"Did it start when you two went into town?"

Chloe vehemently shook her head. "No. I was upset about Tyler, and Aiden knew I needed to get out. I swear. That kiss you saw was the first time we kissed."

Mom exhaled and scooped up a lump of horse crap to add to the wheelbarrow.

Chloe dug in, too. "The day at the diner was the day he told me I deserved better than Tyler, and that he thought Tyler was a manipulative jerk. It actually made me mad, but it stuck in my brain. It's one of the reasons that when I saw the picture of him kissing that other girl, it hurt, but I thought, 'I *do* deserve better.'"

"I've said the very same thing at least a hundred times."

True and then some, which had helped create that awful rift between them. Chloe never wanted it to be there ever again, so she searched for the right words. "I know, and I appreciate it, but you're my mom. You don't think anyone's good enough for me."

Mom straightened and put a fist on her hip. "Because they're not."

"Aiden doesn't think he's good enough for me, either, which is sad because he's a really good guy. He told me he liked me and waited until I'd okayed the kissing to kiss me. I want you to know that I'm not rushing into anything. I know we're leaving soon. I'm not sure what's going to happen with Aiden, or if I'll even get to talk to him before we leave, but no matter what, I'm never going against my better judgment for a boy again."

Chloe meant it, too. So much could've been avoided if she'd stood up for herself. If she'd put her foot down. From now on, if someone didn't respect her and purposely did things that made her uncomfortable, she wouldn't let it slide. "Some of that is because of learning the hard way, but a lot of it has been being here. Learning the difference between true friends and fake friends, and Liza's been working with me a lot on standing up for myself and setting boundaries."

"And the meds? Do you feel better?"

At first Chloe hadn't wanted to take them, but she'd promised she'd try. Liza promised they'd work to find the right combo for her and said there was more to it than simply taking a pill. "I'm still getting used to them, and they make me a little dizzy, but yeah, I'm starting to feel better. There's less noise in my head, which helps me focus on the important stuff." Chloe lowered the pitchfork and peered across at the person who'd comforted her countless times through the years. Who'd always been there. "Like my mom."

Mom blinked at her, her chin quivering. "I'm sure you're buttering me up, but I don't even care. I needed to hear that."

"I'm not buttering you up. I'm serious." Chloe's voice cracked, and tears sprang to her eyes. "I never want to fight again."

"Yeah, let's not do that. It was like there was this Chloe-shaped hole in my life, and no pressure, but since you're only my kid, you get all my affection. Even the mushy stuff you don't want."

Chloe laughed and sniffed. "Bring it on."

Mom dropped her pitchfork, and then they were hugging. Mom took it to the breathless point, squeezing the air out of her, and she'd never been happier to be without oxygen.

"We're literally covered in dust and hugging next to a wheelbarrow filled with horse crap," Mom said. "I'm not sure if I should say look how far we've come, or how far we've fallen."

"Me neither. I never thought I'd enjoy being in the middle of nowhere so much."

"Same."

For most of the time she'd been here, Chloe had been counting down the days to when she could leave and go home. Over the past few days, something had changed, and she found herself wishing she could slow it all down.

Wishing she had more time.

And while Aiden was definitely one of the reasons, he wasn't the only one.

Chapter 32

JESS LIFTED HER HEAD OFF WADE'S BARE CHEST AND skirted her fingertips across his jawline. He nipped at her fingers and she smiled, so much happiness filling her she was in serious danger of floating away.

"I've petted cows, fed cows, learned how to ride a horse, *and* I've had really hot sex with a cowboy going on four nights in a row now." She flashed him a big smile. "I think I'm ready for advanced cowgirl training."

His low laugh vibrated through her, adding another layer of happiness, as well as reawakening parts of her that were pleasantly sore from all the cowboy riding. He swept her hair off her face, then tugged her toward him for a kiss. He slanted his mouth over hers, working her into a state of delirium she didn't think could ever be topped.

"What if I told you that you've already tamed this stubborn cowboy? Pretty sure that's as advanced as it gets."

Her heart swelled so much it could hardly fit in her rib cage anymore. "Are you saying you're my cowboy?"

"Damn straight," he said, hugging her to him like he never planned on letting her go. "You're my cowgirl and I'm your cowboy, and that's that."

She loved it when he called her his cowgirl. And while the way he declared things without an ounce of wiggle room often drove her crazy when it came to the rules, she loved when he did it regarding their relationship.

She dropped her head onto his chest and listened to the steady beat of his heart. Felt her own heart echo it, beat for beat.

They argued remarkably less these days, and even their minor arguments ended in kisses and eventually tumbling into this bed again. The past few days had been nothing short of incredible, and as she lay there, Wade's fingers skimming up and down her spine, she started to think thoughts that'd previously seemed impossible.

Maybe he wanted this as much as she did.

Maybe they could find a way to make it work, even after she returned to the city.

After all, two hours wasn't that long. They could travel back and forth. Call in between visits.

Maybe this time she'd found something real, along with a guy who was willing to fight for her.

"Wade?"

"Hmm," he said, his voice sleepy.

She opened her mouth, but she couldn't do it. Not yet. Right now things were so perfect, and her heart was too vulnerable, practically out there on her sleeve already.

Never mind she didn't have sleeves on, which was only another reason to wait. Being rejected would hurt. Being rejected while naked would be devastating.

"I'm just glad that I came here," she said. "That something amazing could come out of something that'd threatened to crush me."

"Nothing could crush you, Jessica Cook. You're too tough for that nonsense."

The compliment warmed her from the inside out, but she couldn't help thinking: *you. You could crush me.*

Then she went from wondering if they could work it out to wondering if she was relying on him too much.

———————

Wade was going to have to wake up Jessica, but he took a moment to soak in the sight of her in his bed, sheets crumpled from last night's roll in them.

He couldn't get enough of her. Of her lips, her laugh, the noises she made when he was buried inside her.

Of having her body wrapped around him as he drifted off to sleep. It was a level of comfort and peace he'd never felt.

Yet she also revved him up and excited him more than any other woman had. She challenged him, too, making him rethink stances he thought he'd never budge on.

Basically, she was perfect.

Maybe she'll want to stay. He wanted to ask her, but he knew it was selfish on his end. She'd said before she didn't belong here, which was ridiculous, but she did have another life in a city. She had Chloe and a job, and he'd caught the tail end of a phone conversation last night where she'd been assuring her boss that she'd get the work done and email him, and that she'd be back in the office before long.

It was easy to love the ranch temporarily, especially in spring. Right now it was a novelty. Baby animals and sunshine. Horse rides and scenery so beautiful it was like stepping into a picture.

Winters were often rough and lengthy. More work and days when they were stuck on the ranch, no getting out to town, no being outside for extended periods.

How long would she truly be happy cooking morning and night for minimum wage? Hell, for food and board. It wasn't an easy life. But it was his life. The land, the animals, even the youth camp were part of his family's legacy. Part of him.

He'd never be rich, and he'd never be able to travel much, and that suited him just fine.

Most women wanted more, and Jessica had already been denied enough after becoming a mother so young.

He wanted to be enough. But he'd already been down this road, and it didn't end well. Actually, that was an understatement. It ended in pain and disappointment, not just for him but for his entire family.

Jessica stirred, and he straightened and walked over to her, extending one of the steaming mugs in his hands. "Mornin.'"

"A girl could get used to this," she said, and his mind went down that dangerous *what-if* path again. She reached for the mug, but her gaze was on his shirtless torso, and she missed the handle by a few inches.

He repositioned it for her, and she gave him a sheepish grin.

"Mmm," she said after taking a sip. "Do I detect the chocolate creamer I like in there?"

"I picked some up when I ran into town yesterday."

"For me?"

"Nah, I just thought I'd start having grossly sweet coffee for the hell of it." He sat next to her and kissed her lips. "Of course for you."

"Thank you. Now maybe I won't fall asleep on my walk to the kitchen. See, this guy's been keeping me up late, giving my body quite the workout."

"You're the one who has the audacity to walk around looking like that." He kissed her again, and when her tongue darted out to touch his, it was like a match to gunpowder. He set his mug on the nightstand, took hers and placed it next to it, and then he crawled over her and kissed her again.

"We're gonna be late," she said, but she hooked her leg around his waist as she said it.

"I'll put in a good word with management."

"Oh, I'm not sure that'll help. Management is really against making exceptions."

"I'll help you make breakfast, then," he mumbled against her lips, and then he reached between them and stroked between her thighs. He swallowed her gasp as she went pliant underneath him, and then they were making love, fast and furious, the urgency he felt driving him to hold her tighter.

To make sure that he didn't take a single second of his time with her for granted.

Chapter 33

JESSICA'S AND CHLOE'S FINAL WEEK AT THE RANCH WAS suddenly here, its loud ticking-clock sensation completely unwelcome.

Since the Dawsons were going to have to advertise for the cook position again, and that meant Kathy would have more to do, Jess spent a lot of extra hours in the kitchen, freezer cooking and stocking up as much as possible.

Kathy kept telling her she didn't need to worry, but that didn't stop her from feeling like she was leaving them in the lurch. If she wasn't going to stay, though—and Wade certainly hadn't asked her to—she wanted to leave them as well-prepared as possible.

While she and Wade still spent most nights together, conversations didn't flow as smoothly. Even their kisses and lovemaking held a frantic edge that worked a wedge between them.

He was distancing her even when he held her close, and she'd instinctively pulled back because she couldn't afford to be out there all alone.

On Friday morning, Jess showed up at Liza's office fifteen minutes early for Chloe's last counseling session. They were going to go over everything she and Chloe could do to help her anxiety and discuss the next steps to ensure Chloe kept on top of it.

The stack of booklets Liza had in the lobby of her office caught Jess's eye, and she picked up one on addiction. Lately she'd formed an addiction—to a guy, not a substance—but she was afraid withdrawal was going to be difficult, and she could use any tips she could get.

"Why are you reading that?" Liza asked, and Jess jumped.

She quickly whipped it behind her, even though it was too late. "No reason."

Liza pursed her lips and gave her the kind of stern-mom look she gave her twins.

"Uh, I mean, so I'm well-informed and prepared. I like learning stuff. Like how I learned to cook and to make awesome friends who let me cling to my denial."

"Cowboys aren't an addiction." Two creases formed between Liza's eyebrows. "That's coming from a former cowboy addict, though, so..." She sighed and stepped closer. "Do you really have to go?"

A giant lump formed in Jess's throat, and she was pretty sure her lungs were caving in on each other. "I promised Chloe."

"Have you asked her if she still wants to leave?"

Jess ran a hand through her hair and let her shoulders sag with the weight she felt more and more of as their time ran out. "If she says she wants to stay, that'd just be another reason why I shouldn't. Not just because of Aiden, but because we're already getting too attached."

A compassionate expression overtook Liza's features as she looked her right in the eye, managing to be soft yet firm at the same time. "It's okay to form attachments."

"I..." It was easy enough to feel like her relationship with Wade was independent from her life with Chloe while her daughter was living in the girls' cabin. But now that she was finishing up her time here, Jess had to focus on what was best for her and Chloe's future. "It's not that simple, and you know it."

"Things that are worthwhile are rarely simple," Liza responded.

Any man Jess pulled into her life needed to stick around. He needed to want to be in not just her life, but her and Chloe's life, and Wade hadn't expressed the desire to be part of their lives past their time here. Not in a long-distance capacity or any other capacity.

In some ways, it was expected. It'd happened plenty in her life, which was why Jess was so glad she'd learned to depend on herself. Sure, there would be days when she was barely fine, but she would be fine.

Chloe walked into the office, and Jess caught her glancing back at Aiden as he headed toward the stables.

After spending time tutoring Aiden, Jess had seen that he was a respectful, straightforward kid who'd had a rough go in life. While she understood why Chloe wanted to be the person to soothe that, he was still a teen boy, and Jess would rather remain cautious. Not to mention Chloe needed to learn how to take care of herself before she tried to fix someone else.

They needed to get back to their life where it was just the two of them, and then they'd decide if they could handle adding more people.

Even if a tiny part of their hearts would be stuck back here at the ranch.

———

It was ridiculous how much sorrow had flooded Chloe's chest as she'd tossed her bag in the trunk of Mom's car a few minutes ago. She'd felt the same hopelessness the day they'd arrived at Turn Around Ranch, sure her life was over. All she'd wanted to do was go back home, back to her life and her friends. She almost wished she still felt that way because it'd make it a lot easier to say goodbye.

Her eyes burned as she walked into the stables, and it wasn't from the smell. She stopped in front of Rowdy's stall, and he automatically trotted over, happy to see her as always. She ran her hand down his long face and peered into those big horse eyes. "Thank you for being such an awesome horse. For listening to my rambling and taking me away for a bit when things got too heavy here."

Yep. Tears were already forming, and she'd only managed to get halfway through saying goodbye to a horse. Izzy had left a few days ago, and while Chloe had hugged her goodbye and her throat had been way too tight, she'd managed to choke back the tears.

But how did she say goodbye to racing across the ranch and afternoons spent brushing down a friend who always listened and never judged her? Equine therapy was something she would've rolled her eyes over before, but after experiencing the lung-loosening effects, she was glad it existed.

Maybe even glad that she'd done something stupid enough to land her here, since it was the first time she'd managed to deal with her anxiety without the mind-numbing effects of weed or alcohol.

Now she had other tools, but she couldn't cram the horse in the trunk—although Mom was bringing one of the kittens, and she was glad they'd have at least one tiny piece of this place.

The sunlight streaming through the entryway dimmed, a shadow figure blocking part of the light for a second or two. Then the figure walked toward her, more details standing out the closer he got. Dark hair, green eyes. Crooked, dimpled grin, although it looked like he had to work hard for it.

"Hey," Aiden said. "They told me I could come say goodbye. We have ten whole minutes before they'll charge in."

Oh crap. More tears pressed against her eyes, hot and multiplying by the second. She wanted to say so much, but if she opened her mouth, she'd cry for sure, and she wasn't sure she'd be able to stop.

Aiden extended his hand, his fingers reaching for hers, and she met him halfway. A warm tear trailed down her cheek, and she gave up on fighting them back.

"I don't want to say goodbye," she croaked. "I already told Rowdy goodbye, and it was too sad, and I don't think I can bear another."

His fingers curled around her palm, and he tugged her in for a hug. "Don't say it, then. I'll write you all the time. You'll be sick of me."

"Impossible." A part of her worried that once she left, Aiden would forget about her, sort of like Tyler had. There'd be messages here and there that would gradually slow to a trickle and then fade away completely.

"I promise I'll never leave you on Read. If you get a random letter and nothing else—like an A or a C or Z—that means they were dragging me away from the computer before I could finish, but I'm thinking about you, and I'll eventually make it back to write more."

"Okay, but just know I'll probably respond with three

letters if you do that, and they'll be *W-T-F*." She hugged him tighter when he laughed. She was funnier around him, and he laughed more, and if she thought about how she might not laugh in a long time, this would only be harder. "I promise the same thing. About always answering."

"If you get busy and it takes you a few days, I'll understand. And if you meet someone else…" The words came out raw, as if he'd had to force them out and despised them as much as she did. "Just be upfront with me. Otherwise, I'll be here waiting for you to visit."

"I'll work on convincing my mom." Chloe wasn't worried she wouldn't want to visit, because Mom had obviously made friends here—she'd never seen her so social or happy. It'd be hard for her to come back, though. She waved it off, but she was as sad to leave Wade as Chloe was to leave Aiden.

This morning Chloe had asked, "What if we stayed? I could do another semester at the school." Somehow she was trying to talk herself *into* summer school, and in that moment she wasn't even sure who she was. Except she did know, and that was why she was willing to make crazy sacrifices.

But Mom had given her a sad smile and said it'd only get harder to leave the longer they stayed, and that she'd already worn out her forced welcome. There was something in there about getting back to work and their lives, and when Chloe asked about Wade, Mom said they always knew it was temporary.

"Two more minutes," a voice called. Brady was apparently their babysitter for their goodbyes.

"Have I told you that I think you're amazing?" Chloe asked, and Aiden ducked his head, his cheeks coloring slightly. How freaking cute was that? It struck her again how opposite he was from Tyler, who would've given a cocky response and treated her like his trophy to show off instead of a real person.

"You sort of terrified me when you first got here," Aiden said, and she snorted a laugh, killing any image of her being tough. "There was the pretty, smart, and funny thing, but that arctic glare you pulled out sometimes…"

She did her best to whip it out, but she was smiling too much for it to be very effective.

Aiden reached up and lightly tugged the ends of her hair, giving her stomach that fresh-from-the-roller-coaster drop. "Just give it to any guy who so much as looks at you, okay?"

She laughed again. "Deal. Because in case you didn't hear, I'm totally into cowboys now."

"I'm hardly a cowboy."

"Keep on telling yourself that, cowboy." She peered up at him, committing every curve and line of his face to memory. "I'll miss you."

"I'll miss you, too."

A loud throat clearing came from near the doorway, and Chloe tipped on to her toes and kissed Aiden before she lost her chance at a proper goodbye.

Wade helped Jess convince the orange tabby into a carrier. "I still can't believe you named your cat Ed of all things."

"Ed *Sheeran*. Like the singer." Jess stuck her finger through the carrier's slats to pat her kitten's head. "You know, because both of them have ginger hair."

"Yeah, that makes it better."

"This from a guy who has dogs named after old cowboy movies."

"*Crocodile Dundee* is hardly a cowboy movie."

"Semantics." It was probably silly to take home a kitten that she'd never be able to look at without thinking about the ranch and Wade and her time here. But Jess had to pour her attachment into something, and Ed Sheeran now came running when he heard her voice. So she'd snuggle him and love him, and he'd never break her heart, not like the cowboy at her side had somehow done, in spite of repeatedly telling herself they only had the here and now.

Sleeping with Wade had made it harder, yet the thought of missing out on those nights also made her ache. Even as he walked her to the car, her suitcase and the extra bag of stuff she'd acquired already crammed in the trunk he'd fixed so it'd latch and stay that way, she wanted him to ask her to stay longer. To tell her they'd find a way to make it work, even though she told herself she was asking too much.

Well, mentally asking too much.

It's for the best. Chloe needs stability.

Home, a familiar school with a broader curriculum so she can quickly catch up and then graduate on time. New friends, Jess hoped. Part of her also worried that punk kid would get his hooks into Chloe, and she'd have to use her newfound skills to hog-tie him. Maybe drag him around in manure.

But as Wade had pointed out, she couldn't put her daughter in a bubble or lock her in a tower.

Unfortunately, she couldn't live in daydream land with Wade forever, either.

Besides, it'd be good for Chloe to face her demons and know that she could slay them.

Jess's throat tightened to the painful point as the staff gathered around. Chloe was in the mix, next to Aiden. They were holding hands, and Jess found she was glad her daughter had someone to hold hands with during this painful goodbye.

"I'll never forget you guys," Jess said. "I can't thank you enough for taking us in, for eating my cooking when it was really bad..."

Chuckles went around the circle.

"For teaching me all about ranch life, from petting cows to feeding them, to driving big trucks and riding horses. I'm even going to miss sitting on a saddle as I order dinners I pretend to make myself."

Liza gave a half laugh, half sob, and Elise asked why she was crying, and the thin thread Jess had on her emotions snapped, the faces around her blurring as tears filled her eyes. "Most of all, thanks for teaching me about acceptance and unconditional friendship and second chances."

She sniffed, and Liza surged forward and hugged her. They made promises of keeping in touch, and then Jess went down the line, giving and accepting hugs. She kissed the twins' cheeks and ran her fingers through their soft hair. She tried not to wobble when Brady patted her hard on the back. Tanya was there next to him, and Jess hugged her, too, before moving on to Kathy.

Kathy whispered kind things in her ear, told her she was welcome anytime, and followed it all up with "Don't be a stranger now, you hear?"

And then she had one last person to hug goodbye.

Everyone backed up a few steps, giving her and Wade a semblance of privacy that really meant they'd be straining harder to hear.

Jess wound her arms around Wade's waist, dropping her head on his chest and taking the chance to inhale the scent of him one last time. Grass and sunshine and diesel and musk and cowboy.

Her cowboy.

She'd hold on to the way he'd called her his cowgirl, even if he hadn't meant it in a permanent way. "Thank you for everything."

His arms finally wrapped around her fully, squeezing and securing and making her ache all over again. "By everything, do you mean voting against hiring you, yelling at you when you got stuck in the mud, and making you so mad you saluted me?"

She laughed, and it came out strangled with tears. "Man, when you put it that way, I guess I should say good riddance."

He pulled back, cupped her cheek, and peered into her eyes. His jaw tightened, and when he brushed his thumb across her cheekbone, it felt like she might crumble to dust and float away.

That was what he reduced her to, and yet she still clung to him.

"You are the most stubborn, beautiful, caring woman I've ever met."

Tell me to stay. Tell me you love me.

She never should've thought the word *love* because it hit her that she'd gone and fallen in love with him. She'd come to him in over her head, and she was leaving the same way.

Wade cleared his throat. "If you ever find yourself in this neck of the woods…"

It was almost the same as asking her to stay, only it fell too short. It was more *if* than *need*.

"Same to you. If you ever find yourself in the city…" Okay, she was being a big, old wimp, doing the same thing. "Goodbye, Wade Dawson."

He nodded, again and again, and then he pulled her into his arms, his embrace tight enough that her toes left the ground. His lips touched hers, a light brush, and she thought that was for the best with their audience and with—

His lips captured hers again, and she clung to him as he moved his mouth over hers, tasting and teasing and then delving his tongue inside. It felt as though he was committing every inch of her to memory, possibly because that was what *she* was doing.

Memorizing the way he held her so tightly as he kissed her. The feel of his callused fingertips on her lower back, where he'd slipped them just underneath the hem of her shirt. Of how he anchored her to him as he kissed her breathless and the rest of the world fell away.

When he lowered her back to her feet, it was completely silent, the cows, dogs, and other animals not even bothering to make a sound.

He didn't say goodbye. He simply opened her door and waited for her to climb inside. Aiden did the same thing to the passenger door, waiting until Chloe was settled and belted in before closing the door.

Chloe reached across and gripped Jess's hand, and Jess held on tight enough that she was cutting off her own circulation.

"We have to wave," Chloe said, tears choking her words.

"I know," Jess said, even though she didn't know how she was going to find the strength to smile and wave.

Reverting to autopilot mode at the same time she shifted

her car into gear, she propped a smile on her lips and waved until the figures in her rearview mirror disappeared in a cloud of dust. Then she took hold of Chloe's hand again, and they cried off and on the entire way home.

Chapter 34

IRRITATION COURSED THROUGH WADE AS HE LOOKED AT the guy occupying the seat opposite the desk he was perched on.

"Wow, you trained at the Colorado Culinary Academy," Ma said, reading from the guy's résumé.

"Yes. Graduated top of my class."

Wade crossed his arms that much tighter. "We're not really interested in fancy dishes here. We like simple. Stuff we can pronounce."

"Give me a menu, and I'll follow it. I do hope I'll be able to make some tweaks and add my own touches. I bet you'll be surprised to find you like having the variety."

Variety was for suckers. Wade liked the same old same, over and over again. When he let something new and amazing into his life, he got used to it, and then it went away, and life seemed dull and pointless. He was sticking with plain and boring from now on.

Ma asked a few more questions, smiling and nodding at the answers, and Wade hoped she wasn't seriously considering hiring the guy.

"What would you do if you burned breakfast?" Wade asked. "Say you burned the biscuits?"

Offense pinched the man's already rigid features. "I'm far too careful to burn food, but I'd make it again. I'd pay for the ingredients since it was my mistake, of course. I also bake these delightful little scones, and just you wait until you taste them."

Scones. Like when he accused Jessica's biscuits of being more like scones, and she told him that proper scones were actually more like American biscuits. How did every single damn thing make him think of her?

"We'll be in touch," Wade said, standing. He was over this interview.

Ma thanked the guy for his time, and the two of them ushered him out to his fancy car that would never survive the daily drive from town if it was rainy or snowy.

Liza sat on the porch swing, and she called the twins to her while the guy backed out. Brady was on the porch, too, hammering a loose rail into place.

"You weren't very friendly," Ma scolded. "That's the first candidate we've had in three weeks, and you practically growled at him the entire time and then showed him the door."

Wade shrugged. "It's not a good fit. He doesn't belong here."

Mom sighed, and Liza leaned forward in the swing, the creak of the chains coming to an abrupt stop. "Sorry to eavesdrop," she said, and he shot her a look, because they both knew she wasn't sorry. "But what Wade means to say is that Jess is the one who belongs here."

"I don't need you to use your fancy degree to take everything I say and tell me what I mean."

"Oh, I don't even need a degree to know what's wrong with you, Wade Dawson." She turned to Everett and Elise. "Kids, can you tell me why Mr. Wade is so grouchy?"

"He's sad about Miss Jessica leaving." Elise grabbed his hand and patted it. "Iss okay. I miss her, too."

Everett wrinkled his nose. "You and Miss Jessica kissed. *A lot.*"

Wade grunted.

"Brady?" Liza turned to his brother. "Care to weigh in?"

"You're downright insufferable, man." Brady dropped the hammer into the old metal toolbox they'd had since the dawn of time. "We all see it, and we all think you should at least call her."

As if Wade hadn't picked up the phone to call her a dozen times. He wanted to hear her voice and to talk to her, but he knew it'd only drag out the misery. With so much of it pumping through his system day in and day out, he needed to get it all out and then move on.

"This is why I never should've gotten involved. I knew everyone would get too attached, just for her to leave." Wade started down the porch steps. "Now if you'll excuse me, I've got a lot of work to do."

"Maybe she wouldn't have left if you'd asked her to stay," Ma said, and he froze in place. Over and over, he told himself that she was always going to leave, end of story. "She's not like Serena, who only liked the idea of the ranch. Jess belongs here, and so does Chloe. Did you tell her that?"

"Or that you wanted to try to make it work?" Liza added, and he couldn't help turning back to face her. "Anything that would give her any indication you cared? That you're in love with her?"

Everyone looked at him now. He wasn't even sure which question to start with, although they all boiled down to the same thing. What good would it have done to pour out his heart and have her leave anyway?

Then again, what good had holding back done? Now he had to wonder over and over *what if*. What if he'd asked her to stay? What if he'd told her he wanted to keep dating her, even if it meant dealing with way too much distance between them?

He'd tried to convince himself he hadn't quite fallen in love, but when Jessica left, a piece of his heart went with her. A big piece that left his heart struggling to beat the way it should. No matter how much work he filled his days with, he saw the lack of her everywhere.

The space between him and Brady in the truck that she no longer filled.

The side of his bed that he'd started to think of as hers.

No one chased the cows around the corral and treated them like overgrown puppies.

He'd strolled in the kitchen so many times only to find it glaringly empty.

Ma was back to juggling too many hats, and that meant he should tell Mr. Fancy-Pants Chef he could have the job. But that would mean admitting Jessica wasn't coming back, and he wasn't ready to do that.

He'd *never* be ready to do that.

"I think he might finally be getting it," his mother said to Liza, and he wondered how many meetings they'd had to discuss it.

"Of course I'm in love with her," he said. "How could I not be? She's funny and smart and beautiful, and she does belong here. She belongs with me."

Brady snapped the toolbox lid closed and stood. "What are you going to do about it?"

Wade looked at his family. Liza and her kids were part of his family now, too, and as many people as they had here on the ranch, they were missing two very important members. It might take him a while to convince Jessica of that, but he couldn't keep going along, pretending he didn't need her in his life.

It wasn't working, and clearly he hadn't been doing a good job of hiding that.

"Do we have her address?" he asked.

A triumphant smile spread across Ma's face. "I've got all the paperwork she filled out tucked away in the office. I'll go get it."

He glanced down at his clothes, dirty from feeding and checking horses and cows. He should probably shower and change, but then it'd get so late, and now that he'd decided to go plead his case, he couldn't wait another minute.

The screech of the screen door he'd never gotten around to greasing up punctured the air, and Ma came out waving a paper. Wade charged up the porch steps, took it from her hands, and hugged her. He reached out and squeezed Liza's hand and then glanced at Brady.

"Will you be okay if I cut out early?"

"Do what you gotta do, man. We'll cover you."

Aiden came around the corner of the porch, and his forehead creased as he took in the scene. He glanced at the paper in Wade's hand, and his eyes widened. "Does this mean…?"

"I'm gonna go get my cowgirl."

"Can I come?" Aiden asked, so much desire coating the words and shining in his features that Wade knew the kid had been as miserable as he had. Then Aiden quickly schooled his features. "Never mind. It's probably a bad idea, and I'm sure you don't want me in the way."

"Hell, considering your girl's at least talking to you, I need your help." Wade clapped Aiden on the back. "Hop in the truck, kid. We've got just over two hours, and you're gonna coach me on what to say to get her back."

Chapter 35

"I saw that," Chloe said after Jess quickly minimized the screen on her laptop. Dang it, she thought she'd been fast enough. Her daughter sat next to her on the couch, a gallon of ice cream and two spoons in her hands.

"Rough day?" Jess asked, nodding at the ice cream.

"No, I just really wanted ice cream."

Jess narrowed her eyes. During the adjustment period with her meds, Chloe said they'd made her feel not exactly like herself because situations that'd normally freak her out didn't as much, but Jess saw more and more of the Chloe she used to be. It was still a daily process, though, one she carefully monitored.

"I promise, Mom. I'm good. Tyler did hit me up yesterday..."

A muscle-clenching mixture of unease and agitation crept across her shoulders, and she did her best to keep her voice level. "And?"

"And I told him that he'd have to go tell his sad story to another girl who'd believe his bullshit. Then I casually mentioned that I needed to go because my boyfriend was calling." Chloe extended a spoon to Jess, and they both dug into the container.

Ed Sheeran jumped up, appearing out of nowhere now that food had been brought out, and Jessica patted her kitty's head and tried to keep him from getting chocolate sauce on his fur. "How is Aiden?"

"He's good. They've had a lot of changeover with people leaving and new teens coming in, so they're crazy busy. With it getting warmer, the grass is getting tall enough they won't have to feed the cows hay much longer, so they'll be changing them to a new pasture. That means Aiden gets to herd the cows on horseback, which he secretly loves." Lovestruck was the best way to describe her daughter's expression. "Silly cowboy who doesn't think he's a cowboy. It's so cute."

With all the talk of the ranch, Jess's heart quickened and splatted in that disconcerting way it did whenever the subject came up. This was what she'd been reduced to— begging for crumbs from her teenage daughter. "Did he say anything about Wade?"

Chloe cocked her head, a hint of pity in the tilt. "Did you want me to ask about him since you're too big of a wimp to just call him?"

"It's called respecting myself. Aretha Franklin sang a whole song about it."

"There are also songs about telling someone you're in love with them. "Say Something," "Into You," "You Belong with Me"… Ed Sheeran, don't you have a few?" Their kitty meowed, and Chloe gestured toward him. "See. Maybe you should listen to some of those."

Jess frowned and waved her spoon at her daughter. "Just eat your ice cream, smarty-pants."

Chloe took a giant bite and then spoke around it. "Go ahead and pull up that website you were looking at again. We both know you want to."

Instead of arguing, Jess gave in and opened up her laptop. This was how she got her fix these days. She pulled up the website to Turn Around Ranch, looked through the pictures, and clicked on the link for the "Cook Needed" job posting to see if it was still there.

The day it disappeared, she'd probably have an ugly crash. At least she'd still have the pictures. The same pictures she'd seen dozens of times but was studying yet again.

I knew I should've brought home one of those addiction booklets. She'd called Liza one night after the twins were asleep, and they'd chatted and it was awesome and painful at the same time.

"If it makes you feel any better," Chloe said. "I miss the ranch, too."

"The ranch or the boy?"

"Yes." Chloe pointed her spoon at Jess. "Same as you, and don't even try to deny it."

Longing wrapped itself around her heart, winding tighter and tighter and making it hard to breathe. "He didn't ask me to stay."

"Did you tell him you wanted to?"

Jess sighed. "You sound like Liza."

"Well, she is super smart and so am I, so that makes sense."

"But we needed to come back home. You needed stability and to face your demons, and I needed to get back to work, and…" There were a hundred reasons why she'd made the right decision, so why did her entire life feel so wrong?

Probably because when they'd arrived back home, it no longer felt like home. She was surrounded by the possessions she'd been so proud of because she'd built this life herself, through a lot of hard work, and yet it seemed so empty.

"Mom, that's a load of crap, and you and I both know it.

You're not working your dream job, and our apartment is nice and all, but home's wherever we go."

"Are you saying *I'm* your home?"

Chloe wobbled her head, obviously not wanting to admit to the mushiness of her statement, but then she shrugged. "That's what it boils down to, yeah. And I'm not a knight who has to complete some quest. My demons aren't my old friends or Tyler, and I have nothing to prove by coming back here. My demons are mental, and I take my brain everywhere I go."

"You right, you right," Jessica said, using one of Chloe's common phrases to lighten the mood. "I hate that you have to deal with anxiety at all. I wish I could take on all your worries and cares so you wouldn't have to."

"You take on plenty. It's a daily struggle, and sometimes I still have to take a break and work on calming down my breathing, but at least now I know how to better deal with it. It's nice knowing that it's part of how my brain works and not that I'm just broken and unable to deal with life."

Jess pulled her into a side hug, resting her head against her daughter's. "You're perfect."

"No, I'm not. And that's okay."

"Look at you, being all wise beyond your years." A little scrolling on her laptop pad, and the link for her old ranch job was front and center. Jess hesitated a second or two and then clicked on it. Clearly, she was not wise beyond her years.

"Fill it out," Chloe said.

"The application?" Honestly, Jess was sort of surprised the ranch was technologically advanced enough to have the online application option, and she wondered if it was something new that they'd put up after she left, or if it'd been there before.

"Yeah. If Wade calls, that means he wants you back. If not, at least you tried."

The logic was sound and gave her a much-needed bravery boost. Her hands still trembled as she moved her fingers over the keyboard, and her nerves tangled themselves into a jumbled-up wad in her gut.

At this point, she figured she didn't have anything to lose—besides her last shred of hope. But what good was it doing her, drowning in how much she missed Wade? Not just him, but everyone on the ranch and the ranch itself.

Ed Sheeran joined in typing as Jess filled out her name, and when she ended up with a dozen extra letters that'd turned her name into Jes;kajdicca Coumjk, Chloe took the kitty and distracted him by tossing a toy mouse filled with catnip.

Then she leaned in and helped fill in the form.

Under experience, Jess put: *To be honest, I've only worked as a cook once before, for barely for six weeks, and I had no clue what I was doing and I sort of burned a lot of stuff, but I was hoping you'd make a BIG OL' EXCEPTION and give me a chance anyway.*

Under education, she put that her cowgirl training was completed under a very strict teacher who never made any exceptions, but that she was now certified in petting calves, driving a stick shift, and riding a horse (for short periods of time and after help with the saddle), and that she was efficient in buying food from local diners when needed.

In the comments section, she added that she also had an assistant chef, who she was hoping they'd make an exception for as well.

"Ooh, add that your assistant is willing to help saddle the horse if needed," Chloe said, and Jess typed it in.

Then every box was filled out, and Jess hovered her finger over the button that'd send it. "This was fun, but I'm not sure it's a good idea. After all, they need an actual cook, and I'm not sure we can truly survive on just food and board. What happens when you want to go to college? My boss isn't going to let me continue working on the side out of the office, either. He was already at the end of his patience when—"

Chloe reached over and clicked the send button. "*Oops,*" she said in an exaggerated way that made it obvious she didn't mean it at all.

At the knock on the door, they looked at each other, as if the other person would know why someone was knocking.

"Were you expecting someone?" Jess asked.

"No. You?"

Jessica shook her head. No one came over. Before she'd had a group of people who'd inserted themselves into her life, she'd thought she liked it that way. She set her spoon on the coffee table, wiped her hands on the thighs of her jeans, and walked to the door. She looked through the peephole, and everything inside her screeched to a halt. Her heart, her lungs, her thoughts.

"Who is it?" Chloe whispered.

Jess forced her limbs into motion and peeked again, thinking that filling out that application had her imagining things. Even though she watched through the tiny circle of distorting glass as Wade lifted an arm to knock again, she still jumped. "It's Wade. Unless I'm hallucinating."

"Well, open it," Chloe said, and Jess smoothed a hand

over her hair and then sucked in a steadying breath, flipped the lock, and twisted the knob.

Her steadying breath was in vain, every ounce of oxygen whooshing out of her as she took him in. Was he taller? More muscular?

He was hotter for sure, his worn jeans hugging his body in a way that made her jealous of pants, his shirt stretched tight across his built chest, and that ever-present hat shading his stormy gray eyes.

Aiden stepped out from behind him and gave her a polite nod. "Hi, Miss Jess."

Chloe was suddenly behind her, nearly shoving her through the open doorway into Wade's arms—where she wanted to be, but she was still trying to put together the fact that he was here, and why was he here, and how broken would her heart be by the end of tonight if he was simply in the city and swinging by?

A squeal escaped Chloe as she threw her arms around Aiden. Jess smiled at how happy they both were and found that her worries over teenage boys were considerably less now that she knew the boy. It helped that Chloe had shown her a lot of his sweet messages and that they were back to being open with each other.

Aiden reached out and smacked Wade's arm, and Wade cleared his throat. "I need to tell you something. A lot of things."

"Okay," Jess said, her mouth bone dry.

"Aiden, how about you and Chloe go inside for a few minutes?"

They started past them, and then Wade snagged Aiden's shirt. "On second thought, you kids stay out here, right under this bright porch light, and I'll go in." Wade's eyes met hers. "As long as that's okay with you."

Jess glanced at Chloe. "Be good."

"You too," Chloe said with a grin.

Then Wade stepped inside her apartment and closed the door, and Jess didn't know what to say or do, and if her pulse beat through her head any faster, she was seriously going to pass out.

"You look good," he said, and warmth swirled through her.

"You do too."

He took a step forward, slowly running his hand down her arm and linking their fingers together. "I miss you, Jessica. I should've told you before you left that I didn't want you to go. I was trying not to be selfish, but now I don't care about being selfish if it means I don't have to be without you. I'm willing to keep us going, even if it means long distance, but the truth is, I think you belong out on the ranch with me—both you and Chloe. Everyone misses you. But I more than miss you. I…" He gripped her hand tighter as he brought it up to his lips and kissed her knuckles. "I need you. I need my cowgirl back. I told myself I wasn't leaving without some kind of assurance we'd find a way to make us work, no matter what it takes."

So many emotions hit her at once, hope and joy and affection. "I miss everyone, too. And I miss the ranch. To be honest, I've been kind of miserable without my cowboy."

A smile spread across his handsome face. "If you need time, I'm willing to wait. If you want to start slow or—"

She threw her arms around her neck and crushed her lips to his.

He wrapped her up in his embrace, deepening the kiss and giving her another reminder of why she'd missed him so much.

"I have a small confession," she said, and he dragged his thumb along her jawline, as if he was making sure she was real. "I just applied for a new job. I was hoping I could use you as a reference."

His eyebrows drew together. "Does this new job bring you closer to the ranch?"

"Really, really close. You'd probably see me every day."

"I'm completely on board, then."

"It's at this place called Turn Around Ranch—not sure if you've heard of it, but apparently they're in need of a cook."

"I heard about that, actually."

"I thought you might've. I'm just a little worried because I asked for a lot of exceptions, and I know for a fact that one of the guys who does the hiring doesn't like to make exceptions."

"Sounds like a real idiot."

She laughed. "He can be pretty stubborn sometimes, but his heart is in the right place." She moved her hand over the center of his chest, where she could feel that very heart beating against her palm.

"I have a confession, too." He wrapped one arm around her waist, securing her to him. "I was gonna throw it out earlier, but I thought I'd better see if you wanted to go slow first. I didn't want to scare you away."

"I'm afraid it's too late to scare me away, and slow sounds...painful." She tipped onto her toes and brushed her lips over his. "Don't you agree?"

"Completely agree—see, look at how well we're getting

along." He kissed her, a way too short kiss, and then he rested his forehead against hers. He exhaled a warm breath, and his gaze locked on hers. "I love you, Jessica Cook."

The words sank in, settling deep inside her soul and mending the part of her that'd felt broken ever since she'd driven away from him. He loved her. He wanted her.

"I know a lot of people have walked away from you in your life, but I'm in this for the long haul. I never want to experience what it's like to be without you again, and if you'll have me, I'm yours."

Jessica's eyes went shiny with tears, and he held on tight. He'd put it all out there, and while he'd been sure she felt the same, he still held his breath.

"I love you, too," she said, and his heart flooded with the knowledge, plugging the gaping hole that the loss of her had left him with. She was coming back to the ranch. They were going to make it work.

She loved him.

She linked her hands behind his neck, bringing her body tight to his as she kissed him. He lowered his hands to her butt, lifting her into his arms and moving his mouth against hers.

"Hey, cowboy?" she murmured against his lips.

"Yes, cowgirl," he said, and she grinned.

"Take me home."

Epilogue

CHLOE BROUGHT ROWDY TO A STOP AT THE SPOT NEXT to the creek where, in a lot of ways, she'd first fallen in love with Turn Around Ranch.

Aiden pulled Koda up next to her, and they shared a grin. Two months ago, she and Mom had moved back to the ranch, and life felt right. Once in a while she'd stop and marvel at how much happiness she'd found in a place that she'd originally called hell.

At how much happiness she'd found with the boy on the horse next to her. It'd taken her a while to convince him he deserved to be happy and that he was good enough for her, but he was finally realizing what a great guy he was.

He dismounted and walked over to help her down, although she didn't exactly need help. She turned in his arms and leaned in for a kiss. He gripped her hips and parted her lips with his, making the most of the limited seconds they had.

Any minute, the teens in the program would be coming through the trees to join them in the open meadow. She and Aiden still didn't get to go many places alone, besides the occasional trek into town. They had plenty of rules and a strict curfew, but it'd gotten a whole thirty minutes later after she'd turned sixteen and regained her mom's trust. It wasn't something she took lightly.

Aiden swept her hair behind her ear, affection swimming in the depths of his green eyes. He made her feel so cared for. When the storms of anxiety began roiling and gathering strength, he helped calm them. "I love you, Chloe. I just wanted you to know."

Sunshine spread through her chest, warmer than the summer rays beating down on them. She wound her arms around his waist and lowered her head onto his chest. "I love you, too."

The rest of the horses and teens broke the tree line, and they stepped apart but kept their fingers laced together. A few of the friends she'd made in the program, like the Double D's, were still on the ranch, working on the issues that'd brought them here. But there were also several new people, along with a girl named Alyssa, who reminded Chloe a lot of herself. She missed Izzy, but they kept in touch through messages, and she was due to visit early next month so she could get the extra boost she'd need to face the school year.

"By the way," Aiden said, "I think Wade's gonna ask your mom to marry him. He kept patting his pocket on our ride back from the city, and I swear it looked like a ring box."

Chloe smiled. "He's been asking me about her favorite foods and places, so I figured he was up to something." It was about time, honestly. No one knew when or if Nash would come back, which meant they couldn't really decorate or settle, and they'd been talking about moving in with Wade for a while. It was for more than just logistical reasons. Mom and Wade were ready for the next step. But Mrs. Dawson was old school, and she'd rather they be married before they live together. Not that it was the only reason Wade would ask, but Mom deserved a little traditional after a very nontraditional start.

Suddenly, Chloe's smile faded as a new thought took over. "I just realized something."

"Yeah?"

"If you're Wade's brother and they get married, then…" She didn't finish, but his scrunched-up expression made it clear he got where she was going. "I'm just gonna pretend that's not a thing. We met at the same time, so…"

"I'm fully on board with denial."

Jess reached over and grabbed Wade's hand as they watched the seconds tick down on the timer. There was that saying about how a watched pot never boiled, but she'd watched one start boiling from across the kitchen, and even though she'd sprinted to catch it, it'd not only boiled but boiled over and created a huge mess on the burner, so she thought that saying was crap.

"It's okay either way," Wade said, slipping his fingers between hers. The diamond engagement ring on her finger caught the light, yet another reminder of how big and life-changing the past month had been. "I'm happy with our life. Happy with you and Chloe and Aiden."

This was so different from the first time she'd taken a pregnancy test. Since she'd had a supportive guy—make that a supportive *fiancé*—by her side for over three months now, she should be less nervous, but drunken butterflies still swerved and crashed together inside her stomach. There was a tingling undercurrent of excitement, too, one she worked to keep under control in case… Well, she wasn't even sure what outcome to wish for.

She'd been in the middle of wedding-planning madness with Kathy and Liza when she realized she was late. By a few weeks. Then she'd had to keep a poker face because she didn't want Wade finding out from his family, who would immediately get carried away, and now she was back to nervous.

A big part of her had never thought she'd have another baby.

For a long time, she'd felt complete with just her and Chloe. *Fine*, as she'd once told Wade.

Now her life was better than fine, filled with friends and almost in-laws she worked with on a daily basis and a fiancé she couldn't stop kissing.

Speaking of… Jess leaned over and kissed him. The remaining two minutes were gonna pass either way, so they might as well pass them kissing.

The timer *bing*ed, and she dropped her head against Wade's shoulder. "You look. It's too much pressure."

"It's not a test you pass or fail. It's just…"

"Our future?"

He laughed. "What exactly our future entails—we already know it's gonna be awesome because we're going to face it together." The couch cushions shifted as he scooted forward. He exhaled a heavy breath, and that ringing silence that she'd only heard out here on the ranch buzzed through her.

She lifted her head, and Wade grinned at her.

Tears filled her eyes. She couldn't help it. "We're gonna have a little cowboy or cowgirl?"

He nodded, and his words came out thick with emotion. "We're gonna have a baby."

Happiness flooded her, and she flung her arms around her sexy fiancé.

The door swung open, and Chloe and Aiden walked in. They paused, undoubtedly sensing something different in the air.

"Sorry, we were just going to grab a snack and"—Chloe's eyes went wide—"O-M-G, is that a pregnancy test?"

Jess nodded, figuring there was no use in hiding it now, and honestly, she'd never make it more than a few hours before spilling the news to Chloe anyway. "We're having a baby."

Chloe squealed and then tackle hugged her. "I'm gonna be the best older sister, just you wait."

"I have no doubt."

"And I'm gonna be the best uncle," Aiden said, and the kids frowned at each other, the way they always did when they discussed how weird figuring out titles was going to be once their families had merged.

"Dude, we're gonna sound like the biggest hicks to other people." Chloe rolled onto the couch on Jess's other side and kicked her feet up on the coffee table. "Maybe we shouldn't bother explaining about how Aiden's adopted and you guys got married *after* he and I started dating and just freak them out."

Jess laughed. "Hey, we've never done things the normal way. Why start now?"

No, none of her plans for life had gone the way she'd originally intended, and as she sat there with her family, more love and happiness filling her than she even knew was possible, she was grateful for all the wrong turns she'd taken that'd led her to right where she belonged.

Acknowledgments

Huge thanks to Deb Werksman for saying yes to my new series, for giving it a home with Sourcebooks Casablanca, and for being so lovely to work with. Thanks to the entire team at Sourcebooks, from marketing to publicity to content and to anyone who helps in the process of getting my books from my computer into the hands of readers.

I'm so grateful for my agent, Nicole Resciniti, for not only understanding the vision I had for my career, but also pushing my goals to be even bigger and then helping me reach them. I adore you.

I can't thank Aaron Huey and the rest of the staff at Fire Mountain Residential Treatment Center enough for letting me come in and ask questions and check out the treatment center. They do such amazing things for struggling teens, and the Beyond Risk and Back podcasts were also great help and something I highly recommend to parents of tweens and teens. Thanks to the teens at Fire Mountain who let me have lunch with them while I asked a bunch of questions for my book. I made sure to add your "aggressive dance party" to the book as promised.

To my daughter, thank you for letting me use some of our experiences learning about and finding tools to deal with your anxiety in my book. You are brave and amazing, and I'm so proud at the way you've used those tools to help others. My whole family deserves all the thanks for putting up with deadline brain and burned meals and the times I'm locked in my office for hours on end. Thank goodness I have a husband who helps me juggle everything and has been my biggest supporter from the beginning. Michael, I couldn't do it without you.

Gina L. Maxwell and Rebecca Yarros, words cannot express my adoration for you both. Thank you for the plot calls and the catchup calls and for being my lifesavers in writing and in life.

Thanks, dear readers, whether this is the first book of mine you've read or if you've read dozens, I appreciate every single one of you. You make dreams come true.

About the Author

Cindi Madsen is a *USA Today* bestselling author of contemporary romance and young adult novels. She sits at her computer every chance she gets, plotting, revising, and falling in love with her characters. Sometimes it makes her a crazy person. Without it, she'd be even crazier. She loves music and dancing, and wishes summer lasted all year long. She lives in Colorado (where summer is most definitely *not* all year long) with her husband and three children.

Read on for an excerpt of

CAUGHT UP
in a
COWBOY

by Jennie Marts

Chapter 1

BITS OF GRAVEL FLEW BEHIND THE TIRES OF THE CON-
vertible, and Rockford James swore as he turned onto the
dirt road leading to the Triple J Ranch. Normally, he enjoyed
coming home for a visit, especially in the late spring when
everything was turning green and the wildflowers were in
bloom, but not this spring—not when he was coming home
with both his pride and his body badly injured.

His spirits lifted and the corners of his mouth tugged up
in a grin as he drew even with what appeared to be a pirate
riding a child's bicycle along the shoulder of the road. A
gorgeous female pirate—one with long blond hair and great
legs.

Legs he recognized.

Legs that belonged to the only woman who had ever
stolen his heart.

Nine years ago, Quinn Rivers had given him her heart as well. Too bad he'd broken it. Not exactly broken—more like smashed, crushed, and shattered it into a million tiny pieces. According to her anyway.

He slowed the car, calling out as he drew alongside her. Her outfit consisted of a flimsy little top that bared her shoulders under a snug corset vest and a short, frilly striped skirt. She wore some kind of sheer white knee socks, and one of them had fallen and pooled loosely around her ankle. "Ahoy there, matey. You lose your ship?"

Keeping her eyes focused on the road, she stuck out her hand and offered him a gesture unbecoming of a lady—pirate or otherwise. Then her feet stilled on the pedals as she must have registered his voice. "Ho-ly crap. You have got to be freaking kidding me."

Bracing her feet on the ground, she turned her head, brown eyes flashing with anger. "And here I thought my day couldn't get any worse. What the hell are you doing here, Rock?"

He stopped the car next to her, then draped his arm over the steering wheel, trying to appear cool. Even though his heart pounded against his chest from the fact that he was seeing her again. She had this way of getting under his skin; she was just so damn beautiful. Even wearing a pirate outfit. "Hey, now. Is that any way to speak to an old friend?"

"I don't know. I'll let you know when I run into one."

Ouch. He'd hoped she wasn't still that bitter about their breakup. They'd been kids, barely out of high school. But they'd been together since they were fourteen, his conscience reminded him, and they'd made plans to spend their future together.

But that was before he got the full-ride scholarship and the NHL started scouting him.

And he had tried.

Yeah, keep telling yourself that, buddy.

Okay, he probably hadn't tried hard enough. But he'd been young and dumb and swept up in the fever and glory of finally having his dreams of pursuing a professional hockey career coming true.

With that glory came attention and fame and lots of travel with the team where cute puck bunnies were ready and willing to show their favorite players a good time.

He hadn't cheated on Quinn, but he came home less often and didn't make the time for texts and calls. He'd gone to college first while she finished her senior year, and by the time he did come home the next summer, he'd felt like he'd outgrown their relationship, and her, and had suggested they take a mini break.

Which turned into an *actual* break, of both their relationship and Quinn's heart.

But it had been almost nine years since he'd left; they'd been kids, and that kind of stuff happened all the time. Since then, he hadn't made it home a lot and had run into her only a handful of times. In fact, he probably hadn't seen her in over a year.

But he'd thought of her. Often. And repeatedly wondered if he'd made the right choice by picking the fame and celebrity of his career and letting go of her.

Sometimes, those summer days spent with Quinn seemed like yesterday, but really, so much had happened—in both of their lives—that it felt like a lifetime ago.

Surely she'd softened a little toward him in all that time.

"Let me offer you a lift." The dirt road they were on led to both of their families' neighboring ranches.

"No thanks. I'd rather pedal this bike until the moon comes up than take a ride from you."

Yep. Still mad, all right.

Nothing he could do if she wanted to keep the grudge fest going. Except he was tired of the grudge. Tired of them being enemies. She'd been the best friend he'd ever had. And right now, he felt like he could use a friend.

His pride had already been wounded; what was one more hit? At least he could say he tried.

Although he didn't want it to seem like he was trying too hard. He did still have a *little* pride left, damn it.

"Okay. Suit yourself. It's not *that* hot out here." He squinted up at the bright Colorado sun, then eased off the brake, letting the car coast forward.

"Wait." She shifted from one booted foot to the other, the plastic pirate sword bouncing against her curvy hip. "Fine. I'll take a ride. But only because I'm desperate."

"You? Desperate? I doubt it," he said with a chuckle. Putting the car in Park, he left the engine running and made his way around the back of the car. He reached for the bike, but she was already fitting it into the back seat of the convertible.

"I've got it." Her gaze traveled along the length of his body, coming to rest on his face, and her expression softened for the first time. "I heard about the fight and your injury."

He froze, heat rushing to his cheeks and anger building in his gut. Of course she'd heard about the fight. It had made the nightly news, for Pete's sake. He was sure the whole town of Creedence had heard about it.

Nothing flowed faster than a good piece of gossip in a small town. Especially when it's bad news—or news about the fall of the hometown hero. Or the guy who thought he was better than everyone else and bigger than his small-town roots, depending on who you talked to and which camp they fell into. Or what day of the week it was.

You could always count on a small town to be loyal.

Until you let them down.

"I'm fine," he said, probably a little too sternly, as he opened the car door, giving her room to pass him and slide into the passenger seat. He sucked in a breath as the scent of her perfume swept over him.

She smelled the same—a mix of vanilla, honeysuckle, and home.

He didn't let himself wonder if she felt the same. No, he'd blown his chances of that ever happening again a long time ago. Still, he couldn't help but drop his gaze to her long, tanned legs or notice the way her breasts spilled over the snug, corseted vest of the pirate costume.

"So, what's with the outfit?" he asked as he slid into the driver's seat and put the car in gear.

She blew out her breath in an exaggerated sigh. A loose tendril of hair clung to her damp forehead, and he was tempted to reach across the seat to brush it back.

"It's Max's birthday today," she said, as if that explained everything.

He didn't say anything—didn't know what to say.

The subject of Max always was a bit of an awkward one between them. After he'd left, he'd heard the rumors of how Quinn had hooked up with a hick loser named Monty Hill who'd lived one town over. She'd met him at a party and it had been a rebound one-night stand, designed to make him pay for breaking things off with her, if the gossip was true.

But she'd been the one to pay. Her impulse retaliation had ended in an unplanned pregnancy with another jerk who couldn't be counted on to stick around for her. Hill had taken off, and Quinn had ended up staying at her family's ranch.

"He's eight now." Her voice held the steely tone of anger, but he heard the hint of pride that also crept in.

"I know," he mumbled, more to himself than to her. "So, you decided to dress up like a pirate for his birthday?"

She snorted. "No. Of course not. One of Max's favorite books is *Treasure Island*, and he wanted a pirate-themed party, so I *hired* a party company to send out a couple of actors to dress up like pirates. The outfits showed up this morning, but the actors didn't. Evidently, there was a mix-up in the office, and the couple had been double-booked and were already en route to Denver when I called."

"So you decided to fill in." He tried to hold back his grin.

She shrugged. "What else was I going to do?"

"That doesn't explain the bike."

"The bike is his main gift. I ordered it from the hardware store in town, but it was late and we weren't expecting it to come in today. They called about an hour ago and said it had shown up, but they didn't have anyone to deliver it. I was already in the pirate getup, so I ran into town to get it."

"And decided to ride it home?"

"Yes, smart-ass. I thought it would be fun to squeeze onto a tiny bike dressed in a cheap Halloween costume and enjoy the bright, sunny day by riding home." She blew out another exasperated breath. "My stupid car broke down on the main road."

"Why didn't you call Ham or Logan to come pick you up?" he asked, referring to her dad and her older brother.

"Because in my flustered state of panic about having to fill in as the pirate princess and the fear that the party would be ruined, I left my phone on the dresser when I ran out of the house. I was carrying the dang bike, but it got so heavy, then I tried pushing it, and that was killing my back, so I thought it would be easier and faster if I just tried to ride it the last mile back to the ranch."

"Makes sense to me." He slowed the car, turning into the long driveway of Rivers Gulch. White fences lined the drive, and several head of cattle grazed on the fresh green grass of the pastures along either side of the road.

The scent of recently mown hay skimmed the air, mixed with the familiar smells of plowed earth and cattle.

Seeing the sprawling ranch house and the long, white barn settled something inside of him, and he let out a slow breath, helping to ease the tension in his neck. He'd practically grown up here, running around this place with Quinn and her brother, Logan.

Their families' ranches were within spitting distance of each other; in fact, he could see the farmhouse of the Triple J across the pasture to his left. They were separated only by prime grazing land and the pond that he'd learned to swim in during the summer and skate on in the winter.

The two families had an ongoing feud—although he wasn't sure any of them really knew what they were fighting about anymore, and the kids had never cared much about it anyway.

The adults liked to bring it up, but they were the only kids around for miles, and they'd become fast friends—he and his brothers sneaking over to Rivers Gulch as often as they could.

This place felt just as much like home as his own did. He'd missed it. In the years since he'd left, he'd been back only a handful of times.

His life had become so busy, his hockey career taking up most of his time. And after what happened with Quinn, neither Ham nor Logan was ever too excited to see him. Her mom had died when she was in grade school, and both men had always been overprotective of her.

He snuck a glance at her as he drove past the barn. Her wavy hair was pulled back in a ponytail, but wisps of it had come loose and fell across her neck in little curls. She looked good—really good. A thick chunk of regret settled in his gut, and he knew letting her go had been the biggest mistake of his life.

It wasn't the first time he'd thought it. Images of Quinn haunted his dreams, and he often wondered what it would be like now if only he'd brought her with him instead of leaving her behind. If he had her to wave to in the stands at his games or to come home to at night instead of an empty house. But he'd screwed that up, and he felt the remorse every time he returned to Rivers Gulch.

He'd been young and arrogant—thought he had the world by the tail. Scouts had come sniffing around when he was in high school, inflating his head and his own self-importance. And once he started playing in the big leagues, everything about this small town—including Quinn—had just seemed...well...small. Too small for a big shot like him.

He was just a kid—and an idiot. But by the time he'd realized his mistake and come back for her, it was too late.

Hindsight was a mother.

And so was Quinn.

Easing the car in front of the house, he took in the festive balloons and streamers tied to the railings along the porch. So much of the house looked the same—the long porch that ran the length of the house, the wooden rocking chairs, and the swing hanging from the end.

They'd spent a lot of time on that swing, talking and laughing, his arm around her as his foot slowly pushed them back and forth.

She opened the car door, but he put a hand on her arm and offered her one of his most charming smiles. "It's good to see you, Quinn. You look great. Even in a pirate outfit."

Her eyes widened, and she blinked at him, for once not having a sarcastic reply. He watched her throat shift as she swallowed, and he yearned to reach out to run his fingers along her slender neck.

"Well, thanks for the lift." She turned away and stepped out of the car.

Pushing open his door, he got out and reached for the bicycle, lifting it out of the back seat before she had a chance. He carried it around and set it on the ground in front of her. "I'd like to meet him. You know, Max. If that's okay."

"You would?" Her voice was soft, almost hopeful, but still held a note of suspicion. "Why?"

He ran a hand through his hair and let out a sigh. He'd been rehearsing what he was going to say as they drove up to the ranch, but now his mouth had gone dry. The collar of his cotton T-shirt clung to his neck, and he didn't know what to do with his hands.

Dang. He hadn't had sweaty palms since he was in high

school. He wiped them on his jeans. He was known for his charm and usually had a way with women, but not this woman. This one had him tongue-tied and nervous as a teenager.

He shoved his hands in his pockets. "Listen, Quinn. I know I screwed up. I was young and stupid and a damn fool. And I'm sorrier than I could ever say. But I can't go back and fix it. All I can do is move forward. I miss this place. I miss having you in my life. I'd like to at least be your friend."

She opened her mouth, and he steeled himself for her to tell him to go jump in the lake. Or worse. But she didn't. She looked up at him, her eyes searching his face, as if trying to decide if he was serious. "Why now? After all these years?"

He shrugged, his gaze drifting as he stared off at the distant green pastures. He'd let this go on too long, let the hurt fester. It was time to make amends—to at least try. He looked back at her, trying to express his sincerity. "Why not? Isn't it about time?"

She swallowed again and gave a small nod of her head.

A tiny flicker of hope lit in his gut as he waited for her response. He could practically *see* her thinking—watch the emotions cross her face in the furrow of her brow and the way she chewed on her bottom lip. Oh man, he loved it when she did that; the way she sucked her bottom lip under her front teeth always did crazy things to his insides.

"Okay. We can *try* being friends." She gave him a side-long glance, the hint of a smile tugging at the corner of her mouth. "On one condition."

Uh-oh. Conditions are never good. Although he would do just about anything to prove to her that he was serious about being in her life again.

"What's that?"

"I need someone to be the other pirate for the party. I already asked Logan if he would wear the other costume, and he refused. I was planning to ask Dad, but I have a feeling I'll get the same response."

He tried to imagine Hamilton Rivers in a pirate outfit and couldn't. Ham was old-school cowboy, tough as nails and loyal to the land. He wore his boots from sunup to sundown and had more grit than a sheet of sandpaper. The only soft spot he had was for his daughter. And Rock had broken her heart.

If there hadn't been enough animosity between the two families over their land before, Rock had sealed the feud by walking away from Quinn.

And now he had a chance to try to make it up to her. And to keep an eight-year-old kid from being disappointed. Even if it meant making a fool of himself.

He squinted one eye closed and tilted his head. If he was going to do it, might as well do it right.

Go big or go home.

"Aye, lass," he said in his best gruff pirate impression. "I'll be a pirate for ye, but don't cross me, or I'll make ye walk the plank."

Her eyes widened, and she laughed before she could stop herself. An actual laugh. Well, more like a small chuckle, but it was worth it. He'd talk in a pirate accent all afternoon if it meant he could hear her laugh again.

She took a step forward, reached out her hand as if to touch his arm, then let it drop to her side. "All right, Captain Jack, you don't have to go that far." She might not have touched him, but she offered him a grin—a true grin.

Yeah, he could be a pirate. He could be whatever she needed. Or he could dang well try.

The front door slammed open with a bang, and Quinn jumped. As if on cue, her brother stepped out on the front porch.

Anger sparked in Logan's eyes as he glared at Rock. "What the hell are you doing here?"

Chapter 2

Quinn was thinking the same thing.

What the hell was Rockford James doing standing in front of her? And offering to fill in as the pirate at her son's birthday party, no less.

But the righteous indignation was hers to carry, and she held up a hand to her brother. "Rock gave me a ride home. That stupid car broke down again, and I would have had to walk the whole way if he hadn't stopped to give me a lift."

"Why didn't you call me?"

"I forgot my phone."

He gave a grudging nod to Rock. "Well, we've got it from here. Thanks." He pulled the screen door open, then turned back and mumbled, "Sorry to hear about your head. That guy was an asshole."

She felt Rock stiffen beside her. He obviously didn't like to talk about it. But she was glad to see her brother being civil—maybe this could be the start of a truce between the Rivers and James families. She tried to keep a light tone in her voice. "Rock is coming to the party. He's going to help out by filling in as the other pirate."

Her brother raised an eyebrow, then shook his head, any remnants of a truce disappearing behind his scowl. "Like hell he is. We don't need another pirate. And we dang sure don't need *his* help."

Leaving the bike on the porch, she automatically reached for Rock's hand and pulled him up the stairs. "Too bad. He's

staying. Max wants a pirate, and I'm giving him a pirate."
The nerve of her brother, telling her what to do. She fought
to hold back the eye roll. He was only two years older than
she was, but she'd always be his baby sister. Annoying.

It wasn't until they had stepped onto the porch that she
realized she was holding Rock's hand. The shock of touching
his skin and having her hand in his after all these years took
her breath away. His fingers curled around hers, making her
hyperaware of the wall of male standing next to her.

"You heard the lady," Rock said with a smirk.

She led him through the house and into her bedroom,
where the other costume was. It was strange having him in
her room again.

He looked around with interest. "Wow, you're still in
your old bedroom. You've changed it up though. Got rid of
the pom-poms and the boy band posters."

Pushing the door shut with her foot, she dropped his
hand as if it were on fire. "That's because I'm an adult now.
And a mom. I have my own boy, and he's the one I cheer
for."

Memories of Rock being in this room with her flooded
her mind, and her heart ached at flashes of recollection.
Lying on the floor as they listened to music or worked on
homework, curled on her bed kissing and touching in the
frantic way that teenagers discover each other. The pictures
in her head were as clear as if they had happened yesterday.

But they hadn't. She pushed the memories away—back
into the spaces where she kept them, sealed off so they
couldn't hurt her. That was the past. She needed to focus on
the present, on Max and the birthday party that was going
to start any minute now.

She pointed to the pirate costume laid out across her bed. The outfit consisted of a thin muslin shirt, a faux leather vest, and a pair of brown, striped pants. A long scarf served as a belt, with a black hat and a sword completing the costume.

"You can put that on. The guests will be here anytime, so we've got to be ready. If the pants don't fit, just wear your jeans." She glanced at his thighs, thick and muscular from years of ice skating. "Yeah, you should probably just wear your jeans."

He chuckled as he reached for the hem of his T-shirt and tugged it over his head.

She sucked in her breath.

Holy hot cowboy. The guy's chest was a solid mass of muscle.

The last time she'd seen him without a shirt, they'd been teenagers. He wasn't a teenager now. He was a man with a man's body.

The muscles in his arms flexed as he tossed the shirt onto the bed, and she almost choked at the size of them. He had the body of an athlete, toned and firm. A tattoo of his team's logo covered the top part of his right arm. She hadn't known he'd gotten a tattoo.

She didn't really know anything about him anymore. Just the bits of gossip around town and the occasional stories she heard about him from his family or on one of the sports channels on TV. She wouldn't admit it to anyone else, but she'd seen several of his games, watching him when he was on the ice and searching the player's box for glimpses of him when he wasn't.

She tried to look away but was mesmerized by his body, so foreign yet so familiar. Her gaze traveled over him, discovering new scars and marks that hadn't been there before, that he must have earned in his years on the ice.

His hair was still a little too long, curling along his neck, but it had darkened to a dirty-blond color, and his eyes were still the same greenish blue. She'd always thought they were the same color as the pond they learned to swim in, a mixture of the shades, depending on his mood or what color clothes he was wearing.

There were so many new things about him, yet he still felt like the same guy that she'd grown up with—the one who'd shown her how to ride a horse, who'd tutored her in chemistry, and who had taught her how to French kiss. And he'd been quite a teacher.

He reached for the shirt on the bed, turning slightly, and she gasped at the mass of ugly purple bruising down the side of his rib cage. She reached out as if to touch him, heard his sharp intake of breath as her fingers barely skimmed his side, and quickly dropped her hand.

"Is that from the—" She didn't want to bring up the fight again. Apparently, she didn't have to.

A scowl settled on his face, and he swiped at the discoloration as if to wipe it away. "Yeah, I guess. It's no big deal though—just a few bruises. We're always getting banged up. These are already starting to fade."

They didn't look like they were starting to fade. But the subject obviously made him uncomfortable, so she let it go and concentrated on a problem that had just surfaced in her mind. "They didn't send along any boots or shoes."

He pulled the shirt over his head. It was snug, hugging his muscled chest and stretching over his thick upper arms. "My boots will do fine."

She glanced down at his leather, square-toed cowboy boots. "A pirate wearing cowboy boots?" Oh geez—that sounded kind of hot, especially when the cowboy/pirate was Rock.

Stop it. This was the man who'd broken her heart—who'd left her behind. She wasn't about to fall victim to his charming grin and a few well-toned muscles.

He tugged on the vest and picked up the long, red scarf, a baffled look on his face. "What do I do with this?"

"You tie it around your waist. Like a belt." She sighed at his blank look and took the scarf. Sliding her arms around him, she wrapped the scarf around his waist and tied it in a knot at his hip. Her hands shook a little as they brushed over his hard abs, their solidness visible through the thin shirt.

Taking a step back, she picked up the sword from the bed and passed it to him. They needed to get out of her bedroom. She could try to push the memories away, but the ghosts of them as a couple—as young lovers—were thick. As if their souls were floating in the air, taking up all the space and making it hard for her to breathe.

The sound of a truck coming up the driveway pulled Quinn from her thoughts. Thank goodness. The guests were starting to arrive.

The door of her room burst open, and Max rushed in. "Mom! Mom! They're here! Come on! The party is starting!" He grabbed her arm and pulled, then stopped when he caught sight of Rock.

He pushed his small glasses up his nose and grinned at her. Her heart did that gushy mom thing it did every time her son smiled because she'd gotten something exactly right. "You found a pirate."

That smile on her son's face made every awkward moment with Rock worth it. "Yep, this is Captain…um… James." That was original. She gave Rock a small shrug of her shoulders, hoping he would play along. "He sailed the seven seas to be here for your birthday party today."

Max's eyes widened as he looked at Rock. "You're a pretty big pirate," he whispered.

Rock puffed out his chest and lowered his voice, affecting a deep, pirate accent. "Aye. That's from spending so much time working aboard me ship, matey. I heard some scallywag named Max was having a party, and I thought I'd stop by for some rum." He glanced up at Quinn. "Er, I mean some grog. You got any grog, boy, or am I going to have to make you swab the poop deck?"

"You said 'poop.'" Max dissolved into giggles as Rock wielded his plastic sword in the air. "You're funny."

He *was* funny. Was he seriously *still* doing a pirate voice?

She tried to keep from laughing, but the sound of Max's giggles was too much. Shaking her head, she looked down at her son. "Why don't you go say hello to your guests, and I'll try to find the Captain here some *grog*."

"Okay, Mom." Max offered Rock a wave, then raced from the room. "See ya later, Captain James."

"Nice work, matey," she said, trying to mimic his accent as she held the door for him. "You think you can keep it up long enough to entertain a dozen hyper eight-year-olds?"

"Aye. I love a challenge." He crossed the room, stopping behind her and lowering his voice as he leaned closer to her ear. "And might I add, ye've got the finest pirate booty I've ever laid me eyes on."

She raised an eyebrow, trying to hold in a laugh. "Are you seriously flirting with me using pirate lingo?"

He winked and gave her a sharp nod of his head. "Aye, me beauty. Would you like to shiver me timbers?"

Her eyes widened, but even he couldn't hold a straight face for that one, and they busted out laughing.

It had been a long time since they'd laughed like that together.

It felt good. Right.

He held up his hands in surrender. "Sorry. That one went too far. It sounded better in my head."

"Keep that up, and you're gonna be the one walking the plank." She tried to sound gruff but couldn't quite pull it off. With a slow smile, she turned and headed for the kitchen, ignoring the butterflies careening around in her stomach at the fact that not only was Rock in her bedroom again, but he was flirting with her—and she kind of liked it.

Three hours, seventeen cupcakes, and three water-balloon fights that Rock instigated later, she sank onto the bench seat of the picnic table.

He dropped down next to her and pulled off his pirate hat. The scent of his aftershave wafted around her, and his thigh came dangerously close to touching hers. His hair was tousled from the hat and the warm day, and she had the strongest urge to reach out and smooth it down.

Her dad and Max had left to take the last of the kids home, and the scent of grilled hot dogs and sunscreen lingered in the air.

She'd thought her dad would have a coronary when he saw Rock at the party, but she told him he was doing it for

Max and to chill out. Ham had grunted, and the two men had mainly stayed out of each other's way.

"Wow. You were right. Eight-year-olds are tough." He puffed out a breath, sounding more like he'd gone into triple overtime instead of wrangling up a group of rowdy children.

"You were pretty great with them." Surprisingly great. She'd had no idea he could work a crowd like that. He was funny and charming, and he'd had the kids and half of the parents eating out of his hand. Especially the moms.

One of the kid's moms fell all over herself trying to help Rock pass out the cupcakes.

And speaking of falling, if Carolyn Parker had displayed any more of her cleavage, her boobs would have popped right out of her top. Not very becoming of the PTA president and self-professed "room mom."

The moms were bad enough, preening around Rock, but the dads were just as ridiculous, trying to act cool and buddy up with him. So what if he was a famous hockey player and on television? He was still the same guy that half of them had gone to school with. Why were they treating him like such a celebrity?

Because he was. He wasn't just *some* hockey player. He was Rockford James, the star, the hockey-playing cowboy and a major player on the Colorado team. A team he was going back to, she reminded herself.

"They were fun." Rock's deep voice rumbled through her and dragged her out of her musings. "And I do have *some* skills." He nudged her leg and cocked an eyebrow. "But I do my best work when I'm not in front of a crowd."

She shook her head, the start of a smile tugging at her lip. "You're awful."

"Awful handsome for a pirate, you mean?" He flashed her one of his charming grins, teasing her as he bumped her leg with his again, then leaving his knee lightly against hers.

She could feel the heat of his skin, even through his jeans. The cotton texture of the denim rubbed against her bare leg, causing her earlier butterflies to return, swooping and swirling wildly in her belly.

Was he flirting with her? Or just laying on the charm like he'd been doing all afternoon with the other guests? Ugh. The very thought of him flirting with Carolyn Parker made her stomach go sour.

What was that about?

Actually, she knew what it was about.

The green-eyed monster was rearing its ugly head, and she didn't like it. Not one bit. She wasn't usually jealous. But who would she have to be jealous of? So much of her life was spent focused on her role as a mom: laundry, bath time, making lunches, tucking Max in at night, and reading books with him. So many books. That kid loved to read and loved being read to.

She didn't have time to think about men or flirting. Not until now, when she had Rock James sitting in front of her, the ridiculously cute guy she'd loved for half of her life, the one whose leg now pressed snugly against hers as he'd somehow moved even closer.

And the one who had torn her heart to shreds when he'd broken up with her.

No matter how cute and charming he was, there was still that.

She sighed. "What are you doing here, Rock?"

His playful grin fell, but before he had a chance to

answer, her brother walked up holding a chocolate cupcake and leaned his hip against the edge of the picnic table next to her.

"Looks like you two were the hit of the party," Logan said. "Your picture will probably make tomorrow's news as the pirate couple of the year."

"What are you talking about?" she asked.

"Didn't you see Carolyn Parker taking pictures of you guys? I'm sure you'll be in tomorrow's edition of the *Creedence Chronicle*. She just got hired on there and is trying to start some new section like the society pages. I'll wager that you'll be her feature story." He peeled back the wrapper of the cupcake and took a bite. "Unless she sells the pictures to that reporter who was lurking out front earlier," he said around a mouthful of cake.

Rock's head snapped up. "What reporter?"

CAUGHT UP IN
A COWBOY

USA Today bestselling author Jennie Marts
welcomes you to Creedence, Colorado,
where the cowboys are hot on the ice

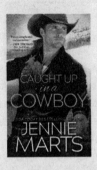

After an injury, NHL star Rockford James returns to his hometown ranch to find that a lot has changed. The one thing that
hasn't? His feelings for Quinn Rivers, his high school sweet-
heart and girl next door.

Quinn had no choice but to get over Rock after he left.
Teenaged and heartbroken, she had a rebound one-night stand
that ended in single motherhood. Now that Rock's back—and
clamoring for a second chance—Quinn will do anything to
avoid getting caught up in this oh-so-tempting cowboy...

"Funny, complicated, and irresistible."

—Jodi Thomas, *New York Times* bestselling author

For more info about Sourcebooks's
books and authors, visit:
sourcebooks.com

BIG CHANCE
COWBOY

**At Big Chance Dog Rescue, even
humans get a second chance**

After a disastrous mistake disbanded his army unit, Adam
Collins has returned home to Big Chance, Texas. He doesn't
plan to stay, but when an old flame asks him to help her train her
scruffy dog, he can't say no. As his reluctant heart opens up, the
impossible seems possible: a place where he, his friends, and
the other strays who show up can heal—and a second chance
with the woman he's always loved…

> "A real page-turner with a sexy cowboy, a sassy
> heroine, and a dog that brings them together."
>
> **—Carolyn Brown, *New York Times* bestseller**

HOT FOR
A COWBOY

**More sizzling romance from Kim Redford's
Smokin' Hot Cowboys series**

Eden Rafferty has lost it all: big-time career, high-profile marriage, and just about everything she owns. Coming back to Wildcat Bluff with her tail between her legs, the only person who can help her heal is cowboy firefighter Shane Taggart. But nothing is simple, and their high-octane past is just the beginning of their current problems...

"This passionate love story has everything."

—*Fresh Fiction* for *A Cowboy Firefighter for Christmas*

For more info about Sourcebooks's
books and authors, visit:

sourcebooks.com